THE
CANDIDATE

A POLITICAL THRILLER FROM THE AUTHOR OF THE FALCON TRILOGY

C. H. COBB

DOORWAY
PRESS

Published by Doorway Press,
Greenville, OH, USA
doorwaypress.com

Signed copies are available by ordering from chcobb.com.
Print version is available on Amazon.com,
and wherever books are sold.
An E-version is available from Amazon for the Kindle.

ISBN: 0-9848875-5-5
ISBN-13: 978-0-9848875-5-2
Library of Congress Control Number: 2016906925
First Edition, 2016

Cover design by Dani Snell,
www.refractedlightreviews.com.
Cover photo © Moth Owl Photography
Used by permission.

Scripture quotations taken from the
New American Standard Bible® (NASB),
Copyright © 1960, 1962, 1963, 1968, 1971, 1972, 1973,
1975, 1977, 1995 by The Lockman Foundation
Used by permission. www.Lockman.org

Federalist Papers quotations come from *The Federalist Papers
(Illustrated)*, Kindle Edition,
(no copyright).

This novel was written using Open Office 4.

Acknowledgments

Of my six books, this has been the most difficult to write. As an opinionated political partisan, I've struggled to be fair and open-handed in my depictions, and to avoid demonizing any of my characters (with the possible exception of one). In a presidential election year in which I am not enamored with the choices, I've tried to avoid taking out my real-life frustrations on my characters—or my readers! But I really do wish I could vote for Henry Marshall!

This is a work of fiction, and the characters exist only in my own mind. However, the details in this novel have been meticulously checked. I trust you will find all the historic references, quotes, places, etc., quite accurate and properly (though not formally) attributed.

You can visit Byron Gillespie's house on Runner Road (it's actually there); however, I recommend you visit by way of Google Earth rather than in person. Buckskin Gulch is really there, as are all the hospitals, restaurants, highways, etc., mentioned in the story. I think I made up a few things out of whole cloth, but not very many.

Thank you, Google Earth, Wikipedia, and the scholars and historians who've generously placed their work on the Internet. Thank you, beta-readers, who pointed out typos and other mistakes. Thanks to John Schmidt, a retired police officer, for helping with details of police investigations.

A special thank-you to my sister Elizabeth, who edits my work with a professional eye, a teacher's comments, and a warm sense of humor. In addition to her editing, Elizabeth is a retired Foreign Service Officer and was able to set me straight on multiple details about the State Department and government service.

And a big thanks to those brave patriots who risked everything in the last half of the eighteenth century to form a new nation and a new government in search of freedom and opportunity for all people. The Founding Fathers were men of incisive and brilliant thought, and it shows in their writings, particularly the Declaration and the Constitution. And thanks to Abraham Lincoln, who finally resolved the issue of slavery, a fatal contradiction between those two documents, and a terrible, tragic injustice to an entire race of people.

Most of all, thanks to the God who gave me redemption through Jesus Christ, and a mind to think, hands to write, a heart to learn, and an imagination to see what's not there.

Any remaining errors of fact or grammar are mine and mine alone. *Soli Deo Gloria!*

Dedication

Discouragement, weariness, busyness, and other obligations repeatedly called me away from this project. I'm a full-time pastor. I squeeze writing in on my days off, vacation days, and evenings when I don't have appointments. I was ready to quit writing this tale on multiple occasions. I would have—if not for my wife.

Doris believes that this is not only a *good* story, but an *important* one. By encouraging me to tell the tale, she willingly sacrificed time with me and quietly and cheerfully tolerated a house and yard in which important chores, tasks, and projects weren't getting done (apologies to my neighbors). She was also my first-layer editor: before I sent stuff to Elizabeth or the beta-readers, Dor read it and in some cases helped me rework it.

Thanks, babe, I love you. I'm dedicating this one to you—I couldn't have done it without you!

Cast of Characters

Adam McKenzie – Reporter, *Chicago Tribune*

Buford Jackson – Corporate lawyer, friend of Marshall, Marshall campaign chief of staff

Byron Gillespie, aka Ares – US Department of State official, assigned to the Global Security Contingency Fund, liaising between the State Department and the DOD

Carlos Estrada – Chief of security, Marshall campaign

Carly Johnson, aka Momma – Office manager, Marshall campaign headquarters

Charity Marshall – Daughter of Henry and Haley

Charlie Marshall – Son of Henry and Haley, identical twin of Conner

Conner Marshall – Son of Henry and Haley, identical twin of Charlie

Grady Wilson – Sergeant, Golden Police Department. Heads the investigative unit

Haley Marshall – Henry Marshall's wife

Henry Marshall – Presidential candidate, 2016

Joshua Cummings – Political consultant, Marshall campaign manager

Lucy Gillespie – Daughter of Byron

Mike Trujillo – State Chairman of the Colorado GOP, Marshall campaign press secretary

Pamela Hastings – Democratic candidate for president, 2016

Roland Yates – NTSB Investigator-in-Charge

Samuel Bergman, Jr., aka SJ – FBI Special Agent, Denver Field Office

Sandy Jackson – Buford's wife

Sarah Dalton – FBI Evidence Response Team leader

Timothy Hardy – IT director, Marshall campaign

Wayne Bushnell – Republican candidate for president, 2016

Chapter 1

IT HAS BEEN FREQUENTLY REMARKED THAT IT
SEEMS TO HAVE BEEN RESERVED TO THE PEOPLE OF
THIS COUNTRY, BY THEIR CONDUCT AND EXAMPLE,
TO DECIDE THE IMPORTANT QUESTION, WHETHER
SOCIETIES OF MEN ARE REALLY CAPABLE OR NOT OF
ESTABLISHING GOOD GOVERNMENT FROM
REFLECTION AND CHOICE, OR WHETHER THEY ARE
FOREVER DESTINED TO DEPEND FOR THEIR
POLITICAL CONSTITUTIONS ON ACCIDENT AND
FORCE.

Alexander Hamilton, Federalist #1

Friday, September 23, 2016

Uncle Sam needed a good, presidential butt-kicking—a turn-over-the-tables, throw-the-bums-out house cleaning—and Henry Marshall wanted to be the man to do the job. *But, he thought glumly, there's not much chance of that happening, is there?* Marshall's candidacy was a shot in the dark. Running as an independent he'd garnered only thirty percent at the polls with little over six weeks to go—the election was as good as lost. *Still, I've got nothing to complain about. I've done much better than I thought I would. Got on the ballot in all fifty states. That counts for something, anyway.*

He stared at the square-jawed face looking back at him in the bathroom mirror. At sixty-two his once jet-black hair now had streaks of grey and was thinning in places, but his grey eyes had lost none of their intensity over the years; a steely glare could still freeze a subordinate in his tracks. Marshall tugged on his tie, making a few adjustments. He grinned at himself. *At least I won't have to wear one of these dumb things for the next four years. And I won't have a Secret Service entourage following me everywhere I go. And, I'll get to drive myself. I guess it's okay.*

The United States Code stipulated that *major* presidential candidates and their spouses would be provided Secret Service protection within one hundred twenty days of a presidential election. It was the prerogative of the Secretary of the Department of Homeland Security to identify who was a "major" candidate. Though by the Fourth of July Marshall was polling at twenty-five percent nationally, the Secretary determined he was not a major candidate. Lacking the bureaucratic inertia that the federal security apparatus produced, Marshall was able to be light on his feet, showing up at events and photo opportunities on an almost impromptu basis. When Marshall gained three points in the polls between July and August, the campaign manager of the Democratic candidate appealed privately to the President, also a Democrat, pointing out that the absence of a Secret Service detail was a great advantage to the Marshall campaign. Consequently the President reversed his cabinet secretary's decision and the Marshall campaign was offered a federal security detail. They declined, though Marshall's security chief did accept the offer to meet with a Secret Service liaison officer for thrice-weekly security briefings.

Henry maintained an optimistic front for the sake of his campaign staff, but as the pages of the calendar turned and the polls did not improve hope was fading. *So why keep going? Because it's the right thing to do. My ideas are right. My vision is right. But they can't be explained in twenty-second sound bites. I've been painted as an extremist, a political jihadist—a bomb thrower—by the mainstream media. Perhaps hanging in there for six more weeks will give me the opportunity to sell a conservative vision to a few more people. Maybe I am building the base for the guy that will win in 2020. In any case, I'm going to see it through to the end.* After one more pull on his reluctant tie, Henry turned on his heel and went downstairs.

Haley was in the kitchen pouring coffee and putting some donuts on the table. She looked at the time as he walked in— it was quarter till six. "Your flight for Chicago leaves at ten. You've got time for a bit of breakfast. What else is on your schedule today, Hank?"

"Morning, babe. Got a strategy meeting this morning with senior staff, then I'm off to the airport. The Illinois Education Association is trying to decide whom to endorse, and they invited both major-party candidates to speak to the membership this afternoon. Apparently Adam McKenzie of the *Chicago Tribune* shamed them into inviting me as well, so I'm going as the token loon. That's going to take up my afternoon and early evening. Tomorrow morning I'm headed for the south side of Chicago where we'll shoot our final campaign ad in front of another failed HUD housing project. I fly home tomorrow afternoon."

Sitting down at the table, Haley sipped her coffee, a quizzical expression on her face. "I thought the IEA was in bed with Pamela Hastings, the Democratic candidate. The teacher's unions are the most reliable constituency the Democrats have, so why this interest in the Republican and you now at this late date?"

"They aren't interested in me. But Wayne Bushnell has been making noises about raising the Department of Education's budget by fifty percent. He's dangling enough carrots that the rank and file are revolting against the foreordained endorsement of Hastings. In the end I think it's going to be little more than a bidding war between the Republicans and the Democrats." He reached for another donut, hoping Haley wouldn't notice that he'd already had two.

She'd noticed. "Go easy on the fat pills, there, buster," she cautioned. Marshall quickly took a bite so she wouldn't insist he put it back, and winked at her. Both devoted runners, Hank and Haley were fit and trim but Haley wanted to ensure they stayed that way. She raised her eyebrows, shaking her head, and then resumed her comments about his schedule.

"Hank, you could have turned this opportunity down, you

know. It's a little over six weeks before Election Day. Don't you think you should be spending time on the undecideds, rather than those whose minds are made up to vote against you? Three-quarters of the education associations in the country think you're the second coming of Attila the Hun, and the other quarter thinks you're an ignorant knuckle-dragger. Why are you spending time and money to talk to them?"

Marshall put his pastry and coffee down and reached across the table, taking his wife's hands in his. "Haley, we're going to lose this race. I don't say that to anyone else, but you know it's true. There's just too much ground to make up between now and the 8th of November. The country hasn't had a fair hearing of my vision. It's being filtered, slanted, and spun through the mainstream media. Based on the cockeyed national coverage of my platform, I wouldn't even want to vote for me! Most of the country thinks I want women barefoot and pregnant, I want to feed the homeless to the wolves, push granny over the cliff, and destroy the planet with fossil fuels.

"I know it's over, babe. So when I have a chance to talk directly to educators, no filters, no interviewer cutting me off, I'm going to take it. Maybe I can convince two or three that Leviathan has gotten too big and doesn't know education half as well as they do. Maybe I can convince them that local control of standards and objectives and curriculum is far superior to federal mandates handed down from an entrenched, marginally competent bureaucracy a thousand miles away.

"My goal in these final weeks is to convince as many as I can that we need to rein in the feds and pick up the slack on a local level. That's why I'm going."

She squeezed his hands, her dark brown eyes sparkling. "Just my luck to fall in love with Don Quixote," she said. What she loved most about her husband was his commitment to do what he thought was right, no matter the consequences. Time and time again it had proven to be a costly commitment, but he never wavered.

Henry and Haley were married in '84, six years after his first wife, Rose, had been killed by a drunk driver. Alcohol had taken his wife and it nearly killed him, too. Unable to cope with the loss, Marshall found comfort in a bottle. For a year he stumbled about in a drunken, grief-filled fog.

Everything changed when he woke up one morning in a cheap hotel on the south side of Cheyenne. His car was parked outside the door but he had absolutely no memory of the previous three days, and no clue as to how—or why—he had driven to the hotel. Deciding that death was preferable to his empty, painful life, he began rummaging around the room looking for paper on which to write a suicide note. Instead of paper he found a Gideon Bible. It happened to open to the Gospel of John, and Henry Marshall began to read. Three hours later he placed his faith in Christ and never touched the bottle again. Everything had changed.

"So what are you up to while I'm tilting at windmills?" he asked, admiring her shoulder-length blond hair. Even at fifty-six, Haley was still a woman who turned men's heads. He started clearing away the breakfast dishes.

"Well, let's see. I've got two sections of advanced math this morning and I'm subbing for the algebra teacher this afternoon. The twins are driving down from Boulder this afternoon, and tonight we are going to the game. The Jags play Evergreen, and the boys really wanted to be here for that. Tomorrow morning Josh Cummings has me scheduled to speak to the Colorado Association of Wheat Growers, trying to convince them that your plan for unsubsidized markets are better for the country than the federal crop subsidies they've become accustomed to. It's a tough sell, Hank. *Vote for my husband and he will cost you thousands of dollars.*"

Joshua Cummings was Henry Marshall's campaign manager. A brilliant political operative, Cummings had plenty of experience masterminding presidential campaigns. Six feet tall, two hundred ten pounds, and packing all the stress of a high-powered consultant, Cummings should have been a heart attack waiting to happen. Instead, to the everlasting marvel of his doctor he was as healthy as the proverbial ox, a good thing considering the rigor of campaigning across fifty states. He had constructed the ultimate marriage between hands-on retail campaigning, social media, and the Internet. The result was a legitimate three-way race for the presidency. Marshall was polling at thirty percent, the GOP candidate at thirty-one, and the Democrat at thirty-five, with four percent undecided. Whether or not Marshall won he'd already made history by mounting an effective campaign as an independent.

"That's why Cummings is sending you instead of me. You're better looking and he figured maybe they won't throw things at you while you're being escorted from the podium." He turned off the coffee pot and put the cups in the sink.

"Thanks a heap, buster."

Marshall turned around and embraced his wife. "Listen, Haley, in several weeks it will be over. You and I can resume being Mr. and Mrs. Nobody, and life goes back to normal."

She shook her head. "No, it doesn't, Hank. It will never go back to normal. This *is* the new normal. You've become the spokesman for the opposition to the two political parties. The Dems are the party of big government. The Repubs are the party of slightly smaller big government. There are very few people out there who can mount a credible challenge to the status quo, but you are one of those who can. This isn't the end, Hank, it's just the beginning. It will go on for the rest of our lives, but it is a fight worth having. So let's saddle up our horses and do this. I've got your back."

****

They say every man has his price. I guess mine is only twenty grand. Tim Hardy stared at the laptop battery in his hand. *Do I really want to go through with this?* he asked himself. *This is the point of no return . . . no, actually that was when I accepted the first payment. If I back out now they'll expose me, or maybe blackmail me. Or worse. I don't have a choice—I've got to do it.* He sighed and clicked *Shut down* on his boss's laptop. Stealing a furtive glance behind him, he growled to the computer, "Get on with it, will ya?" He wanted to finish the job before his boss showed up. He removed his glasses and nervously cleaned them while he waited. Hardy was thirty-seven and unmarried. He wrestled frequently with the dark suspicion that life was passing him by, and that it was someone else's fault. Though he had made the choice to work for the Marshall campaign as IT director, he still resented the fact that the salary was lower than a commensurate position in business.

He groaned. The laptop's screen was petulantly announcing "**Windows is installing updates. Do not shut down or unplug the computer.**" *Why did it have to do this now? Come on, COME ON, you stupid computer!* Mercifully, the laptop completed its updates and shut down. With shaking hands he swapped the battery pack with the one he'd found sitting on the front seat of his car when he left the house for work this morning. Sweat beaded on his brow, though the room was a cool sixty-eight degrees.

The lure of fast, easy money had been more than Hardy could resist. It hadn't taken much of a sales job to buy his betrayal. His conscience nagged him. *Am I really that cheap? Is that all it takes to get me to betray a friend and employer?* Hardy was a confessing Christian. He was also, now, a traitor.

Two months ago a burner phone had showed up in his man bag—he still wasn't sure how it got there. But someone claiming to be a journalist writing a book on the inside story of Marshall's campaign began contacting him through the phone, wanting inside information and paying generously for it. At first it was just harmless bits of information, but the demands had steadily grown—as had the payouts. As time went on, Hardy realized that the "journalist" story was in all probability mere window dressing for something a great deal more nefarious. He began to suspect that it was actually an attempt by one of the other campaigns to sabotage Marshall's bid for the presidency.

Three days ago the journalist had texted him:

> *Verifying he'll be in hotel room, 21:00 Chicago time, Friday.*

Correct. Scheduled to skype with chief of staff at that time.

R u sure?

Looking at schedule now. I'm sure, ok?

Just checking. Package will be delivered Friday AM. Inform when installed.

The phone was in his pocket. He felt as though it was radioactive. The thrill of all that nice luscious money had faded within twenty-four hours. Since then he'd been miserable, sick to his stomach and depressed. His conscience was working overtime.

"Hey, Tim! What's up?"

Hardy whirled around, feeling exposed. He forced himself to calm down and remember his cover story. "Morning, Mr. Marshall. I decided to replace your laptop battery before you headed for Chicago. The network management client sent me two messages this week indicating that the battery is wearing out. Wouldn't want this thing to die when you're on the road."

"Really? Hadn't a clue. It's a good thing you caught it, Tim. I'm glad you're our IT director—you do a great job."

"Thank you, sir. It's a pleasure to work for your campaign." *I wish you hadn't said that, sir. You're giving kudos to Judas Iscariot, the man who's just betrayed you. Why don't you come a little closer, sir, and I'll just stab you in the back? Oh, Lord God, what have I done? What have I become?*

Tim had been told by the anonymous journalist that the replacement battery pack contained some hardware that would allow him to spy on the machine remotely, giving him access to its files and allowing him to connect to its microphone and camera surreptitiously. The data would be invaluable as an inside look at what the Marshall headquarters came up with in the final days of the intense presidential campaign. That's what he had been told the battery pack contained, anyway. It was nowhere near the truth.

****

"I'm sorry, Mr. Marshall, but you'll have to put your laptop away. The captain is ready to back away from the gate," the flight attendant reminded him. She leaned over and added privately, "I'm pulling the lever for you on November 8, sir. Best wishes. I hope you win!"

He flashed his trademark toothy grin and replied, "Thanks, Barbara. This campaign has been a long, almost surreal experience. I'm glad it's finally winding down, one way or another. Can I tell you a secret?"

Joshua Cummings, his campaign manager, was sitting in the window seat next to Marshall. He paled and muttered under his breath, "Um, sir, I'm not sure—"

"Relax, Josh, I'm only going to tell her the most juicy one."

Cummings rolled his eyes and sighed.

The pretty flight attendant looked around conspiratorially, then in a mock whisper purred, "Oh, tell me! I'm the soul of discretion."

He nodded, glanced around, then said in a stage whisper, "I wish I'd bought twice as much stock in Southwest!"

"Really? Well, I'll tell you a secret, sir. I've heard from Corporate that if you win, we're going to be renamed *Presidential Airlines.*"

"That's not funny," Cummings groaned. Marshall just grinned.

When Marshall declared his candidacy he'd had to put his investments—of which he had millions—into a blind trust, including the large blocks of stock in Southwest Airlines he'd purchased two weeks earlier. Rather than chartering aircraft he'd decided that his campaign travel would be on Southwest whenever possible; he liked the airline and how it was managed and the spunk of the employees. The *bags fly free* had helped as well. His campaign staff sought to organize travel and events around Southwest's standard commercial schedule. It was a decision that was saving the campaign thousands. It was also catching the eye of the public: travel on Southwest was burgeoning.

Marshall had taken a great deal of heat over the stock purchase. The Securities and Exchange Commission threatened to look into the matter, but that had turned out to be little more than political posturing. A media storm raged for three months as a team of federal lawyers sought to find a way to turn the transaction into a case of insider trading. They finally backed off when the attorney general sent them a private memo advising that his office had investigated and concluded there was no case.

The purchase didn't fit the currently reigning politically correct populist narrative. Both major party opponents had trashed the move, calling it crony capitalism. Reporter after reporter attempted to maneuver Henry Marshall into some sort of *mea culpa*. Adam MacKenzie of the *Chicago Tribune* landed an exclusive interview with Marshall.

"You purchased eight million dollars of stock in Southwest Airlines two weeks before you announced your candidacy, knowing that you were going to use them as your primary airline, is that right?"

"That's right."

MacKenzie studied him with a curious look. "But why did you do that, sir? Surely you must have known it would come out in the news?"

"Of course I knew."

"So why did you make the purchase?"

"Because I wanted to make money when Southwest's stock went up, which I figured it would probably do," replied Marshall, looking the reporter straight in the eye.

MacKenzie blinked. "And you admit that? On the record?"

"Sure, why not?" Marshall replied casually. "What part of this troubles you, Adam? You look as if you're smelling a horrible odor. Do you object to wise investing? Is it profit that troubles you? Perhaps capitalism itself is odious to you?"

"But isn't what you did unethical?"

"How so? I have benefited every other investor in Southwest. I gambled on how the traveling public would respond to my use of the airline. I was right, but I could have been wrong. I have no ties to Southwest, other than what I own in stock, so how is my purchase unethical?"

"It's unfair. You had special knowledge."

"By that standard you'll have to disavow this interview. How is it fair that I picked you, and did not pick one of the other dozen reporters clamoring for some time? Because now *you* have special knowledge, too. That's not fair to them, is it? So if you are going to live consistently by this notion of fairness you profess, surely you won't take advantage of your special, exclusive knowledge, will you? After all, it might mean that your paper profits by your reputation, selling more Internet subscriptions. You could even wind up with a raise. Maybe someday a Pulitzer, based on your knack for getting exclusive interviews. By your sense of ethics, that's not fair. Or does this sort of ethic only apply to other people?"

MacKenzie deftly changed the topic of the interview. But inside he was mortified. Marshall had challenged one of the pillars of his personal worldview and dismantled it with ease. At the end of the interview, Marshall had asked to go off the record for his final comment.

"Adam, I like you. I like your sense of integrity and, yes, your fairness when reporting—that's why you got this exclusive. When you post your article I'm sure you'll put your own spin on it, but I'm equally confident that I won't be misquoted or taken out of context. You and I inhabit different worldviews, I realize that, but I want to challenge you. You'll be much more formidable as a thinker if you start questioning your own premises and presuppositions to see where they lead. The liberalism of one hundred years ago had a well-earned reputation for its intellectual acumen. Unfortunately modern-day liberalism displays very little of that heritage—it's become intellectually flabby."

MacKenzie had driven from the interview to an Internet cafe to type up his notes. But Marshall's parting comment rankled him, and he promised himself he'd be ready if the tables were ever turned again.

****

Tim Hardy was consumed with guilt. Every greeting, every

comment, every smile shared with coworkers was phony. He felt like a hypocrite, estranged from his friends and coworkers though they were ignorant of his betrayal. *There's no way the money is worth this. I feel miserable.*

Guilt became paranoia. As he went about his duties he found it difficult to resist the notion that people were watching him, pointing at him, and talking about him behind his back. *Nonsense! Get a grip! No one knows what I've done.* But the feelings intensified.

Stealing furtive glances about him to see if he was being watched, Hardy entered the men's restroom and locked himself in a stall. Using the prepaid cellphone provided by the journalist, he texted him.

> *it's done.*

The response was almost immediate.

> > *good. at precisely 10:30am go to sbucks. buy bagel. leave phone in bagel bag on table & walk out.*

> *ok.*

> > *remaining pymnt will hit acct by morning.*

> *ok.*

> > *do not attempt further contact.*

He turned off the phone and stuck it in his pocket. Flushing the toilet, Hardy exited the stall and washed his hands. Thirty minutes later he'd ditched the phone at the Starbucks across the street. He didn't hang around to see who picked it up, figuring the less he knew the better. It didn't take a genius to see that they were eliminating any evidence that could tie them to the replacement battery. It never occurred to him that there was one more major piece of evidence to be eliminated.

****

Henry Marshall sighed as he surveyed the crowd. Some two hundred officers, board members, delegates, teacher's union reps, and sundry notables connected with the Illinois Education Association milled about in the auditorium, finding seats and chatting with friends. He knew it would be a decidedly hostile audience. *Maybe Haley was right*, he thought, *this meeting probably is a waste of time.*

He was scheduled to speak first, followed by the Republican. The Democrat had the last word. Marshall was allotted ten minutes, the other two thirty apiece. Soon the assembly was called to order and almost before he knew it he was being introduced. In no time, it seemed, the meeting was over and he was driving his rental back to the hotel. He dialed Josh Cummings at a stoplight.

"Cummings."

"Hey, Josh, it's me. I'm headed for the hotel."

"How'd it go?"

"Okay, I guess. Nobody was there to hear me—they wanted to know how much money Bushnell was willing to pay for their support. He promised the moon in federal dollars. Then Hastings took the stage and promised the moon plus half of Mars. This is after I got up and said I'm kicking the feds out of the equation."

"Hmm. Let me guess: they decided not to endorse you?"

"Right you are. I'll be back at the hotel in twenty minutes, where are you?"

"Just pulling into the parking garage. I met with the videographer and his crew. We're all ready for the shoot tomorrow."

"Good. I'll see you there. Get us some room service, will you? Order something light for me. We can do some strategizing while we eat, before I call Buford at nine."

****

Tim Hardy checked the backup server to make sure it was set for the evening's automated backup. He scanned the system logs of his small server farm, on the lookout for hardware problems and other anomalies. Everything looked green and clean. Next he turned to the firewall log. Other than the customary IP scans from would-be hackers and other things that go bump in the night, all was well. Tim was proud of the fact that no network for which he was responsible had ever been successfully hacked. Shutting down the monitors, he turned off the lights and locked his office.

"Yo! Hardy! Watching the game on Sunday?" The speaker was Joe Albaugh, one of the campaign's principal strategists. An import from DC, he'd quickly fallen in love with Mile High and all things Broncos.

"Wouldn't miss it, Joe. I want to see the Broncos clobber the Bengals. Been waiting for this one since the season began. What about you?"

"Oh, I'll be watching. Looking forward to it. Just wish it was a home game."

"Yeah, me too. I thought you guys never took any time off, especially this close to the election."

"I've carved out a five-hour block on Sunday. I'm turning off my phone and shutting down my iPad. For five glorious hours I'm just going to be a football fan. I've got a big-screen TV, and I'm gonna start with all the pre-game nonsense. When the game is over, it's back to the grind."

"Well, at least you've got your priorities right. Go Broncs!"

"Darn straight. Go Broncs! Have a good weekend, Tim."

The Marshall campaign headquarters was located at 1600 Jackson Street in Golden, Colorado, occupying the entire top floor of the building. Hardy stepped out of the building and looked up at the sky. Cloudless, it was a picture-perfect fall afternoon for the Front Range of the Rockies. To the west the peaks already had snow on them. The air was dry and crisp, the sky as brilliant blue at the horizon as it was at the zenith. North Table and South Table Mountains stood like quiet sentinels over the city. Beautiful as the scene was it could not erase the gloom in his heart. Marshall was a friend and fellow church member. Hardy had just turned him into little more than a meal ticket.

He started across the three lanes of Jackson Street for his customary end-of-day cup of Starbucks. Absorbed in his thoughts, he did not notice the white Cadillac Escalade pull out of 16th Street and accelerate toward him.

"Look out!" someone screamed. Hardy snapped out of his reverie just in time to see the Escalade bearing down on him. He tried to leap out of the way but it was too late. The bumper caught him midair, spinning him upside down. Slamming into the windshield, he was launched into the air and flipped over the accelerating vehicle before crashing onto the hard pavement. Hardy groaned, and descended into pain-wracked blackness.

****

Job complete.

Good! Did you get the phone?

Of course.

Destroy it. Hang around until expiration verified. The money will be in your usual account.

Roger that.

****

Sergeant Grady Wilson was at his desk when the call came in at 5:45 in the evening. A hit-and-run on Jackson was looking more and more like an attempted vehicular homicide to the responding officer. An eyewitness reported that the driver appeared to target the victim. The officer had requested the assistance of the department Investigations Unit, which was under Wilson's supervision. He checked the duty sheet; every available investigator was out on other calls. He'd have to go himself. The union would complain, but as far as Wilson was concerned the union could stick it in their ear.

"Tag, you're it," he said to Janice Ortega, the desk officer as he walked past.

"Where you off to, Grady?"

"That call on Jackson. Dispatch says they need an investigator and I've got no one else to send. Call me if you need me."

"Will do," she replied, making a note in the log.

By the time Wilson arrived the ambulance had already left with the victim. A portion of the street was cordoned off and he observed two officers taking detailed measurements and photographs as they bagged physical evidence. A third policeman directed the bottled-up traffic into the west lane.

"Who's the officer in charge?" Wilson asked.

"That would be me," responded Billy Blake, clipboard in hand. Blake was a five-year veteran with the force. "What are you doing out here, Grady? I thought you were handcuffed to that desk."

"Somebody's got to do the work, Billy. You beat cops are spending too much time at Dunkin' Donuts, so they sent me out to pick up the slack."

Blake smirked, "Well, it's good to know you still remember how real police work is done, old-timer. No, seriously, why are you here?"

"Sanchez quit last week. Thought you heard about that. He's accepted a job as police chief in Buena Vista. Anyway, it left the Investigations Unit short-handed so I thought I'd take this call, and here I am. Whatcha got for me?"

"The victim is Timothy Hardy, thirty-seven, male Caucasian. He was crossing the street—"

"Jaywalking?"

"Of course. He was hit by a white, late-model Cadillac Escalade. The Escalade didn't hang around. We have two witnesses who saw the accident occur, plus three more who heard the impact, turned, and witnessed the Escalade driving away. No one got the license plate number, although two witnesses verified it was a Colorado tag."

"Figures." Wilson examined the scene for a moment, measuring distances in his head. "Any evidence from the car, broken pieces, anything fall off?"

"A few pieces of the grill, part of a windshield wiper."

"Well, that's something, at least. If we can locate the

vehicle there should be threads from the victim's clothing hung up on the broken parts. Have to check all the body shops. But it's gonna be hard to find the vehicle with no plate number."

"Uh-huh. He stepped off the curb over there," Blake pointed. "The area of impact was here, according to the witnesses."

Wilson walked the path the vehicle had traveled just before impact. "I don't see any skid marks—not even a hint. Didn't the driver try to stop?"

"Nope. That's why we called you guys. We've taken statements from all the witnesses. The two that actually saw the accident stated independently of one another that the driver of the Escalade appeared to target the victim. One of the witnesses had to leave after we got her statement—she had something of a family emergency—but the other witness is still here. I asked him to stay until a detective arrived to interview him."

"Okay, I'll talk to him. How about the victim? How is he?"

Blake shrugged. "Well, he was alive when they took him to Saint Anthony's, but he was in bad shape. I don't know that he'll make it, Grady. He was drifting in and out of consciousness when the EMTs were working on him. They said he kept muttering something about a battery."

"A *battery?*"

"That's what they said."

"Hmm. Odd. Must be a nerd. Most people talk about their momma when they're about to die. Okay, where's your witness?"

Blake nodded toward his cruiser, "Squad car."

Seated in the back of the car was a seventy-something old man with shoulder-length grey hair and a matching beard. His leathery face held a pair of bright blue eyes and the unlit stub of a cigar clenched between his yellowed teeth. A torn denim shirt draped on a thin frame, well-worn jeans, and scuffed work boots completed the outfit. All that was lacking, Wilson mused, was a burro laden with a prospecting outfit.

Wilson introduced himself, and after a moment of small

talk to put the old fellow at ease he began his questions. "What did you see?" the detective asked.

"Well, that man, see, he started across the street from t'other side, front of that building—"

"Was there much traffic?"

"No more 'n usual, Officer. Jackson's always a little dicey to get across, but this boy shoulda been fine."

"So what happened next?"

"Well, as I was saying, he starts across the street, an' then this here white Caddy jumps out, comes after him."

"Wait—what do you mean, 'jumps out'?" Wilson asked, as he scribbled in his notebook.

"He'd been parked over there on the side street for ten, mebbe fifteen minutes. I knowed it 'cause I was watchin' him. Son's got hisself a car just like that, and I like those Escalades, so I guess I was just sort of enjoyin' the view."

The detective stopped writing and frowned. "Was there anyone in the car while you were watching it?"

The geezer held the stub of cigar and stared at it as though he'd forgotten it was in his mouth. "Huh. Dang thing went out again! What? Oh, couldn't tell. Tinted windows, you see. But must'a been, because I never saw anyone get into it."

"Alright. What next?"

"The fella was in the far west lane, had just stepped off the curb. The car jumps out and zooms across all three lanes, all the way over to that lane. By that time, the poor guy was in the middle lane and the Caddy moves back into the middle like he was aimin' for 'im. So I shouted and just then the feller sees the car. Tried to dart out of the way but that ol' Caddy just tracked him, step for step. Boom! Nailed him, hit him full on."

The detective made a few more notes, then asked, "As far as you could see, the driver didn't try to avoid the man?"

"Avoid him? Heck no! Looked to me like he was tryin' to hit him. Didn't even hit his brakes—not once. Almost chasin' him, like."

The detective questioned the old man for a few more minutes then let him go his way. It would have been a fairly simple hit-and-run except that two witnesses were positive the driver was trying to run the victim down.

Sergeant Grady Wilson had interviewed thousands of witnesses, perps, and victims in his thirty-year career. After twenty years beating the streets in New York City, he'd come to the Wild West thinking maybe life would slow down. It hadn't happened. He'd found that people were pretty much the same everywhere—only the accents were different. As a detective he'd been treated to just about every fanciful tale, excuse, and rationale for crime that the warped human mind could invent. He'd interviewed many skilled liars, but something in his gut told him the old guy was shooting straight.

He walked back to Officer Blake and asked, "Billy, did you get anything else?"

"Yeah, I've got a few more statements to give you. One of the victim's coworkers showed up to see what all the excitement was about and recognized the name. Turns out that Tim Hardy was—or still is, I should say—the IT guy for the Marshall campaign headquarters—you know, that guy who's running for president as an independent."

"No kidding?" Wilson scratched his chin, thinking, and then muttered, "Well, that adds an unpleasant little twist to our investigation."

"Really? Why?"

"We shouldn't assume Hardy's occupation is unrelated to this accident, especially since it appears he was targeted."

Blake stared at him for a moment before responding. "Whoa. That would put this incident on a whole different level. Don't you think you're being a little premature, Grady?"

"Nope. Far better to send out the warning and be wrong than sit on it and let someone take a free shot at the candidate."

Blake removed his hat and ran his fingers through his hair. "Okay. So what now?"

"Tell you what—you finish cleanup here, and I'll call Dispatch and have them send an officer to the hospital to keep an eye on Hardy. After I write up my report I'll sit down with the chief and let him make the next decision. It's not mine to make."

* * * * * * * * * *

Haley Marshall looked at her watch: it was 6:30 p.m. If they were going to eat before the game they'd have to hurry. She called to the twins from the top of the stairs, "Hey, boys, let's get a move on! I thought we'd grab a sub on the way to the game. How does that sound?"

"Great, Mom," Charlie answered from his room. Charlie and Conner had driven down from Boulder earlier in the afternoon, where each was enrolled at the University of Colorado. The Jaguars of D'Evelyn High School were playing the Arvada Bulldogs, a rivalry sufficiently intense to bring the twins back from college. Though neither boy had played, football was a passion for the whole family.

Turning to go downstairs, Haley accidentally missed the edge of the first step and stumbled. She cried out as she pitched forward. Flailing, she grabbed for the banister but missed, and tumbled head over heels down the stairs, slamming her head onto the flagstone landing at the bottom.

Charlie and Conner raced to the stairway and looked in disbelief at the unmoving form of their mother sprawled at the bottom of the stairs, her left arm trapped underneath her body at an unusual angle. "MOM!" Charlie cried as he raced down the stairs. "Conner, call 911, NOW!"

He knew enough not to move her. Kneeling beside her unresponsive form, he assured himself that she was still breathing. A small pool of blood puddled under her head. *Oh, Lord, please help!*

It seemed an eternity before the emergency crew arrived. Charlie had never felt so helpless as he did while waiting on the EMTs. The boys followed the ambulance to the hospital, Charlie driving while Conner tried to reach his father. He wound up leaving a message on his dad's cell. "Dad, it's Conner. Mom's had an accident and she's in an ambulance headed for St. Anthony's. Please call as soon as you can."

* * * * * * * * * *

"Thanks for the update, Sergeant Wilson. I'll tell Mr. Marshall. Let me know if anything else turns up, and we'll keep eyes wide open on our end." Carlos Estrada ended the call and dropped the phone in his pocket. He looked at his watch—it was after seven-thirty in the evening, central time. He knocked lightly on the door connecting the adjacent hotel rooms. Henry Marshall's room was in the center of the block of three rooms, his on one side and Joshua Cummings' on the other.

"Come in, Carlos."

The big man let himself in. Forty-five years old, Estrada was the chief of security for the campaign, doubling as Marshall's personal bodyguard and driver. Tipping the scales at two hundred thirty pounds, the six-foot-four-inch Mexican had become a naturalized US citizen at nineteen. When the landscaping service he worked for went belly-up two years later, he found himself unemployed. Desperate for work, Carlos enlisted in the Navy and fell in love with the life of a sailor. His Navy career eventually led him to the SEALs. After seventeen years spent wearing the SEAL "Budweiser," much of it on deployment downrange doing things that remain classified to this day, Estrada retired with the rank of Chief Petty Officer.

For the last four months he'd been running security for Marshall with a staff of four assistants, two of whom usually stayed at the headquarters liaising with law enforcement, the FBI and the Secret Service, running down leads, assessing potential threats, and making security arrangements at venues where Marshall was speaking. All five men were operationally capable. Besides Estrada one was a retired SEAL, another was a retired FBI agent, and the remaining two had retired from the Denver PD.

Marshall and Cummings were sitting at the suite's small dining table, papers scattered everywhere. Marshall looked quizzically at his bodyguard and asked, "What's up?"

"Sir, I just took a call from the Golden PD. It's bad news. Tim Hardy was hit by a car while crossing Jackson Street this afternoon."

"Tim? My word! That's terrible! Is he—how is he?"

"He's in the ICU at St. Anthony in pretty bad shape. The officer wasn't specific about the nature of his injuries, sir," Estrada replied.

Cummings offered, "I'll call Carly, Hank, and ask her to check on him and get back to us. She can notify the staff." Carly Johnson was the office manager of the campaign headquarters.

"Thanks, Josh. Let me know what she finds out. Let's pray for him right now." Estrada sat at the table and the three men bowed their heads while Marshall prayed for Tim Hardy, that his life would be spared and that he would not sustain any debilitating injuries from the accident.

"There's more, sir. The head of the investigative unit believes there is a strong probability that Hardy was targeted by the driver. Two witnesses reported that the car actually moved to intercept Tim as he crossed the street."

"But why would anyone want to harm Tim? I don't understand."

"Sir, there are three people in a tightly contested race for the presidency of this nation. Tim just happens to work for one of them," Joshua Cummings said as Estrada nodded.

"The Golden PD thinks it could have something to do with my campaign?"

"They don't know if it's related, but they want to make us aware of the possibility," replied the security chief, as he stood up.

"What do you think, Carlos?" Marshall looked up at his bodyguard, knowing how he would answer. As he watched the big man, it struck Marshall that Estrada looked like a pirate, or perhaps a Mexican Mr. Clean. Completely bald and clean-shaven, he sported a thick gold ring in his right ear. On the left side of his face was an old scar running from his mouth to his ear. *A memento from a dearly departed bad guy,* Estrada had called the disfigurement, chuckling, when asked about it. He had refused to go into detail.

"I think it's time to bring in the Secret Service, sir. There's a little over six weeks to go—but a lot can happen in six weeks."

"You've been arguing that point for months now," noted Marshall wryly.

"Yes, sir, I have. We've been lucky. But now I must insist, sir. You must accept Secret Service protection."

Marshall looked at Cummings, who nodded and said, "He's right, Hank. Don't tempt fate—please."

"Alright," Marshall sighed. "You're the security expert. You can call them on Monday morning, Carlos."

"No, sir. I'm calling them right now," the bodyguard said over his shoulder as he returned to his room.

Marshall felt his phone vibrating in his pocket and realized he'd neglected to turn the ringer back on after meeting with the IEA. He groaned, thinking there would be a raft of messages waiting. There was only one and it was from Conner.

"Hang on a minute, Josh. Got a message from my son." While Henry dialed his voice mail, Josh followed Carlos into his room to discuss the details of Secret Service protection. When he returned Marshall was just hanging up, his face ashen. "I've got to return to Denver immediately," Marshall said, rubbing his face with both hands.

"What is it, Hank? What's happened?"

Marshall looked up, his eyes glistening but his voice steady. "I just learned that Haley's also in St. Anthony's ICU. She fell down the stairs at home and struck her head. Thank God the boys were there—they heard her fall and called the rescue squad. Conner was on the way to the hospital when he called. I just spoke with him. Haley hasn't regained consciousness. They know there's a concussion, but they're fearing worse.

"I've got to return home right now, Josh. Call Carly, have her book Carlos and me on a flight that will get us back to Denver as soon as possible. You stay here and shoot that ad tomorrow."

"Me? I can't—you're the candidate, Hank. We'll just reschedule—" Cummings objected. He hated getting in front of a camera.

"Can't, not enough time. The election is in six weeks.

We've already purchased the airtime. Just rewrite the script so that the message is from you."

"But—"

"Josh! Listen! We're out of options! Are you going to vote for me on Election Day?"

"Well, of course! But—"

"Just tell 'em why, then. You know my position on HUD. Explain it. Sell it. I need your help on this one, Josh. I've got to get back to Haley."

Cummings nodded. "Okay. I'll do it. You pack, I'll contact Carly and then tell Carlos to pack up, too."

Soon Carly had secured tickets on an 8:50 p.m. departure. Hank and Carlos had to rush to make the flight.

****

Ares was the Greek god of war. He was also a State Department employee. Sometimes the fit was perfect.

After spending thirteen action-packed years on SEAL Team 8 in various parts of Africa, training local troops, kidnapping troublesome warlords, rescuing hostages, taking down pirates and being involved in multiple black operations, Ares had precisely the skill sets and African contacts needed to implement the Global Security Contingency Fund (GSCF), authorized by Section 1207 of the fiscal year 2012 National Defense Authorization Act. The purpose of the GSCF was ostensibly to carry out security and counterterrorism training. It was also charged with helping at-risk nations develop a stable judicial infrastructure by implementing rule-of-law programs. The funding for GSCF initiatives came from combining budget portions from the Departments of Defense and State.

But like many good ideas that hovered in the grey margins of legality, the GSCF experienced mission creep, and before long the State Department found itself involved in both intelligence and quasi-military operations. But State Department political appointees lacked the experience and skills of high-ranking military officers, and soon the GSCF was making hundred-million-dollar messes, as the Benghazi debacle in September of 2012 demonstrated.

When Ares retired from the SEALs the State Department snapped him up and used him as a three-way liaison officer between State, the DOD, and the African governments involved in the GSCF program. It wasn't long, however, before Ares had decided he was no longer in the game for mom and apple pie—not when there were massive amounts of money floating about with few controls and little account-ability. Ares discovered that many African leaders and militias were more than willing to provide a twenty-percent kickback for American aid dollars. Soon he'd established a Swiss bank account that was prospering like a Vegas casino.

And then that meddling presidential candidate Henry Marshall appeared on the scene. The man was a radical, as far as Ares was concerned, filled with idiotic notions about states' rights and slicing the federal government down to size. At first his campaign could be easily ignored, but when he started polling above twenty percent nationally and his platform began to push the major party candidates in a more conserva-tive direction, Ares realized he had to do something before it got out of hand.

Among Marshall's other ridiculous notions, he held that America should not be spending money on foreign military aid unless it was clearly, directly, and explicitly in the national interest. Foreign military aid to the African nations such as those under GSCF did not qualify; Marshall wanted to termi-nate the program.

If the lunatic had just kept his bright ideas to himself there would have been no problem. But as luck (or unluck, Ares mused) would have it Marshall's idea struck a nerve with the American public, and after the two major campaigns poll-tested it and found it to be a winner, all three campaigns were calling retreat on the GSCF. As Ares saw it Marshall was threatening his livelihood. That simply would not do. At first Ares had tried a series of dirty tricks to discredit the Marshall campaign. But nothing had worked and it was time to escalate the tactics. The fix, as Ares saw it, was straightforward: Marshall was pushing the other two campaigns toward isolationism by his constant pressure on the foreign aid issue. Eliminate Marshall and the pressure—hence, the problem—goes away.

And how to eliminate Marshall? Perhaps a nine-cell laptop battery, two cells of which were packed with C4 explosives on a timer, would do the trick. It would be done when the man was alone, minimizing collateral damage. Ares had no desire to kill Americans—he just wanted to eliminate Henry Marshall.

****

Between his pockets and his briefcase, the man whose code name was Ares was carrying four phones. One, a burner phone—a prepaid cheapo—contained the text messages to and from Tim Hardy. It would be destroyed as soon as he was able to get away from the office. Another was a standard iPhone used to contact him by family, friends, and coworkers. The third was the official, secure State-Department-issued phone employed for his official-but-confidential legitimate business. And finally was his personal Boeing Black Smartphone, complete with a biometric security package and 8192-bit-third-party encryption, something the NSA couldn't even come close to cracking. This phone he used only for his personal nefarious activities. Whenever asked about it, he intimated that it was for an authorized GSCF black op in the you-don't-want-to-know-about-it category.

Ares stayed late in his office. He had a contact in China he had some business with—on his State Department phone—regarding the purchase of ten thousand Russian-licensed but Chinese-made Kalashnikovs for a GSCF project in Ghana. Later he would communicate with a government official in Ghana—on his Boeing Black—and clear a personal fifty thousand on the deal.

He was on the phone with his Chinese contact when he

felt the iPhone vibrating in his pocket. Ignoring it, he wrapped up the deal and completed the call. Then he pulled out the iPhone and checked the screen: his only child, Lucy, had left a message.

Ares was a very wealthy man, compliments of the US taxpayers, but he was also a very lonely man. His wife had succumbed to cancer twelve years ago and it had left him bitter and angry. Though he did not believe in God, he blamed God for taking his wife. In the years since, a cold fury had grown in his heart and he began lashing out at God in any way he could, living recklessly on the razor edge of life. It was the grief and rage of that loss which pushed Ares over the thin line from patriot to predator. His buddies in the SEALs saw what was happening and realized he'd be a danger to any operation he was attached to. They talked him into retiring for his own safety as well as theirs. Shortly after that the State Department had picked him up. But the canker of his anger and bitterness had corrupted the man, and it was not hard for him to justify skimming cash off the top of his GSCF operations.

His only real pleasure in life was his daughter, Lucy. She was twenty-two, a beautiful, loving girl who doted on her daddy. If there was one area of his personal life he handled with the utmost care, gentleness, and integrity it was his daughter. She was his one remaining reason for living. He would do anything for her.

Ares swiped his finger across the screen of his iPhone to access his voice mail, and listened to the message.

"Hey, Daddy, it's Lucy. Listen, if I lose you it's just that my battery is almost out of juice. I'm on my way to Denver for a job interview. You'll never guess who's on my flight, Dad. It's that guy Henry Marshall—the independent candidate for president. It's so cool! I really like him, Dad, and I think you wou —"

At that point his daughter's phone dropped out and the message terminated. *What? Marshall's on Lucy's flight? He's supposed to be in his hotel room. Oh, dear God, no, not Lucy!* Frantically he called her back, but the call was immediately directed to voice mail. His legs turned to rubber and he sank to the floor, groaning, "Oh, God, no, please, no!" He looked at his watch: it was six minutes before ten eastern, six minutes before nine, Chicago time. Six more minutes. He stifled a sob. "Baby, I'm so sorry, I'm so sorry." He broke down and cried.

Mechanically, he clambered to his feet and stumbled through his tears to his office door. He locked it and then opened his office safe. Ares pulled out an M45A1 handgun, a remake of the venerable Colt .45 M1911 designed for special operations forces, and placed it on his desk. Reaching into his safe again, he withdrew a bottle of Johnnie Walker. Dumping the cold coffee from his mug into the trash can, he refilled the cup with scotch. He placed the cup next to the handgun then turned on his office television, which was more or less permanently tuned to CNN. Taking a large swallow, Ares looked at his watch—in two minutes the last vestige of happiness would be wiped out from his life, and it was his own doing.

Chapter 2

> NOTHING IS MORE CERTAIN THAN THE
> INDISPENSABLE NECESSITY OF GOVERNMENT; AND IT
> IS EQUALLY UNDENIABLE THAT WHENEVER AND
> HOWEVER IT IS INSTITUTED, THE PEOPLE MUST CEDE
> TO IT SOME OF THEIR NATURAL RIGHTS, IN ORDER
> TO VEST IT WITH REQUISITE POWERS.
>
> *John Jay, Federalist #2*

Twelve years earlier: Friday August 6, 2004

"Are you satisfied with this? You're sure this is what you want?" asked Buford Jackson. The tall, silver-haired lawyer was holding the contract for the sale of Econnect, Inc., a high-tech company Marshall started in 1990, and which was now worth something north of one hundred fifty million dollars.

Henry Marshall looked at his attorney and nodded. "Yep. Let's do it. I'm ready to open a new chapter."

Jackson measured him with a cool look. "And just what does this new chapter entail?" The lawyer thought Marshall was being precipitous, acting too soon. Marshall was selling his company for one hundred million cash plus forty percent of the stock.

"Gonna do something I've always wanted to do. I want to write so I'm going to start a blog."

Jackson gathered up the stacks of papers, agreements, and forms necessary for the sale and shoved them into his bulging satchel. "A blog? Hmm. No money in that," he observed.

"Don't need money, Jacks. Look, I built this company from the ground up. I've poured my blood, sweat, and tears into it and it's been far more successful than I deserve. I've given it fourteen years of my life but now I'm ready to turn the corner."

"Yes, Hank, but you don't know what's *around* that corner," rejoined the lawyer as he shut his office safe and spun the dial.

"Jacks, I don't *care* what's around that corner. I've far more money than I'll ever need. Haley and I are going to have fun giving it away. And I'm going to write—be a political gadfly. I've already started building my website. Can't wait!" Marshall stood up, briefcase in hand, as the two headed for the door of Jackson's spacious office. Western Law Associates (WLA) was founded by Jackson and occupied the entire twentieth floor of a large office tower in downtown Denver, Colorado.

The lawyer stopped and turned to Marshall. "Who's your audience?"

"Beats me," Henry grinned.

Jackson snorted derisively, "You haven't a clue what you want to do! You know what they say, Hank: 'A fool and his money are soon parted.'"

"Thanks a heap! That's a real vote of confidence, pardner."

"No, actually, *pardner*, it's not."

"You're just jealous, Jacks," Marshall laughed.

"Of your bank account, yes. Of your plans, no. You'll go bonkers within six months. You'll be at my door begging me to set up a new corporation for you. Don't say I didn't warn you." He checked his watch and added, "We've got to be there in fifteen minutes and Denver traffic is going to make it difficult. Let's wiggle."

****

The summer of 1984 had been an exciting time for the thirty-year-old Marshall. He graduated with a degree in Electronic Engineering from Colorado State University, he married Haley, and he began his career at Intelligent Solutions, Inc., a Silicon Valley startup that designed intelligent microcontrollers and application-specific integrated circuits (ASICs). The couple lived modestly and plowed their savings into stock at Intelligent when the company went public with an IPO. The value of the company skyrocketed, helped by the fact that the rapidly expanding Internet was demanding new infrastructure at a breakneck pace. By 1990 Marshall was able to resign his position and move to Golden, Colorado, where he launched his own company, Econnect, Inc., designing and manufacturing ASICs for Internet routers. The business expanded so fast Marshall was barely able to keep up with it. In twenty years he'd gone from a thirty-year-old college student struggling to make ends meet to a debt-free multimillionaire. It had taken a schedule of sixty-hour weeks, and not a few seventy- and eighty-hour ones, but he was now financially independent.

Buford Jackson was one of his best friends—more of a mentor, actually. Marshall had picked the corporate lawyer out of the phone book in 1990, checked out his references, and retained him to set up his corporation. Though Jackson was fourteen years older the two men quickly became close friends. Both were avid runners and enjoyed trail running together. Like Marshall, Jackson was a believer and attended the same church as his friend. Both served as volunteers at Build Denver, a charitable corporation that refurbished, remodeled, and repaired the homes of needy people in the Denver metro area. As the years went by, Marshall found himself increasingly trusting the older man's wisdom and judgment.

****

Finalizing the sale of Econnect took most of the day. That evening Henry and Haley celebrated by taking Buford and his wife Sandy out for the best steak Denver could provide.

"So, Hank, what are you *really* going to do with yourself?" Buford asked. "I just can't imagine you sitting on the couch in front of a keyboard in your pajamas, popping chocolates and haunting the Internet."

"Well, tomorrow we're getting ready for a camping trip. Haley and I are taking the kids to the Flat Tops Wilderness Area for a week of backpacking and trout fishing before school starts. When we return I'm going to finish building my website and start blogging."

"What will you write about?" asked Sandy. At five eleven Sandy was almost as tall as her husband. She'd been a standout on the William and Mary women's basketball team in 1970. Also a trail runner, she retained much of the athletic grace of her youth.

"Politics. I'm sick and tired of both political parties and the mess they've made of the federal government."

"I thought you were a registered Republican."

"Oh, I am," he affirmed, "but the Republicans have lost their moorings and are all over the map. Color me disenchanted, maybe even disenfranchised. They used to be the party of small government and fiscal responsibility but they've been taken over by the RINOS. So I'm going to start lobbing some verbal grenades and see what happens. Someone's got to call them to account."

"And this is not going to produce any revenue?" Buford observed, half-questioning, half-stating.

"Nah. I told you before, Jacks, we don't need money. We're set. I'm going to put in twenty hours of community volunteer time each week, and then spend another thirty hours writing and researching. It's going to be a blast."

Jackson didn't respond. Hank could tell by the set of his friend's jaw and his slow nod that he was pondering something. Conversation lulled and they resumed eating. After a moment, the lawyer said, "This will go somewhere, Hank. You're not going to be a blogger the rest of your life. Something will come of this. You watch—you'll see."

****

When in doubt, read the instructions!
Posted 10/5/2004
By Henry Marshall

When was the last time you read the Constitution of the United States? Reading that august document answers many questions about why our President, judiciary, and legislators do the things they do. But it also raises a lot of questions, like, *Why is the federal government involved in this, or doing that? Who gave the feds the right? Wasn't that reserved to the states?*

The founding documents of our country place limits on the powers of the federal government. Over the years, however, there has been an inexorable creep by the feds toward powers never granted by the Constitution. This is evident in all three branches of the government. Congress has passed laws intruding into the rights of the states on issues ranging from the conduct of elections to environmental protection, education, energy policy, commerce, and many others.

The judiciary has morphed from its role as the guardian of the Constitution and existing law into an ad hoc legislative body, creating law by judicial fiat. One of the travesties of our day is the overturning of popularly approved state referenda by the federal judiciary on the dubiously subjective grounds of the "penumbra" of the law rather than the objective letter of it.

Perhaps the greatest malfeasance is found in the executive branch. The President and his Justice Department selectively enforce—or not—laws that have been passed by Congress, signed by the President, and found constitutional by the courts —laws that the President is sworn to uphold. Favored companies are granted waivers to laws on no basis other than presidential whim. The regulatory bodies are out of control, having become a law unto themselves. Numerous government agencies now have SWAT teams. I can understand why the FBI might have one, but why does the Railroad Retirement Board require a Special Weapons and Tactics team?

Thomas Jefferson once said, *"In questions of power, then, let no more be heard of confidence in man, but bind him down from mischief by the chains of the Constitution."* It's good advice, and high time we heed it.

Friends, the government is no longer capable of controlling itself. We the People need to rein it in through the power of the ballot box. Throw the bums out, and let's elect men and women who do not think of themselves as rulers, but as servants and stewards.

****

Buford Jackson's observation was prophetic. Over the next several years Henry Marshall's blog went viral among conservatives and libertarians, gaining a national following of over eight million regular readers. Whether in praise or censure, his pieces were cited regularly in the *New York Times*, the *Washington Post*, the *Chicago Tribune*, the *Dallas Morning News*, the *Denver Post*, and the *San Francisco Chronicle*. Fox News issued numerous invitations to appear on their news shows but Marshall turned them all down. He had no interest in celebrity and no desire to leave his beloved Colorado. Originally nothing more than a quasi-hobby by which he could share his viewpoints, his blog created a movement that took him by surprise. It was becoming increasingly difficult to lead a private life.

Chapter 3

[W]E HAVE NO GOVERNMENT ARMED WITH POWER CAPABLE OF CONTENDING WITH HUMAN PASSIONS UNBRIDLED BY MORALITY AND RELIGION. AVARICE, AMBITION, REVENGE, OR GALLANTRY, WOULD BREAK THE STRONGEST CORDS OF OUR CONSTITUTION AS A WHALE GOES THROUGH A NET. OUR CONSTITUTION WAS MADE ONLY FOR A MORAL AND RELIGIOUS PEOPLE. IT IS WHOLLY INADEQUATE TO THE GOVERNMENT OF ANY OTHER.

John Adams, in a letter to the officers of the first brigade of the third division of the militia of Massachusetts, 11 October 1798.

May, 2006

"Thanks for meeting with me, Hank." US Representative Dallas Chamberlain was trying to be friendly but felt as if he were greeting the enemy. Marshall had written a series of posts accusing Chamberlain of being a go-along-to-get-along establishment Republican. Chamberlain was the ranking minority member of the powerful House Ways and Means Committee and over the last year had supported tax increases sponsored by liberal Democrats in return for favorable votes on boondoggle projects in the congressman's Sixth District. Chamberlain had complained loudly about "Democrat profligate spending," but bellied up to the federal trough to get his share of the booty whenever there was an opportunity. Marshall's contention was that Chamberlain's sort of behavior, shared by establishment politicians on both sides of the aisle, was precisely why the House was unable to reduce the federal deficit. Marshall's posts were causing a noticeable drop in Chamberlain's support, and the congressman was facing a tough primary election in three months.

"You are quite welcome, Congressman," Marshall replied as he sat down and picked up the swanky steakhouse's menu.

"Dinner's on me, Hank, and please, call me Dallas," said the politician, perhaps a little too expansively.

"You are most kind, sir, but I'm turning the tables on you. I don't want the taxpayers footing the bill for my steak, so this is my treat, Congressman, er, Dallas. I've already talked to the server so there's no point in arguing."

Chamberlain chuckled, ignoring the jab. "I see I've been out-maneuvered. Well, thank you. Next time I'll pick up the tab. Before we get down to business, let's order."

After ordering the two men enjoyed rehashing the Denver Broncos' 2005 season. Jake Plummer had done well and the team made the playoffs, beating the Patriots but falling short in the AFC Championship game against the Pittsburgh Steelers. Both men were avid Broncos fans and they buried the hatchet long enough to enjoy reliving the season. Chamberlain finally turned the conversation back to the purpose of their meeting.

"Hank, I wish you would be as supportive of my reelection campaign as you are of the Broncos."

"Dallas, I wish I could, but I can't. You talk a good conservative fiscal game but your record says, 'big government.'"

The politician pushed his plate aside and said, "Look, Hank, I hear you. But Colorado is no longer a red state. We are a purple state trending blue. My opponent might win the primary but he'd never take the general. If we want to retain control of the House we've got to run moderates. The American people aren't going to elect conservatives."

"So you say."

"It's true," the politician insisted confidently.

Marshall motioned to the server for a refill of his water, then turned back to Chamberlain. "Dallas, there are several problems with your statement. One, I believe the Republican conservative base is much larger than the Republican moderate base. The party will get a much higher base turnout with conservative candidates. Two, let's suppose we win the election with a slate of moderates. Then what?"

Chamberlain blinked, surprised by the question. "Well, obviously, then we govern. Then we are able to carry forward a Republican program for the country, especially if we capture both the House and the Senate."

"Yes, you can carry forward a Republican *moderate* program, which is right back to big government and business as usual. So from a conservative's perspective, what's the point of winning at all?" Marshall took a sip of his water as he watched his opponent.

"Well, with reference to the Senate for example, how about the Supreme Court and other high judicial appointments? If we don't control the Senate we can't influence who gets on the courts," the congressman insisted.

"True. So what's the record on Republican appointments to the bench? Mixed at best! We conservatives have no guarantee that moderates in the Senate will even listen to us on judicial appointments. So what do we gain by electing moderates? Nothing!" Marshall declared.

"And just what do you gain by throwing the election to the Democrats? Worse than nothing!" Chamberlain asserted heatedly.

"Not true. We cut out the establishment deadwood by eliminating the power of the incumbent, and give the conservative a better shot at winning the primary in the *next* election. It is a long-term, multi-cycle strategy. That's something you moderates don't understand about us conservatives: we aren't after political power, Dallas. We want *change*, systemic change from the status quo."

Dallas leaned forward, "Marshall, listen to me! Governing is about compromise. You never get everything you want and you never get anything done unless you're willing to work with the other team."

"I hear you, and I agree. But those of us who are conservatives feel like the guys in the middle and on the left keep moving the goal posts. Conservatives are the only ones being told to march to the middle and the middle keeps moving further left. You clearly don't understand the difference between a moderate and a conservative, Dallas." Henry motioned to the server for the bill.

"Okay, I'll bite," the politician responded sarcastically, "What's the difference?"

"Moderates, Dallas, have policy *preferences*. Conservatives have policy *convictions*. Moderates are pragmatists, pursuing whatever works. But conservatives tend to live by a consistent ideology, a worldview. That's why the two approach compromise so differently."

Chamberlain played with his coffee cup for a moment before he spoke. "So there's no convincing you—you will not support me in the primary?"

"No, I'm endorsing your challenger."

The politician stood and reached for his wallet. He grinned at Marshall, "Will you compromise on the bill? Let me get the tip?"

Marshall smiled back, "No, Congressman, no compromise. I've got the whole thing."

****

Dallas Chamberlain stormed back into his Sixth District office, chafing over his failure to move the blogger to his side. As he swept past his secretary she said, "Congressman, your flight for Washing—"

"NOT NOW!" he snapped, disappearing into his office and slamming the door. He paced around the large, well-appointed space trying to calm down. *Somehow,* he thought, *I've got to mitigate Marshall's impact, otherwise he'll throw the primary to my opponent. And for the first time in eighteen years, I'll be out of work.* "Can't have that," he mused aloud.

Anger exhausted, he dropped into his plush leather chair and massaged his temples. An idea slowly emerged and he picked up the phone and buzzed his secretary.

"Gladys, get Ezra Raikes on the phone for me."

****

The cab dropped Henry Marshall off under the overhang at the Mayflower Hotel on Connecticut Avenue in DC on Thursday evening, June 15, 2006. It was drizzling lightly, the tail end of a vigorous thunderstorm that had delayed the landing of Marshall's flight at Ronald Reagan National Airport. He walked into the ornate lobby with his carry-on and checked in. Though he hated traveling without his wife on this weekend it could not be avoided. Haley was scheduled to speak at the Colorado Republican Women's Club in Fort Collins on Friday night. He was participating in a Heritage Foundation conference on morality and politics in DC and had the keynote address on Friday night. Both invitations had been very short notice; coincidentally, the originally scheduled speakers at both events had fallen ill and were unable to attend.

The conference workshops began at 8:00 a.m. Friday and kept him busy all day. He delivered his keynote that evening at 7:00 p.m. and arrived back at the hotel after ten, exhausted. He changed into a pair of gym shorts and parked on the bed in front of the television set. *I really shouldn't be watching this, especially since it's pay-per-view,* he thought to himself. *I'll only watch for five or ten minutes. Haley would die if she knew.* But before he knew it he'd fallen asleep with the TV on.

****

Marshall was sitting in his study working on a blog post five days later when the phone rang. They still used an old-fashioned landline for their main telephone, and he heard Haley calling from the kitchen, "Hank, it's for you. Some guy from the *Chicago Tribune.*"

He picked up the phone. "This is Henry Marshall."

"Mr Marshall, Adam MacKenzie, *Chicago Tribune.* How

are you, sir?"

"Fine, Mr. MacKenzie. How can I help you?"

"I'll be publishing an article about your recent trip to DC and I wanted you to get a chance to look at it and respond before it goes to print. May I email it to you?"

Henry provided his email address and assured the reporter he'd read the article. When it arrived in his email he printed the attachment and sat down to read it, expecting to see a report of his keynote address. He was shocked, however, when he looked at the headline: CONSERVATIVE BLOGGER PREACHES MORALITY, WATCHES XXX-RATED VIDEOS.

He didn't realize Haley had come into the room and was reading the headline over his shoulder. "What?" she cried, snatching the article out of his hand. "What's this, Hank?" she demanded, rapidly scanning the piece, tears welling out of her eyes. "Hank, is this true?"

He stuttered and stammered and then shot back, "Well, how should I know if it's true, Haley? You didn't even let me read it!"

"*Read it?*" she snapped angrily. "You don't need to read it —just look at the headline! Is that true?"

"No, of course not! You know me better than that!" he protested.

"Do I?" she replied icily.

He held up his hands. "Look, sweetheart, I haven't a clue what this is about. Give me a chance to read the article and we'll sit down and talk about it calmly. I'll answer any question you have. But I am assuring you right now—whatever that thing says, I did *not* watch any x-rated video. And it really hurts me that you are even wondering about that."

She nodded and placed the papers in his hand. Turning on her heel, she left the room without a word. He sat down and read the piece carefully. An unnamed source had provided MacKenzie with a copy of the hotel bill for Marshall's stay at the Heritage conference, a picture of which was included in the article. Marshall himself had never seen the bill, and assumed his expenses were paid by Heritage. But sure enough, listed under extra charges was a pay-per-view bill for a porn film. He shut his eyes and shook his head, *I can't believe this.*

****

The next two weeks were a nightmare for Marshall. MacKenzie published the piece in the *Chicago Tribune,* complete with Marshall's denials. But the evidence was damning and Marshall had no good explanation for it. Traffic on his blog was halved in the space of four days. The comments posted left no doubt that his readers felt betrayed. Other writers and political figures who had felt the sharp end of Marshall's pen rejoiced in his apparent downfall, joyfully accusing him of abject hypocrisy.

After many long and painful conversations Henry had just about persuaded his wife he didn't do it. Her acceptance of his story was guarded at best and suspicious at worst. It frustrated him to see how the entire affair had rocked her confidence in him. Marshall had prided himself on his integrity but now his reputation was in tatters.

One day not long after the exposé his pastor called. "Henry, you've been going through a rough time. Let's meet at IHOP and have a cup of coffee. I might be able to help."

An hour later the two men were sitting in a booth at the restaurant. "Thanks for meeting with me, Pastor Joe. This thing has turned my world upside down and I have no idea what to do about it."

Joseph Johnson was about ten years older than Henry. He'd been at the church for twenty-five years and was well respected for his wisdom and Bible knowledge. Silver-haired with a crew-cut and goatee, he looked like a college professor. "What hurts the most, Hank?"

"That no one seems to believe me, Pastor. I think that's the worst. People are questioning my honesty, now. They're not sure whether they can trust me. Never had that before. Hurts."

Johnson nodded. "As a believer your integrity is one of

your most precious possessions. But maybe I can bring a little perspective to the issue.

"The problem of pornography is widespread, both in the church and out of it. The statistics say more than sixty percent of men use it monthly. For many unbelievers, it's no big deal. Sex is a natural urge, pornography appears to some as a victimless way of satisfying the drive; it's not true, but that's what they claim.

"It's different for believers, though. The use of pornography is sinful. Jesus labels it adultery—a betrayal of the marriage covenant. Paul calls it *pornia*, immorality. Pornography takes God's marvelous gift of sexuality—something that reaches to the core of our being and identity as humans —and warps it, turning it into nothing more than a cheap thrill. What God intended as a special joy for marriage is corrupted. And there are *countless* victims. Porn is the driving economic engine of sexual slavery around the globe; to some degree all who indulge in it bear responsibility.

"Now, Hank, because there is such shame attached to pornography in Christian circles, there's another sin that frequently gets attached to it as well. Christian men addicted to porn begin to lie about their sin in order to cover their tracks. Deception is the brother of most addictive sins, and pornography is highly addictive. It might begin with just a few lies but rapidly expands to the point where a man's life is defined by deception. This is why, Hank, you're having a hard time getting people to believe your denial. The Christian consumer of pornography usually becomes an inveterate liar."

Marshall's shoulders slumped, "So you don't believe me, either?"

"I didn't say that. As it is, I am choosing to believe you until you give me reasons to decide otherwise. Better for me to believe you and be proven wrong, than to wrongly accuse you of lying. If you are lying, the Lord will reveal that in His time."

"That's not exactly a ringing endorsement."

"I'm just being honest with you, Hank. I *do* believe you, but I've done enough counseling to know that sometimes I'm proven wrong."

Hank nodded. "Okay, I understand. What's the best thing for me to do now?"

"I think, first of all, this should be a reminder that you aren't above falling—none of us are. Proverbs 28:26 says that he who trusts in his own heart is a fool. Jeremiah 17:9 tells us our own hearts are so capable of deceiving us they are unknowable. So don't get your nose all bent out of joint just because people think you've fallen. Instead let the Lord use this to humble you and to remind you that you are just as capable of falling as any man.

"Second, I'd say that you need to let this experience drive you closer to Christ. Isaiah 57 says that the high and holy God dwells with the broken and contrite. Seek your comfort and sufficiency in Him and His Word. Remember: He is sovereign: for His own good purposes He permitted this allegation.

"Finally, if it's possible, clear your name. Your credibility as a Christian and a political commentator is in the toilet if this allegation stands. Men of integrity are rare and the world knows it. Hypocrites are a dime a dozen, and we usually don't give them the time of day."

They talked for another thirty minutes. Marshall walked out of IHOP feeling lighter than he had in days. It was helpful to be reminded that Christ was in control.

Later that day he called Buford Jackson. "Jacks, I need your help. Somehow I need to prove that the allegations against me are false."

The lawyer asked quietly, "Henry, what happened to you in DC?"

"Not you, too, Jacks! I didn't do it! I don't look at porn, okay?"

"What about the evidence, Hank?"

"I don't know what to tell you, Buford, other than *I did not do it!*"

There was silence on the other end of the phone. Then the lawyer said slowly, "Hank, my gut tells me you didn't. But I'm a lawyer and the evidence as it now stands is pretty doggone conclusive. All I can say is this: I'm standing by you.

If you did it, I'll help you work through it. If you didn't do it, I'll help you clear your name and reputation."

"That's why I'm calling. Maybe I can hire a private investigator to dig into this thing and find out what's going on."

"Okay, what do you need from me?"

"Do you know any PIs in DC?"

"No, I don't. Wait! Yes, as a matter of fact I do. I have a friend who used to be an FBI agent here in Denver. He spent most of his years working out of Seattle before coming to the Denver office near the end of his career. Retired several years ago, moved to Annapolis, Maryland. Got himself a boat on the Bay. He set up a small private investigations firm just to keep himself busy."

"That's just what I need. What's his name and how do I contact him?"

****

For the second time in as many weeks Marshall found himself standing in the passenger-pickup area of Reagan National in DC. A tall, grey-haired man emerged from a dark blue Ford S10 pickup and waved at him. "Over here, Mr. Marshall."

"You must be Jim Stewart?"

"That's what it says on my driver's license. Got any bags?" Wearing dark sunglasses, the man was dressed in a pair of blue jeans, loafers, and a black short-sleeve shirt. A faded blue CVN-70 *Carl Vinson* hat was perched on his head.

"No, this is just a quick turn-around trip. All I have is my briefcase. Why don't you drive us to some place we can grab breakfast?" Marshall motioned to the ball cap, "I thought you were retired FBI. Buford Jackson didn't say anything about you serving in the Navy."

"That's because I never did," Stewart said, as he navigated the traffic. "The hat's a souvenir from an old case I worked on years ago, back when I was in the Seattle office. Nope, only job I ever had was FBI. Retired several years back. Now I fish on the Bay darn near full-time. Only show up for my PI business if the fish aren't biting or there's not enough wind for a good sail."

The two men engaged in small talk until they were seated in a booth in Bob Evans. Jim Stewart looked narrowly at Marshall and demanded, "Okay, Hank, you have to explain a mystery to me before I agree take the case. You've just dropped five or six hundred dollars flying out to talk to me. If you hire me, I'm gonna cost you six, seven, maybe eight thousand dollars. Maybe more than that. And for what? An allegation you watched a dirty movie? C'mon, what's the big deal? So you got caught looking at a few forbidden treats, so what? Most of the guys I know have bought a magazine here and there; I know I have.

"So why are you sweating this? Even if you didn't do it, why pour all this cash into proving you didn't? Why's it so important to you?" Stewart poured them both a cup of coffee from the pot the waitress had left.

"Jim, I'm a believer in Christ—"

Stewart held up his hands, "Whoa! Let's get something straight right out of the box. I'm not interested in your religion, man. Buford's a great guy but he was always trying to sell me on Jesus. Came close to ruining our friendship. So if you're going to talk to me about Jesus I'm gonna drive you back to Reagan right now."

"Wait a minute, Stewart! *You* asked *me* a question," rejoined Marshall rather heatedly. "The answer has something to do with my faith, okay? Are you unable to extend me the courtesy of listening to my answer to your question?"

The PI shrugged sheepishly, "Sorry. Jumped the gun. Please continue."

"As I said, I am a Christian and holiness matters to Christians. Whether or not it means anything to you or anyone else for that matter, if I actually watched that movie I've dishonored Christ and I've dishonored my wife, and that's very important to me.

"I was accused of watching it when I was here in DC giving a talk on morality and politics—"

"Ouch!" Stewart chuckled. "Bad time to get caught. I don't imagine that went over very well."

"Yeah, well, it didn't come out until afterwards. But here's the thing: I'm not going to be known as another one of those self-righteous blowhards who preaches one thing and lives another. I'm a writer—"

"Yeah, that's what Jacks told me," the investigator interrupted again. "Said you've got quite a following—or did, anyway, until this little deal went down."

"Right. I do—or, did. Anyway, my whole life is wrapped around calling this country back to its constitutional roots and a basic level of morality. My personal integrity is essential. If readers think I don't live what I advocate they won't listen to a thing I say. I need to prove that I didn't do this. And when I do I'm going to call the *Chicago Tribune* reporter who broke the story and see if he'll write another article."

"Good luck with that. Reporters are never too keen on retractions. Bad news sells better than good news." Stewart studied the earnest man sitting across the table, his sharp blue eyes missing nothing. "Okay, I get it. It really is that important to you, isn't it?"

Marshall nodded. "It is."

"Alright. I'll see what I can do. It's gonna cost you three Gs right now for me to take the case. Add another two thousand for every week I'm on the case, the first week payable in advance. If you're prepared to write a check for five grand, you've hired yourself an investigator."

Marshall pulled out his checkbook, wrote a check for five thousand, and slid it across the table. Stewart folded it and stuck it in his wallet. "I'll probably be needing affidavits from you allowing the release of personal information. This whole privacy thing has been blown way out of proportion. Pain in the butt. Businesses won't release information on their customers without explicit permission."

"Contact Buford Jackson. He has comprehensive power of attorney for me and will provide those documents as you need them." He withdrew a file folder from his brief case. "This contains the hotel bill with the pay-per-view charges. The first charge is the porn flick. The second charge is for a Jane Austin flick I did watch—certainly not a dirty movie. Also in the folder is the conference schedule showing when I was speaking. Other than this, I don't have anything for you to go on."

"This ought to do it. You, Hank, have no idea how lucky you are," grinned Stewart as he put the folder in his briefcase.

"How's that?"

"Maryland's early season for striped bass ended last week so I can get started right away on your case."

Marshall laughed. He liked the crusty old agent. "That's not luck, Jim, it's providence. No such thing as luck."

****

Throughout July the readership on Marshall's blog continued to fall off until it was a mere fifth of what it had been prior to the MacKenzie article. Republican incumbent Dallas Chamberlain, who'd been polling in second place and fading behind a strong conservative challenger prior to the exposé on Marshall, saw his numbers edging back up steadily. The final poll numbers a week before the primary gave Chamberlain a four-point advantage.

Marshall was sitting in Starbucks with his pastor when his cellphone vibrated. It was Stewart.

"Call a meeting, Hank!" the investigator said abruptly when Marshall answered.

"Well, hello to you, too, Jim! What's up?"

"Call a meeting," the gravelly-voiced agent repeated, "I've got all the evidence and it puts you in the clear. It was a setup from the very beginning, Hank. I want Buford there, I want your wife there, and I want Adam MacKenzie there, because he's got one heck of an investigative piece to write."

Marshall couldn't speak for a moment. Pastor Johnson saw Hank's eyes well up and wondered what the call was about.

"Hello? Hank? Can you hear me?" Stewart asked, afraid he'd lost the connection.

"Yeah, Jim," he said hoarsely, "I'm here. That is great, great news, man." He cleared his throat, and asked, "When do you want the meeting? MacKenzie is already in town, he's been nosing around trying to dig up some local dirt on me for a follow-up article."

"Set the meeting for one o'clock tomorrow. You can pick me up at the airport at noon."

"Deal. See you then."

****

Adam MacKenzie of the *Chicago Tribune* was irritated. He'd been invited to a meeting hosted by Henry Marshall's attorney but the invitation was more like a summons and MacKenzie didn't like to be summoned. He'd been in Denver for three days interviewing friends and former employees of Marshall, digging up information for a follow-up article to his initial exposé. From what he'd been able to uncover so far Marshall was a real boy scout. No employee complaints, no sexual harassment accusations, no hint of marital infidelity, no known track record of pornography usage. He'd discovered that Marshall had gone on an almost non-stop alcoholic binge the year after his first wife died in an auto accident but that was nearly thirty years ago. Other than that it was slim pickings.

Admit it, Adam. What you don't like about Marshall is that he is a well-spoken intellectual conservative, and by your reckoning intellectual and conservative don't belong in the same sentence. You don't like it when someone challenges your worldview as easily as this guy does. MacKenzie clenched his jaws and shook his head, wishing he could get rid of that little voice in his conscience. *Yeah, this isn't journalism, Adam, it's a vendetta. Marshall's blog posts have had the audacity to pick apart your views and you want to poke him back.*

A graduate of the University of Southern California's prestigious Annenberg School for Communication and Journalism, Adam MacKenzie was the poster boy for left-wing

American journalism. He was unaware of his own bias because he considered his viewpoints to be the standard setting for "normal." But lately his settled progressive world had become uncertain. When writing an article on a Chicago Board of Education fight over the history curriculum he'd done some first-hand research, reading from cover to cover the textbook recommended by the Common Core standards. Then he read a history textbook used by the school system fifty years prior. And finally he studied three volumes covering early American history, each written by highly regarded historians. When he had finished he was shocked by what he'd found. The textbook recommended by Common Core was little more than an exercise in revisionist history, especially concerning America's founding and its early documents. It was not education at all, but indoctrination, and it disgusted the reporter.

The discovery was an inconvenient truth that was leading in some very disconcerting directions. For the first time in his life Adam MacKenzie began questioning his a priori commitments to the moral and intellectual superiority of progressivism. His carefully constructed personal reality was beginning to totter. The uncertainty, combined with the growing suspicion that somewhere along the line he'd been sold a bill of goods, made him angry.

The reporter left his rental in the underground parking garage and took the elevator up to Western Law Associates, Buford Jackson's firm. He was ushered into a conference room decorated with original western-themed paintings by cowboy artist Bill Owen. The secretary got him a cup of coffee and he sat down at the highly polished table, getting ready for the meeting.

A few minutes later Buford Jackson walked in. "You must be Adam MacKenzie, from the *Tribune*. Thank you for making time for us. I'm Buford Jackson, Henry Marshall's attorney. The others should be here any minute."

"Good to meet you, Counselor. I'm wondering, sir, if I should have legal representation at this meeting?"

Jackson looked surprised, "I don't see why. What is your

concern, Mr. MacKenzie?"

"I just published a piece very unfavorable to your client and I'm in Denver working on a follow-up. I am assuming this meeting is related to that, perhaps an opening shot to some sort of legal response. If so, I'll have to reschedule a time when my own legal counsel can be present."

"Mr. MacKenzie, I assure you that is not at all what this meeting is about. Henry Marshall has no plans whatsoever to bring action against you nor would I advise him to. We wanted you to be here in your capacity as an investigative journalist. There's going to be some new evidence presented regarding Marshall's activities in DC several weeks ago, and as you wrote the original piece we wanted to offer you an exclusive on what we hope will be a follow-up."

"Sorry, sir, but I don't do articles on demand. I'm a journalist, not a publicist."

"We didn't invite you here to be a publicist," the lawyer explained patiently. "We are just offering you the first shot at this evidence. If you have no interest in what we are about to share, fine, there are many other journalists who will find it fascinating. But please at least hear us out and then do with it what you will."

"Fair enough—I can do that." Adam sat down and pulled out his notebook and a digital recorder. "May I record this meeting?"

"Yes, but please consider everything you hear to be off the record. At the conclusion of the meeting if you are interested in what has been presented we can talk about what's on and what's off."

A few minutes later Henry and Haley Marshall walked in, followed by Jim Stewart. Introductions were made all around and the meeting began.

"Two weeks ago I spoke at a Heritage Foundation conference in DC on politics and morality. Several days later I was informed there was a charge on my hotel bill for a pay-per-view porn flick. Somehow, MacKenzie, a copy of that bill came into your possession and you, understandably, used it to write a very unflattering article accusing me of being a moral hypocrite.

"Naturally, I denied watching any such movie. Nevertheless you went forward with the article, which makes perfect sense—if I had watched the movie why *wouldn't* I lie about it in an effort to protect my reputation?" The reporter nodded.

Marshall continued, "However, I could not leave the accusation unchallenged. My integrity is important to me personally and it's vital for the audience for whom I write. I had to do something and I realized that no one was going to take my word on the matter without solid evidence. So I hired Jim Stewart to look into the matter. Jim is a part-time private eye who is a retired FBI agent. That's why we're here today—to hear the evidence Jim uncovered."

Adam nodded again, scribbling furiously on his pad.

Stewart plugged his laptop into the conference room projector and displayed an image of the hotel bill on the screen. "First things first," he said, grinning. "There are *two* movies on this bill, not one. What I want to know, Marshall, is what you were doing watching a Jane Austin chick flick when you could have been watching something manly, like *Saving Private Ryan*? What's with *Emma*, for crying out loud?"

"You watched *Emma*? You're kidding? I've been trying to get you to watch that with me for years, and you go off and watch it by yourself?" Haley demanded.

Marshall smiled sheepishly. "Look, sweetie, men just don't watch that Jane Austin stuff."

"No? Then why did you?"

He spread his hands, "You always rave about what a good movie it is, so I was curious. I thought if it was good enough, then you and I could watch it together sometime at home."

"And?" she queried dubiously.

"I don't know. I fell asleep after the first five minutes."

Haley rolled her eyes and shook her head.

Marshall looked at the reporter and stabbed the table with his finger, "That," he said, "is definitely *off* the record." He turned back to Stewart. "Can we move on, please?"

The investigator grinned maliciously and chuckled. "*Emma? Emma?* You gotta do something to renew your man-card, old boy. Okay, moving right along, the hotel management told me who handles their pay-per-view streaming video services, so I contacted Eastern Seaboard Entertainment, Inc. They wouldn't talk to me until I produced your affidavit, Hank. Apparently they like to keep their customers' private viewing habits private. They did confirm that they streamed the video to Hank's room that night. I talked to the IT management company contracted by the hotel, and their techs checked the router logs and verified that the Quality of Service, or QoS, protocol was active to Hank's room that night, meaning that streaming video was received."

Marshall frowned, "Wait a minute, Jim. I thought you said you found evidence that *cleared* me!"

"And so I did," Stewart responded. "The dirty movie was streamed from 6:30 until 8:15 p.m. that night."

"But I was at the conference, speaking, all afternoon and evening. I didn't get back to the hotel until nearly ten."

"Bingo," Stewart said with a smile.

MacKenzie sat up straighter in his chair. "Then who was watching the movie?"

"That's the question, isn't it? Who watched the movie? So who was sharing your room, Marshall?" Stewart asked.

"No one!" Marshall snapped.

"He's right," Stewart continued. "No one. So I got curious and contacted the firm that handles security for the Mayflower Hotel. Every time a key card is used to unlock any door at the hotel the access is recorded in a log file. At 6:15 p.m., a key card assigned to the housekeeping staff was used to open Marshall's door. I got a little more curious, and kept looking. That same key card opened the outer stairwell door at 6:12 p.m., and that was our friend's big mistake."

"How so?" asked Jackson.

"Because the stairwell has security cameras in it and I have a perfect shot of the man who came through the door." He brought up the high-definition black and white picture on the conference room screen. "I have no idea who this character is. None of the hotel staff or management recognized him. But this is our man—this is the guy who watched the dirty movie in your hotel room, Hank, and then changed the channel back to ESPN when the movie was over."

"Small world," MacKenzie muttered, staring at the picture on the screen.

"What?" Stewart asked.

"I said it's a small world," the reporter repeated. "Unbelievably, I know who that guy is. He's Ezra Raikes. Two years ago he served on Dallas Chamberlain's reelection campaign, doing oppo."

"Doing what?" Haley asked.

"Chamberlain?" exclaimed Stewart.

"Yes, Chamberlain," the reporter affirmed. He turned to Haley and explained, "Oppo is opposition research. He's one of the guys who digs up dirt on a candidate's opponent. But I wonder how on earth he got involved with this, and who's behind him?"

"I think I can answer that. Your identification of the creep, MacKenzie, actually confirms my findings," the investigator said. He turned to Hank, "When it became obvious this was a setup I started digging a little deeper. Getting caught watching a porn flick when you're speaking on morality—that's just a little too rich, a little too coincidental. So I looked into the conference arrangements. Each speaker at the conference is underwritten by an anonymous sponsor, a donor who covers all the expenses for that particular speaker: travel, meals, lodging, the speaker's fee, the whole shootin' match."

"Really? Never knew that," Marshall observed.

"Your anonymous sponsor was Dallas Chamberlain," Stewart said.

The room went silent. The only sound was MacKenzie scribbling in his notebook. After a moment the reporter looked up and asked quietly, "Mr. Marshall, hadn't you endorsed Chamberlain's primary opponent?"

Marshall nodded, and MacKenzie resumed writing in his notebook.

"Well, there's one more piece of the puzzle—" said Stewart.

"No, actually there are two more pieces," interrupted the

reporter, "but you go first, sir, please."

The investigator nodded. "When I learned who sponsored Hank at the conference I got a little curious about the coincidence that you, Mrs. Marshall, were not with your husband. As I understand it your practice is to travel together whenever possible."

"Correct," affirmed Haley. "The only reason I did not go with him this time was a last-minute speaking engagement with the Colorado Republican Women's Club."

"Right," continued Stewart, "I made a few more phone calls and learned that the invitation you received to speak to the Republican Women's Club, Mrs. Marshall, came at the urging of Congressman Chamberlain. Apparently Chamberlain wanted to ensure you would not be with your husband on this trip." Stewart turned to MacKenzie, "You have something to add to this?"

"Yes. The individual that provided me a copy of the Mayflower Hotel bill is connected with the Chamberlain campaign. I'd never connected all these dots, however."

"It was Chamberlain all along," mused Jackson. "In order to counteract your blog and your endorsement of his primary challenger, Hank, he had to take you down. And it was effective. He's presently a four-point favorite."

"Jim, I don't know how to thank you," Marshall said. "I feel like I have my life back."

"You might not be so grateful when you get my bill," Stewart laughed. "I had to grease a few palms along the way. By the way, Hank, the Heritage people were not involved with this nasty business. They had no idea of Chamberlain's machinations."

Buford Jackson looked at the journalist. "MacKenzie, I had no clue as to what we would learn today. But I figured it would be important for you to hear it in case you wanted to take another shot at this whole sordid episode. We are offering you an exclusive and there is only one string attached: you must publish at least one week before the primary. You don't have to accept what you've heard today. Draw your own conclusions, hire your own investigator, whatever. Write it the way you see it. So tell me, are you interested in an exclusive?"

"Yes, I am." He turned to Jim Stewart, "Will you share your research and contacts with me so I can independently verify everything?"

"If Hank has no objections, certainly."

"Just one thing, gentlemen," Hank said, "that *Emma* business? It's off the record."

****

With five days to go before the Colorado Republican primary Adam MacKenzie published his article in the *Chicago Tribune*. The story was picked up by all the networks and the story headlined CNN and Fox for three days. The evening the story broke Dallas Chamberlain held a press conference, complete with manufactured fury, promising to fire anyone on his campaign staff found to be responsible for the underhanded trick. The national exposure Marshall's blog received almost swamped his hosting service and he soon regained his audience, plus many more.

Chamberlain lost the primary, but his challenger was defeated in the massive Democratic sweep that occurred in the general election. The Republicans took a beating, losing control of both the House and the Senate. Democrats also gained the numerical advantage in the gubernatorial races, finishing the evening with twenty-eight of fifty governorships.

Chapter 4

THE PROPOSED CONSTITUTION, SO FAR FROM IMPLYING AN ABOLITION OF THE STATE GOVERNMENTS, MAKES THEM CONSTITUENT PARTS OF THE NATIONAL SOVEREIGNTY, BY ALLOWING THEM A DIRECT REPRESENTATION IN THE SENATE, AND LEAVES IN THEIR POSSESSION CERTAIN EXCLUSIVE AND VERY IMPORTANT PORTIONS OF SOVEREIGN POWER. THIS FULLY CORRESPONDS, IN EVERY RATIONAL IMPORT OF THE TERMS, WITH THE IDEA OF A FEDERAL GOVERNMENT.

Alexander Hamilton, Federalist #9

December, 2006

Mike Trujillo sat in the Starbucks in Pueblo and absent-mindedly stirred his coffee as he read Henry Marshall's latest blog post on his iPhone. "Right on," he muttered to himself. The chairman of the Colorado Republican Party, Trujillo was becoming increasingly disillusioned at the direction the national party was taking. It wasn't just a leftward drift—although that certainly bothered him—it was the ascendancy of a new pragmatism. When the RNC had gathered the state party chairmen earlier in the year, one of the speakers who'd garnered the most applause had used the line, "Winning isn't everything; it's the only thing." Trujillo had gotten up and quietly walked out during the thunderous ovation. *What*, he'd asked himself, *is the point of winning if we've compromised all we hold dear in order to win? Why bother running at all if that is the case? Are we after nothing more than power?*

Trujillo stared at Marshall's blog for another moment and

thought, *Time for you to get in the game, Marshall.* He knew that Marshall lived in Golden. *Golden. Hmm. That's Jefferson County, Buford Jackson's turf. Wonder if Buford knows him?* Jackson was the Jefferson County chair of the Republican Party. Trujillo put his coffee down and dialed Jackson's number.

"Hello, Mike. What's up?"

"Hey, Jacks. Do you read Henry Marshall's blog?"

"Every day. Why?"

"He's there in Golden, in your stomping grounds. Have you ever met him?" Mike sipped his coffee and frowned. Not enough sugar.

"Yes, I know him quite well. He's a good friend. I've done legal work for him, we go to the same church, we run together several times a month."

"Is he a registered Republican?" Trujillo asked as he stirred another little bag of sugar into the hot, black brew.

"Right now he is. Not sure how long that will last, though. He's really disgusted with the RNC."

"Aren't we all," Trujillo averred. "Can you put me in touch with him?"

"Yeah, I can put you in touch with him. In fact, I'm having breakfast with him this Saturday. Why don't you join us? The IHOP, on South Colorado Boulevard, just off US 87, 7:00 a.m."

"Excellent. Thanks for the invite. I'll be there." He took another sip. Perfect.

"Mike, can I ask what this is concerning?"

"Yes, of course. I think it's time Marshall got in the game. I want to convince him of that. I'd like to see him on a ballot in the not-too-distant future."

"As far as he's concerned, he *is* in the game. And he's got a large audience that follows him."

"Can he deliver them on Election Day?" Mike stood up and headed for the door, coffee in one hand, phone in the other.

"He's not interested in *delivering* them, Mike, he's interested in *developing* them into voters of conviction. Marshall isn't into red state-blue state, he wants to influence his audience at a far deeper level—he wants to change their thinking. Look, Mike, let me give you two cautions. First, don't burn any bridges. He's gonna turn you down cold, but what he probably needs is the idea run up the flagpole several times before he's willing to think seriously about it. So don't try to score a home run with him, or even a double or triple—just get on base. Second, he wants nothing to do with power grabs or intraparty politics. To Henry elective office is a means of serving the country, not a personal bucket-list item."

"All the better, from my perspective."

"You may not think so after you've talked to him."

"Why's that?" queried Trujillo. He put his coffee cup on the roof of his car as he stood in the early morning cold, fishing for his keys. A chilly, moisture-laden west wind was blowing off the Pueblo Reservoir, and the forecast was calling for snow in the next several days.

"Henry is not a good old boy, Mike. I know you aren't either, but Marshall takes it to a whole new level. He won't compromise or bargain if it's an issue that touches his core convictions. He won't play the *if you vote for my bill, I'll vote for yours* game. For him, every vote should be decided by the merits of the bill, period. He thinks legislators should be fully exposed by being forced to vote on single issues. Marshall hates the practice of tacking an unrelated amendment onto a bill, and then saying you really opposed it but voted for it because of the amendment. Modern parliamentary procedure is disingenuous, as far as Marshall is concerned."

The politician patted down every pocket, looking for his keys. No luck. Engrossed in the conversation, he didn't realize he was trying all the same pockets a second time. "Does he elevate every issue to major importance? Would he ascribe the same importance to a bill setting a state holiday for the jackalope as he would to a vote on the minimum wage?"

"Oh, no. He's got a good sense of discernment regarding which are hills to die on and which are of little consequence. But he won't budge on matters of conviction."

"That's why I want to talk to him. That's the kind of

candidate we need. Hang on a minute, I've got to put you down." Trujillo set the phone next to his coffee and searched his pockets one more time. No keys. With a sinking heart he peered through the tinted windows of his Ford Escape 4x4 and spied the keys dangling from the ignition. "Oh, for crying in a bucket!" he exclaimed. He picked up his phone. "Locked myself out of the car. What an idiot! And it's freezing out here."

"Did you try the door, Mike?"

"No, I didn't try the door! I always lock it!" he rejoined, irritated with himself.

"Try the door," Jackson patiently advised.

It opened easily. "How'd you know, Jacks?" he asked incredulously.

"Oh, I know you better than you think, Tru. And by the way—don't forget to get your coffee off the roof before you drive away."

****

Saturday morning dawned with three inches of snow on the ground in Denver and more expected. Henry Marshall was sitting in the booth at IHOP nursing a cup of coffee when Buford Jackson arrived and slid in the seat opposite. Jackson was wearing a red and black checkered wool lumberjack shirt, blue jeans, and old leather hiking boots. He looked more like a ranch hand than an eminently successful corporate lawyer.

"Mornin', Jacks. Glad the snow didn't slow you down."

"If three inches of snow slows a guy down, he's got to seriously consider living somewhere else," the old lawyer carped. "Listen, Hank, Mike Trujillo called me earlier this week, wants to meet you. I invited him to join us this morning."

"Trujillo? Isn't he the chairman of the state GOP?" Marshall asked. Jackson nodded. Hank continued, "Be glad to meet him—but I'm not going to use my blog as a shill for GOP candidates."

"I know that, Hank. Relax. That's not why he wants to meet you." Jackson perused the menu. He was in the mood for a stack of hot pancakes, slathered in real butter, with a liberal dollop of honey dribbled over them.

"Why, then?" demanded the younger man.

"I'll let him tell you. Just . . . be nice, okay?"

Marshall rolled his eyes and picked up his own menu. As they waited the conversation turned to the Broncos' waning chances for post-season play. Ten minutes later Mike Trujillo entered, brushing snow off his overcoat.

"You're late, Mike. We're starving," Jackson grouched. He motioned to the waitress.

"Well, a cheery hello to you, too, Jacks," Trujillo grumbled as he sat down and picked up his menu. "I suppose it could have had something to do with the weather," he said.

"Meh! Excuses! What's three inches of snow to a Coloradoan?" Jackson replied, winking at Marshall.

"Try twelve inches plus whiteout between Pueblo and Fountain, Buford. That would have stopped you Denver wussies cold."

"Touché. Twelve inches, huh?" Jackson raised his eyebrows. He'd not bothered to listen to the weather that morning.

"Yeah, and Denver is next. It's coming from the southwest. Hope you've got an extra room. You might need to invite me to spend the night, Jacks." He turned to Henry and shook his hand, "You must be Henry Marshall. I'm Mike Trujillo. Pleased to meet you."

"Hi, Mike. Glad to meet you." Marshall tried to be warm but couldn't help being a little reserved and not a little suspicious.

After breakfast was well underway the state GOP chair said, "Been reading your blog, Hank. I like what you have to say—especially your emphasis on principled conservatism."

"Thanks, Mike. If you've been reading my blog you know I'm not big on business as usual."

"Kind of hard not to notice that," Trujillo chuckled. "You know, Henry, it's one thing to criticize the modern political scene. It's another to wade in and start changing it. When are you going to throw your hat in the ring?"

Marshall let the question hang in the air while he refilled their coffee cups from the pot on the table, and then answered carelessly, "Oh, probably never. Being a politician is not one of my dreams in life, Mike."

"Perhaps not. But how about being an honest man representing the people who elected you and fighting for what you and your constituents believe?" Trujillo persisted. "You've done a good job critiquing the system, Hank. What about rolling up your sleeves and fixing it?"

The blogger shook his head. "That might be some people's calling, Mike, but I'm not convinced it's mine. I'm writing and exposing the flaws in the system and I'm proposing ideas of how we can do it better, but I've no interest in becoming a legislator. I'm not a lawyer and don't want to be one.

"Besides, I'm unelectable anyway because I say what I think and I tell the truth. I don't use 'diplo-speak.' And there's a significant portion of the electorate, maybe more than half, who doesn't care what a program costs as long as someone else is paying for it. They haven't a clue what the tax rate would need to be if Congress submitted a balanced budget at the current level of spending. And the politicians are happy to oblige the voters' ignorance and kick the can down the road. I don't think I could work within the system without throwing up every twenty minutes."

"Hmm. I've got two big problems with your objections, Marshall."

"Really? Fire away."

"First, your objections to the system reveal no real hope for change. Why are you even bothering to write if you have no hope? What's the point? It sort of makes you a political nihilist."

Buford Jackson looked down at his coffee cup and smiled. *Score!* Trujillo had just made a point his young friend could not answer. *Good job, Mike. You've just planted the seed that will eventually do the trick.*

"Second," Mike continued, "are you suggesting that out of

all our politicians, you would be the only honest, principled guy among them, the only guy who really cares? Are you really ready to flush them all down the toilet? No offense intended, but doesn't that strike you as just a little unfair, maybe a little arrogant?"

Ouch! Jackson thought to himself as he continued grinning into his coffee. *Hank, ol' buddy, you needed that, whether you know it or not.*

Marshall was silent. He wasn't accustomed to being challenged and wanted to angrily deny Trujillo's observations. But in a humbling moment of insight he realized the man sitting across from him was right. His blog had done so well and attracted so many admirers that his ego had become inflated —leaving him blind to his own flaws. He sensed the hand of the Lord behind the rebuke.

His Internet cheering section would never confront him as Mike Trujillo just did. He'd known the man for less than an hour but God was already using the politician to tell him things he needed to hear. This was a man, Marshall decided, that he needed as a friend.

****

Seven months later Mike Trujillo pulled his Ford SUV into the parking lot of the Montrose Holiday Inn Express. It was a gorgeous late afternoon in July. The four-hour drive from Pueblo to Montrose on US 50 had been a treat, the scenery ranging from an alpine wonderland of alternating stands of aspen and fir to stretches of semi-arid high-plains beauty. Trujillo loved the Rockies—there was nowhere else he'd rather be.

Montrose is a picturesque little town nestled in the southern Colorado Rockies. In the latter part of the nineteenth century when the track layers for the Denver and Rio Grande Railroad finally reached Montrose the town quickly became an important shipping center for ore from the mines in the area. But the mining business, while still significant, is no longer the mighty economic force it once was. Montrose remains something of a regional travel hub, but mostly for skiers coming to the San Juan Mountains.

But Trujillo had not come on a sight-seeing trip. The Madison Group, of which he was a member, was meeting in Montrose. The town had been chosen because it was not frequented by the high and mighty. No one dialed it into their GPS as anything more than a waypoint to somewhere else. In Aspen or Vail you might meet a high ranking political colleague on vacation, be it December or July. But hang around Montrose outside of ski season and you're going to bump into ranchers, truck drivers, and blue-collar workers coming off their shifts at the mine. It's the perfect place to be if your intention is flying below the radar, and the Madison Group was trying to stay at terrain-hugging level.

The Madison Group was a clandestine rebellion growing within the Republican Party. Its core convictions—indeed, the fact that it *had* core convictions—were anathema to a rudderless political party cast adrift on a sea of opportunists and rent-seekers. Everyone wanted a piece of the US budget: Big Business, Big Environment, Big Renewable Energy, Big Healthcare, Big Education, the Big Military-Industrial Complex, Big Welfare, Big Wall Street, Big Hollywood, Big Race-Hustlers, you name it, there were plenty of eager porkers gathering at the federal trough and plenty of politicians willing to dole out the slop. Meanwhile the country was drowning in a sea of red ink and the middle class was groaning under a confiscatory tax burden.

Although there were notable exceptions, much of Washington had become an insular world of political prostitution: an incestuous ruling class of legislators, lobbyists and bureaucrats sucking the life from average Americans. Politicians had two clients: the moneyed donors who contributed to their reelections (expecting favors in return), and the voters who had become dependent on government entitlements. Government was growing by leaps and bounds and the federal debt was somewhere north of unpayable. Both Republicans and Democrats were complicit.

The forty-odd men and women of the Madison Group were all patriots possessing significant political clout. Most were Republicans, a few were Democrats, several were Libertarians, but they all self-identified as constitutionalist conservatives. Though disagreeing on numerous issues they came together to forge a common platform they could all support while agreeing to disagree on peripherals. They knew that reforming the institutions of government would never happen without a political uprising of the slowly shrinking middle class. It was their goal to put forward a presidential candidate that would tell the truth and bring the executive branch with all its regulatory and enforcement powers under control.

But they also knew the major parties at the national level would stop at nothing to maintain the status quo. Which explains why the group remained secret and met in Montrose as opposed to Chicago.

****

After settling into his room, Mike Trujillo drove the short distance to his favorite Montrose restaurant, The Camp Robber, for a salad and a bowl of their signature Green Chile Chicken Potato soup. He sat by himself in a booth and took inventory. Sitting two tables away was one of the US senators from Texas. The governor of Indiana was in a booth against the far wall with his attorney general. The speaker of the house of the Utah state legislature had been leaving the restaurant as Trujillo was being seated. All were members of the Madison Group.

Trujillo pulled out his phone and texted Buford Jackson.

> *You here yet?*
>> *Yep*
> *Where?*
>> *Owl Creek, near Chimney Rock*
> *Whatsa matter? Take a wrong turn?*

No! Got here early, TRYING to fish! Go away! You're bothering me and scaring the trout!

Ha! One look at your ugly mug, they'll be terrified! See you in the AM.

Trujillo chuckled as he put his phone away. The crusty old lawyer was more like a brother than a friend.

****

To gain admittance to the secretive Madison Group, a prospect had to be sponsored by a current member. Two years ago Trujillo had sponsored Buford Jackson. Jackson had been full of questions and challenges.

"What's your position on abortion?" the lawyer had asked.

"The Madison Group believes it's a matter for each state to decide," answered Sam Sebastian, a former undersecretary of the US State Department who was currently serving a two-year term as the chairman of the Madison Group. Rotund and short with a bald head encircled by snow-white hair, eyebrows, and mustache, Sebastian bore an uncanny resemblance to the banker appearing on the Monopoly game board, minus the top hat. With a sharp, inquisitive mind, an undergrad degree in American history and a law degree from Harvard, Sebastian was well equipped to add intellectual heft to the Madison Group.

One of the functions of the chairman was to interview prospects and decide whether or not to admit them to the group. The screening process preserved the anonymity of the rest of the group in the event the prospect was rejected.

"But abortion is murder. How can you not have a position on it?" insisted Jackson.

"We *do have a position*: we believe the matter should be decided by each state individually. The big mistake in *Roe v. Wade* was taking the matter out of the hands of the states. Many of us agree with you that abortion is murder. Some of us don't. But we are all united around the idea that the matter is one to be decided at the state level."

"What about gay marriage?"

"That's a horse of a different color because the government has a compelling interest in the health of families as the basic building blocks of the state. Marriage as an institution has always been about more than sex: it's about procreation—raising children—and those children represent the future of the nation. Gay marriage threatens the family unit and treats children as though mothers and fathers are interchangeable. A great deal of research demonstrates that they are not interchangeable and that children do best with both biological parents in the home. If the family is weakened the future of the state is jeopardized. Economic statistics, health statistics and crime statistics all agree: healthy family units promote a healthy nation. That makes gay marriage a legitimate matter for federal involvement. The Madison Group opposes gay marriage, per se, as well as the adoption of children by gay couples. However we believe the matter of civil unions should be left to the voters in each state."

Jackson nodded, and then replied, "You don't even see the inconsistency, do you, Sam?"

"Inconsistency? Regarding what?" Sebastian asked, furrowing his brow.

"The state has a compelling interest in preserving families and the environment in which children are reared, which is why the Madison Group takes a firm position opposing homosexual marriage, correct?"

"Correct."

"And yet the state has no compelling interest in protecting the most helpless of its citizens, the unborn child? It seems to me that if there is a role at all for the federal government that role would certainly include protecting the lives of its citizens."

Sebastian held up his hands in mock surrender, "Buford, I hear you. But we are trying to establish a coalition that will unite around basic conservatism. Just like there are factions in both major parties, there are factions among us. The only hope we have of beating the liberals is to unite around what we can agree on, not fight about what we can't."

"I understand that, and to a point I agree. But by punting on abortion and yet opposing homosexual marriage, the Madison Group has created a crack in its foundation that any college-age philosophy major could drive an eighteen-wheeler through. The state has a compelling interest in both situations; you've only recognized it in one of the two. This is going to come back to haunt you."

"Perhaps," Sam Sebastian replied, shrugging his shoulders. "But our platform is more strategic than philosophical. The only way to shrink Leviathan is by turning everything we can back over to the power of the states. Our core strategic principle is states' rights, not social conservatism. But we haven't abandoned social or moral conservatism; we believe that when the power has been returned to the states it will be easier for the citizens of a state to move it in a conservative social and moral direction. But if we don't push the power back to the states first, then every time a state votes to, say, ban homosexual marriage, the federal courts will feel compelled to intervene and overrule the will of the electorate."

"I understand. But the Madison Group is not going to help itself with this kind of inconsistency in its central principles."

"Objection noted. More questions?"

Jackson thought for a moment before asking, "Okay, how about legalization of marijuana?"

"Remove marijuana from the federal list of controlled substances and let the states sort the rest of it out."

"Minimum wage?"

"Leave it to the states. Listen, Buford, while we are correcting the overreach of Uncle Sam we have to be very careful how we do it. If we stake out comprehensive positions on every issue we will find ourselves advocating a federal government just as illegitimately intrusive as the current one.

"The imposition of federal laws and regulations is strangling the country. The national government has usurped the role granted it by the Constitution. Complicating the problem is an activist judiciary transforming the Constitution and Bill of Rights into something never intended by the Founders." Sebastian paused for a moment and lit his pipe. The rich smell of cherry-flavored tobacco filled the room.

Sebastian puffed on his pipe for a moment and then continued. "The Madison Group unites around the vision of allowing the people in each individual state to choose the path for their state. In the best sense of the expression we want to encourage the states to become laboratories of democracy."

Buford raised his eyebrows, "You're misusing Justice Brandeis' expression when he wrote the dissent in *New State Ice Co. v. Liebmann.* He didn't mean what you think he meant, Sam."

"I am well aware of what Brandeis meant. A study of his legal opinions makes clear that he only liked 'laboratories' that produced the 'right' results—in other words, that supported progressive causes. But the Madison Group has co-opted the expression. What *we* mean by it is that the federal government must never intrude in the business of the states except as explicitly provided for in the Constitution. The states must be allowed to manage their own affairs within the limits specified by the Constitution. We don't believe the Constitution has a *penumbra*," Sebastian added dryly.

"Well, that's a relief," muttered Jackson.

Sebastian nodded. "Quite. The role of the federal government is to ensure that the liberties specifically enshrined in our founding documents are preserved in all the states, whether or not state laws and regulations pass muster with a progressive agenda. If a state goes too liberal or too conservative and a citizen does not care for it, he can either become active in local politics and try to pull it back, or he can vote with his feet and move to a state more to his liking. The important thing is that he does not have the burden of trying to get forty-nine *other* states to agree with him, only the residents of his state."

****

Sam Sebastian looked about at the gathered Madison Group members. "I propose that we run a presidential candidate in 2016. I think we'll be ready. We should stay within the two-party system as long as possible, but if it looks like he will not win the nomination then he—or she—jumps ship and runs as an independent."

"No," replied the normally quiet Joshua Cummings. All heads turned in his direction. "Run a candidate in 2016? Yes, we can do that. Switch over from one of the majors to run as an independent halfway through? No, that's a surefire formula for failure. If he's going to go independent he needs to start that way," he insisted. Cummings was a widely respected political consultant who'd managed several successful presidential campaigns, consulted on others, and had written authoritative books on the shifting political landscape. Both CNN and Fox News used him as a political analyst. No one else in the room possessed his expertise in managing and leading national political campaigns. Frankly, there weren't many consultants in the whole country who could match Josh Cummings' breadth and depth of experience.

"You can't make a presidential campaign materialize out of thin air, no matter how much excitement you generate. Getting functioning campaign teams in all fifty states is a massive undertaking, impossible on short notice. Then you've got to collect enough signatures to get on the ballot in each state. And that's just the beginning of troubles. If you think the calendar is the big problem, just wait until you consider the money necessary to make all that happen." Cummings paused and rubbed his face with both hands.

"Go on," Sebastian urged.

"Well, you're going to be working with very limited funds. So you've got to come up with a strategy that will put at least two hundred seventy electoral votes in your column on election night. That plan will drive your expenditures, ad buys, meet-and-greets, and so forth. You don't necessarily have to be competitive in every state, but you do have to attain two-seventy. And even though the early states are small from an electoral standpoint—Iowa, New Hampshire, Nevada, South

Carolina—they are crucial from a momentum standpoint. Ignore them to your peril. Doing poorly in the early states can dry up contributions overnight. None of this planning and preparation," Cummings concluded, "happens on short notice. You need lots of lead time. If our guy is going to run as an independent, he's got to start there."

"I guess you've got your work cut out for you, then," smiled Mike Trujillo.

"Say again? What's that supposed to mean?"

Sam affirmed, "Josh, if anyone can solve these problems and map a road to victory, you can. And we happen to know you're taking the 2008 presidential campaign season off. So why don't you put that super-computer brain of yours to work on this problem? Pro bono, of course."

Cummings rolled his eyes. "Of course, of course, of course," he mimicked. "Why did I know you'd say that?" Money was not an issue for Cummings. Between his books and his consulting he was well set.

"Well?"

"Yeah, I'll tackle it," he said. "Why not? It will be a challenge. Maybe I can use it for my next book, call it *How to Win a Presidential Campaign with neither Money, Party, nor Candidate*. Piece of cake," he snorted sarcastically. "Come to think of it, I've got the easy part. The rest of you guys have the hard part."

"How's that?" asked Buford Jackson.

"You guys have to come up with the candidate. It's 2006 now: if we can't name our candidate by New Years Day 2013, we'll have to push the project back another four years. Listen, people," he asserted, rapping his knuckles on the table for emphasis, "the two established parties have had all this machinery set up, well oiled and functioning for over one hundred years. We have nothing. Nothing! We're facing a near-superhuman challenge just to mount a credible campaign, not to mention winning. If we don't have an outstanding candidate by dawn of January 1, 2013, we can forget the 2016 election. And even if we do have our guy, it's going to be an exhausting four-year sprint."

The next two hours were spent discussing strategies, resources, potential donors, and handling the press. The one thing not discussed was the matter most needing discussion: who might the candidate be?

Though he shared his thoughts with no one, Buford Jackson had a name in mind. But the problem was, that person had neither interest nor experience in political office. It was, in some ways, ludicrous to even consider him.

****

We're Being Played for Fools
Posted 9/1/2008
By Henry Marshall

In two months and four days Americans will exercise the highest privilege of citizenship the United States can offer. Millions will go to the polls to cast their vote selecting the next president to govern this great country.

Every presidential election is a high-stakes event. The person who sits behind the Resolute Desk in the Oval Office is arguably the most powerful human being on the planet. The fate of nations has often been in the hands of the President of the United States. Since the beginning of the twentieth century a short list of countries affected by the exercise of the power of the American presidency—for good or for ill— would include Germany, Italy, Japan, England, France, the Netherlands, the Philippines, China, Korea, Vietnam, Cuba, Egypt, Israel, Kuwait, Iraq, Libya, Iran, Panama, Nicaragua, and many others. It is indisputable that the next administration will add to that list, whether by military intervention in one of the world's hotspots, fighting AIDS or some other disease in Africa, or providing disaster relief somewhere.

And yet the election campaign has not proven to be about wise governance and good policy but rather a bidding war for votes among various constituencies. To a certain degree both the Republican and Democrat candidates have trivialized the great trust they are seeking by pandering to various voting blocks. They are treating the Office of the Presidency as if it were for sale, and the purchase is made at the cost of your tax dollars and mine. The country is ill-served by treating its highest office as a commodity to be purchased at an auction.

We are in a fiscal crisis and we need serious leadership. Social safety net entitlements, corporate welfare, sweetheart deals with big business, and what our legislators call WAM, or "Walking Around Money" are combining to sink our fiscal ship. Washington spends money like a drunken sailor, and the solution proposed for our spending problem is yet more spending.

Every tax dollar taken from your pocket is a dollar largely wasted by the government. As was famously stated by Ronald Reagan in his first inaugural address, "In this present crisis, government is not the solution to our problem, government IS the problem." Some might find this statement humorous, but to me it's no laughing matter. The federal government has become the primary problem that plagues America. Uncle Sam is ruining the economy and destroying the middle class. The *Code of Federal Regulations* has over 157,000 pages of regulations printed in over 200 bound volumes, strangling small business, squashing innovation, and diminishing the freedom of the average American.

These are the sorts of serious issues that face our country today, and judging from their platforms and speeches both major party candidates seem bent on fueling the fire rather than fixing the problem. The American people deserve better. We should demand better!

The solution is simple to understand but difficult to achieve. It involves two words: *states' rights*. From the beginning of the twentieth century to the present time we have seen one long usurpation of power by Uncle Sam. In order to save our country and ensure that it continues to be a bastion of freedom in an autocratic world, this unconstitutional power grab by the feds must be reversed. The federal government needs to be restricted to the very few duties granted it by our Constitution. Everything else must be returned to the fifty states.

In his first inaugural address President Reagan said "We must act today in order to preserve tomorrow." It is unfortunate that in the current election we are not provided a candidate who will "act today." We need a presidential candidate who is committed to *dismantling Leviathan*, not perpetuating it. Neither of the current major party presidential candidates qualify. We are being played for fools. I hope and pray the American voter will cultivate a long memory, for we cannot afford in four years to have another such selection.

****

"Josh, c'mon, help us out! The Democrats are eating our lunch. It's only two months until the election, so you won't be in it that long. We need you, buddy."

Joshua Cummings sighed and closed his eyes, shaking his head. He felt like throwing his iPhone in the Arkansas River, rather than the yellow and black Mepps spinner dangling from the tip of his ultra-light spinning rod. He reluctantly waded to the bank and sat down on a rock. "No, Buzzy, for the last time, no, no, no, no! Why should I help you guys? Your candidate is a RINO. I'm not interested in putting a RINO in office."

"Ah, but what about the Supreme Court? There are two probable appointments in this next term. Do you want a Democrat making those appointments?"

"No, I don't. Of course not! I want a conservative to make those appointments!"

"Well then, there you go. Welcome aboard! I'll see you in Washington tomorrow morning at Campbell's campaign headquarters."

"No, Buzzy, you won't. Campbell is not a conservative. I'm not going to help put him in office. There would be little—if any—discernible difference between his Supreme Court nominees and those of the Democrats."

"Look, Josh, if we can get a Republican slate elected, maybe in 2012 we'll run a conservative."

"Buzzy, how many times do you think the rank and file will fall for that cruel bait-and-switch? It's a RINO strategy that's keeping the libs and the establishment types in control of the party. The result has been predictable: more big-government programs, more spending, more national debt. If the Republicans are nothing more than Democrat-lite, why should the electorate vote for them?"

"Josh, wake up! You need to deal with realpolitik, man. We've got to run someone who is electable."

"*No*, you have to run someone who has convictions, otherwise there is no point in winning and the voter winds up with a bad choice or a slightly better bad choice. I'm not interested in winning elections, Buzzy, I'm interested in changing the country, pulling it back to its constitutional founding principles. "

"Josh, you are one of the top political consultants in the country. Most people, including me, consider you to be a political genius. I've seen you pull elections out of the swamp and win, time and time again. Please, please, please work with us! We need you, man."

"No, Buzzy. When the RNC anointed a left-of-center moderate as the heir apparent, they left me and most of the base behind. I'm done with the RINO game. You guys made your bed, now you have to sleep in it."

"Josh—"

"I'm hanging up now, Buzzy, goodbye." Joshua Cummings terminated the call and turned his cellphone off. Turning around, he studied the water. A slight riffle thirty feet from him and slightly upstream looked very promising. Cummings expertly cast the Mepps just above the other side of the riffle and began his retrieve. He observed a flash of silver under the water just downstream of the riffle and was immediately rewarded with a hard strike. "Yeah, baby!" he exulted, grinning as he played the large Brown trout.

Chapter 5

> IF ANGELS WERE TO GOVERN MEN, NEITHER
> EXTERNAL NOR INTERNAL CONTROLS ON
> GOVERNMENT WOULD BE NECESSARY. IN FRAMING A
> GOVERNMENT WHICH IS TO BE ADMINISTERED BY
> MEN OVER MEN, THE GREAT DIFFICULTY LIES IN THIS:
> YOU MUST FIRST ENABLE THE GOVERNMENT TO
> CONTROL THE GOVERNED; AND IN THE NEXT PLACE
> OBLIGE IT TO CONTROL ITSELF.
>
> *James Madison, Federalist #51*

Early November, 2008

As expected the progressive Democrat candidate for president clobbered the moderate Republican in the general election on the 4th of November. And, also as expected, the Republican National Committee engaged in the standard GOP establishment post-mortem: "If our man had positioned himself a little farther to the left he could have made a better showing. If only he hadn't picked such a conservative for his vice presidential candidate. It's that darn conservative wing of the party! They say the dumbest things and frighten the moderates and independents." Unnoticed, of course, was that truly conservative Republican legislators and gubernatorial candidates won nearly every race in which they were represented. This, despite the fact that the overwhelming swing of the election was Democratic, and despite the mainstream media's best efforts to portray the conservatives as wild-eyed radicals obsessed with giving Granny a last meal of dog food before pushing her over the cliff in her wheelchair.

****

Well, duh! What did you expect?
Posted 11/7/2008
By Henry Marshall

The title of today's post is intended to be prophetic: I will be posting a blog article under this heading after the State of the Union address in 2012. But I can already tell you much of what will be in that future post. Why am I able to do so? It's simple: our country, having elected a "progressive" to the Office of the Presidency earlier this week and having granted him a solid congressional majority, has opened a Pandora's box of trouble—trouble that's entirely predictable as to its outcome.

Let's cut to the chase, shall we? Progressivism is simply socialism with a shiny new name. When she was being interviewed for *Thames TV This Week* on February 5, 1976, Margaret Thatcher put her finger on the great weakness of socialism—a weakness that has been demonstrated historically in every case. She said, ". . .Socialist governments traditionally do make a financial mess. *They always run out of other people's money.* It's quite a characteristic of them."

Socialism is claimed to be a transitional stage between capitalism and a communist utopia in which the need for a central government will have withered. In socialism, the means of production are owned by the state and managed by the workers. But the sad judgment of history is that socialist enclaves, be they nations or local projects, have proven to be inherently unstable. They always fail to deliver what they promise.

There are at least two glaring weak points of socialism. The lesser of the two is that the creation of legitimate wealth in a socialist society is virtually impossible, consequently socialism can not survive inefficiency. A socialist society produces—theoretically—only what is needed. The value of the commodities produced is not based upon demand but the labor output necessary to manufacture them. In actual practice, socialist societies have produced far less than what is needed. Unless an artificial means of propping them up can be found, they collapse under their own weight.

The second essential flaw of socialism is its inability to deal with the sinful nature of man. Socialist theory—usually atheistic—denies the inherent evil in man. If men were angels a socialist society might do well, but when push comes to shove, the laborers are not sufficiently motivated by the altruism of the socialist project to work harder than their neighbor. In effect, they have no skin in the game because under socialism one is not supposed to build personal wealth. Socialism possesses a glorious inconsistency: while denying the sinful bent of men, it accuses capitalism of playing to man's greed. Say what? Isn't greed sinful?

At the end of our new socialist presi-dent-elect's fourth year, we will be suffering devastating unemployment, an unpayable federal debt, a new round of massively intrusive government regulations with a corresponding loss of personal freedom, an unparalleled government takeover of portions of the US economy, and a new generation of people and corporations dependent upon federal government hand-outs and subsidies. This is the legacy of socialism.

And when I write that post, I will ask: *what did you expect?*

****

Buford Jackson punched in Marshall's number and waited for the cellular network to connect the call. It was January 2009, and the Front Range was blanketed in snow. The lawyer had been following Marshall's blog and was impressed by what he'd seen. With over ten million followers, Marshall's web host had been forced to create a small server farm just to handle the traffic surrounding his blog. Not that they minded: click-through advertising traffic was generating a revenue stream more than sufficient to make the effort worthwhile.

"Hey, Jacks, what's up?"

"I'm calling you out, you couch potato! Want you to run the Garden of the Gods Ten-Miler with me this year," Jackson insisted. The lawyer turned in his chair so he could see the mountains. With the snow cover gleaming in the morning sun, they looked like burnished silver.

"Ten miles? Whoa! I'd have to throw on a little extra training. There's quite a bit of up and down in that race, isn't there?" asked Marshall.

"Yes, plenty."

"When is it?"

"June 14, Hank. Plenty of time to train—as long as your wussy butt can run in the cold," challenged Jackson.

"Ha! If you can do it, Buford, I can do it."

Jackson grinned to himself. The fish had taken the bait. "Really? What have you been doing lately?"

"Oh, maybe twenty miles a week, but no real climbing or altitude."

"Hmm. We'll have to change that. Okay—you work out on your own during the week, but I own you until noon every Saturday. What do you say, Hank?"

"Let me check with Haley to be sure, and I'll get back to you."

"Sounds good."

Buford Jackson hung up the phone, and swiveled around in his black leather chair. "And thus begins your preparation, Hank," he said aloud, "but not for the Garden of the Gods race. Oh, no, no, no—I've got a different race in mind for you."

That Saturday they drove up to Red Rocks and ran a six-mile loop trail. As they ran, Buford quizzed Henry about his blog.

"So, I see you've got, what, around ten million followers? Is that about right?" he asked. They were doing somewhere around eight-minute miles, the lawyer guessed.

"Yep. It's been growing like crazy. I think we're averaging fifteen thousand new visitors each month."

"Did you ever think that it would take off like this?"

"No, not in my wildest dreams," Marshall admitted. "I think I've hit a nerve in the conservative movement. Based on the comments, the readers feel like somebody's finally put their finger on how they feel and what's wrong with the country."

Both runners fell silent as they navigated some icy patches. They reached a dry, straight stretch and Jackson continued, his breath creating puffs of condensation that froze on his beard and mustache. "So, what events have you planned?"

"What do you mean, Jacks?"

"Events! Like a speaking tour. What do you have planned?" Jackson pressed.

"None. Don't plan to, either." Marshall's response was

emphatic, if a little breathless due to the altitude and the incline.

"Oh, I'm sorry. I guess I misunderstood what you are trying to do," confessed Jackson, his gravelly voice tinged with an edge of sarcasm.

"What's that supposed to mean, Buford?" asked Marshall defensively.

"Oh, nothing, really. I guess I thought you were trying to educate the populace about a government constrained by the Constitution, the division of powers, and what it means to be a republic. I didn't realize your blog was just a personal outlet to vent your frustrations with Washington."

Hank didn't respond and the pair continued to run in silence. Jackson knew his friend was processing what he'd just said, and he didn't want to offer a fig leaf. The silver-haired attorney was following the advice he'd often given to younger lawyers: *when your opponent is convicting himself, don't get in his way.*

The parking lot was in sight, and Jackson had icicles on his beard when Marshall finally responded. "So what would these events look like? How would this work?"

"It won't be too difficult. Pick a topic you are passionate about—something that captures your own heart—perhaps something on why the Founders wrote checks and balances into the Constitution, or why it is necessary to place restraints on government. Develop a good, well-researched speech. Craft a punchy two-or-three-sentence pitch for your topic, and get a graphic artist to create a reproducible image that captures your theme.

"Put a survey on your blog to assess interest—something like, 'I am planning a speaking tour on this topic for late spring. I still have open dates. If you'd like me to come to your area, give me your zip code and email address.' Have your webmaster weave the survey, the pitch, and the graphic together in an eye-catching way. Then see what sort of response you get. Your webmaster should build a database of the responses. You pick the, say, eight zip codes with the greatest response and that's where you go.

"Carve out several weeks when you and Haley can travel—always, always, always take your wife to these sorts of things. It keeps you out of trouble; it makes your wife a full participant—a partner; and it lets people get to see and know you much better."

"What about the logistics of renting and setting up a venue, making all the arrangements, and so forth?"

"If you decide you're serious about this, I'll find someone to handle that part. Just don't schedule your speaking tour during the Garden of the Gods Ten-Miler!"

****

"Buford Jackson really had a weird idea yesterday morning. He thinks I ought to schedule some sort of speaking tour, some public appearances connected with my blog."

"Really? Why is that a 'weird' idea, Hank? Why not just a 'good' idea?" Haley's brown eyes sparkled as she looked across the table at her husband. She considered her husband to be an intelligent and perceptive man in all matters except where it concerned himself. She knew he was still mystified by the success of his blog.

He cocked his head, surprised, and queried, "You think it's a *good* idea?"

"I do."

"But—"

She cut him off with a wave of her hand. "Hank, haven't you been reading the comments on your blog? You're tapping a deeply felt frustration with Washington and the status quo. People know the system is not working the way it was designed to. Your blog pieces are identifying what's gone wrong. You're giving your readers an 'aha!' experience by explaining and validating why they are so frustrated."

"This blog thing was supposed to be a hobby, Haley. Do we really want it to grow beyond that? Are you prepared for that? Because you will be just as involved as I will."

"Hank, the Lord is in control. It will go as far as He wants it to, and no farther. So, yes, I am prepared to move to the next step and however many steps there might be beyond that."

"Buford says it's essential you come if I set up a speaking tour. Says I need you to keep me out of trouble," Marshall added, smiling.

She laughed, a musical sound that had captivated Henry the first time he'd heard it. She reached across the table and with a mischievous twinkle in her eye responded, "He knows you well! I guess we'll have to schedule it around my teaching calendar."

He nodded. "I still feel uncertain about this. Besides, I'm not convinced anyone would take an evening to hear me speak. Let's pray about it for several weeks before we decide."

****

Western Law Associates, Inc., (WLA) was a prestigious Denver legal firm specializing in corporate law, patents, and intellectual property rights. Owned by five partners, Buford Jackson was the senior partner and founder, having run it solo for the first four years. But after winning a fifty-million-dollar patent-infringement judgment against a medical equipment manufacturer on behalf of a Denver high-tech firm, he found himself with more business than he could handle. Eventually he had taken on four partners, two women and two men, all people of high integrity with hard-nosed courtroom experience. Jackson retained managing control, owning fifty-five percent of the firm.

An athletic sixty-eight, Jackson was a Christian who did not suffer fools. He tended to be bluntly honest, but not brutal. Jackson took his faith very seriously, seeking to live consistently the implications of what he believed. He practiced corporate law because he genuinely enjoyed it. He loved the research and finding the one nugget that would seal a favorable verdict. He enjoyed the challenge of the courtroom and the effort required to present a persuasive argument. He was a lawyer of conscience and didn't take on cases or clients that went crosswise to his own convictions.

Jackson was an imposing figure topping out at three inches above six feet. His rugged, tanned face and silver-grey hair with close-trimmed beard and mustache combined to produce an image of a wild-west sheriff. He had a deep, gravelly voice that commanded attention. By a constant regimen of running with just enough weight-lifting to keep his upper body tight, he maintained excellent cardiovascular fitness. His wife Sandy joked that he was Omar Sharif's taller brother, and the resemblance to the actor was uncanny.

Buford Jackson was a natural leader and a born mentor. Though neither man would have expressed it in these terms, Henry Marshall was Jackson's protégé. His influence over the younger man was considerable. Marshall's convictions and ideas were his own, but the manner and tone in which he communicated them to the world, his interactions with those around him, and the character with which he lived out each day was—at least partially—a consequence of his friendship with the lawyer.

But the lawyer was ready to make some changes in his own schedule. Though WLA had an active load of clients, Jackson himself had not accepted any new cases in the last six months. His own docket was clearing up and his long-term cases were being turned over to his associates. A year ago WLA had renegotiated its retainer contracts so that Jackson was not mentioned by name in any of them: the firm, not Jackson himself, was now on retainer. He'd even been hinting about a potential buyout. As the lawyer slowly put distance between himself and the firm he had a growing amount of freedom in his schedule—and he knew exactly how he wanted to spend the extra time.

****

"Have you read this?" Buford Jackson reached into the back seat of his car and retrieved a shrink-wrapped copy of

Walter McDougall's classic, *Promised Land, Crusader State: The American Encounter with the World Since 1776*, and put it in Henry Marshall's hands. The two men and their wives were standing in the church parking lot after the Sunday morning service. A warm Chinook wind was sweeping off the Front Range and it was a balmy, sunny sixty degrees.

"No, why?" Hank set his Bible on the car and started digging for his keys.

"As you continue to write, Hank, it might help to actually know what you're talking about."

"Well, thanks a lot, Jacks. With friends like you—"

The lawyer cut him off with a dismissive wave of his hand. "Oh, stick it in your ear! Listen, Hank, you need to read more widely than the strictly constitutional issues. You know why? Because government policies should be the outworking, the implementation, of the Constitution and the laws that have been added since. Foreign policy, such as that in McDougall's book, is all about the face America presents to the world. There are philosophical underpinnings that drive it—it's just as important as domestic policy in some respects. When American blood and treasure are spent it's in consequence of foreign policy. Foreign policy is an area of American politics in which you need more fluency.

"When you go on your speaking tour you're not going to sit on top of Mount Olympus and lecture the hoi polloi from on high, you know. People will have questions. Their questions won't be scripted and much of the time they won't even be on topic. You've got a powerful critique of the current political scene—they'll want to know your opinion on other matters, too. So it's high time you start boning up on a wider spectrum of issues, such as foreign policy."

"But I haven't decided whether or not to do a speaking tour," Marshall protested.

"Oh, you will. I'll quiz you on McDougall during our run on Saturday."

****

Two months later, February of 2009, Marshall still had not committed to a speaking tour. Jackson didn't press the issue, knowing his designs would amount to nothing if Hank himself was not committed. Haley and the kids, however, were in favor. Their eldest, Charity, a precocious fifteen-year-old who'd inherited her parents' mind for numbers, thought it would be "cool" but that Dad would have to "stop dressing like a dork." Charlie and Conner, their thirteen year old identical twins, thought it would be neat as long as they could travel with Mom and Dad and add to their scrapbooks of US states they had visited.

Hank knew he was dragging his feet, but he wasn't sure why. He just knew he really didn't want to commit to it. He and Haley had prayed together about the idea and she thought the answer was a clear yes. He was resisting, and felt a growing reluctance to launch a speaking tour even if he thought the Lord was in it. Fighting with himself, he grew irritable and snappish with his family, which just made matters worse.

One night Haley stood at the doorway of his study, watching him. Hank sat motionless at his desk staring blankly at his monitor, unaware she was there. After observing quietly for several moments she walked behind his chair and began kneading his shoulders. They were tight with tension. "Hank, are you okay?"

He touched her hands. "The joy is gone. I'm not enjoying writing anymore. Truthfully, I'm not enjoying much of anything anymore. I wish Jacks had never mentioned that stupid idea of going out and speaking. The thought will not turn loose of me. I can't shake it, but I know I don't want to do it. I don't want to. I just—don't want to."

She continued rubbing his shoulders. "Then don't do it, Hank," she said softly. "It's okay. No one is forcing you to."

He swiveled in his chair until he was facing her. "That's just it, sweetheart. I think the Lord wants me to do it. I have the distinct sense that I'm fighting against Him, and that's why I'm so miserable. I don't want to go on a speaking tour. I don't want the hassle and the headaches. I don't want to travel. I—I don't want the exposure."

She sat on the edge of his desk, not speaking. He shook his head, then turned back to his monitor. They sat in silence for a few minutes and then she said, "Why don't you get away for a few days and clear your head. You could head for Leadville, or Buena Vista, or Crested Buttes, and have some time to yourself—think, pray, relax. Don't take your phone or your computer. Take a couple of good books, maybe a novel. Take your cross-country skis and have a couple of days to just bump around. When you come back we'll sit down and talk it out. I'll support your decision either way."

He pursed his lips and exhaled slowly. "You know, that sounds really, really good. I'll do it."

"You can make your plans tomorrow. It's late, why don't you come to bed?" She raised her eyebrows and smiled, flirting.

"Whoa! That sounds really good, too." He turned the computer off and followed her out of the room.

Chapter 6

IF A NUMBER OF POLITICAL SOCIETIES ENTER INTO A LARGER POLITICAL SOCIETY, THE LAWS WHICH THE LATTER MAY ENACT, PURSUANT TO THE POWERS INTRUSTED TO IT BY ITS CONSTITUTION, MUST NECESSARILY BE SUPREME OVER THOSE SOCIETIES, AND THE INDIVIDUALS OF WHOM THEY ARE COMPOSED. . . . BUT IT WILL NOT FOLLOW FROM THIS DOCTRINE THAT ACTS OF THE LARGE SOCIETY WHICH ARE NOT PURSUANT TO ITS CONSTITUTIONAL POWERS, BUT WHICH ARE INVASIONS OF THE RESIDUARY AUTHORITIES OF THE SMALLER SOCIETIES, WILL BECOME THE SUPREME LAW OF THE LAND. THESE WILL BE MERELY ACTS OF USURPATION, AND WILL DESERVE TO BE TREATED AS SUCH.

Alexander Hamilton, Federalist #33

Tuesday, February 10, 2009

Flurries of snow scampered around his Mitsubishi Outlander Sport as Marshall loaded the vehicle with skis and snowshoes, hiking boots and gators, a heavy parka, and an emergency pack designed for traveling the high country in winter. He didn't know exactly what he would need because he had no idea what he'd be doing—he just needed to get away. He took his cellphone but kept it turned off. No computer.

"When should I expect you back?" asked Haley when he went back into the kitchen.

"No later than supper time on Saturday, babe," he replied as he poked around in the cabinets looking for his travel mug.

"Ah ha!" he said triumphantly, and then filled it with hot coffee.

"What if Buford calls?"

"Tell the old rascal that I've gone on a *thinking* tour," he smirked. "That'll fix him."

Several hours later he was driving on US 285, descending into the beautiful South Park basin, between the Mosquito and Park Mountain ranges. A quarter mile south of Kenosha Pass, South Park spread out before him on his left as the road wound down to the valley floor. He stopped at the overlook and got out of the car. The air was fresh and cold, with just a hint of sage. A frigid gust explored the neck of his wool shirt, and he reached back into the SUV for his parka. It was over-cast and there were snowflakes on the wind, but nothing serious at the moment. An eighteen-wheeler was laboring up the pass, diesel throbbing, but otherwise the road was bare of traffic.

Invigorated, Marshall drank in the beauty. The valley extended south until it was lost in the mist of distance, snow-capped mountains towering on either side like sentinels, with streaks and faces of black granite showing starkly wherever the snow refused to stay put. Closer to him, a stand of white-barked aspens off to his right bowed their heads before the cold wind in graceful synchronized ballet. Further up the mountain at the edge of a forest of blue spruce, five deer grazed. There was something simple, primeval, head-clearing about the mountains. Going into the high country had always felt like coming home for Marshall—he couldn't explain it.

"The glory of God on display," he murmured to no one. "It gets in your blood."

Shivering, he climbed back into the car. He passed Fairplay and the Route 9 backdoor into Breckenridge and continued south to Buena Vista. Turning north on Route 24 towards Leadville, Henry decided to stop for coffee at the Roastery. "Why not?" he said to the steering wheel. "I'm not on a schedule. Don't have to be anywhere. If I want to spend thirty minutes enjoying a cup of coffee, well, that's exactly what I will do!" He grinned, enjoying the freedom. Getting away was exactly what he needed!

The shop was warm, crowded, buzzing with noisy conversation. He got his coffee and sat down at a tiny table in the corner, lost in his own thoughts as he studied his odd resistance to the idea of a speaking tour. Hank didn't intend to eavesdrop on the two young men at the neighboring table, but his ears perked up when he heard his name mentioned and then he did listen.

"You're kidding, Joe, right? You read Henry Marshall's blog? He's crazy, he hasn't a clue what he's talking about. Anyone with even a modest education can see that!" The speaker was a young man in his mid-twenties, Hank guessed, wearing a black tee shirt with large white lettering that proclaimed, "TAX THE RICH."

"Whoa, Clem! We both got our Masters in Poli Sci at Boulder—same graduating class. And as I remember I ranked *ahead* of you, didn't I? So I'd say my modest education matches yours and I think Marshall knows exactly what he's talking about." Joe was wearing a lumberjack shirt, blue jeans, and a pair of muddy boots. A Colorado Rockies ball cap was perched backwards on his head.

"Listen, Joe—if Marshall had his way, when you and I came out of high school we wouldn't have been able to *go* to college. We couldn't have afforded it. I *had* to borrow money to go to school—tuition, room and board, books, they're all crazy expensive. Marshall wants to eliminate federal student loans. No way, man!"

"But Clem, have you ever considered that the reason college is so expensive is because there's so much money floating around to pay for it?"

"That is the *dumbest* thing I ever heard!" rejoined Clem hotly. They glared at each other. Marshall could feel the tension even from a table away. The two fell silent and brooded over their coffee, evidently not wanting to escalate the disagreement.

Hank picked up his cup and stood next to their table. "Excuse me, guys, couldn't help but overhear your conversation. I've read Marshall's blog, too, and I think I could explain his point about federal education dollars if you'd give me the opportunity. Do you mind if I join you?"

Joe looked like he was trying to formulate a polite way to say *yes, we mind, please go away*, when Clem beat him to the punch and said, "Have a seat. If you can explain how college would be less expensive with less financial assistance from Washington, I'm all ears. What's your name, stranger?"

Marshall answered, "Hank. How about you guys?"

"I'm Clem, and this genius sitting across from me is Joe. I'd love to hear how taking away loan money for college will make it more affordable. That's like claiming if Jill has four apples and Jack takes two of them, Jill will now have five. It's bad math, and what Marshall is arguing for is bad policy." Clem took a slow slip of his coffee and studied Hank over the edge of his cup.

Hank nodded, "If you put it that way, I think Marshall would probably agree with you, Clem. But that's not how things work. Since you brought it up let's stay with the Jack and Jill scenario. Let's say Jill is selling apples. For the sake of simplicity, we'll ignore the whole dynamic of market competition. How will Jill set the price for her apples?"

"How should I know?" said Clem, rolling his eyes.

"Wait a minute, Clem," Hank responded patiently. "Work with me. Does she need to cover her costs?"

"Okay, I'll play along. Sure, she needs to cover her costs. Whatever she pays to purchase the apples, transport them, and—"

"Don't forget the costs of regulatory compliance," Joe said sarcastically. "You know, apple inspectors, OSHA inspectors, tax complia—"

"Butt out, small government boy! I know you've got a burr under your saddle, but you're wearing it on your sleeve and it's irritating. So back out and just listen, okay?" Clem shot back.

Joe held up his hands in mock surrender but kept his mouth shut.

"Now," Marshall said, "Let's say we've accounted for Jill's costs. Do you think she wants to make a profit?" He took a bite of his donut.

"Probably."

"How much profit?"

"I don't know, Hank," Clem said, exasperated. "It depends on whether she is socially conscious; whether she wants to gouge or help people."

"Fine," Henry nodded in agreement. "Let's say she is socially conscious and she's selling apples in the poorest part of town."

"Then she'll keep them affordable, otherwise she won't be selling many apples."

"True," Marshall agreed. "A modest profit, then?"

"Yeah, sure," Clem shrugged.

"Okay. But now, what if she moves her apple stand to the wealthiest part of town? Big money people live close by, lawyers, doctors. Will that change what she charges for apples?"

Clem sensed a trap and became wary. "Not necessarily."

Joe exploded. "Oh, get real! Sure it will! Listen, Clem, she'll charge more for her apples because sellers always charge whatever the market will bear. If your clientele is wealthy, your prices are higher."

"Not if you're socially conscious," insisted Clem.

Joe looked at his friend and paused for a moment, obviously weighing what he was about to say. When he continued, his tone was no longer contentious, "I regard you as socially conscious," admitted Joe. "I truly believe that you are genuinely concerned for your fellow man. But just last week, Clem, you sold your old iPhone on Ebay and you're still bragging about how much you got for it. You squeezed every dime you could out of that old piece of junk."

"That's different," Clem replied sheepishly.

"Why is that different? You eat three good meals a day, you've got a decent car, a reliable job, you're not sinking in debt. You didn't need the extra hundred bucks you got for that phone."

"But I've got financial goals," Clem asserted, not liking the turn the conversation had taken.

"Don't we all?" Joe replied dryly.

"Guys, guys, stop," Marshall said, spreading his hands. "The reality is that sellers *do* sell for what the market will bear, generally speaking. If your customers have more money in their pockets and they need your product you'll probably set the price for your product higher than you would if they're all living from paycheck to paycheck," Hank said. "That's just a basic reality of the marketplace."

Clem conceded, "Okay, I'll grant you that. That's probably true. But what does any of this have to do with federal student loans?"

"The easy availability of government loans meant that students had more cash available. So the schools charged what the market could bear with each fresh infusion of cash from the government. And it wasn't because they were trying to rip students off. Educational institutions have financial goals, too, you know. There's that new football stadium, the new science lab, the new wing for the library. Maybe a new performing arts hall. A new benefits package for faculty. More administrators to manage the growing campus. These aren't bad goals but they do require big bucks. More cash accessible to students through federally subsidized student loans meant colleges could raise their tuition without losing their customers—the students. Hence, college gets more expensive." Marshall took the last bite of his donut and finished his coffee.

Clem shook his head, "No. Correlation doesn't mean causation."

"True," Marshall agreed. "But it *can*. And in this case it *does*. The history of our government demonstrates that whatever the government subsidizes always gets more expensive. There are plenty of studies demonstrating the link between an increase in federal student loan dollars and rising college tuition. Bill Bennett, Reagan's secretary of education, demonstrated in 1986 that tuition was rising at four times the rate of inflation. *Four times!* Another study showed that for every one dollar increase in subsidized student loans, tuition goes up by sixty to seventy cents."

Clem blinked. "That can't be true."

"But it is," affirmed Marshall quietly. "Marshall is absolutely correct on his blog. The data supports his point."

"I won't believe it until I see the studies myself," the young man replied obstinately.

"Fair enough," Marshall admitted, "I respect that. But let me ask you this: hypothetically, now, just hypothetically, if the figures I cited to you were in fact accurate would you agree that the availability of federal dollars is driving tuition costs up? Hypothetically, of course."

"Yeah, I would. But I *don't* believe you," responded Clem.

Marshall pushed a pen and his empty donut bag across the table. "Give me your snail mail address. I'll mail the studies to you. You can read 'em yourself."

Clem stared at Hank for a moment then picked up the pen and scribbled his address. "Okay, I'm game—I'll take the challenge. You show me the data and as long as the study was conducted by qualified people I'll change my mind on this. Who are you anyway?"

Hank folded the donut bag and put it in his pocket. He stood up and fished for his car keys, and then winked at Clem. "Henry Marshall," he said, smiling.

****

Marshall checked into the Delaware Hotel in Leadville. For three days he puttered around the town. He made a few side trips and did some cross-country skiing on trails close by, but mostly he was reading and praying, trying to get a grasp on why the idea of a speaking tour was so obnoxious. He was no closer to a decision but he felt the tension draining away.

Thursday night he decided to check out the next morning and drive to Alma. From Alma he'd take County Road 8 up Buckskin Gulch to Kite Lake. He doubted the road was open all the way so he planned to drive as far as he could and then ski the rest of the way, returning before dark. Friday night he'd spend at Dillon, then drive home on Saturday.

Kite Lake was a favorite location for the whole family. The Marshalls visited several times every summer, camping and fishing. It was close enough to Golden that even just driving up for a day hike was reasonable. At twelve thousand feet the lake was above the timberline and the surrounding meadows were carpeted in colorful wildflowers during the summer months. Cutthroat trout made the lake a favorite spot for fishermen, and several of Colorado's fourteeners could be climbed from the trailheads at the parking area.

Marshall wanted to bring back pictures of what the area looked like when it was snowed in. Before going to bed he checked the avalanche report; the danger was low for the Kite Lake area. Even though the weather report showed a significant snowstorm moving up from the southwest, a powerful bubble of high pressure over Idaho was expected to hold the storm to the south, forcing it to track east across northern New Mexico and the southern tier of Colorado before moving more northerly into Kansas. It looked as though he could follow through with his plans to visit Kite Lake. Wanting to get an early start, he didn't take time to look at the weather report in the morning before checking out. Unbeknownst to him, the high pressure area had unexpectedly dissipated overnight with the result that the storm turned north. It now had a new track, bore-sited on the mountains of central Colorado.

When Marshall turned onto Route 9 at Fairplay the sky was grey and lowering and the wind had picked up out of the southeast. The temperature had risen slightly, climbing to fifteen degrees. By the time he turned onto Buckskin Street in Alma it was flurrying. Marshall didn't take much notice. In the Colorado high country weather is often more local than regional—in one high valley a snow squall could be putting down three inches of new powder while it is sunny in the neighboring valley and the regional forecast is calling for clear skies.

Marshall had gone perhaps a mile and a half up Buckskin Gulch before the road became impassable. He parked and put on his cross-country gear. It was four miles up and a climb of about fourteen hundred feet, a mildly challenging trek for Marshall.

Hank grinned as he started for the lake—he couldn't help it. The world about him was utterly silent save for the wind in the trees. There was no one in sight, nor had he passed any vehicles on the way up—he had the place to himself. He felt like he was in a child's snow globe: the snow was falling steadily, scurrying on a fresh breeze blowing up-canyon. Had he checked the tiny thermometer attached to the zipper pull on his jacket, he'd have seen that the snow was not the only thing falling.

About a mile further on, a movement in the corner of his eye grabbed his attention. He stopped and stood perfectly still. Across Buckskin Creek in the edge of the alpine willows stood a bull elk, head high, sniffing the wind. Close by four smaller elk grazed on the willows. Hank watched for a moment and then slowly reached inside his parka for his camera, but the sharp eyes of the big bull detected the movement. The elk made a barking sound and wheeled about, loping down-valley into cover, with the other animals following.

By the time Hank reached Kite Lake it was snowing heavily and the wind was whipping and gusting, blowing the snow horizontally. He was thankful for his yellow ski goggles, otherwise it would have been impossible to look into the wind. He told himself it was nothing more than a strong squall. Marshall skied around the frozen lake, snapping photographs with his digital camera. Finally he skied over to a small, locked Forest service shed and sat in its lee, eating a light lunch of jerky and trail mix.

The clouds were thick and dark and the light had faded when he put his food and water bottle back in his bright red daypack. Though several hours from sunset, the intensity of the growing storm created a dusk-like atmosphere. In the dim light the deepening snow was featureless and Marshall found that he'd lost much of his depth perception. It was blizzard conditions, near whiteout.

"Hank, old boy, this is not good. Methinks you've over-stayed your welcome by an hour or so. Me also thinks the weatherman needs to find himself a different job. That storm has landed right on top of me," he muttered to himself as he started back down. It was hard to identify the road and his tracks had long since been covered.

He wasn't too worried. He knew the area around Kite Lake like the back of his hand. He was only four miles or so above the car and no more than six from Alma. All he had to do was follow the canyon down and it would deposit him right on Alma's main street. He finally located the road and started down the valley.

A quarter mile below Kite Lake, Buckskin Creek runs under the road in a culvert. With the whiteout conditions and dim lighting Marshall didn't realize he was on the edge of the culvert. His right ski went off the edge and as he tumbled down onto the frozen creek his left ski tip hung up on something. For some reason the binding did not release and he wrenched his knee. Fiery paroxysms of pain screamed through his left leg and he cried out in agony. He released his bindings and lay in the snow, trying to make sense of what had just happened.

Gritting his teeth, Marshall rolled to his back and held his knee, trying to give the searing throb a chance to subside. But it didn't. After a few minutes he got his legs under him and tried to stand up. The pain was so intense he cried out again as he collapsed back into the snow. Now he was worried.

"This I had not counted on. And like a complete novice I didn't even let anyone know where I was going. Break the rules just once, Hank, and look what happens. No one knows where I am. What an idiot," he growled to himself.

Unsure of what to do, he fished around in his pockets for his cellphone. No service. "Oh, great. Just great." He lay in the snow and prayed for help and guidance. After a moment he thought, *Haley hasn't a clue where I am, nor does anyone else. It's not likely anyone else will be up this road until April at the earliest. And it's not getting warmer anytime soon. So if I'm going to get out of this mess, I've got to take the initiative.*

He knew the Lord was in control, he just had no clue as to what the Lord intended. *Okay, pain or no pain, Hank, you've gotta drag your carcass down this canyon or you're gonna turn into a popsicle.*

Hank lined his skis up and rolled on to them, groaning with pain. After fastening the bindings he fought his way to a standing position, using his poles to help. The pain was excruciating. It was hard to remain standing, much less move forward. He discovered that he could pole plant, edge forward carefully on his right ski working against his poles, and then twist his hips to drag his left foot forward without involving his knee too greatly.

It was slow, exhausting work and Hank couldn't remember ever being in so much pain. His shoulders and arms gradually wearied of the increased load. Within a quarter of a mile he began to perspire, a situation that would put him in greater danger than his knee. If his clothing became damp he could freeze to death. He was facing a catch-22 dilemma. The only way to get back to the car was to keep going, but if he kept going he would sweat and eventually make the situation worse.

After struggling another half mile he finally admitted to himself that it was impossible to continue. Pain, exhaustion, perspiration, and nightfall put an end to his progress. He checked the thermometer on his zipper pull. Five below. And the wind was now howling. He was freezing, and he knew that his thinking had slowed down. He was fighting mental confusion.

Marshall removed his skis and planted them upright in the deep snow, where they might be seen if someone came along. Working quickly he dug a snow cave. He crawled inside, finished the last of his jerky and water, and fell fast asleep, shivering.

****

"South Park District Ranger Office, this is Cindy speaking, how may I help you?" She glanced at the thermometer just outside the window. Eight below. The Forest Service vehicles in the parking lot were covered under fourteen inches of snow and it was still coming down.

The voice on the other end of the phone sounded worried. "Yes, this is Tom Johnson. My son went winter-camping with a group of friends in Buckskin Gulch. They were going to camp at Kite Lake. Anyway they were supposed to return home last night and none of us have heard anything from them. I'm concerned something must have happened, especially with the storm."

Cindy got the make and model of their vehicle, their names, and as much of their itinerary as Johnson knew, and promised to look into it. She looked at the clock as she time-stamped her log entry. It was 1:30 p.m., Saturday afternoon.

She turned around in her chair. "Randall, we've got some college kids that were snow-camping at Kite. Should have returned yesterday. No one's heard from them."

Randall was a west Texas product, a long, tall, lanky man with a lazy drawl that would have made a Mississippian sound as though he hailed from Maine. Where five words were necessary, the laconic Randall might manage two. He was working intently on a plug of tobacco at the moment. He sighed and spit into an empty coffee can he kept next to the desk. "Cat fixed?" he asked. Their LMC 1500 snow cat had been out of action for two weeks with engine trouble.

"Um-hmm," Cindy replied. "Picked it up in Denver yesterday. It's still on the trailer."

He nodded. "Ah'll check on 'em." He started for the door, stopped and turned. "Av'lanche danger?"

"I'll check," Cindy replied. He nodded again, grabbed his parka and ambled out of the office.

The snow cat fired up on the first try and Randall let the motor run for several minutes to warm it up, and then topped off the tanks with gasoline. He checked the emergency supply locker on the cat, and added four Mylar blankets, several extra quarts of water, and a box of energy bars.

It was still snowing heavily, but the wind which had created blizzard conditions overnight had died down. Randall beat the snow off his shoulders and hat, then stepped back inside the office. He collected his spittoon can from his desk, then looked at Cindy with raised eyebrows.

"Avalanche danger is high, Randall. Be careful." She looked at the coffee can he was clutching and frowned, wrinkling her nose. "Try to hit the can, okay? That stuff is gross when you miss, you know?"

He grinned and winked at her, and then clumped out into the snow. After putting chains on the truck, he trailered the rig to Alma and pulled into the town hall parking lot. Locking the truck, he climbed into the snow cat; it started on the first try again. *Huh. They finally got it fixed.* After situating his spittoon and buckling up, he turned on the two-way and adjusted the frequency. "Radio check," he drawled, keying the microphone.

"Five-by-five," came Cindy's response over the radio. "If I don't see you by seventeen hundred hours, I'll send in a Saint Bernard."

"Make sure he's carryin' Red Man chewin' 'bacca. Runnin' low."

She didn't respond, and he grinned again.

Thirty minutes later Randall was passing the Mineral Park Road turnoff. The snow was about four feet deep on the flat, drifted in places to eight or ten feet. He'd not seen a soul since leaving Alma.

****

Hank wandered through the house but nothing looked familiar. Nothing seemed right, nothing was in the right place. He looked out through the front window. The lawns and street were buried under snow that had not been plowed, but he didn't recognize the neighborhood. *This isn't our house, but somehow I know it is our house. What is going on?*

Conner, one of his twins, walked in. "Mom said you wanted to talk to me, Dad. What's up?"

"I want to talk about your plans when you graduate, son. I understand you're thinking about not going to college."

"Not interested in college, Dad. I'm going to work in Vail

during the winters, and pick up a landscaping job each summer."

"Conner," Marshall responded patiently, "God has uniquely gifted you with an amazing aptitude for mathematics. You take after your mom. And you've told us many times— you love math and science."

The teen frowned, "But I also love to ski, Dad. And I don't want the hassle of a real job."

Hank choked back a frustrated response. Raising his voice wouldn't help a bit. "Skiing is fun, son, I agree. And there is nothing dishonorable about working on the lifts or bussing tables in the lodge. But you have the ability to do so much *more* with your life—to make a rare contribution as a teacher or researcher. Your test scores are off the charts, Conner. God did not give you those abilities so you could bury them at a ski lodge. You're a steward of the gifts and talents God gives— don't waste them." As he spoke, Marshall realized that the house was freezing. He could even see his breath. He gritted his teeth to keep them from chattering. But Conner seemed not to notice the chill in the air.

"But what about you, Dad?"

"What do you mean, what about me?"

"No disrespect, Dad, but you're not practicing what you preach. You're telling me not to waste my gifts, but you are wasting yours."

"What are you talking about, Conner?" Henry tried to act surprised, but in his heart he knew exactly what his son was talking about.

"You are an excellent communicator, Dad. You're passionate, well spoken, and you connect well with high schoolers, college kids, and older adults. But you are refusing to use your gifts."

"But I *am* using my gifts, Conner. I have a very successful blog and I'm quite convinced that I am doing what God wants me to do." Marshall began to look for a way to end the conversation. Somehow his son had turned the tables on him and it was time to beat a hasty retreat.

"But you've turned down the speaking tour thing, Dad. It's

one thing to connect with people over the anonymous Internet, but it's another thing entirely to connect face to face. I think you could do so much more with your blog if you took Mr. Jackson's advice and went on this tour. It's sort of like that parable in the Bible, Dad, about the man who buried his talent."

"Conner, that parable is about money. The talents in the story actually refer to an amount of money, not skills and abilities."

"I understand that. But even so, isn't it really about stewardship?"

Ouch! Busted! I should have known Conner is sophisticated enough to understand the real point of that parable. "I'm not exactly burying my talent, son. I've got a very popular blog." He made an excuse and cut the conversation short, knowing he had no defense. Conner had distilled the whole matter to its bare essentials: the stewardship of his gifts. Marshall had been trying to avoid thinking about the subject in those terms ever since Buford Jackson had suggested the idea.

When Conner left the room, Hank decided to turn up the heat in the house. He looked where the thermostat should have been, but it wasn't there. After thinking about it he realized he had no idea where to find the thermostat. He shivered and pulled his parka more tightly around himself and discovered he was wearing his ski gloves. *What on earth is going on?*

****

The snow was still falling heavily and it was getting dark. Randall was a quarter mile short of Kite Lake when his radio crackled.

"Randall, can you read me?"

"Gotcha loud and clear. Go ahead, Cindy." Both rangers knew the formal radio protocol but used it only when there was more traffic on the frequency. There had been none since Randall started up the gulch, however, so they kept it simple.

"Just got a call from Tom Johnson. His kids have checked in, they're all safe and sound. You can turn the cat around and come home."

"Roger that, turnin' 'round, comin' home. By the way, the snow cat is runnin' smooth as silk. Those mechanics did a fine job."

Randall flipped the switch to turn on the extra halogen worklights that had been mounted above the cab and his surroundings filled with light. Staying on the road was guess-work, but the grade off the road to his right was too steep for traversing. The layer of snow underneath the fresh stuff was covered with half an inch of ice from freezing rain that fell a week ago. If he ran off the road he'd wind up sliding sideways all the way down to the creek.

The wind lessened to a light breeze, and finally died completely. The snow turned into the fat, lazy flakes that signal the trailing edge of a storm. Suddenly Randall felt the cat tilt and realized that he'd run off the road. The vehicle began side-slipping and picked up speed laterally as it slid downhill. "Whoa, Bessie!" muttered the lanky Forest Ranger. If the leading edge of the downhill track dug in or caught on something, it could roll the cat. Randall was glad he'd belted in. For the briefest instant he wavered, deciding whether to turn uphill and fight the slide, or turn downhill and ride it out. "Downhill it is," he said to himself as he spun the cat and faced downhill. The snow cat slid almost all the way to the creek before it finally stopped.

Randall turned the vehicle downstream and decided that rather than attempting to climb back to the road he would head down-canyon and intersect the road where it entered the narrows, just above the Sweet Home Mine. As he approached the narrows something to his right front caught the glare of his headlights and gleamed back at him. Curious, he steered the cat closer. It was a pair of skis stuck into the snow; reflec-tive strips on the skis were picking up the light of his headlights.

"Now, that's just downright strange," Randall drawled to himself, staring at the skis through the windshield. He grabbed the radio microphone, "Cindy, this is Randall. Anyone else 'sposed to be up Buckskin?"

"Let me check." After a moment she radioed back, "Nope, not as far as we're concerned. No one notified us, and that batch of kids has already turned up on the other side of the mountain. Seems that instead of snow-camping, they got hotel rooms in Dillon and have been skiing Breckenridge. Why do you ask, Randall?"

"'Cause I'm starin' at a pair of Rossi Positracks stickin' in the snow just outside my cab. Nobody's gonna walk off and just leave those things. They're 'spensive skis."

"Where are you?"

"Oh, mebbe a tenth mile above Sweet Home. I just took a little ride. Got too close to the edge in that steep section and slipped down almost to the creek. Hadn't been for that, I'd never seen these skis. I'm gonna get out, tramp around a bit, see if I can find anything else. I know it's quittin' time, but I need you to stay by the radio, Cindy, 'case I find anything or get m'self into trouble." He spit into his coffee can.

"No problem, Randall. I'll wait until you get back to Alma."

"Obliged."

It was now fully dark. Randell idled the snow cat and grabbed a powerful flashlight and an avalanche probe and stepped out of the cab. Standing on the tracks, he strapped on snowshoes and then walked over to the skis and examined them closely. He walked concentric circles around the skis, probing the snow, expanding his circle by three feet with each circuit. On his third go-round he saw the entrance to a snow cave, almost covered.

"Hello? Hello?" he shouted as he shined his light into the small hole. There was no response. Working rapidly he cleared away the snow and unearthed a man, dead or alive he could not tell. There was no obvious injury, so he gently carried the unmoving form into the extended cab of the snow cat. Removing his snow shoes, Randall climbed into the cab himself and turned the heater on full. Carefully he arranged the man on the floor of the cargo area. He was barely able to detect a pulse, but it was there though weak and erratic. He pulled out his pocket knife and held the blade up to the man's open mouth. The slightest bit of condensation formed on the blade. "Huh," he grunted to himself. "He's still breathin', but barely." The ranger grabbed an epitympanic thermometer from the snow cat's advanced medical kit and gently inserted the probe into the victim's ear. The man's temperature registered as twenty-nine degrees Celsius, or about eighty-four degrees Farenheit. Randall shook his head, "Ain't much hope for you, pilgrim, but I'll do my best."

The victim's clothing was slightly damp but Randall knew better than to wrestle it off of him. Too much movement could bring on cardiac arrest. He unzipped the victim's parka and applied several chemical hot packs wrapped in thick cloth to the man's neck, chest and groin, and then zipped the parka back over them.

The lanky ranger had a dilemma. Protocol called for him to stay with the victim and monitor him in case he went into cardiac arrest. But that meant he would have to stay put—he couldn't drive the cat and monitor the victim both. But if he stayed put, the nearest help was hours away, even if he radioed for help. It was too dangerous to put a chopper down in this narrow part of the canyon, and there weren't any ground rescue teams closer than Breckinridge. Without competent emergency care soon, the man would die.

"Sorry, pilgrim, but you're gonna to have to fend for yourself back here while I drive. Don't die on me, okay?" He wrapped the unconscious form in a mylar blanket, then belted himself into the driver's seat.

"Cindy, you there?"

"Still here, Randall."

"I've recovered an unconscious Caucasian male, probably in his forties or fifties. Moderate to severe hypothermia, body temp twenty-nine. As of right now he's got a pulse, very weak, and is breathin' on his own. I need a rescue chopper in the municipal parking lot in Alma as soon as you can get it there. My ETA to the lot is thirty-five minutes. Did you get that?"

"Roger, Randall. You need a chopper in thirty-five minutes

at Alma. I'll call Flight for Life and get it set up. You can tell me all about it when you get back. Do you have a name?"

"Negative. Right now he's John Doe, and he's gonna be dead John Doe unless we can get him some help soon. This is Randall, out."

Chapter 7

A DEMOCRACY IS ALWAYS TEMPORARY IN NATURE; IT
SIMPLY CANNOT EXIST AS A PERMANENT FORM OF
GOVERNMENT. A DEMOCRACY WILL CONTINUE TO
EXIST UP UNTIL THE TIME THAT VOTERS DISCOVER
THAT THEY CAN VOTE THEMSELVES LARGESSE FROM
THE PUBLIC TREASURY. FROM THAT MOMENT ON,
THE MAJORITY ALWAYS VOTES FOR THE CANDIDATES
WHO PROMISE THE MOST BENEFITS FROM THE
PUBLIC TREASURY, WITH THE RESULT THAT A
DEMOCRACY WILL FINALLY COLLAPSE DUE TO LOOSE
FISCAL POLICY, WHICH IS ALWAYS FOLLOWED BY A
DICTATORSHIP.

Authorship unknown

Saturday, February 14, 2009

"Boys, come on down for supper," Haley Marshall called up the stairs. Charity, their fifteen-year old, was spending the night with one of her friends. Haley had been holding supper in the oven, hoping that Hank would get home in time to eat with them.

"Finally! Is Dad home?" asked thirteen-year old Charlie as he came bounding down the stairs with his twin, Conner, a few steps behind him.

"No. I reckon I'd better feed you two bottomless pits; I know you've got to be starving."

"Mom, we're always starving!" Conner said cheerfully. "Thirty minutes after we're done, we'll be hungry again."

Haley rolled her eyes, but smiled at her twins. "Don't I know it! I've gotta teach you two how to cook for yourselves.

Either that or hire a full-time cook."

The boys looked at each other and grinned. "Our own cook? That'd be cool," said Charlie.

"Yeah! I'd order steak every night! Anyway, where's Dad, Mom? I thought he was supposed to be here by now," said Conner.

"Well, that's what I thought, too. Maybe the storm has delayed him a little, I don't know. I'm sure he'll be here before bedtime." She didn't say so, but Haley was a little worried. She'd called his cellphone thirty minutes ago, but it went right to voicemail.

They were just finishing supper when their landline phone rang. Caller ID indicated "St. Anthony's Hospital." Fearing the worst, she picked up the receiver. "Hello?" she said, trying to keep the concern out of her voice.

"Hi, this is Walt Bruggeman. Am I speaking with Mrs. Haley Marshall?"

"Yes, this is she. How can I help you?" She sat down in her chair. The boys were clearing the table and she snapped her fingers to get their attention, and then pointed upstairs. Charlie looked at Conner and shrugged, and the two trotted upstairs to their bedroom.

"Mrs. Marshall, I'm the chaplain at St. Anthony's Hospital in Frisco. Your husband was admitted through our ER about thirty minutes ago. He's now in the Critical Care Unit receiving treatment for a severe case of hypothermia. I am so sorry to bring you this news, but I can assure you that our medical staff is doing everything they can for your husband."

"Is he—is he . . . ?" Haley struggled for words, not knowing what to ask and fearing the answers she might receive. "But is he okay? Is he going to make it?"

"Mrs. Marshall, he is in critical condition. I'd say the situation is very serious. But we have one of the best doctors this side of the Mississippi when it comes to treating hypothermia, and you must not lose hope. I was notified just before calling you that the staff believes his vital signs are stabilizing, but they are continuing to characterize his condition as critical. If you are able to get here this evening, I would—he's still at the point where anything could happen."

"I'll be there as soon as possible."

"Can I pray with you?" Bruggeman asked gently.

"Yes, please do. Both my husband and I know Christ as Savior."

Bruggeman prayed briefly, asking the Lord to preserve Marshall's life and to keep Haley safe as she traveled to the hospital. He closed his prayer by asking that whatever happened Christ would be glorified.

"Amen, Chaplain. Thank you for calling."

Haley sat at the table for a moment, weeping quietly and praying. Then she dried her eyes and went up to the boys' room. "Charlie, Conner, something has happened to your dad. He's got a bad case of hypothermia and has been admitted to the hospital in Frisco. His condition is very serious but the man I talked to was hopeful that it was improving. Let's pray for Daddy and then I need to drive to Frisco to be with him."

"Can we come, Mom?" asked Conner. Both boys looked worried.

"No, I don't think that would be a good idea. They have to keep him very quiet and very still right now. I'm going to call Charity and have her come home so that all three of you are together."

****

When Henry Marshall arrived at the Critical Care Unit of St. Anthony Summit Medical Center in Frisco at 7:15 p.m. his vital signs were very weak. The doctor decided it was too dangerous to transfer him to the Level I Trauma Center in Lakewood. Victims of severe hypothermia typically have a very slow, weak heartbeat and very little in the way of respiration. Too much jostling or movement can cause a victim to go into cardiac arrest. The medical staff began treating him immediately with warm intravenous fluid and heated oxygen in a mask.

Haley called Buford and Sandy Jackson and asked them to

notify the church's prayer chain as she rushed her preparations to leave for the hospital. She packed an overnight bag, called Charity, and was about to leave when there was a knock on the front door. She answered the door and found Buford and Sandy standing on her porch. Haley was already having a hard time controlling her emotions and to see her dear friends coming to her aid was more than she could handle—she broke down in tears. Sandy hugged her and said, "We're driving you."

Haley sniffed and dabbed her eyes with a tissue. "I can't ask you to do that, Sandy. It's after eight already, and—"

"It's decided, so don't argue," Buford said firmly in his gravelly voice. He picked up Haley's overnight bag and continued, "We've packed our own bags, and we'll get a room in Frisco tonight. Besides, you're going to need help getting Hank's vehicle home and you won't want him driving."

She looked up at the old, silver-haired lawyer and threw her arms around him and squeezed tight. "Thank you, Buford. I won't argue. I can't tell you how much you and Sandy mean to me, especially at a time like this."

Interstate 70 was plowed but icy, and the normal seventy-minute drive from Golden to Frisco took about an hour and a half. The skies had cleared and the night was frigid and windy, the thermometer reading below zero when Buford let the women out at the entrance to the hospital. He caught up with them in the Critical Care waiting area, and it wasn't long before a doctor came out to update Haley.

"Mrs. Marshall, I'm Dr. Paramjeet. Chaplain Bruggeman called you, yes?" Haley nodded. "Good. Please, sit down." The doctor motioned her to a chair and then sat across from her. "Your husband's vital signs have improved. He's still listed as critical, but I'd say he's stable. His core temperature is now at thirty-three degrees Celsius, or a little better than ninety-one degrees Fahrenheit. He has hypoxia—a lack of oxygen in the tissues, particularly his extremities. It gives him a blue pallor, but I don't want you to worry when you see him—his color will improve soon. We're giving him warmed, moist oxygen, which will help his oxygen level and bring up his temperature.

We are also monitoring him for fluid in the lungs, pneumonia, and several other complications often associated with moderate to severe hypothermia, but so far none of that has developed. Your husband was in pretty bad shape when he arrived and he's fortunate to be alive, but his outlook is improving rapidly. It's a credit to the good judgment and quick actions of the Forest Service employee who found him, and the Flight for Life crew that transported him here."

She swallowed hard, fighting the lump trying to form in her throat. "Thank you, Doctor. Will he have any long-term damage from this?"

"No, I don't think so," Paramjeet replied carefully. "Neurologically he appears to be fine, but that's a very preliminary judgment and he'll be tested more thoroughly when his core temperature gets back to normal. Although his heart and respiration slowed dramatically, which is what caused his hypoxia, the drop in body temperature slowed his metabolism and actually protected his brain from the lack of oxygen. It is not uncommon to see severe hypothermia victims recover with no neurological damage at all.

"He has no signs of frostbite or any other condition that a couple of days of taking it easy won't remedy. Assuming no complications develop, you'll notice a rapid improvement once his core temperature returns to normal, but he's going to be very tired for a few days."

The doctor consulted a clipboard he was holding. "He is complaining about pain in his left knee. Unfortunately until his vital signs return to normal we can't give him any painkillers and we don't want to move him around. Hypothermia victims tend to have a very irritable heart and moving them too much can make bad things happen. So we'll wait until morning before we send him for an MRI to see what's going on with his knee. If all goes well tonight, tomorrow I will move him from Critical Care into a telemetry unit and we'll continue to monitor him tomorrow night. Barring unforeseen complications you can take him home Monday."

"Can I see him?"

"Certainly, but keep it very brief and don't tax him with questions. Though he has stabilized somewhat we want to keep him as still as possible until his core temperature has returned to normal. You'll find him a little confused, but that's par for the course, considering his current core temperature." The doctor stood up and motioned to a nurse. "The nurse can take you to him."

"You go, Haley. We'll stay here—we can see Hank tomorrow. Buford is getting us some rooms in Frisco," said Sandy. The two women hugged again and then Haley entered the CCU.

She stood at the door of his room. Hank was wearing an oxygen mask, he was hooked up to an IV drip, and had a catheter, a heart monitor, and various other tubes and wires disappearing under his blanket. He looked like he was sleeping.

"Hank?"

His eyes fluttered open, searched the room, and then rested on her. She could see a weak grin form under the oxygen mask.

"Hey, babe." His voice was muffled by the mask.

She held his hand and squeezed it. It felt cold. "Seems like you've had quite an adventure."

"Uh-huh. Decided to do some snow-camping without my sleeping bag. Got a little chilly."

She shook her head, smiling. "Can't let you go anywhere by yourself. You're always getting in trouble."

"Yep. That's why I married you. Needed someone to keep me out of trouble."

"How do you feel, honey?" It came out before she remembered that she wasn't to ask any questions. It unnerved her to see him looking so weak, hooked up to so many monitors.

He grimaced. "Really drained. The room feels kind of hot. My left knee is throbbing."

She nodded. Suddenly he gripped her hand. "Tell Conner he's not going to be a ski bum. I'm going to do it so he has to, too. He's going to college."

She hadn't a clue what he was talking about, but replied

soothingly, "I'll tell him, sweetheart. You just rest."

Hank nodded and shut his eyes. Haley quietly left the room. The questions would have to wait until tomorrow.

The next morning Haley returned to the hospital with the Jacksons. Dr. Paramjeet met them in the CCU waiting room. "Don't you ever go home?" Haley asked with a sympathetic smile, surprised to find him there on a Sunday morning.

He grinned at her, "Well, yes, occasionally. But I'm the local hypothermia specialist, and we received two more severe cases overnight. When it rains it pours, I guess.

"Henry is doing much better this morning. His temp is normal, his color is normal, and his mental confusion is gone. I asked about his knee, and he told me that he took a bad fall while cross-country skiing and wrenched it. An MRI this morning revealed a bucket handle tear of the medial meniscus in his left knee. Now, that's not my area of specialty and I am recommending that you get him to an orthopedic surgeon in Denver early this week. I still want to keep an eye on him overnight tonight, but we can release him first thing tomorrow morning, as long as everything continues to look good. He's being moved out of the CCU into a telemetry room right now. Give us another twenty minutes or so, and you can see him." He gave her a slip of paper with Hank's room number.

Half an hour later she was standing by his bedside. "Good morning, Trouble," she said with a smile.

"Trouble, eh? You are a sight for sore eyes, Mrs. Marshall. I hope you're here to spring me out of this joint." He looked much better than he had the day before. He was sitting up, a Gideon Bible open on his lap.

"Slow down, buster! You're not going anywhere today. You've got another night in the Frisco Hilton."

She sat down next to the bed and they bantered for another moment or so, holding hands, until she finally asked, "Hank, what happened up there?"

"Got careless, sweetie. The Rockies are wonderful, but they aren't very forgiving. On Friday morning I left Leadville and drove to Alma. I wanted to ski up to Kite Lake and bring home some pictures of what it looks like in winter. I'd checked the weather the night before, and heard that the big storm was supposed to stay well south of us. I got up on Friday morning and, like an idiot, checked out without watching the weather report. By the time I got to Buckskin Gulch snow was flying, but I thought it was just a squall. Anyway, the road became impassable about four miles below the lake so I skied the rest of the way.

"I was really enjoying the snow, the whole thing—it was gorgeous, so peaceful. Got some great pictures and started back down, but by this time it was getting dark with nearly whiteout conditions. On the way down I accidentally skied off the road and fell—wrenched my knee terribly. Couldn't walk, couldn't ski, couldn't hardly move. No cell service, no nothing. So I dug a snow cave and crawled in. I was freezing and my knee was killing me. I started praying but I must have fallen asleep. Next thing I know, I'm waking up in this hospital."

A little later the Jacksons entered the room. Buford took one look at him and sighed with a disgusted expression on his face. "You wimp. I knew you'd do just about anything to get out of that Garden of the Gods race, but I never thought you'd stoop to this."

Henry grinned. "Good to see you, too, Jacks. Did you ever think about working on your bedside manner?"

"But I have! You should have seen how I used to be," Jackson growled.

The two women looked at each other and rolled their eyes, shaking their heads. "Let's let these two spit at each other in private, Sandy. C'mon. We'll find the cafeteria and I'll buy you a cup of coffee." The ladies left and Jackson sat down beside the bed and pulled out a book.

"Brought along some reading for you."

"Why am I not surprised? What is it?"

"Volume one of Blackstone's commentaries on English law. Blackstone forms much of the foundation of American jurisprudence. He's big on common law. I think you'll find his thinking helpful as you blog about the current state of our government."

"Thanks, Jacks," Hank said. He flipped through the book and found that he was actually looking forward to starting it. That surprised him because he had been a little resentful of Buford's pushes. But the resentment was gone. And the book looked fascinating.

"What? No snide comments?" Jackson's eyes narrowed and he frowned.

"Nope. Can't wait to read it."

"Hmm. Evidently you're still suffering the mental confusion of hypothermia. You are truly not yourself."

Marshall laughed. The two talked for another ten minutes and then Jackson said, "Tell me where your car is. Sandy and I will leave Haley here with you and go recover your vehicle."

****

Hank shut Blackstone with a snap and said, "We need to talk, babe."

Haley was sitting by his bed reading her book. She closed it and looked at him. "Okay. You first."

"Are you still in favor of me doing the speaking tour thing?"

She nodded, "I am. I think it's the right thing to do, Hank. I feel like God is nudging you to do it."

He agreed. "So do I. I had a dream while I was in that snow cave. Conner was trying to explain to me that rather than go to college and pursue more study in mathematics, he was going to be a ski bum. I told him that God had uniquely gifted him and that God expected him to be a steward of the gifts and opportunities he had received." Hank fell silent for a moment, remembering the dream.

"So what happened?" Haley asked.

"He threw it right back in my face. Said something to the effect that since I wasn't using my gifts he didn't feel compelled to use his, either. And suddenly, in my dream, I knew he was right. I'm using some of my opportunities but not all of them. I've been taking a lazy way out and have been digging in my heels when Buford tries to push me."

Haley didn't answer but just squeezed his hand.

"You knew it, too, didn't you?" he asked, surprised.

She nodded. "I did. But I also knew you had to figure this out on your own. If I had pushed you, you'd have started to resent me just like you were getting irritated with Buford. So I backed off and just started praying that God would help you see it."

"Am I really that bull-headed?"

"Yes, you are. You really are. But I love your bull-headedness. Especially when it's pointed in the right direction." She leaned over and kissed him.

"Then if it's okay with you, when Buford gets back I'm going to tell him to sign me up for that crazy speaking tour thing." He shook his head, "I just *know* I'm going to regret this," he said, only half smiling.

"No, you won't and neither will I. And," she laughed, "neither will our budding mathematician or his brother and sister. Not as long as you take us with you!"

****

Dr. Paramjeet was just leaving Marshall's room when Buford and Sandy Jackson returned late Sunday afternoon.

"So, what's the word?" asked Sandy as they seated themselves around Henry's bed.

"As long as everything still looks good in the morning, I can take him home tomorrow," said Haley. "The doctor said everything is pretty much back to normal now. They just want to observe him for another sixteen hours. When we get home tomorrow, I'll make an appointment to get his knee looked at."

"Excellent," said Buford as he handed the keys to the Mitsubishi to Haley. "Thank the Lord. Henry, I am very relieved and thankful that you're doing so well. There are half a dozen ways this *could* have ended, none of them good."

"Praise the Lord, indeed," Marshall affirmed. "This whole

experience has been one answered prayer after another. Any trouble finding the car?"

"Nope. It was right where you said it would be. Started up fine, no problems. It did take us a while to dig it out of the snow."

"Buford, do you realize this whole shebang is your fault?" asked Hank, a serious expression on his face.

"My fault?" the lawyer responded. He looked at Haley and quipped, "You'd better get the nurse, I think his mental confusion has returned." He turned back to Marshall and demanded, "How do you figure it's my fault?"

"It's that stupid speaking tour idea. Ever since you first mentioned it I haven't been sleeping well, I've been anxious, irritable, snapping at Haley and the kids. I think you'd better ante up for some marriage counseling. I took this little excursion in the mountains to clear my brain."

"Evidently it didn't work," Jackson observed dryly.

"Oh, but it did! Sign me up. I'm ready to do it."

"Seriously?" Jackson queried, eyebrows raised. He studied Marshall's face.

"Uh-huh. If you are still willing to help, I'll do it. I'm serious," replied Hank.

Jackson blinked and was speechless for a moment. Then he asked, "Okay, when do we start?"

****

"Have a seat, Hank. How's the knee?" Buford asked as Hank limped into the conference room. Marshall had had knee surgery about two weeks before, and while he wasn't on crutches he was wearing a brace that kept him from bending his knee.

"It's improving a little every day. I'm getting therapy three times a week, and they've given me exercises to do on the off days. I don't think I'm going to be able to do the Garden of the Gods race with you this year, Jacks. Maybe next year. So! What do you have for me?"

"I've drawn up the documents for your company, *The Marshall Plan, LLC*, with you as the sole owner. You've got a federal employer identification number. Everything is set, Hank, you are ready to do business."

"Great! Thanks for your good work on this, Buford. What's first, then?" Marshall took a seat across the polished mahogany table from his friend.

"Write a blog piece advertising the fact that you are doing a speaking tour, and that you will go to the ten locations with the most responses, by zip code. Include a 'respond by' date. Have your webmaster create all the necessary forms and databases. Make sure he captures the full name and mailing address, email address, and phone number of each responder. Our target date for the beginning of the speaking tour should be September." Jackson slid several papers for Marshall's signature over to him, and he signed them and slid them back.

"Okay. I'm gonna get right on it. Now that I've agreed to this whole cockamamie scheme, Jacks, I'm actually looking forward to it."

"This may be the beginning of a long journey, Hank. I'm glad you've taken the first step."

A phone call came for Jackson at that moment from a client, and Marshall had to get to his physical therapy appointment so the two men parted company. As Hank limped to the elevator, he wondered what Jackson meant by saying it was the first step of a long journey. He pondered it for a moment then shrugged and dismissed the thought.

Chapter 8

THE ADMINISTRATION OF PRIVATE JUSTICE BETWEEN
THE CITIZENS OF THE SAME STATE, THE
SUPERVISION OF AGRICULTURE AND OF OTHER
CONCERNS OF A SIMILAR NATURE, ALL THOSE
THINGS, IN SHORT, WHICH ARE PROPER TO BE
PROVIDED FOR BY LOCAL LEGISLATION, CAN NEVER
BE DESIRABLE CARES OF A GENERAL JURISDICTION.
IT IS THEREFORE IMPROBABLE THAT THERE SHOULD
EXIST A DISPOSITION IN THE FEDERAL COUNCILS TO
USURP THE POWERS WITH WHICH THEY ARE
CONNECTED; BECAUSE THE ATTEMPT TO EXERCISE
THOSE POWERS WOULD BE AS TROUBLESOME AS IT
WOULD BE NUGATORY; AND THE POSSESSION OF
THEM, FOR THAT REASON, WOULD CONTRIBUTE
NOTHING TO THE DIGNITY, TO THE IMPORTANCE, OR
TO THE SPLENDOR OF THE NATIONAL GOVERNMENT.

Alexander Hamilton, Federalist #17

Friday, June 22, 2012

Henry Marshall stood with Jackson, Ashton Bancroft, and Joshua Cummings on the floor of the University of Dayton Arena where Marshall had just finished speaking. Marshall's speech dealt with foreign policy and the often ill-fated, clumsy attempts of current and past administrations to influence events in other countries through foreign aid. Marshall's contention was that attempts to create an American-style government and economy in countries that did not have a deep Judeo-Christian background were doomed to failure, and that much of American foreign aid money was simply winding up in the personal bank accounts of dictators and warlords.

The large group of well-wishers, autograph-seekers, and atten-dees finally dwindled after forty-five minutes and the four men were talking as the arena cleared out.

"You seem quite well versed in foreign affairs, Henry. How did you come by your knowledge?" asked Bancroft. Ashton Bancroft had served in the US Congress for ten years and now was in private law practice in Dayton. He'd been the local contact who handled the details of Marshall's speaking engagement in Dayton.

Henry pointed at Jackson. "The man has been force-feeding me books for years. He once remarked that it would be helpful if I actually knew what I was talking about. I figured he might be right. Haley and I have taken some vaca-tions out of the country and I've done quite a bit of traveling for business in years past. My view on US involvement in foreign affairs has developed from my reading and from a careful observation of what the administrations of the last twenty or thirty years have accomplished, as well as where they have failed."

Haley and the boys stood by waiting patiently (Haley), and not so patiently (Conner and Charlie). Haley had promised to take them to a late movie and they were beginning to worry about missing it. Jackson noticed Conner nervously looking at his watch and, ever the manager, stepped in. "Well, gentlemen, I've got to hustle this group away. Haley and the boys are headed for Huber Heights to take in a movie, and Hank and I are going to drop them off before we get a late bite to eat."

"I've got an idea—why don't we go out together?" suggested Joshua Cummings. "Hank, your wife can take the rental and Ashton and I will take you and Buford to get some-thing to eat and then drop you off at your hotel."

Marshall had noticed Cummings attended each of his prior five engagements: Jacksonville, Atlanta, Nashville, Albu-querque, and Richmond, Virginia. And now Dayton, Ohio. Hank had humorously asked this friend of Buford's if he was being stalked. The political consultant replied no, but he had business in those cities and simply arranged his travel to enable him to take in Marshall's speeches. Hank had the feeling something more was involved, but let it go.

Hank and Buford looked at each other and shrugged. "Sounds good," replied Henry, "thanks, Josh. I'll enjoy having someone to talk to besides Buford," he said, flashing a devilish smile at his friend. Jackson shook his head and raised his eyebrows.

After Haley and the kids left, Cummings asked, "Where are you guys staying? Any places to eat close to it?"

"Drury Inn on Miller Lane," Jackson answered.

"Oh, yeah," exclaimed Ashton, "Miller Lane is restaurant row. Plenty of good places to eat."

Thirty minutes later the men were seated in a booth at Panera Bread, located right next to the Drury. "I've been reading your blog, Hank. I really enjoy your take on things. How are your speaking tours going? I thought you were originally going to do ten, but there's been a lot more than that, hasn't there?" asked Ashton.

Hank finished a bite of salad before he answered. "This man," he said, tilting his head toward Jackson, "has somehow managed to leash me to a speaking treadmill. I still don't know how he did it. But since 2009, I've actually spoken in every state except Hawaii." He cast a sidelong glance at Buford before continuing, "I don't know why he's never put me in Hawaii—I'd love to take the family there."

"It's very simple, Hank. Nobody in Hawaii likes you," Jackson replied.

"You see what abuse I put up with?" quipped Marshall. "Anyway, Buford manages the whole shebang and I just go where he tells me to go. The whole thing was his idea. Originally I didn't want anything to do with it. But after a while it became fun. I bring the family, we get to see the sights and enjoy different places. The kids love it. You saw my sons this evening, I also have a seventeen-year-old daughter, Charity. She's with the youth group on a short-term missions trip to Honduras this week, so she wasn't able to come."

Joshua Cummings asked, "Has the speaking tour had an effect on your blog? Have you noticed an uptick in traffic since you started?"

"Yeah, but not as much as we expected. The number of hits grew pretty rapidly at first, but the growth has since slowed quite a bit. I think we've pretty much saturated the market and I'd be surprised if it grew much more. I've got about forty-five million visitors to the blog, but they're not all from the US and they certainly don't all agree with me. The comments on my posts often amount to little more than a flame war. But I've got five volunteer moderators who do a good job keeping a lid on things."

Bancroft's phone vibrated, and he looked at it briefly before asking, "So, what's next for you, Hank?"

"Nothing, I hope! Tonight's meeting is the last one on the schedule. I'm looking forward to a quiet summer with the family. I don't know how Buford does it—he's been managing his law firm and managing me and the Marshall Plan, Inc. We talked last week and agreed that we're both exhausted. So I'm looking forward to slowing down a bit."

"Except for your reading," Buford reminded him. "No slowing down there."

Marshall sighed. "Yes, Jacks. Except for my reading."

They stopped chatting and busied themselves with their meals for a few minutes and then Jackson prodded Bancroft, "Abe, tell us about your background. I don't really know much about you other than what Cummings has told me, and he thinks you walk on water."

"Abe?" Hank asked, confused.

"My nickname," Bancroft responded. "Comes from my initials A.B. I spent some time in the military in my younger days and my commander found that Abe was easier to say than Bancroft. Anyway, the nickname stuck—"

Cummings cut him off. "Spent some time in the military? Ha! He'll never tell you this, but Abe is a highly decorated veteran. He was a sniper with the Marines 1st Recon Battalion. Spent the final years of the Vietnam war sneaking around in the jungle disguised as a bush, plinking Viet Cong."

Marshall raised his eyebrows, "Special forces?"

Bancroft shrugged, slightly embarrassed, and muttered, "It wasn't that big of a deal."

Cummings continued, "Hank, I had to research this guy to find out anything about him. He hardly ever talks about himself—humble to a fault! He graduated top of his class from Harvard Law Sch—"

"Joshua!" Jackson interrupted firmly, "Let him tell his own story."

"Oh, right. Sorry!" said Cummings.

"Anyway, I've done a stint as the AG here in Ohio," Bancroft resumed. "I spent ten years in Congress, and did time on the Intelligence and Foreign Affairs Committees—"

"He *chaired* Foreign Affairs," Cummings interrupted. Jackson shot him a dirty look and Cummings shrugged.

Bancroft chuckled. "Whatever. I left the Washington rat race in 2008, and now I'm practicing law here as well as teaching a few courses at UD."

"Why did you get out?" Hank asked.

"Ten years in Washington is plenty, Hank. Our Founders anticipated citizen legislators; I don't think they foresaw the development of a professional class of politicians. And besides, it's the regulatory agencies in Washington, the entrenched bureaucrats, who have the real power. I got the impression sometimes that it didn't really matter what laws Congress passed, the executive agencies interpreted the legislation and wrote the regulations the way they wanted, no matter what the law said. When I realized I was getting cynical about the political process, I knew it was time to leave."

"Do you think you'll ever go back to Washington?" asked Jackson.

"I've lived too long to make categorical statements about what I will or won't do, Buford. But I have no desire to go back. Washington is a kind of la-la land. You lose perspective very quickly there. Millions become billions become trillions and the average Washington pol doesn't blink an eye. They know there is a day of reckoning coming but it's going to hit on someone else's watch so they don't worry about it. People there live a vastly different life and are clueless about what the average American faces. The real work of the nation is done out here, in flyover country."

They talked for a few more minutes and then Marshall yawned. "I'm sorry, guys, but I'm beat—can't keep my eyes open. I'm gonna bail out. What time do we have to be at the airport tomorrow, Jacks?"

"If we're there by two in the afternoon we'll be fine."

"Good. I'm sleeping in. Abe, it's been a real honor to meet you—thank you for your service to our country. Good night, gentlemen." Henry left the restaurant and walked across the parking lot to the Drury Inn.

"Well, gentlemen, I've still got a bit of gas in the tank, if you do. There's a Cold Stone Creamery just down the street several hundred yards. If we hoof it we can walk off our dinner and make room for ice cream, all at the same time," suggested Joshua Cummings, knowing of Bancroft's weakness for ice cream.

"I'm game," replied Abe.

Jackson, who had some matters to discuss with the two, nodded. They left Panera and dodged their way across the busy traffic on Miller Lane. In a few minutes they were eating ice cream at Cold Stone.

Buford opened his mouth to begin the discussion but Cummings beat him to the punch. "I think we have our man, Jacks. I think Henry is our guy."

Jackson laughed, "I was just about to say the same thing to you. I've felt that way for the last five years or so. I've been grooming him."

"Is that what the books are all about?" Cummings asked, accidentally dripping ice cream down his shirt. "Aw, rats!"

"You're supposed to put it in your mouth, Josh, not your pocket," snickered Jackson. "But, yes, that's what the books are about."

"What are you guys talking about?" asked Bancroft.

"Abe, how long have you been in the Madison Group?" asked Jackson.

"Three months. Josh sponsored me," the former congressman replied.

"Oh, that's right, I'd forgotten. I saw your name in last month's newsletter. We haven't met in session yet this year, so you probably don't know what's going on. I need to ask you to keep a secret, Abe. No one, including the Madison Group, knows about this, although we will be suggesting it to them soon. Do I have your word on the secrecy of what I am about to tell you?" asked Buford Jackson.

"Sure. I spent enough time on the Intelligence Committee to know how important secrets are. You have my word."

"The Madison Group is going to run an independent for the 2016 presidential election. We've been looking for a candidate, with the goal of having him or her identified by January 1, 2013. Josh and I are going to recommend Henry Marshall. That's why Joshua has been at his last six speeches, including tonight. Josh has been evaluating how he speaks, how he handles questions off the cuff, and how, well, *presidential* he seems. For my part, I hired a private investigator several years ago to vet Marshall—it was the same guy who cleared him of the porn flick charges back in 2006, Jim Stewart. Stewart is former FBI. He's been doing oppo on Marshall since 2008, on my dime. I got his final report last month. Marshall has no skeletons in the closet. There are some things that will come up during a campaign, such as the year Henry spent in a booze bottle after the death of his first wife, but all of them can be turned into strengths." Jackson accidentally tilted his cone, and ice cream dribbled down the side and into his lap.

"What goes around comes around," murmured Cummings innocently.

"But Marshall is a total neophyte. Has he ever held political office, or even run for it?" objected Bancroft.

"Nope. But that's not a weakness—it's a strength," replied Jackson, dabbing his pants with a napkin.

Ashton furrowed his brow, "How so?"

"You tell him, Josh."

"Abe, I've been tracking the polls, watching what Gallup is doing as well as RealClearPolitics. And both parties have been asking a lot of focus group questions as the primary campaigning season wraps up. There are a lot of conservative Republicans who feel betrayed; they feel like the RINO establishment has ensured that a moderate wins the primaries.

There is a decided lack of enthusiasm for the candidate. We're only two months from the Republican National Convention and the mood of the country is clear: the electorate is disgusted with professional politicians. 'Hate' is not too strong a word. We are likely to come out of the convention with a moderate. If that happens and we lose the general election, I predict that what is now anger at Washington will grow to *outrage* in the 2016 campaign.

"If I'm right, Marshall's lack of political experience and his established reputation as a clear-thinking, plain-speaking gadfly will be two very, very powerful points in his favor. And it does not hurt that he already has massive name recognition among conservative voters because of his blog."

"Okay, I can buy that, but the Republican power structure will never run him as a candidate. They'll sink you before you get out of the starting gate," Ashton asserted.

"You didn't hear me. I said a moment ago that we're not going to run him as a Republican. We're going to run him as an independent," replied Buford patiently.

"But Buford, there's no way you can create the ground game necessary to get him on all the ballots, much less get him elected—there won't be enough time. It's a noble cause but it's doomed to failure. You'd need strong organizations of committed volunteers in every state. Where's that going to come from?"

Jackson smiled. "Why do you think Marshall's been speaking in every state except Hawaii since 2009? Henry doesn't know this—yet—but I've amassed several hundred thousand names and addresses of people who think he's the greatest thing since Margaret Thatcher or Ronald Reagan. In forty-nine of the fifty states I already have thousands of people who are committed to his ideas, and many who worked hard as volunteers to set up his speaking engagements. Like, for instance . . ."

"Me?" asked Bancroft.

"You."

Ashton—who'd managed to finish his ice cream without wearing it, sat back and stared at the ceiling. After a moment he grinned and looked at Buford. "I can't believe I'm saying this, but you might have a chance. It's a long shot but it sounds like you've got many of the big pieces in place already. It just might work. And the more I think about it the more I love it. In fact, it's exciting. I'm in! Whatever I can do that you need done in the Dayton area, I'd love to help."

"Well, we haven't told you the hardest part yet, Abe," admitted Jackson reluctantly.

"What's the hardest part?"

"Somehow I've got to talk Marshall into being the candidate. He hasn't a clue about this crazy scheme. He nearly died in 2009—literally—when he was agonizing over whether to commit to this speaking tour. I don't have any idea how to broach this with him. I'd probably have more success talking him into flying to the moon."

****

"So what's with all the secrecy, Jacks? What am I doing way out here in the mountains eating a bag lunch with you? Is this thing wired?" Mike Trujillo quipped, looking underneath the picnic table. They were sitting at the Collegiate Peaks Overlook just off Highway 24, above Buena Vista. It was late September 2012, and there wasn't a cloud in the sunny sky. Trujillo was thankful that the table was in the pavilion—sitting in the sun would have been too hot. Buford Jackson had called him a week ago to set up the meeting, and had warned him not to tell anyone.

The silver-haired lawyer didn't respond right way. He munched slowly on a Reuben sandwich as he stared into the distance. After a moment he turned to his friend. "Tru, just look at that, will you? Mt. Harvard, Yale, Princeton. Stands of bright yellow aspen, dark green fir, black granite, the snow above the timberline. Those snow-covered peaks look like burnished silver under this sun. Have you ever seen anything so glorious?"

Trujillo sighed and turned back to the vista in front of

him. It was glorious, he admitted to himself. "It is quite a view, Jacks, it truly is. I hope I never get used to it."

"People who get used to it don't deserve to live here," Jackson murmured. He took another bite of his sandwich, then slapped the table with the palm of his hand, startling his friend. "Okay! Business! Let's talk business, Mike. When did you give up your post as the state GOP chairman?"

"End of last December. Figured I'd served there long enough. Plus with things heating up in the Madison Group, I was feeling a conflict of interest." Trujillo washed down the last of his roast beef sandwich with a swallow of Pepsi.

"Good, good. I've been waiting for you to do just that. Mike, I need your help, and I need you to keep a secret."

"A secret? Okay, let me guess . . . um, Sandy is pregnant, and you two are expecting sextuplets?"

"Thank the Lord, no! That would require an actual miracle, for reasons that I won't go into." The old lawyer fixed his grey eyes on his friend. "Seriously, Mike, I know who the Madison Group should put forward as its independent candidate for the 2016 presidential election. That's the secret."

Trujillo grinned at Buford and asked, "Who? You?"

"Tru, I'm serious. We've got our man. We need to run Henry Marshall," he replied earnestly.

Trujillo studied his friend's face briefly before responding, "You're not kidding, are you?"

"I'm dead serious. He's perfect."

"No, he's not perfect, he's awful, Jacks! What's got into you, man? Marshall has zero political experience and he's not interested in getting into politics. I asked, remember? He's made enemies out of virtually every politician on the planet. And he's been entirely honest about eliminating all subsidies and rolling back the federal government. The teachers' unions would eat him for breakfast and AFSME would serve whatever's left for lunch. There is not a single interest group who would be for him. And the money guys would hate him, because he can't be bought. Marshall's not just rocking the boat, Buford, he wants to point the deck gun at the hull and blow giant holes in it." Trujillo shook his head, "No, Buford, you're nuts. It's a good thing I brought my fly rod with me, otherwise I just wasted my time driving out here."

Buford turned back and gazed at the mountains in the distance. After a moment he looked at Mike and said, "Don't you see it, Tru? The items you just named don't disqualify him; on the contrary, they are some of his best qualifications. He's a man of integrity. No one owns him. The groups you've identified as being against him will be against anyone but a RINO. Not so the people who will become our voter base; the list you just enumerated they will consider the basic requirements for any candidate they would support."

Mike flicked away a large black fly trying to land on his can of Pepsi. "Look, Jacks, I know you like Hank. So do I—"

"—And so do about twenty million other people," Jackson interjected.

"I know, Buford. But let's be realistic, okay? He knows the Constitution, I'll grant you that. But he has no political experience and zero experience governing. And what about his knowledge of world affairs? Can he tell the Malvinas from the Maldives? Has he ever traveled outside of the States? Does he know even the most basic procedures and protocols of the House or Senate? And what if he did run? He'd get eaten alive in the debates. And besides, he's somewhat of a bomb thrower—I think he would scare off moderates." Trujillo wadded up the trash from his lunch and tossed it in the garbage can chained to one of the pavilion supports.

"Mike, why are you even part of the Madison Group?" the lawyer snapped, exasperated. He stood up and looked around; there were no other picnickers or cars in the parking lot. Trying to control his frustration, he began to pace as he spoke to his friend. "It sounds to me like you're making an argument for the establishment! What? Do you really think we can run a milquetoast moderate or a laid-back conservative and straighten this country out? Washington is so entrenched in the wrong direction it's going to *take* a bomb thrower to straighten it out! Everyone of us in the Madison Group is supposed to be willing to risk losing everything in order to do the right thing. What's happened to you? You recruited me into the MG, for crying out loud, and now it sounds like you want to drop out!"

The Pueblo politician didn't answer. He turned away from his friend and walked to the far side of the pavilion and stood looking off into the distance. Jackson waited silently. Finally Trujillo turned around. "I do want to drop out, Jacks. I've lost hope and I'm not sure if it's worth the fight anymore. The country has reached the tipping point and I don't think we can pull it back. Once fifty percent of the people decide to vote for the guy offering the most free stuff, we're done. Game over. And, my old friend, I'm afraid we are already there."

Buford sighed. "Come here, Mike. Sit down. Let me tell you a little story."

Trujillo laughed, a dry, cynical sound. "Story time with Uncle Buford, huh?"

"Humor me," the lawyer demanded in his gravelly voice.

Trujillo shrugged his shoulders and muttered, "Why not?" He sat down across the table from Jackson and said cynically, "Okay, have at it."

"What do you think of when I say Trenton?"

"The capital of the most corrupt state in the Union. Politicians on the take. Dirty cops."

"All that may be true," Buford acknowledged, "but let me tell you what I think about when someone mentions Trenton. I think of the battle that saved not only the Continental Army but the entire cause of independence.

"In December of 1776, the morale of the Continental Army was in the toilet. The Brits had 'em on the run. Our boys had not shown they could stand up to the British regulars or their European mercenaries, the Hessians. Fully ninety percent of Washington's men who'd been with him at Long Island were gone—for some their enlistments had expired, many others simply deserted, disappeared into the night. The politicians in Philadelphia weren't helping: not only were they breaking promises to provide food, clothing, and military supplies, they'd cut and run themselves, relocating from Philly to Baltimore. Washington wrote to his cousin, saying that he thought it was pretty much game over—just like you said a moment ago.

"Against all odds, Washington decided for one last push—a surprise attack against the Hessians who had entered winter quarters at Trenton. There's no way it should have been successful. Crossing the Delaware dodging ice floes, marching a ragtag, malnourished army you could track by following the bloody footprints in the snow, nine miles in freezing, sleeting, pre-dawn conditions. Two men died from exposure during that long slog in the snow and the mud. During the march a courier came to tell Washington that General Sullivan's men were unable to keep their gunpowder dry. Sullivan was commanding half the main body of troops. Washington's response? *Tell General Sullivan to use the bayonet. I am resolved to take Trenton.*

"Parts of the plan of battle fell apart before they even engaged the enemy. The overall timing of the attack was shot to pieces because of delays. More than fifty percent of Washington's force had been unable to cross the river and were stuck where they were of no use to him. And he attacked anyway. And the rest is history, as they say.

"It was a lost cause, Tru. That attack should have never been successful. The tipping point had been reached. It was a last, desperate roll of the dice. Washington gambled everything, virtually the whole Continental cause, on that one action. You know what the password was he gave the troops? *Victory or death!*"

Buford Jackson stood up and looked at his silent, downcast friend. "We've got one more chance, Tru, only one. If we lose in 2016 the American experiment is pretty much over.

"I don't know if we can win, but I do know this: halfway measures and halfway candidates won't do the job. It will take total commitment from us, and it will take a candidate who understands what needs to be done and who is not afraid to do the job. We must have a man who understands that whole pieces of the federal government need to be dismantled, not merely improved—otherwise we will lose even if we win the election."

Trujillo remained silent, and wouldn't look at him.

"Please don't speak of this to Marshall—he hasn't a clue of what I'm thinking." Buford hesitated and when Trujillo made no acknowledgment, he added, "Mike, listen, give Joshua Cummings a call. I know you respect him. Ask him what he thinks about Marshall."

Trujillo sighed. "I'll call him."

"Fair enough, Tru. I'll see you in November at the Madison Group meeting." He gathered up his things, walked to his car, and returned to Denver with a heavy heart.

****

Don't improve it, remove it!
Posted 10/5/2012
By Henry Marshall

When Alexander Hamilton wrote *Federalist #17* to the people of New York on December 5, 1787, he promised them that under the proposed constitution the federal government would never interfere with the "administration of private justice between the citizens of the same State, the supervision of agriculture and of other concerns of a similar nature." Hamilton thought those matters would be left to the states since they would "contribute nothing to the dignity, to the importance, or to the splendor of the national government."

Hamilton had not a clue that by 1862 Abraham Lincoln would create the Department of Agriculture as an independent department of the federal government, and that by 1889 Grover Cleveland would give it Cabinet status. By 1914 the federal government was pouring money into all sorts of agricultural cooperative and extension programs in every county in every state in America. By 1933, the Department of Agriculture was paying farmers not to farm, a consequence of the Agricultural Adjustment Act of 1933. Even though the Supreme Court ruled in 1936 that regulation of agriculture was a state power and not a federal one, the busy bees in the federal leviathan tried again with the Agricultural Adjustment Act of 1938, and we've been paying farmers not to farm ever since —over eight billion dollars in 2004 alone.

In 1941 an Ohio farmer, Roscoe Filburn, grew more wheat than the law allowed him to and he was fined $117.11. He took the case all the way to the Supreme Court (Wickard v. Filburn, 317 US 111) and lost because the Court shoehorned the case into a matter of interstate commerce, which the Constitution does allow the federal government to regulate.

It was an awful decision. The Court said that even though Filburn was growing wheat for his own animals and not selling it across state lines (not selling it at all, actually), it indirectly affected interstate commerce because Filburn was not purchasing wheat for his animals and that *failure to purchase affected interstate markets*. The decision opened a legal Pandora's box, because now virtually any economic activity could be construed as affecting interstate commerce, therefore the federal government could control and regulate economic activity.

Hamilton, Madison, and Jay would be horrified to see how the Supreme Court has virtually shredded the Constitution with boneheaded decisions such as these, the executive and legislative branches going along as willing co-conspirators.

This is the problem with the federal government: it is totally out of control, having usurped powers the Constitution reserves to the states. It's not enough to scale back these unconstitutional Cabinet departments and federal regulatory agencies—they have to be completely eliminated, the programs shut down, the workers let go, the buildings and the assets sold, the lands turned back over to the states.

The best use of the federal legislative branch would be to declare a two-year moratorium on new legislation, and spend the next two years *repealing* all the legislation that usurps the power and rights of the states.

Don't let the politicians bamboozle you: we don't need to *improve* these agencies and departments, we need to *eliminate* them. Totally. We don't need to reduce waste, fraud and abuse—we need to surgically remove it by fully dismantling these unconstitutional cancers.

Someone might ask, "but what if we need some of these programs?" Fine. Let your state and your local government handle it, but don't saddle the taxpayers in the other forty-nine states with your pet programs.

****

On November 6, 2012, the American electorate once again had an opportunity to make their preferences known. The Democrats ran a far left candidate, the Republicans a moderate one. Despite a moribund economy, skyrocketing budget deficits, and a clear turn toward socialism, the incumbent Democrat was reelected. The voters also increased the Democrats' hold on the House and the Senate.

Polls demonstrated that a large portion of the Republican conservative base sat out the election. Joshua Cummings was invited to be one of the election-night analysts on CNN, and he produced charts and graphs demonstrating that had the registered GOP conservative base turned out in greater numbers, the Republican candidate would have won. However, the consensus conclusion of the National Republican Committee and many of the Republican establishment figures was that the candidate presented to the voters was too conservative. The Party argued that if they had put forward a more moderate candidate, he would have attracted a larger swath of voters and carried the day.

And so it was that the nation awoke on November 7 to four more years of business as usual in Washington, DC. The status quo had been maintained, the lifestyles of the powerful and politically connected undisturbed. Four more years of soaring deficits, government intrusions into the marketplace, overbearing regulations, and judicially mandated social change as the country continued the fundamental transformation that began in 2008.

****

Buford Jackson pulled his black Lexus IS 250 into the guest check-in parking spot of the Sheraton Albuquerque Airport Hotel. He tapped Joshua Cummings' shoulder; his friend was snoozing in the passenger seat. "Josh! Josh! We're here. Let's go check in." The seven-hour drive from Golden, CO had been uneventful and Josh had slept a good part of the way. It was mid-November and Albuquerque basked under late-afternoon, sunny skies.

There was still an hour before dinner, so Jackson put on his running gear and went for a jog while Cummings sat in the room and caught up on his reading. At eight o'clock they met with the rest of the Madison Group in the hotel's Gran Quivera meeting room.

Addison Kulp, formerly the governor of South Carolina, was the current chairwoman of the Madison Group. Dressed in a black pantsuit with a white top, she was all business as she called the meeting to order. The first hour was consumed by two speeches from their stable of constitutional lawyers, one on the history and practice of recess appointments, and the other had to do with the various pieces of legislation that created, perpetuated, and extended the Civil Service ranks, and whether presidents could use executive authority to replace Civil Service employees who weren't producing. The last ten minutes of this speech also detailed what would be necessary, legislatively, to begin weakening and dismantling the Civil Service.

Finally the meeting turned to the question of the 2016 presidential candidate. Buford knew that four candidates would be presented. The rules were very strict. No potential candidate could be aware that he or she was under considera-tion. No candidate could be a Madison Group member. Briefing packets had to be compiled on each potential candi-date and distributed to all the members. The brief was required to contain a report distilled from a minimum of one hundred hours of opposition research conducted by a profes-sional firm; a position statement gleaned from the candidate's speeches, writing, and voting record; and a resumé containing a complete account of academic achievements and employ-ment since high school. Additionally, the presenter had to include a ten-page-minimum written opinion detailing why the candidate was a winning candidate.

Each presenter had thirty minutes to make the case for his or her recommendation. The group would reconvene in session the next morning, and each presenter would be ques-tioned for an hour, defending his candidate. The whole group would reconvene the following evening for a vote, each member listing their preferred candidates in order of preference. Finally, the list would be narrowed to the two top vote-getters before the meeting adjourned. Each Madison Group member would then have a month to research the two candidates, and a final vote to select the candidate would be taken at a meeting in mid-December.

Jackson leaned over and said quietly to Cummings, "Let's present Marshall last. We'll get an idea of who the competition might be." Cummings nodded.

Sam Sebastian, the former chairman of the Madison Group, stood up. "Madame Chairman, I move that we add Anthony Zeller to the list." Zeller was the sitting Republican governor of Florida at the moment but he had been voicing a lot of unhappiness with the RNC, and Sebastian thought it would not take much to convince him to run as an independent.

Next was a motion made by the attorney general of Indiana that Peyton Hopkins' name be added. Hopkins was a decorated Navy fighter pilot who went into politics after retiring as a commander. He represented Idaho's 1st Congressional District in the US House of Representatives, and was already listed as an independent.

The third motion came from Joseph Sarber, US senator from Texas. He moved that Elizabeth Montgomery, the other senator from Texas, be added to the list.

Buford Jackson and Joshua Cummings had argued about who would nominate Henry Marshall. He was clearly Jackson's protégé and Buford dearly wanted the honor of nominating his friend, but in the end they had agreed that Joshua Cummings' stature as a political consultant would carry the most weight.

Cummings stood and announced, "I move that we add Henry Marshall's name to the list." A low murmur went through the room. Marshall's name was known by most in the room, but it was also known that he had no experience in political office.

By the time all four nominators had made their presentations it was very late, and the meeting was adjourned until 9:00 a.m. Jackson and Cummings hadn't been back in their suite for ten minutes before there was a soft tap at the door. Cummings opened the door and Mike Trujillo stood outside with a box of pizza and a bag of cold soft drinks.

"Well, come in, come in," invited Cummings, "people bearing gifts are always welcome."

"I didn't get a chance to say hi earlier this evening, so I thought I would stop by. The pizza, well, it's actually a peace offering."

"Peace offering?" asked Buford, as he wrangled plates out of the suite's little kitchen and put them on the small dining table.

"Yeah. Look, Jacks, I know you really like Marshall and I like him, too. But he just has the wrong kind of resumé to be a candidate for president. It's not personal, but tomorrow I'm going to be speaking in favor of Peyton Hopkins. And when I turn in my ballot Marshall's going to be in the number four slot."

"Don't worry, Tru. I'll still be your friend when you lose," jibed Jackson.

Trujillo grimaced and raised his eyebrows. "I'm not going to lose, Jacks. You are. You guys didn't hang around down there after Addy dismissed the meeting. Most of the discussion revolved around comments like *What's gotten into Josh Cummings? I thought he had better sense than that.*"

"Ouch," replied Jackson. "I guess I'm glad you nominated him and not me, Josh." He winked at Cummings.

The consultant stuffed a slice of pizza into his mouth, took a swig of his soft drink, and then declared, "Nothing has gotten into me, Tru. I'm probably the only guy in that room who's been dealing with the polling data on the electorate. We won't win if we put up a politician. It's simply impossible."

The three friends knew they wouldn't agree, so there was no point in belaboring the topic. They turned the discussion to the Broncos, and the success they were having with the newly acquired Peyton Manning under center.

Cummings made his case passionately the next day, but it

was for naught. The two top vote-getters were Peyton Hopkins and Elizabeth Montgomery. Henry Marshall was fourth. That night the Madison Group was sent home with a strict admonition to study and research the two candidates. The next meeting would take place on December 14 in Richmond, Indiana.

Jackson and Cummings checked out the next morning and started the long drive back to Denver under a sky and forecast that was threatening an early season snowfall.

"I can't express how frustrated and angry I am, Josh. I've known since 2006 that Henry Marshall was special. I've been actively mentoring him since then. I was sure that he was the guy for the Madison Group—I am still convinced of that. But it's all been for nothing, apparently. I can't believe they rejected him so decisively. Your presentation was spot on. Just . . . can't believe it," Jackson trailed off, the disappointment thick in his voice.

"I don't know what to tell you, Jacks. We did our homework. He's the right guy. But think about it, Buford: if we can't even convince a bunch of savvy politicos that Marshall's the one, how would we ever convince the voters?"

"Bad analogy, Josh. The professional political class, which describes three-quarters of the Madison Group, if not more, is not looking for what Joe Sixpack looks for when he votes. The voters are looking for an honest, straight shooter who's just as suspicious of the government as they are. The American ruling class has turned politics into an adversarial us-and-them affair, but what they seem to have forgotten is that there are a lot more of the *them*s out there than the *us*'s. And the *them*s are ready to throw the bums out. Marshall is perfect for the voters because they will perceive—and properly so—that he is one of them, one of the disenfranchised.

"After all, that's what your research is showing, isn't it, Josh?" asked Buford, looking over at the man in the passenger seat.

Cummings exhaled noisily. "It is. It's exactly what I am seeing. The other three nominees are great people, Jacks, but they're also just more of the same."

The rest of the trip home was uneventful—quiet conversation about other things. It was the end of a dream for Buford Jackson: not just a dream he had for his friend Henry Marshall, but for America and the turnaround he'd hoped and prayed for.

Chapter 9

IT MERITS PARTICULAR ATTENTION IN THIS PLACE, THAT THE LAWS OF THE CONFEDERACY, AS TO THE ENUMERATED AND LEGITIMATE OBJECTS OF ITS JURISDICTION, WILL BECOME THE SUPREME LAW OF THE LAND; TO THE OBSERVANCE OF WHICH ALL OFFICERS, LEGISLATIVE, EXECUTIVE, AND JUDICIAL, IN EACH STATE, WILL BE BOUND BY THE SANCTITY OF AN OATH. THUS THE LEGISLATURES, COURTS, AND MAGISTRATES, OF THE RESPECTIVE MEMBERS, WILL BE INCORPORATED INTO THE OPERATIONS OF THE NATIONAL GOVERNMENT AS FAR AS ITS JUST AND CONSTITUTIONAL AUTHORITY EXTENDS; AND WILL BE RENDERED AUXILIARY TO THE ENFORCEMENT OF ITS LAWS.

Alexander Hamilton, Federalist #27

Saturday, December 8, 2012

Henry Marshall and Buford Jackson crossed the finish line together. The clock time on the big display over the finish line read 21:43.04, but they had started somewhat back in the pack and Marshall figured that the chip time would be closer to 21:15 or so. He'd been hoping to clock in at under twenty-one minutes, but he knew he'd missed his goal.

The two men had run a charity Jingle Bell 5K race benefiting a local homeless shelter, and both were wearing winter racing gear trying to stay warm in the fifteen-degree morning air. They stood in front of the timing trailer watching the monitor until their chip times scrolled by. Marshall's time was 21:05.17. The RFID timing chips on their bibs placed Jackson twenty-seven one-hundredths of a second faster than his younger friend.

"How's the knee?" Jackson wheezed as they each grabbed a banana from one of the hospitality tables.

"Jacks, you've asked me that after every race since 2009. It's fine!" Marshall put his hands on his hips and leaned over, coughing.

"Just checking, bro. You're getting older, you know. Stuff stops working after a while."

"Older? Older? You're thirteen years older than I am, you old coot!" Marshall exclaimed.

"Who are you calling an old coot? I just beat you in this race, bub," the lawyer crowed, peeling his banana.

"Oh, for Pete's sake, it was by less than a second!" Marshall looked at his friend and laughed. He'd grown to love and respect Buford like an older brother. Buford's friendship was something he held up before the Lord in thanksgiving every day.

"A win is a win is a win," chuckled Jackson. "You're getting slow in your old age, COOT!"

The two men sat on the curb and ate their bananas. "So, Jacks, it's been two weeks since I finished my last book, and you haven't assigned me a new one yet. Have you run out of titles, or what? Am I finally done?"

Buford grimaced. "I don't know, Hank. Maybe you've caught up with me. I guess I'll have to read some more, so I can give you another one."

"Well, don't read too quickly, Buford, I'm enjoying the break. But seriously, you've not been your normal, energetic, grouchy self lately. I feel like you're discouraged about something."

Jackson gave his friend a tight-lipped smile that communicated *I don't want to talk about it*, and said, "I'm fine, Hank." Truth be told, the Madison Group's failure to support Henry Marshall had taken the wind out of the lawyer's sails. But that wasn't something he could share with his friend.

"No, you're not, but I won't press you about whatever it is." The two men chatted about the race for a bit and hung around until the winners were recognized, then Marshall looked at his watch. "Got to go, Jacks. Haley has a honey-do list for me this afternoon. See you at church tomorrow."

****

Peyton Hopkins had just had his questions answered, but he didn't like the answers—in fact he was heartbroken. His wife of forty years, Erin, was just diagnosed with early-onset Alzheimers. For the last six months she'd been forgetting names, missing appointments, misplacing her car keys; and once she'd even gotten lost going home from the grocery store in their suburban northern Virginia neighborhood. In the last two weeks she'd accidentally left one of the stove burners on, almost causing a fire.

Peyton represented Idaho's 1st Congressional District and enjoyed looking out for the people in his district. Hopkins had never jumped on the congressional gravy train. He had the smallest staff of the 435 representatives, and every year in Congress except his first had turned in the lowest expense account figures. His voting record was solidly conservative and he was respected on both sides of the aisle as a man of his word. When Peyton Hopkins committed himself to something he always followed through, win, lose, or draw.

And now his most fundamental commitment was being tested. He smiled sadly: it was no contest. His sweet bride had stood by him for forty years, through long deployments in the Navy, through a painful convalescence from injuries received when the tailhook on his F-14 Tomcat refused to deploy and he went into the barrier and flipped, and through multiple elections. Now it was his turn, and he would stand by her for as long as necessary. There was but one thing to do and that was to resign and withdraw from the political maelstrom.

Finances would not be a problem. He had saved and invested wisely. And they loved their home in Idaho and their neighbors, so moving back from the DC area would be a joy. Erin would be in a home she knew well, filled with many memories.

Hopkins sipped his now-cold coffee and stared at the American flag in the corner of his office. He'd served well. No regrets. He swiveled in his chair until he was facing the wall behind his desk. Mounted there was one of his favorite treasures: a picture of Ronald Reagan and himself at the Reagan ranch. Shortly after leaving office Reagan had run across news of his crash and invited him to come to the ranch for a weekend. It was one of the high points of his life.

No regrets. And he refused to brood. His first phone call was to the governor of Idaho and his second to the Speaker of the House. And finally he gathered his staff and told them. When Congress went into Christmas recess, he was done.

It had been a life well lived, filled with great experiences and unforgettable moments, but now he had a new mission—taking care of Erin—and he embraced it with a heart of gratitude.

****

News about Hopkins' pending retirement and withdrawal from politics spread like wildfire. All the major networks and cable news shows did segments on Hopkins' career. Though a conservative, Hopkins was respected by friends and foes alike, as well as by the media.

But Hopkins' retirement from the political world caused headaches for the Madison Group, as he and Montgomery were the two top picks in contention. With Hopkins' retirement, Montgomery stood to become their pick by default, not by choice. That did not sit well with the group members. What followed was a flurry of emails debating what to do. Sarber, who had nominated Elizabeth Montgomery, was agitating to have her declared the Madison Group candidate. The other members wanted to elevate Zeller, so that they would again have a choice between two individuals. In the end, a decision was reached to replace Hopkins with Anthony Zeller, and the final vote was rescheduled for January 11.

****

Junior Ferris sat in the little diner in Jacksonville eating a heavy lunch of fried chicken, mashed potatoes and gravy, green beans, and the best cornbread he'd ever tasted. The over-the-road trucker was waiting on a text from the dispatcher. Earlier in the day he'd delivered a load of lumber he picked up in North Carolina. He hoped to be assigned a load that would get him closer to his home in Arkansas—he wanted to spend the weekend with his family.

His phone vibrated and he read the text. There was a refrigerated container of citrus going from Jacksonville to the Port of New Orleans. He accepted the haul, finished his meal, and headed for the terminal.

Two hours later he was westbound on Interstate 10. Traffic was moderately heavy, but everyone was clipping along at seventy and Junior was confident he'd have his load to the Port with time to spare.

It was a sunny midafternoon and the heavy lunch he'd had was making him sleepy. He shook his head, trying to clear it. But the drone of the tires, the sunshine, the regular, dashed white line on his left produced an almost irresistible hypnotic effect on him. Suddenly he became aware that while he'd been holding the truck in his lane he really wasn't responding to the subtle moves of traffic around him. He slapped his face a couple of times, shook his head, and decided to pull over at the next rest stop. But within five minutes his senses were again dulled.

A quarter of a mile ahead a cap peeled off the left rear tire of a rig and slammed into the windshield of the Dodge Caravan that was tailgating it. The windshield did not give way but turned into a mesh of cracks impossible to see through. The driver of the Caravan panicked and slammed on his brakes. A flatbed eighteen-wheeler loaded with steel following the Caravan about two hundred yards back started braking rapidly but smoothly and under control. The flatbed was followed by a black Suburban which also hit the brakes.

None of this registered with Junior, who was a good two

hundred yards behind the Suburban. He continued at seventy miles per hour.

****

Anthony Zeller, governor of Florida, was returning to Tallahassee from Jacksonville in a large black Suburban. He was seated in the back seat, his chief of staff beside him, and both men were pecking away at their laptops trying to keep up with the crushing pace that was an unavoidable part of governing a major state.

"Bob, what's the latest in our dispute with the EPA on the Wetlands ruling?" Zeller asked.

His chief of staff looked up from his laptop. "I talked to the AG yesterday. The EPA is asking for more documenta—"

He was interrupted by the driver crying out in terror, "Dear God help us!" as he looked in the rearview mirror.

****

Junior never did regain awareness, at least not in this world. His cab slammed into the Suburban at seventy miles per hour, driving it under the flatbed so hard that the rear axles were torn loose. The top of the Suburban was cleanly sheared off. The cab of the citrus hauler was compressed into a very small space between a forty-foot container filled with fifty tons of oranges and the steel on the flatbed. The fuel tanks of both the car and the truck split. Within seconds the gasoline and diesel fuel ignited, and a raging fire broke out that quickly spread to the tires of all the vehicles.

In a way the fire was a mercy. The occupants of the Suburban died instantly in a scene that would have left first responders with nightmares for months afterwards, but the fire consumed it all before anyone had a chance to see the trauma. The conflagration spread to nearby vehicles stopped in the snarled traffic, but there were no other injuries as the other drivers were able to escape their cars. Interstate 10 was closed for eight hours.

****

"Buford, are you watching CNN or Fox?" asked Mike Trujillo.

"No, why?" asked Jackson.

"Turn it on. Either one."

"Okay." The lawyer held the phone to his ear with one hand and opened the beautifully finished cherry cabinet behind his desk with the other. He powered on the flat screen.

CNN was running their "Breaking News" banner as they broadcast live video from a local affiliate of a raging fire on an interstate highway choked with traffic. A dozen ambulances and police cruisers surrounded the scene in the median and on the shoulders, and four fire trucks were pouring water and foam onto a pair of eighteen-wheelers that were fully engulfed in flames. Buford turned up the sound just in time to hear the reporter say, "A witness at the scene is claiming that there is a vehicle pinned underneath the lead truck. Unverified reports indicate that the trapped vehicle bore the emblem of the governor's office. Wait, I'm getting an update . . . Okay, our CNN affiliate on the scene has contacted the governor's office and confirmed that Governor Zeller and his chief of staff were in Jacksonville earlier today. They were to return to Talla-hassee this afternoon, and they would certainly be on Interstate 10. Attempts to contact either man by cellphone so far have been unsuccessful."

Buford prayed silently for the firemen, paramedics, and police. The scene, apparently shot from a news helicopter hovering over the site, looked awful.

"Are you seeing this, Jacks?" asked Trujillo quietly.

"I am. It's horrific. It's awful."

"I've got a friend in the governor's office and I called him a few minutes ago. It's not been shared with the media, but Zeller was talking to his office about five minutes before this happened. He and Bob Stauffer were on I-10 and he'd given my buddy an ETA of when he'd be back at the office. Unfortunately, that ETA puts him right at or nearby the scene. And Zeller's phone is going right to voice mail, which it would do if—"

"If it had been destroyed," Jackson finished. He sank down into his chair. "Oh, Lord, please no," he sighed. "Tru, Zeller is one of the finest men I know. I've never told you this, Mike, but Zeller is actually my wife's second cousin. We used to get together at family reunions in Orlando, early on. Haven't done it for years because we're all getting older now, but I actually know him quite well and respect him highly. If this is true, it's going to be a real blow to my wife."

Two hours later the news was verified. The remains of three bodies were found trapped under the flatbed. The vehicle was positively identified as the governor's official car. Even though a final identification of the bodies would have to await an analysis of dental records, there was enough in the way of personal effects recovered to make the identification all but certain. Governor Anthony Zeller, his chief of staff Bob Stauffer, and his driver Luis Carmine were dead. Dental records confirmed their identities the following morning.

****

The political landscape had shifted and the Madison Group had to shift along with it. Their two potential candidates were now Elizabeth Montgomery and Henry Marshall; Montgomery by choice and Marshall by default. The final selection meeting was pushed back—again—to February 8. Montgomery won the selection process handily. Joseph Sarber then was charged with the task of asking her to run for president as an independent, with the backing of the Madison Group. Three weeks later Montgomery declared her candidacy and the Madison Group shifted into campaign mode. Buford Jackson, as a Madison Group member, was sworn to support her quest for the presidency. Thus the blow to Jackson's dream of seeing Marshall run for president was final.

****

A Sad Irony
Posted 4/9/2013
By Henry Marshall

In 1777 the Second Continental Congress circulated among the thirteen states a constitution by which the several states in loose union would be governed. It was called the *Articles of Confederation and Perpetual Union*, often referred to as the *Articles of Confederation*. The states ratified the compact by 1781.

It was a document created during our war for independence and, quite naturally, among its chief concerns was to create a central government possessing the authority to wage war, conclude treaties, and provide for international trade.

Article one formally gave to our new nation its name, *The United States of America*. The second article addressed a fear near to the heart of every eighteenth century patriot: having just broken away from a monarch, they did not want to permit the establishment of a central government possessing absolute authority. Consequently the Articles granted to the confederation government only such powers as expressly delegated in the document, all other powers being explicitly reserved to the sovereign states.

The Articles granted Congress the exclusive authority to wage war, exchange ambassadors, enter into treaties, set the terms for commerce with other nations, establish weights and measures, including coinage, as well as several other powers. However, no enforcement mechanisms were provided.

By 1783 the weaknesses of the Articles of Confederation were becoming obvious. For instance, the *Treaty of Paris* ending the war with Britain was drafted in November of 1782 and signed in September a year later. However it was not ratified by Congress until January of 1784. Part of the delay was caused by members of Congress failing to show up—and the confederation government had been given no tools to enforce attendance. Similar problems were experienced as the young nation tried to pay its large war debt. When the states failed to cough up their allotted portion, the central government had no means to force them to do so.

It was apparent that the Articles were inadequate to the task of governing the nation, so a constitutional convention was convened. By late 1787 the new Constitution was submitted to the states for ratification. It was vigorously opposed by some who feared that the creation of a strong federal government would overwhelm the sovereignty of the states and eventually lead to tyranny.

Alexander Hamilton, James Madison, and John Jay thus wrote a series of articles published in New York under the pseudonym Publius that sought to counter the arguments of the anti-federalists. The collection of eighty-five essays known as *The Federalist Papers* set forth the benefits of a strong federal government.

The shocking and sad irony we find at the current time in our nation's history is this: the modern federal government has become so intrusive and has so egregiously usurped the powers reserved to the states that *the arguments in* The Federalist Papers *can now be used to contend for a major dismantling of the federal leviathan*.

In *Federalist #27*, Hamilton argues that: "It merits particular attention in this place, that the laws of the Confederacy, as to the ENUMERATED and LEGITIMATE objects of its jurisdiction, will become the SUPREME LAW of the land; . . . Thus the legislatures, courts, and magistrates, of the respective [states], will be incorporated into the operations of the national government AS FAR AS ITS JUST AND CONSTITUTIONAL AUTHORITY EXTENDS; and will be rendered auxiliary to the enforcement of its laws." The all-caps emphasis, my friends, was original—it was Hamilton's. Notice that he limited the national government to "the enumerated and legitimate objects of its jurisdiction" and "its just and constitutional authority." He's restricting the feds to what the Constitution specifically enumerates as federal powers—all else is reserved to the states.

There is nothing wrong with our federalist Constitution. The problem is that neither the courts nor the legislature nor the executive has acted to limit the authority of the federal government to those powers granted it by the Constitution.

Citing examples of federal tyranny is all too easy. For a simple project, research the amount of land in the western states owned by or controlled by the federal government. Find in the Constitution a provision allowing the federal government the power of determining whether West Virginia shall burn coal to produce electricity, or Alaska drill for oil, or how many miles per gallon an automobile must attain to be manufactured in Detroit, or how much corn a farmer in Iowa is allowed to plant. Study how the Commerce Clause (Article I, Section 8) has been wholly twisted by the courts and legislature to give the feds unprecedented power over the economy.

If we are to reclaim our nation, we must restore sovereignty to the states and wholly eliminate—*not improve, but eliminate*—entire departments of the federal government.

****

In April of 2013, Ohio's congressman from the 10th district lost a long-running battle with cancer, necessitating a special election to fill his seat. Ashton Bancroft was badgered by the GOP until he finally agreed to run. He was unopposed in the primary and handily won the special election in July. As he assembled a staff in his congressional office, he began looking for a domestic policy adviser. Bancroft was ready to turn over some tables and break some furniture to accomplish changes in Washington, DC, and he needed a thinker to help him pick and formulate his battles.

Late one evening in July he sat in the kitchen of his small, rented apartment in Alexandria, Virginia with a large bowl of chocolate ice cream. He fired up his laptop to check Henry Marshall's blog. He loved reading Marshall, who always managed to combine some interesting history with relevant constitutional issues. As he read a blog piece on education it occurred to him that Marshall himself would make a great domestic policy adviser. *Hmm. It can't hurt to try.* He looked at the time; it was 10:30 in Alexandria, 8:30 in Denver. Bancroft picked up the phone and dialed Marshall's number.

"Marshall's residence, Conner speaking."

"Conner, is your dad available? This is Ashton Bancroft."

"Hey, aren't you that guy who was with Marine Recon? A sniper?" Conner and Charlie had been wide-eyed when Joshua Cummings had told them of Bancroft's special forces background several years earlier.

"No, that was my evil twin," Ashcroft chuckled, "kind of like you and Charlie, Conner."

"Yeah, I'm the good twin. Charlie's the evil one," Conner snickered. "Hang on, Mr. Bancroft. I'll go get Dad."

A few seconds later, Hank came on the phone. "Hey, Ashton. I hear from Buford that I need to call you Congressman Bancroft now. Congratulations on your election! But I thought you were done with that rat race."

"Yeah, me too, Hank. But the governor did a little arm-twisting and it was easier to capitulate than resist. It's a replacement term, only a year and a half left, and I probably won't run again when my term is up." Bancroft looked sadly at his empty bowl of ice cream and debated getting another when he was done with the phone call.

"That's what they all say," Henry laughed. "Anyway, what's up, what can I do for you?"

"Hank, I want you on my staff. I want you to come to DC and be my senior domestic policy adviser."

There was a pause, and then Marshall replied, "You are kidding, right?"

"No."

"I don't know what to say, Ashton."

"Try saying yes. It's not hard. Go ahead, try it." Bancroft paced around his little kitchen, willing Marshall to accept.

"What about my blog? That's my vocation now. I can't just walk away from it—I won't just walk away from it," Marshall objected.

"Not asking you to. Nothing about your blog requires you to be in Colorado, Hank," Bancroft replied. "All I would ask is that you put a prominent disclaimer on each post and on the footer of each page, to the effect that the opinions you express are your own and don't necessarily represent my views."

The two men talked for another thirty minutes. The conversation ended with Hank promising to give an answer in the next three days.

****

"What do you think, babe?" Henry asked his wife after recounting the phone call. Haley was sitting across from him stirring a cup of tea.

"I think we should pray about it, but honey, I honestly don't think it's a tough decision. You're being given the opportunity to actually change things, to have a voice in the halls of power. I think we ought to go."

"What about your teaching contract?" he objected. He was grasping at straws and he knew it. "Advanced math teachers aren't exactly flooding the market these days."

"The school can get someone else, Hank. There's still a month before school starts. They won't be happy about it, but they'll understand."

"We'd be moving to northern Virginia, you know. It's crowded, fast-paced, noisy. Nasty," he added.

She smiled behind her teacup. "You're sandbagging."

He grinned sheepishly. "Yep. Don't want to go. Don't want to move to the East Coast. Not even temporarily."

"I think you'd better pray about your attitude, buster."

Marshall sighed. "Yeah. I know. I'm running out of excuses."

"Henry, we need to do this. You need to do this. Somehow

I know this is the next step."

"Next step to where?" Hank objected.

"It's funny," she admitted, pensively, "but I don't know. I just know it's the next step."

Hank got up, walked around the table, and wrapped his arms around his wife. "That's what I love about you—the mystery. And the fact that you are fearless. And, well, the fact that you're beautiful and sexy to boot doesn't hurt either."

She raised her eyebrows quizzically, "Are you making a pass at me?"

"Could be." He grinned at her and winked.

"I'm gonna finish my tea," she said, "and then we can continue this conversation in the bedroom."

Two months later they had rented out their house in Golden, and were living in a condo in Falls Church, Virginia.

Chapter 10

Friday, October 25, 2013

"Just to let our viewers know, Mr. Marshall, can you tell us who you are and what you do?" asked the MSNBC interviewer, Patty Holmes. Marshall had been creating a stir in DC with his strict constitutional viewpoints, and it was hoped that the well-publicized live interview with a man increasingly viewed as a bomb thrower would drive up ratings.

"Sure, Patty. My name is Henry Marshall and I am presently serving as a senior domestic policy adviser for Congressman Ashton Bancroft of Ohio's 10th District. I also write about political issues on my blog at henrymarshall dot org. And let me hasten to add, Patty, that my opinions are my own and do not necessarily reflect those of Congressman Bancroft."

"And he allows you to promote views that many find

rather radical?" she asked doubtfully.

"If he didn't I wouldn't be meeting with you today," Henry responded with a cheery smile.

"Well, let's get started then. Do you have opinions on federal involvement in education?"

"I do," replied Marshall succinctly. He was not going to do this gal's job for her. If she wanted an interview, she would have to ask the questions.

Holmes waited, evidently hoping Marshall would elaborate, but he didn't. Finally she blurted out, "So what do you think about the federal Department of Education?"

"I don't hold it in particularly high regard," Marshall chuckled. He could read the exasperation in Holmes' eyes. She was trying to bait him into a juicy sound bite that could be replayed without context on the evening news, but he wasn't providing it.

"Why are you not supportive of the Department of Education? Surely you are not against improving education in this country?" she frowned.

"Patty, I would love to see our nation do a much better job of educating its young people. Unfortunately, the US Department of Education has contributed very little to that effort. It's a sixty-eight-billion-dollar boondoggle."

"Boondoggle? Isn't that a little unreasonable?"

"Not at all, not when we look at what the Founders intended. Patty, can you cite for me the passage in the United States Constitution that defines the federal government's role in education?" Marshall asked.

The question provoked a momentary deer-in-the-headlights look from his interviewer, but she quickly recovered. "No, but I doubt anyone but a constitutional lawyer could, Mr. Marshall. It's not the sort of thing we read everyday," she said, smiling frostily.

"Unfortunately, you're right—not only could most people not quote the Constitution, I doubt many have even read it. Ignorance about our Constitution is what has permitted our federal government to grow to its present size. I'll quote the passage pertaining to the Education Department: *The powers not delegated to the United States by the Constitution, nor prohibited by it to the States, are reserved to the states respectively, or to the people.* That is the Tenth Amendment, Patty. It's the last one in the Bill of Rights, a document the states ratified in 1791." Marshall sat back in his seat and watched his host, curious to see how she would react.

She studied him for a moment wondering if he'd been joking, and then objected, "But that doesn't say a word about education."

"Actually it does, Patty, it says something critical about education and a whole lot more besides. The Tenth Amendment asserts that the federal government is not to get involved in matters not granted to it by the Constitution. Since the Constitution nowhere *grants* the feds a role in education, the Tenth Amendment therefore *prohibits* it. Education is expressly reserved for the states." He smiled at her.

"Let me get this straight: you're saying that the federal government should not be involved in education?" Holmes asked, barely able to keep the incredulity out of her voice.

"I'm saying the Constitution says that," Marshall reminded her. "So the federal government is spending sixty-eight billion dollars a year on an unconstitutional project. And let's look at what we've gotten for our illegitimate investment: education scores in our country have been steadily sinking when compared with the rest of the world."

"So what is your solution to sinking test scores, Mr. Marshall?" she asked.

"Well, it's not one solution but the prelude to *fifty* possible solutions. First, we have to totally eliminate Uncle Sam's involvement in education. That sixty-eight billion dollars could be, should be, removed from the budget. Then we let the states figure it out at the local level. We might get fifty different solutions, but who cares? Parents in West Virginia care as much as parents in Massachusetts about their children, and both care a whole lot more than some bureaucrat in DC. Washington has no corner on good ideas, and its one-size-fits-all approach is, at best, clumsy."

"But don't you think that the Education Department should be improved rather than eliminated?" she asked stubbornly.

"No. The Constitution gives no role to the feds in education—that's the whole point. Patty, we have a federal deficit of one trillion dollars this year, and one of the reasons we do is because Washington is trying to be all things to all people. Our Constitution carefully and narrowly defines the role of the federal government, all else being left to the states or the people. The Founders did that because in the late eighteenth - early nineteenth century Americans rightly feared governments that had absolute power. And the American experience since then has justified their concerns: the federal government has steadily encroached upon powers the Constitution reserved to the states, aided and abetted by progressive Supreme Court justices who have substituted their own preferences for what the Constitution has clearly and unambiguously said. The consequences of such a radical departure from our Constitution is that we now have a government committed to ponzi-scheme social entitlements and a host of other programs that we haven't a prayer in the world of paying for. There is simply no authority in the Constitution for the feds to have done these things.

"On the other hand, Patty, the fifty states are not limited—unless by their state constitutions—and have been left by the US Constitution with complete freedom to implement education solutions, social safety nets, entitlements, or whatever else the citizens of the particular state care to support. The governmental structures set up in the Constitution are brilliant, Patty, when you think about it. Each state is free to try their own solutions to the problems we face. The only limitations to the state freedoms are those matters the Constitution reserves expressly for the federal government."

The interview went on for another ten minutes and when it concluded Hank sensed none of the polite coldness Patty Holmes displayed at the beginning. She'd become truly curious about his positions, and when the cameras had been turned off and he was walking off the set, she asked him to recommend a few titles she might read to bone up on the Constitution. To Marshall's delight and great surprise MSNBC treated his position fairly in the later rebroadcasts of the live interview, providing sufficient context for the viewer.

One such viewer was Adam Mackenzie, the reporter from the *Chicago Tribune*. Philosophically, MacKenzie was a liberal and he loved history, the Constitution, and the founding documents of the country. But he'd never been so clearly confronted with the practical application of the Constitution to modern government. He felt a grudging admiration for the blogger. The whole pornography episode of several years prior had left him with an appreciation of Henry Marshall's integrity. The MSNBC segment displayed the man as a careful thinker as well. *Adam,* he told himself, *this is a man to watch.*

****

Elizabeth Montgomery's announcement in the summer of 2013 that she was running as an independent for the 2016 presidential election descended on the political world like a bad odor. As a registered Republican currently holding elective office there was no way to sugarcoat the defection, and it caused a great deal of bitterness. She was denounced as a pariah by the Republican establishment and immediately began to experience their wrath in the person of the Senate Majority leader. Legislation containing her name as a sponsor was blocked, highway funds were withheld from her senatorial district, committee appointments evaporated, collegiality disappeared. None of her Republican colleagues sought her collaboration. Even though she continued to caucus with the Republicans, she was wholly isolated.

Since the Madison Group required time to set up the campaign organizations in all fifty states, she needed to make her announcement early—a full twenty months before most candidates show their hand. The early announcement made her the sole target on a battlefield on which no other contenders had yet appeared, and so she absorbed a great deal of negative press from both sides of the aisle. The toxic atmosphere meant that normally reliable donors were spooked, not interested in committing themselves to something they now saw as a losing cause. The members of the Madison Group found that they were alone in donating to the nascent campaign. It didn't take long for members to reach the individual contribution limit. Soon Montgomery's campaign organization was starved for funds even though nothing had been spent on advertising and the salaried positions were modest and few. It rapidly sank into debt.

It was a situation Joshua Cummings had anticipated, but he had not realized it would get as ugly as it did. By February of 2014 Montgomery had had enough and withdrew her candidacy. She shut down her bankrupt campaign and decommissioned what little organization had been achieved.

An additional but unavoidable result was the public disclosure of the Madison Group and the identity of several of its top members. They, too, were ruthlessly disciplined by the party, but stuck to their guns nonetheless and did not reveal other Madison Group members. The Republican Party establishment was now forewarned of an organized rebellion within its ranks. Some hoped that the revelation would draw the party in a more conservative and conciliatory direction, but that didn't happen. Instead the leadership doubled down on moderate positions, vowing to purge the rebels.

The Madison Group's carefully laid plans were in tatters. Resignations brought the membership down to twenty-five. Addison Kulp was nearing the end of her two-year tenure as chairwoman, and she called a meeting in late October to debrief the debacle and discuss the future. Various ideas were kicked around, including the possibility of transitioning into a policy think-tank, but none gathered enough enthusiasm to be acted upon. In the end no action was taken other than to extend Kulp's term as chairwoman. The next meeting was scheduled for November of 2015.

Meanwhile, Marshall continued to serve as Bancroft's policy adviser. He quickly gained a reputation as a straight shooter even among those who didn't like what he had to say.

Henry's command of history, the Constitution, and aspects of policy made him a formidable opponent in any setting, and his careful guidance of Bancroft's positions yielded several legislative successes. Hank showed himself to be a good debater who stuck to the issues and didn't descend into ad hominem attacks.

Henry and Haley enjoyed their time in Washington the way someone might appreciate a lengthy vacation but secretly long to go home. Hank continued to blog and his readership grew significantly during his time in Washington. Congressman Bancroft's term was finished at the end of December 2014, but the Marshalls quietly left his employ in November and returned to their beloved Colorado.

****

Joshua Cummings sat across the table from Adam MacKenzie in Denver's Casa Bonita restaurant. He ran the little flag up the flag pole on his table and an attentive waiter appeared and took Cummings' order for another plate of burritos. MacKenzie watched the political consultant with growing impatience. Cummings had forbidden the use of his digital recorder, but the noise level in the popular restaurant would have rendered it useless anyway. Frustrated, Adam looked down at his notepad—it was blank.

"Mr. Cummings, you can't talk about the Broncos forever. You're the one who called me for this interview. Can we please get started?" he pleaded.

Cummings sighed and nodded. "Go ahead, Adam. Fire away—but remember, this is all unattributed."

"Got it. So what happened with Elizabeth Montgomery?" MacKenzie picked up his pen and prepared to take notes.

"Oh, my. That was awful. It was a major fail on my part. The Madison Group—"

"That's the secretive group of conservatives who have been meeting for the last eight years or so," MacKenzie clarified.

"Correct. Anyway, we were tired of business as usual in the Republican Party, and we wanted to run a true conservative as a presidential candidate. We knew it would never happen within the party itself—the RNC would derail it before we got off the ground.

"So I advised the MG that we would have to run our candidate as an independent from the get-go, and because of that, we would need a lot of lead time to set up campaign organizations in the fifty states. Well, you can't really do that secretly, so we had Elizabeth declare early—really early. And it blew the top off of things. The RNC went nuclear. I had no idea the party would be as brutal as they were. They turned her into the Wicked Witch of the West. She was mercilessly savaged by the party leadership.

"The fallout of all that, Adam, is that I absolutely ruined Montgomery's political career. The sad thing is, she's an outstanding, honest, thoughtful politician. She would have made a superb president. I'll never forgive myself. I know for a fact when her present senatorial term is up, she'll never run again for anything."

Cummings took a bite of his burrito. A wandering mariachi group strolled up to the table and sang a love song in Spanish, halting the conversation until they ambled on to another table.

"She told you this?" MacKenzie continued, scribbling.

Cummings nodded, and then hastily added while chewing, "That, by the way, is totally off the record."

The interview continued with a painful postmortem of the Madison Group experience. Finally MacKenzie started to wrap it up. "Mr. Cummings, you tried and failed to run a conservative candidate who you believed would represent your views and the views of many conservatives around the country. We are now entering the beginning of a new presidential election cycle. The Iowa caucuses are just thirteen months away. Since Montgomery is no longer an option, if you could have any candidate to represent your views, who would it be?"

"That I can answer without hesitation, and you can quote

me on this. I think Henry Marshall would be the best candidate out there, hands down."

MacKenzie blinked, uncertain if he'd heard correctly amidst all the noise of the bustling restaurant. "I'm sorry, but did you say Henry Marshall?"

"I did," Cummings affirmed.

"Really? Why him?"

"Because everyone else is talking about improving the government, saying things like reducing waste, fraud and abuse, negotiating better deals, and starting new programs. Marshall is the only guy talking about removing whole pieces of the federal government."

"Why is that better? What's wrong with improving it?"

"It's like this, Adam. If you dig a foundation to support a two-thousand-square-foot house and then overbuild on it, putting up a four-thousand-square-foot house, you will eventually have big problems like sagging floors and cracked walls. Repeatedly repairing the sagging floor in the overbuilt section is not going to fix the problem, it just perpetuates it. You've got three choices: dig a new foundation underneath the over-built section, tear down the overbuilt parts, or continue to pour money down a rat hole trying to shore up your collapsing house. There are no other choices.

"We have a four-thousand-square-foot government sitting on a two-thousand-square-foot Constitution. No wonder it's breaking down. No wonder it's so inefficient. No wonder it's rife with waste, fraud, and abuse.

"Now, there are three political responses to this conundrum. The progressives in the Democratic Party want to rewrite the Constitution according to the need of the moment. A better way of saying it is that they don't really want a constitution at all, they just want a responsive government that solves the latest problem *du jour*. More government is the answer, no matter what the question. In their thinking, a six-thousand-square-foot house is much better than four, or two and as long as the government is the one designing the additions, all is well and good. They're the guys who want to dig a new foundation under the overbuild.

"The establishment wing of the Republican Party wants to keep things just as they are—shoring up the floor, patching the leaky roof, and even adding new rooms. They want to be the guys who dole out favors to the contractors, the crony capitalists who earn a tidy profit repairing our constantly deteriorating four-thousand-square-foot house.

"The constitutional conservatives are the only ones saying that the original plan was beautiful, a two-thousand-square-foot house is perfect, and we need to tear down the overbuilt sections. Marshall is the man who really, thoroughly understands this and has been communicating it on his blog for years." Cummings pushed back his plate and wiped his mouth with his napkin.

"Okay, but—to continue the house illustration—what if we really do need that six-thousand-square-foot house, Mr. Cummings?" asked MacKenzie, impressed with the cogency of the metaphor.

"But that's the beauty of the Constitution, Adam! Don't you see it? The states themselves can build any size house they want to, implementing whatever is necessary to support their population and its particular needs. Rather than forcing all fifty states to have the same energy policy, West Virginia can go with coal, Michigan with nuclear, California with wind, Utah with hydro. Each state can do as it wishes. And if the citizens don't care for where their government is taking them, conservatives in Wyoming don't have to fight with liberals in California to change conditions in Wyoming. Liberals in New York don't have to fight with libertarians in New Hampshire and conservatives in Texas to change the way New York governs its citizens."

"I have to admit, Mr. Cummings, it's a compelling metaphor. Did you come up with that?" asked MacKenzie, putting his notebook in his briefcase.

"Nope. Marshall did. It was on his blog six years ago."

****

Sunday, January 11, 2015 was dwindling away into the record books. The grey clouds over Colorado weren't all from the weather: Denver had lost earlier in the day to the Indianapolis Colts in an AFC divisional playoff. The whole Marshall family had been at the game to cheer on their beloved Broncos, and they'd come home disappointed. After a noisy supper spent dismantling the Broncos' performance, the twins had driven back to the University of Colorado in Boulder to be ready for classes the next day and Charity had returned to her cozy apartment in Fort Collins, where she was employed as a software engineer for Hewlett Packard.

It was after nine. Hank sat in the family room, snoozing on the couch. The book he'd been reading had slipped from his fingers and was lying on the floor. Haley was sitting in the recliner with her laptop, catching up on the news.

"Oh, my . . . Hank, you've got to see this!" The only response was soft snoring, so she went and sat by her husband and gently shook him awake. "Hey, buster, if you're that shot why don't you just head for bed?"

"What? Huh?" he said groggily, sitting up and scrubbing his face with his hands.

"I said, why don't you go to bed?"

"No, no, I'm just doing some reading . . . huh, must have dropped my book," he said, still a little foggy.

"Hank, you've not been reading for the last thirty minutes, you've been sawing logs. Go to bed. But you've got to read this first. It's an article by Adam MacKenzie, and he quotes Joshua Cummings as saying that you'd be a great candidate for the presidency." She gave him the laptop and pointed to the article.

"What? That's nuts!" he replied, now fully awake. He read the article swiftly and then shook his head. "Josh is crazy. I'm a blogger, not a politician. I think I must be dreaming—I *am* going to bed. Want to come, *ma chérie?*"

****

Two weeks later Ashton Bancroft was a guest on Fox News, and was asked who he'd like to see run for the presidency in the upcoming election. Bancroft spent the next three minutes explaining, uninterrupted, why he thought Henry Marshall would be an excellent candidate. Someone put the clip on YouTube and it went viral within three days.

A week later, Mike Trujillo sat in his study late on Monday night, leafing through his notebook of Marshall blog posts. Trujillo couldn't quite make the transition to a paperless society—he'd printed out every Marshall blog from the very first post, appreciating the blogger's finely tooled analysis of a strict constitutional government. He'd even pulled the tags from the blogs and created an index.

When the Marshalls had moved briefly to Virginia in support of Ashton Bancroft, Trujillo had haunted the DC area news websites like a stalker, watching for anything on Henry Marshall. The more he saw, the more impressed he was. And now in the last month, six writers had expressed in print their belief that Henry Marshall would be a great presidential candidate.

Trujillo put the notebook of blog posts down, leaned back in his chair with his hands behind his head and stared at the ceiling. *I cannot escape the notion that these guys are right. Marshall would make an outstanding candidate. How did I miss it when Buford tried to tell me? Well, maybe I didn't miss it. Maybe Marshall wasn't ready. Maybe nobody else was, either. But we are now. And there's no time to lose!*

Tru looked at the clock. It was eleven thirty. He'd be waking everyone of them up. *No matter. If we're gonna do this, none of us will be sleeping much for the next year or so, anyway.*

He called Buford Jackson first, hoping the old lawyer hadn't gone to bed yet.

"Hello?"

"Jacks, it's Tru. I need a favor."

"At eleven thirty?" Jackson growled.

"No, the day after tomorrow, 3:00 p.m. I need to borrow you, and I need to borrow your conference room at WLA,"

Trujillo announced firmly.

"I'll have to check my schedule, Tru," Jackson cautioned.

"Whatever is on your schedule, Jacks, reschedule it," Trujillo insisted.

"Mike, what's this all about? Why the urgency?"

"Buford, on Wednesday afternoon I am going to talk *you* into talking Henry Marshall into entering the presidential race as an independent candidate."

There was silence on the other end of the phone, and then a dry rejoinder, "Are you sure this is Mike Trujillo, Pueblo politician extraordinaire, who several years ago thought that was the dumbest idea I'd ever had? Is this that Mike Trujillo?"

Mike chuckled, "Yes, this is that guy."

Jackson cleared his throat noisily. "Okay. Now you've got my attention. What did you say you wanted?"

Mike repeated, "I wan—"

"Done. Anything else?"

"No, that will pretty much do it," Trujillo laughed.

"I'll see you in my conference room at 3:00 p.m. on Wednesday. Bring any friends you wish."

Trujillo dialed Ashton Bancroft next, wincing because he knew it was one thirty in the morning in Dayton, Ohio. He heard the phone go off hook, heard something crash to the floor, and then a sleepy and somewhat irritated, "Hello?"

"Ashton, it's Mike Trujillo in Pueblo. Sorry to wake you, sir."

"Mike, it's after one in the morning," grumbled Bancroft. "This had better be good."

"Ashton, I need you to fly to Denver and meet me at the offices of Western Law Associates at 3:00 p.m. on Wednesday, day after tomorrow."

"Mike, I have appointments with clients on Wednesday, I can't just walk out on them."

"Sir, you've said publicly that Henry Marshall would make a good presidential candidate, have you not?"

"Sure, but what does that have to do with this?"

"I think we need to talk Marshall into running. That's what this is about, and we're running out of time in the election cycle to make it happen."

Bancroft sighed, and muttered, "No matter how many times I back out of politics it always comes back to grab me." Louder, he responded to Trujillo, "I'll try. No promises, but I'll try."

Josh Cummings signed on a few minutes later.

"YES!" Trujillo shouted, doing a fist pump. The meeting was on. They would meet at three in the afternoon, and then take Henry and Haley out to dinner that night.

Chapter 11

> THAT GOVERNMENT IS BEST WHICH GOVERNS LEAST.
>
> *Attributed to Thomas Jefferson, actual source unknown*

Wednesday, February 11, 2015

Buford Jackson walked through the expansive offices of Western Law Associates and paused at the door of the conference room. He checked his watch. It was just after two in the afternoon.

"Kathy, see that no one disturbs me, and I mean no one, not for any reason."

"Shall I stand outside the door and guard it, Mr. Jackson?" she asked with a smile.

"If need be, yes," he responded, only half-kidding. He entered the room, locked the door behind him and walked over to the broad expanse of windows. Twenty floors above street level, his conference room provided an unimpeded view of the rugged Front Range of the Rockies. In the distance he could see Interstate 70 snaking into the foothills. A mile west of his office were the sprawling, empty parking lots of Sports Authority Field at Mile High.

He sat at the table pondering the turn of events regarding Henry Marshall and found himself struggling to keep his emotions in check. He'd been mentoring Marshall for years, had always known there was something special about the younger man. When Hank began blogging ten years ago about the history of the country, the Constitution, and current political issues, a wild thought had become firmly implanted in Jackson's mind, one he hadn't been able to shake. Buford knew—somehow he knew—that Henry was destined to become a candidate for the Office of the Presidency. It was a conviction he'd shared with no one but Sandy, his wife.

From that moment Jackson had pushed the younger man, encouraged him, challenged him, sharpened him. Arguing, debating, feeding him books, and slowly introducing him into political circles, Buford had carefully maneuvered Hank into relationships with people he'd need to know. A great unplanned-for boon had been the wild popularity of Marshall's blog. The massive, positive, public response to Hank's ideas made Buford's quixotic dream for his friend seem attainable. And when Marshall began his highly successful speaking tours, more pieces of the puzzle fell into place.

But the bottom fell out when the Madison Group rejected Marshall. Jackson was devastated. He'd not realized how invested he was in the younger man's future until Marshall was passed over with resounding finality. Jackson returned to Denver heartbroken and sank into a depression he battled for months afterward. It was the death of a dream and the lawyer had been caught off-guard by how profoundly he'd been impacted.

Now—unbelievably—the dream was resurrected from a most unexpected direction. Mike Trujillo—who had totally discounted his suggestion in 2012—was now Marshall's most enthusiastic promoter. *Go figure.*

Buford lost the battle with his emotions and put his head in his hands and wept. When he regained control, he got up and paced about the room praying. He prayed for wisdom, he prayed that Marshall and his family would be protected, he prayed that God would build the right team around Hank, and he prayed that God would guard his friend's purity and integrity. To be asked to run for the presidency of the most powerful nation on earth had to be a heady experience—and Jackson prayed that God would keep Marshall humble.

****

Ashton Bancroft, Joshua Cummings, and Buford Jackson sat chatting in the conference room. Trujillo had called to say he was stuck in traffic. Finally he arrived and they got started.

"Buford, I know this is your conference room and Marshall was originally your idea, but may I?"

"Knock yourself out, Tru," Jackson said.

"Gentlemen, in the summer of 2012 Buford asked me to meet him at Buena Vista. He shared an idea—he was planning to recommend that the Madison Group anoint Henry Marshall as its candidate for president. I could not agree."

"That's putting it mildly," Jackson grumbled. "You shot me down with extreme prejudice."

"Yeah, I suppose I did. Anyway, what followed was the Elizabeth Montgomery debacle. Not good. I thought Montgomery would be a great candidate. She would have been, too, except she could not raise any money and she was virtually assassinated by the RNC.

"To make a long story short, I've had a remarkable change of heart. The last two months I've been rereading Marshall's blog posts and it's dawned on me that he knows a great deal more about the Constitution than I do. He's got a feel for the Founders' intentions and he's able to communicate them to the average man. His grasp of policy is great in some areas, adequate in others. He's a man in good control of himself, he speaks and debates well, and he's shown that he can take rebuke and criticism. He's healthy and young, and as a runner displays good self-discipline. And if he was of a mind to he could largely fund his own campaign—he's not dependent on donors. The RNC would have a tougher time derailing him.

"To sum up, I don't think Marshall would be an acceptable candidate, I think he'd be a terrific candidate. I'm convinced that he's the guy we need to pull the country out of the swamp. I am therefore urging that we call the Madison Group back together and rally behind Henry Marshall," concluded Trujillo.

"No, definitely not," replied Bancroft. "The Madison Group is damaged goods and could be finished as an effective organization, at least for some time to come. But otherwise I agree with you, Mike. I think Marshall would make a great candidate and a great president. I say we just run with Marshall on our own."

"But what about our commitments to go with the Madison Group candidate?" objected Trujillo stubbornly.

"Our commitments died with the Montgomery candidacy," answered Jackson. "The Madison Group is no longer contemplating running any candidate for the current cycle. That means we are free and clear as long as we don't portray Hank as a Madison Group candidate."

"He's right, Tru," affirmed Joshua Cummings. "We'll be on solid ground ethically if we run Marshall as a candidate independently of the Madison Group. And my guess is that we'll see most of the remaining members endorse him anyway."

"But won't we need the organizational assets of the Group?" asked Trujillo.

"Actually we have something much, much better," said Buford with a smile. "You may recall that I talked Henry into going on a speaking tour several years back. I sold it to him as an opportunity to teach people about constitutional government—and so it was. But while he was doing it I was busy using the registration form on his website to build a database of names and addresses of the registrants, especially people who were inviting him to speak in their neck of the woods. I have literally hundreds of thousands of names and addresses of Henry Marshall's fans from every state except Hawaii. The speaking tour raised his name recognition and gave people a chance to know him better. I believe those names and addresses can be turned into state and local campaign operations, staffed by volunteers who are already sold on Marshall. And I don't think it will take long to put it together.

"The bottom line, Tru, is that if we can talk Henry into running he is already miles and miles ahead of where Elizabeth Montgomery started. She is well known in Texas and has a great organization there, but Henry is well known in forty-nine states and has the beginnings of an organization in each one."

"Huh. If I didn't know you better, Jacks, I'd say you're brilliant. But since I do know you let's just call it dumb luck."

"Very generous of you, Tru," the lawyer chuckled.

For the next several hours they discussed strategy and batted around ideas. Finally it was time to wrap it up. Buford stood and said, "Now listen! There's one thing I want to make clear, gentlemen. Hank is his own man. To this point I've been sort of shepherding him along. All of us have had a hand in that, to one degree or another. But if he consents to become the candidate, suddenly he's the boss. We can help him only in such ways and capacities as he permits. The policy positions are his, not ours. The decisions become his, not ours. Certainly, it's our decision whether or not we want to be involved—but the level of our involvement will depend on his invitation. Are we clear on that?" he asked, looking around the group. Everyone nodded.

"Okay. I've invited Hank and Haley to join us at my home for dinner tonight. They have no clue that we're going to ask Hank to run. See you all at my place at half past six this evening."

****

"Welcome, Haley! Come in, Hank! So glad you could come. Can I take your coats?" Sandy Jackson welcomed them both with a warm hug.

"Is there anything I can do, Sandy?" asked Haley as she struggled out of her heavy coat.

"Nope, nothing to do. We had the dinner catered tonight —can you believe it?—so *I* don't even have anything to do. Let's go into the den with the guys."

Henry walked into the den and was surprised when he saw who else was there. "Whoa! This looks like a political caucus!" He walked over to Bancroft and shook his hand warmly, "Abe, how are you doing? I'll bet you don't miss Washington, do you?"

"Not a bit, Hank. I'm just relieved my tour of duty is over," said the former congressman.

"Hey, Mike," Henry said, turning to Trujillo. "Great to see you! What are you doing nowadays? Have you pulled out of politics like Abe, here?"

"Nah, Hank, it's just half-time. I'll probably run for something in the next year or two."

"And Joshua Cummings!" said Hank warmly. Cummings was one of his favorite political gurus. "How are you, sir? I'm surprised you've not been snapped up into someone's presidential campaign. Or have you?"

"Good to see you, Hank. No, I'm still unemployed," Cummings affirmed, smiling.

"Is that by choice?"

"Of course it is, Hank," interrupted Buford. "Joshua's phone has been ringing off the hook with offers. He's just playing hard to get."

The group chatted for thirty minutes or so, snow skiing and the Denver Broncos being favorite topics for the Coloradoans. Then Buford walked through the room with a tray of tall, long-stem champagne glasses. When everyone had a glass, Buford raised his. "Excuse me, everyone, I'd like to propose a toast." He waited for a moment while the conversations died down, and then said with a big grin, "To the next president of these United States of America."

"Hear, hear!" everyone replied, and clinked their glasses.

Hank looked at Bancroft and said, "Abe, you sly dog! Are you throwing your hat in the ring?"

The congressman smiled and shook his head, "No, Hank. Not me."

Marshall furrowed his brow, "Well then, Buford, who are we toasting?" he inquired.

"Hank," Buford suggested, "perhaps you and Haley should sit down."

"What are you telling me, Jacks? Is it you? No, wait, that can't be," Hank mused, "you're the one who offered the toast. So Mike, is it you?"

"Hank, please *sit down*," said Trujillo, "in fact, let's all be seated. Haley, please—sit next to him. Thank you." Mike looked around the room, and Buford gave him an imperceptible nod. Trujillo could not wipe the happy smile off his face as he said, "Henry, all of us here are asking you to submit your name as an independent candidate for the presidency. Buford and Sandy, Josh, Abe, me—we all believe you would be an excellent candidate and an even better president."

Hank set his glass down on a coaster. "Very funny, Tru. Now can someone please tell me what's going on? I feel like you guys have gone weird on me all of a sudden."

"Hank, this is not a joke and we are not teasing you," replied Buford seriously. "It is our honest, serious, considered opinion that you would make an outstanding president. We want you to run, and we are pledging our support if you will."

Haley looked like someone had just asked her to walk a tightrope across the Grand Canyon. She blinked and looked at Sandy, who smiled and nodded and squeezed her hand.

The color drained out of Hank's face. "You aren't kidding," he croaked, barely getting the words out.

"No," answered Joshua, "we aren't."

Hank's throat went dry. He sat, speechless. Finally he cleared his throat. He looked at Sandy, "Sandy, could I have a glass of water, please?" She got up and went to the kitchen.

"Well, now. Uh, how 'bout them Broncos?" he said weakly. No one responded. Sandy came back and set a glass of water next to him. Hank took a big swallow and cleared his throat again.

"This, uh, this—this is surreal." He looked at Haley, "Are you hearing what I'm hearing?" She nodded. "Is it making any sense to you?"

She replied quietly, "Hank, I really think you should listen to what they have to say."

He studied her face for a moment then turned back to everyone else. "Okay, fine, I'm all ears," he said, his voice stronger. "What are you guys trying to say?"

Joshua Cummings spoke up, "Henry, we want you to run for president. This is not an impulsive decision for any of us. Abe, Buford, and I were talking about this back in the summer of 2012, when you spoke at UD."

"Okay. How about you, Mike?" Henry asked.

"I was dead set against it, Hank," Trujillo confessed. "But about two months ago I printed all your blog posts and reread them carefully, taking notes. I began to see that you had accurately diagnosed the failure in Washington, and it dawned on me that I had not heard anyone else accurately describe both the problem and the solution, at least not to the degree you did."

"What did you see, Tru?" asked Abe.

"The common theme in all Hank's posts is this: states' rights. The federal government has grown unwieldy, uncontrollable, because it has usurped the roles that the Constitution reserves to the states. Every other politician I know talks about improving Washington. Henry talks about dismantling Washington. Am I right?" he asked, looking at Marshall.

Henry nodded, "Right on target, Tru. That's exactly my point. If the federal government applies the Tenth Amendment, there are a lot of agencies and cabinet-level departments that have to disappear."

Mike continued, "I can admit it when I'm wrong, and boy, my early impression of you, Hank, was wrong! I realized Buford was right all along. So three nights ago I called Buford and told him I'd changed my mind, and that I thought you would be a great candidate. That's why we're here tonight. Somebody just needed to pull the trigger and I guess it was me."

"What about you, Jacks?" Hank looked at his dear friend.

"Well," the lawyer said, his voice slightly husky, "just what do you think all those books were for? And why on God's green earth do you think I pushed you to go on that speaking tour?" He stopped, cleared his throat and wiped his eyes. "All I can say," he growled, "is you're mighty slow on the pick-up, boy. What did you think was going on? It was all in support of what we're asking you to do tonight. I suppose I was the first to see you as presidential material. I didn't know *when* it would happen, but somehow I knew that it *would* happen."

"All this time. . ." Hank murmured, his voice trailing off as he gazed at his friend.

Buford nodded, a lump in his throat, "Uh-huh. Yep."

Hank looked at Haley. She'd recovered from the initial shock. A smile played about her lips, and she tilted her head slightly.

He turned back to the others. "We'll pray about it."

"Good," Cummings responded, "but don't take too long. If you decide to throw your hat in the ring, there is much to do."

The caterer came in and whispered in Sandy's ear. She stood up and announced, "Let's continue this discussion at the dinner table."

****

Henry and Haley fasted and prayed on Thursday and Friday, and then the following Monday and Tuesday. When they sensed that the Lord was not throwing up roadblocks, they contacted the church's prayer chain and asked them to pray about a personal, private request (without naming it) on their behalf. On Friday morning, Hank met with Pastor Johnson.

"Morning, Hank! How's the family?" Pastor Joe asked as he slid into a booth at IHOP.

"Ha! Beats me! Everyone is away at college now, Haley and I are practically empty-nesters. It's a lot quieter, but sometimes a lot lonelier, too. Not as many fights over what college foot-ball game we're gonna watch, but hey, I'd rather have the fights and have my kids at home. I miss 'em." Hank grabbed the carafe and poured his pastor a cup of coffee.

"Thanks." Johnson added a spoon of sugar and took a sip, then said, "Well, don't worry too much, brother. Before you know it you'll have grandkids hanging off the rafters. I've got seven, and they keep us busy. So, what's up Hank? You mentioned that you needed some wisdom regarding a matter."

"Yeah. In a thousand years of guessing you wouldn't even get close to what I'm about to ask you, Pastor Joe."

"Try me."

"I've been asked to run for president, and I want your

advice."

"That's not so big. You've had a lot of corporate experience—I'm not really surprised. So, president of what board, Hank?" his pastor asked.

Hank drew a deep breath and looked around. The other booths nearby were empty. *Here goes nothing*, he said to himself. He looked at his pastor and smiled sheepishly, "President of these United States."

Pastor Johnson raised his eyebrows and just stared at his parishioner. When Hank said nothing more, he narrowed his eyes and clarified, "You mean, you've been asked to run as a candidate for the office of president of our country?"

Hank nodded, "Right."

"You're not joking?" Johnson clarified.

"No, but that was my initial reaction, too. I thought *they* were joking. They weren't. Haley and I have been praying since last Wednesday night, as well as fasting on and off."

Pastor Joe set his cup down. "Hank, tell me the whole story. This I gotta hear."

For the next twenty minutes Hank told his pastor the tale, ending with the dinner party at the Jacksons'.

"Wow. Okay, look Hank, this is a really big deal. But we make decisions on really big deals the same way we make difficult decisions on the garden variety stuff. First you commit the matter to prayer and continue to pray about it until the decision is made. Second, you study the Scriptures to see if there are any direct statements that throw the matter clearly one way or the other. Third, you use wisdom principles informed by the Scripture, and allow them to tilt your heart. Then seek godly counsel; Proverbs states that there is safety in a multitude of counselors. At the end of all that, if you are living for God's glory and nothing decisive has emerged, follow your heart. Do what you want to do, trusting that God is leading the desires of your heart."

Hank nodded. "I'm at the godly counsel part, Pastor. That's why we're meeting."

"So what can you tell me about the people asking you to run? Are they men and women of godly wisdom? Do they know Christ? Do they know anything about politics?"

"You know Buford and Sandy, they go to our church. I respect their knowledge and love for Christ as much as anyone's. Buford is a political junkie from way back. Joshua Cummings is probably the most accomplished conservative political consultant in the country, especially when it comes to national campaigns. He's a Catholic who's made a personal confession of faith in Christ. Abe Bancroft—a lawyer, former congressman—he's a strict constitutionalist in the mold of Madison or Adams. Don't know if he's a believer—I think he's more of a deist, like Ben Franklin. But he's a good moral man, loves the country, wise. I respect him highly. And last, Mike Trujillo. He's a good man, a political animal, but a good man. I don't know what his worldview is, but I know he's not a pragmatist. Trujillo runs on principles, not on what works."

"All these have asked you to run?"

"Yes." Hank hadn't touched his breakfast.

"Would you trust their political judgment on other matters?"

"Sure."

Pastor Joe nodded, and forked a bite of his waffle into his mouth. He took another sip of his coffee, then motioned to Hank's plate, "Are you gonna eat that or just look at it?" Hank grinned and picked up his fork. Johnson said, "Okay, we're tabling this matter until you eat something. Besides, that gives me time to think about what you've said."

The two men worked on their breakfasts for a few minutes, and then Johnson wiped his mouth. "Look, Hank, here's how we don't approach these decisions. We don't put out fleeces. We don't read the tea leaves or look for 'signs.' The same sign could be interpreted by two different believers in diametrically opposed fashions. One might encourage you to do it, saying that Satan's trying to discourage you, while the other says, no, God's trying to prevent you from going that way. Fleeces, signs—they're all bogus.

"What God calls you to is godly wisdom. Sure, you look at the situation and evaluate resources, conditions, etc., but all of that provides the data you plug into wisdom. And if at the end of the day wisdom could argue for either direction, you examine the desires of your heart.

"So Hank, what do you want to do? What does Haley want?"

Marshall sat back in his seat. "Haley wants to jump in with both feet. She's ready to go for it and not look back. I'm more cautious, but the more I think about it the more I long for an opportunity to do whatever I can to put this country back on the right track. On one hand, I have less than a snowball's chance on a hot sidewalk in August to actually get elected; on the other hand if God wants it to happen it will. At the very least I can call attention to areas in which the country has jumped off the rails. Maybe that will do some good."

"Am I hearing you say that you want to do it?"

Marshall looked his pastor in the eye and said, "Yeah. Yes. That is what I'm saying, isn't it? I do want to do it."

"Then I think you have your answer."

****

Hank and Haley stood in the vestibule of the Ruth's Chris Steakhouse in Denver, waiting for Conner and Charlie. Charity was standing with them, having arrived a few minutes earlier from Fort Collins. It was early Saturday evening.

"So what's the occasion, Mom? This is a pretty swanky place!" asked the pretty twenty-one-year old. Charity had graduated a year early from Colorado State University with a degree in computer engineering. Hewlett Packard snapped her up almost immediately, and she was now working for them in Fort Collins as a software engineer, writing firmware for their new Sprout line of personal computers.

Haley looked at her precocious daughter and just smiled. "We have something we want to tell you three, but you'll have to wait until your brothers arrive."

Twenty minutes later the family was seated in a private section of the restaurant.

"Wow, Dad. I think we ought to meet here every Saturday,"

said Charlie, looking at the menu the way a hungry timber wolf might eye a yearling lamb.

"You do, huh?" Hank replied absently as he studied the menu.

"Yeah. I want one of everything."

"And Conner will want what you want, Charlie, so we'll have to order two of everything just to keep you two carnivores fed," Charity sassed.

"Mm mm mmm! Make that three of everything," Hank said dreamily. The girls rolled their eyes and shook their heads.

"Just have 'em bring the whole cow," Conner said helpfully.

After their dinners arrived and they were working on their steaks, Conner managed to ask around a bite, "So, dearly beloved, why exactly are we gathered here together? What's up, Mom?"

Haley didn't reply but looked at Hank and raised her eyebrows.

"We're waiting until dessert to tell you," Hank answered. "Don't want you to choke on your meals."

"So it's big?" Charity asked.

"Really, really big," Haley said, smiling at her daughter.

"Sooo, are you starting a new company, Dad?" Charlie asked.

"Um, we're moving to Hawaii? Or, maybe New Zealand?" Conner guessed.

"Dessert," Hank said firmly. "You won't get anything out of us until dessert."

When their meal was done, the whole family ordered coffee and Chocolate Sin Cake—they were all chocoholics. After the dessert order was taken, Charity tried again. "Okay, Mom, Dad, it's dessert. Time to 'fess up."

"It hasn't arrived yet," said Hank grinning. "You have to wait a little longer."

Finally the order arrived, and the kids looked at their parents expectantly.

"Well?" demanded Charity.

"I have been asked to run as an independent candidate for

the presidency of the United States. Your mom and I have been praying about this for the past ten days, and we've decided to do it."

Three shocked faces stared back. They were too flabbergasted to say anything.

Hank broke the silence by smiling and quipping, "And I'd like to ask for your votes next November."

Charity giggled and replied, "Sure, Dad, I'll vote for you. Can I ride in Air Force One?" Suddenly the kids were laughing and excited, firing questions nonstop, everyone talking at once.

"Who's your veep gonna be?" asked Charlie.

"Cool. Does this mean we get secret service agents following us around?" asked Conner.

"Can we work in your campaign?" asked Charity.

"Will we get to live in the White House, even though we're in college?"

"Do we have to call you Mr. President, or can we still call you Dad?"

"Will you get to drive anymore or will there always be someone driving you?"

"I want to check out Camp David."

"Are there going to be news crews camped outside our dorm?"

"When do you get the nuclear football?"

"Will we get to go into the Situation Room?"

Hank laughed and held up his hands, "Wait a minute! One at a time, one at a time," he insisted. "You're all assuming I'll get elected. It is far more likely I will lose the election, especially since I'm running as an independent. But I will do my dead-level best to win."

"Will you have to go through a primary season, Dad?" Charity asked.

"No. Primaries are designed to select a winner when there are multiple candidates from a party running for the same position. In order to get their party's nomination, a candidate must win enough state primaries and caucuses to accumulate a certain number of delegates. In the 2016 election cycle, for example, the Republican candidate must amass twelve hundred thirty-seven delegates.

"But since I'm running as an independent there will be no primary for me. I'm automatically in. But the flip side of that is I have to qualify for the ballot in each state. It will require tens of thousands of signatures in each state just to get my name printed on the ballot."

"Has an independent ever won the presidency, Dad?" asked Charlie.

"No, never."

"So, what do you think your chances are, Dad?" Conner inquired.

"Very poor, Conner. But I'm going to work as hard as I can to be the first one."

"Yeah, you'd make history just getting there, Hank, even before you'd accomplished one thing," commented Haley.

Charity looked at her dad and felt as proud of him as she ever had. "Daddy, I think you'd make an outstanding president. I'm sure gonna vote for you. And if God wants you to be president you'll get there, and if He doesn't you won't. It's that simple."

Hank smiled. It was the same thing he'd said to Pastor Joe. *Nuts don't fall too far from the tree*, he thought, filled with gratitude for his daughter's simple trust in God's will.

Then he became serious. "Kids, this will obviously mean a lot of life changes for you, even during my campaign. You'll need to be very careful what you say and how you say it. You'll need to keep secrets, because you'll know stuff on the inside of the campaign and every reporter from California to Massachusetts will want to know what you know. Even though I'm the one running for president, your lives will become an open book and many unscrupulous reporters will think you are fair game. At some point you'll probably decide this isn't fun anymore. You might even have a small security detail. Your private lives won't feel so private any more. And if I should win the election, it will even get worse. Are you okay with that?"

The three kids sat thinking about what their dad had just

said. Clearly there could be a dark side to their dad's celebrity. Conner spoke first. "Dad, are you convinced the Lord wants you to run?"

"I am, Conner."

"Then I am willing to live with whatever it takes, Dad," the college student said firmly.

"That goes for me, too, Dad," affirmed Charlie.

"And me," agreed Charity.

****

Beep beep beep beep be—

Hank shut off his alarm and sat up in bed, then swung his feet to the floor. He groaned. Five a.m. came entirely too early.

Haley stirred behind him, got up, and began making the bed. He stood and helped.

"Did I really agree to this, babe? Am I really going to run for the presidency?" It was Monday, two days after the dinner with the kids, and at this hour of the day it sure *seemed* like a dream—maybe a bad dream.

"Uh-huh. You did agree to it—we both did—and starting this morning you're a candidate for the presidency even if no one but you and I and a few others are aware of it. So, saddle up your horse, buster, and let's get this show on the road. Why don't you start the coffee while I finish up in here?"

"Capital idea," he mumbled. He grabbed a pad and pen off his nightstand and wandered off to the kitchen.

Half an hour later they were both showered and dressed and sitting in the kitchen going over the daily schedule.

"Today's a parent-teacher conference day so classes are canceled, otherwise it's a normal work day for teachers. Since calculus students are usually pretty motivated kids, I won't have many conferences and I'll be able to get tomorrow's classroom preps done at school. When I get home I'm grabbing the sewing machine and heading for Charity's place. We're going to make some new curtains for her apartment. I'll be home by ten but you'll be on your own for supper," Haley said as she filled her travel mug with coffee.

"What are we going to do about next year, Haley? You can finish up the current school year, but if I'm campaigning I'm going to need you with me. You won't be able to teach, at least, not a full schedule."

"I know. When next year's contracts come out in a few weeks, I'll talk to the administrator. Maybe I can drop back to just a few sections of advanced math and then do some subbing as the schedule permits," she suggested.

"And that's okay?"

"Hank, I love my students and I love the school. For that matter, I love Colorado and don't really want to leave it. But we made a decision together and I promise you, I'll do whatever it takes. We're in this rodeo together, cowboy."

He smiled at his wife, admiring her courage and willing spirit. "I know you'll do whatever it takes. That means so much to me. But I also know how much it's costing you."

"Well," Haley said as she stood and shoved a few more items into her briefcase, "just remember what they say." She kissed him, grabbed her coffee travel mug, and headed for the door.

"What do they say, babe?"

"Behind every successful man is a *much more talented* woman!" She grinned and winked at him as she closed the door.

A few hours later he was sitting with Buford Jackson in the lawyer's conference room discussing how he would launch his campaign. The windows facing the Front Range were flexing under the assault of a strong Chinook wind. It was sixty-five degrees outside, but by midnight Denver would be under a Winter Storm Warning.

"The first thing I want to do is announce my candidacy on my blog. If it weren't for my faithful readers, no one would consider this project as anything more than a vanity addition to my resumé," Marshall said. "And after that I'll send out news releases to the major media outlets, maybe schedule a news conference."

"What about campaign staff? Are they going to be in place by then?" Jackson asked.

"Yeah, they are. I'll need a functioning staff to handle the media attention. So, I guess I should start hiring staff *before* I write the blog post."

"Can I make a suggestion?" Jackson asked.

"Of course, Jacks, anything."

"Don't grow your staff too big too soon, because it will waste a lot of money and create unnecessary management overhead and headaches. I'd suggest hiring a chief of staff who'll handle the day-to-day operations of the campaign. Get a few policy advisers for foreign and domestic policy. Work with them to start developing your platform. You'll need a campaign director, a campaign spokesman, a media and advertisements guy, a money and donors guy, an IT guy, and a small handful of secretaries. You're going to want someone to coordinate and recruit volunteers. Plus, you're going to need a headquarters. Once things get into full swing it will become clear where else you need to start making staff additions."

Marshall was scribbling furiously as Jackson spoke. Then he looked up from his pad and said, "Some of these positions I've already thought about and filled in my head. For example, chief of staff. Buford you've served as my lawyer since I arrived in Denver years ago. There is no one I trust more than you. Would you be willing to serve as my chief of staff? What sort of salary would you require?"

Jackson grinned, "I was hoping you'd ask, and that's the position I wanted. As for salary, I'm willing to do it for a dollar a month. Just enough to establish a legal contract."

"Thanks, Jacks! Consider yourself hired as of right now," Hank said, smiling with delight. "Would you draw up the necessary forms and paperwork?"

"Of course. I have several staff recommendations for you. Tell me what you think: Joshua Cummings, campaign director."

Hank frowned. "Do you really think he'd do it? He's the best there is, and I'm almost certainly going to be a losing proposition. He could work for anyone out there—he can pick his ticket, and I'd think he'd want to go with someone who has a better chance of winning."

Buford put down his pen and looked at his friend. "Okay, first off, Hank, that's the last time you'll ever tell anyone other than your wife that you're going to lose. Got it?"

"But—" Marshall protested.

"No buts. It's that simple," the lawyer insisted. "None of your people, none of your staff, none of your supporters, and certainly none of your volunteers want to hear you say anything about losing. All of the rest of us will be committed to winning and we are going to spend ourselves, sacrificing blood, sweat, and tears to put you over the top. You'd better be committed to winning, or this campaign will implode faster than Elizabeth Montgomery's did. Are you hearing me?" Jackson demanded. He was as serious and severe as Marshall had ever seen him.

"Yes, I do. I understand," replied Marshall, chastened. It was clear private doubts needed to remain private.

"Remember, Hank," Jackson continued, "this campaign organization is *for* you, but it's not *about* you. It's about the ideas you are championing. It's about our country. It's about our own dreams and aspirations to leave our children something better than what we received. We're going to work for you because we believe your ideas represent what is best for our country."

"Thanks, Jacks, I needed to hear that. From now on this campaign will be about winning, not competing. But mind you, Jacks, it's not about winning at any cost, but winning with our integrity intact. Have *you* got that?" Marshall challenged.

"Of course! I wouldn't sign on to serve you if it was any other way," Jackson replied, irritated.

"Good! Whew! Well, now—our first campaign confrontation. Glad that's over," Marshall chuckled.

Jackson relented, and smiled. "I'm sure it won't be the last. So, what about Cummings?" he asked. "Campaign manager?"

"Yep. Let's get him, Jacks. He's the best and we need the best. Who else?"

"Ashton Bancroft, senior foreign policy advisor," Jackson

suggested.

"Great choice. Abe knows his stuff, is well respected in DC. Who's next?"

"Sam Sebastian, senior domestic policy advisor."

"I don't know him, Jacks. Who is he?" Marshall asked, writing the name on his tablet.

"Sam served in Reagan's State Department as an undersecretary," the lawyer explained as he refilled their water glasses from a pitcher. "He's got a graduate degree in American history and a law degree, both from Harvard. He's, oh, maybe in his mid-sixties. Sam's not going to line up with you everywhere, Hank. Part of his value will be the fact that he'll argue with you in domestic policy matters. But he'll be loyal even when he disagrees. Sam rides for the brand, as they say."

"Let's bring him in as an outside consultant, Buford, until I've had enough time to know if I'm comfortable with him. That way if we have to cut him loose it doesn't cause a stir."

"Sounds good. Okay, one last major position to consider, for now anyway: campaign spokesman. For the time being he can also head up the media and advertising effort, until we get someone else for that position."

"You have any names in mind, Jacks?"

"I think we ought to give it to Tru."

Hank nodded. "Yep. I'm good with that. I like Mike, and he's been used by the Lord several times in my life since you first introduced us. I'd love to have him close by, if he'll do it."

"That's all I've got for now. Who do you want to talk to, and who do you want me to talk to?" asked the lawyer.

"You take Sebastian and Bancroft. I'll take Cummings and Trujillo," answered Marshall, writing a reminder on his pad. "We've still got the IT position to fill, and I don't have any ideas there."

"How about Tim Hardy, from church?"

"Oh, right! I forgot about him. He's looking for work, too. He was the IT director of a small defense contractor in Arvada, but they just went belly up. I'll talk to him," Jackson said, scribbling a note to himself.

"Excellent. Buford, find us a place for our headquarters

here locally. I'm guessing something on the order of eight thousand square feet, with room to grow. Get the ball rolling with the filings and legal work, and open a bank account. I'll seed it with half a million dollars of my own to give us enough money to begin operations. But let's try to get donor funds flowing quickly. One of the positions we didn't cover was the money guy to recruit and manage donors. We've gotta get him in place as soon as possible."

"When do you want these guys to start, Hank?" asked Jackson.

"Monday, if possible. They can help get the headquarters set up and then assist with all the paperwork and filings for the fifty states."

****

I need your help!
Posted 3/2/2015
By Henry Marshall

The Founders of our country were animated by several ideas. Most important among them was that human rights were inalienable—they came from God and it was not the province of government to take them away. They were also convinced that even good men could be corrupted by too great a grant of authority. As a conse-quence, the men who designed our Constitution and our form of government, with its three centers of authority—the executive, the judiciary, and the legislative —created a system of checks and balances by which excesses in one branch could be restrained by another. Although we don't really know if it was Jefferson who first said this, a political proverb frequently expressed in the early nineteenth century affirmed "*that government is best which governs least.*" It was clearly the intent of the Founders for government to have a light hand, not a heavy one, in our affairs.

This same trajectory toward a minimalist federal government can be seen in the Tenth Amendment, which restricts the interests and authority of the federal government to those matters expressly given to it by the Constitution, all other matters being reserved to the several states. At each turn the government is restrained because the Founders knew from the painful lessons of history what happens when a government is granted too much authority by its citizens.

That wise sentiment which surrounds the federal government with fences and boundaries designed to limit its power and restrict its authority has been forgotten, and we now have a federal government that can be most accurately described by the biblical term *leviathan*, which speaks of a great sea monster. The feds have become a many-limbed octopus, stretching forth massive tentacles into areas the Founders never intended.

It's time for this usurpation of power to stop, and for authority to be returned to the states and the citizens. I am asking you to join hands with me as I run for the presidency of this great country on a platform not of improving Washington, but of dismantling its illegitimate departments and agencies. If elected I will champion the Tenth Amendment and the rights of the

states to recover the authority the federal
government has stolen.

You can read my position papers on
HenryMarshall.org, and you can donate to
my campaign there as well. Let's work
together to restore a constitutionally faithful
government in America!

****

"In other news today, the presidential race just got a little
more interesting. We have a new contestant for the job, a little-
known blogger from Golden, Colorado named Henry
Marshall, who has announced his intentions to run as an independent candidate. Marshall declared his candidacy on his
blog three days ago, but it's taken until today for the
announcement to trickle beyond the bounds of the blogosphere into prime time news coverage." The attractive blonde
anchor smiled at the camera, displaying a row of perfect,
white teeth. She obviously considered her show to be prime
time coverage.

"Here in the studio today to discuss the latest happenings
is my expert Campaign 2016 panel. The panel members are
Rosalyn Jansen-Canford, Democratic political consultant,
Thomas Bayfeld, Republican strategist, and finally Adam
MacKenzie, the senior political reporter for the *Chicago
Tribune*." She swiveled her chair to face the panel off to her
left and said, "Welcome, everybody. Before we discuss the
latest contender, Rosalyn, let's talk about the lineup of candidates on the Democratic side of the aisle. How many are
there now? I think I've lost count."

"All of us are struggling to keep track of the field, Susan.
In the last two weeks we've gone from four to seven."

"Seven? Wow. How many do you think will survive the
summer, not to speak of the long slog from now until the
Iowa caucuses?"

"Oh, I would not be surprised to see all seven on the

ballot in Iowa a year from now, Susan. We've got four senators or former senators, a congressman, and the governors of New Jersey and California running. Each of them has a solid organization and deep pockets behind them. In a political campaign at this stage of the game it is usually cash on hand that distinguishes the stayers from the eventual dropouts, and right now all seven are in good shape." Jansen-Canford took a sip from the coffee cup in front of her.

"If you had to identify the strongest of the candidates, who stands out at this early date?" the anchor queried.

"Well, you're asking a political question, you know," Jansen-Canford said with a smile.

The other panelists chuckled, and Thomas jumped in, "You realize, Susan, that both Rosalyn and I are hoping to work for one of the current candidates on our respective sides of the aisle. Adam is the smart one here, he doesn't have to worry about a job. So it's a little hard to answer a question like that."

Susan persisted, "I know what you're saying, but still——. I'm not asking you to criticize any of them, Rosalyn, but in your opinion who are the standouts?"

"I think the clearest leader is Governor Mason of California, and that's because he enjoys strong support from many of the richest people in Silicon Valley. In the last month, three PACs that will be championing his issues have registered with the Federal Election Commission. A distant second is probably Pamela Hastings, senator from Pennsylvania. She's the right gender for the direction the political winds are blowing this year, she has a solid background in foreign policy, and she's distinguished herself as one of the most effective Democrats in the Senate. The other five are strong candidates," Jansen-Canford said, the other two panelists chuckling at her transparent attempt to keep future employment options open, "but Mason and Hastings are clearly leading the pack right now."

Susan directed her attention to Bayfeld. "What do you see on the Republican side, Thomas? It looks to me like there are so many Republicans running there won't be anyone left to vote, they'll all be voting for themselves."

"Well, that's just it, Susan. I think everyone and their brother have either filed or announced their intentions to file. With apologies to Rosalyn, the last six years under a Democratic administration is seen as a disaster by the voters in flyover country. When you combine the fact that we have a lame-duck President whose favorability ratings are somewhere south of abysmal, with a record of governance that even the Democrats are running from, many Republicans are seeing the current election cycle as one that will certainly produce a Republican president. They all want to be that guy, Susan."

"Or gal," the anchor corrected.

"Yes, of course. As it now stands there are no fewer than eighteen who have already filed with the FEC and five more who are seriously considering it. We might be looking at one of those rare elections, Susan, in which we won't know who the Republican candidate is until the convention."

All three panelists nodded in agreement, and Rosalyn added, "I agree with Thomas. It's conceivable that neither major party will know who their nominee is until after their convention."

"Well, Adam, how would this election cycle be affected if the nominees are not determined until the respective conventions?" Susan asked.

"The biggest problem, and it would be really big, is that both nominees would be entering the final leg of the race already bearing battle scars from their own side—friendly fire, if you will. Between now and the nomination all of the Democratic ammunition will be aimed at other Democrats, and the same problem applies to the Republicans. Whoever limps out of the convention and into the general election will already have all of his weaknesses, failures, and dirty laundry exposed. Can you imagine the ads that will be made? The Democrats will be able to take video clips of Republicans attacking the Republican nominee, and use them mercilessly. And the Republicans will do the same to the Democrats. It's not going to be pretty, Susan."

"How can anyone win in such an environment? It seems

like it will be the voters themselves who lose, Adam," the anchor mused.

"The candidate who wins, Susan, will be the one who offers the voters a positive and detailed rationale for supporting them, rather than just lambasting the other party's nominee. It will take a great deal of media discipline to avoid wasting all your airtime criticizing your opponent. The cheap shots are just that: cheap. But politics isn't like football, in which a great defense can win championships. In politics you need a great offense—in other words, you need to score points explaining to the voters why they should vote for you. That requires a positive vision, and a relentlessly negative campaign cannot provide a positive vision."

"Hmm. Interesting. Let's move on to the latest news." The anchor glanced down at the laptop in front of her before continuing. "Two days ago a relatively unknown, radically conservative blogger by the name of Henry Marshall announced on his blog that he was running for president as an independent candidate. Comments? Rosalyn, you first."

Jansen-Canford scoffed and shrugged her shoulders. "Henry who? I've never heard of him. I don't think he will garner enough attention to even qualify as a sideshow, Susan."

"Thomas? Have you heard of him?"

"Yeah, Susan, I've heard of him. This is a guy who probably sits in his parents' basement in his pajamas popping chocolates and pontificating on the web. Maybe a digital Barnum and Bailey—"

"A sucker born every minute?"

"Something like that. Rosalyn's right—he's a total nonfactor. He's gotten his five minutes of fame right now on your show and will sink back into obscurity at the next commercial break."

Susan compressed her lips. "Adam, I see you shaking your head. You disagree?"

"I do. I've interviewed Henry Marshall, I've written two articles about him, and while he might be obscure in the rarified atmosphere of Washington politics, he's garnered a massive following on the web. I think it would be a mistake of the first order to discount him, especially on the Republican side."

"Why do you say that, Adam?" asked Thomas, unable to conceal his surprise.

"Two reasons. Three, actually. First, he's wealthy enough to fund his own campaign if he wishes. So he's not going to run out of money—which means he's in it for the long haul. Second and maybe more important, he is a formidable thinker who is able to communicate in Joe Sixpack's lingo. He can explain the Constitution in understandable ways to people who've never even read it. He makes a compelling case for what's wrong with the federal government, and it revolves around the Tenth Amendment—states' rights. And third, there are way over twenty million people who read his blog. That's not an insignificant number.

"If you don't stray from the I95 corridor you'll miss this, but John Doe Citizen in flyover country is just about ready to march on Washington and burn it down. The disgust and anger of the middle class taxpayer—the sense of betrayal—is widespread and growing. If the major political parties miss that fact and continue to operate business as usual, it's going to be a very interesting election. Because Henry Marshall's got their number."

Chapter 12

IF THE FEDERAL GOVERNMENT SHOULD OVERPASS
THE JUST BOUNDS OF ITS AUTHORITY AND MAKE A
TYRANNICAL USE OF ITS POWERS, THE PEOPLE,
WHOSE CREATURE IT IS, MUST APPEAL TO THE
STANDARD THEY HAVE FORMED, AND TAKE SUCH
MEASURES TO REDRESS THE INJURY DONE TO THE
CONSTITUTION AS THE EXIGENCY MAY SUGGEST AND
PRUDENCE JUSTIFY. THE PROPRIETY OF A LAW, IN A
CONSTITUTIONAL LIGHT, MUST ALWAYS BE
DETERMINED BY THE NATURE OF THE POWERS UPON
WHICH IT IS FOUNDED.

Alexander Hamilton, Federalist #33

Tuesday, June 9, 2015

Buford Jackson stopped outside Carly Johnson's office and asked, "So how goes the battle, Momma?"

Johnson was a slender, grey-haired, ruthlessly efficient general. The actual title of the sixty-five-year-old widow was campaign headquarters office manager. She was demanding, she was detailed, and she did not tolerate fools or slackers. Johnson could outwork anyone on the staff, and she often did. She was wholly committed to getting Marshall elected and would do the job all by herself if she had to. But the young volunteers at headquarters had made an important discovery: underneath Carly's tough Kevlar exterior was a woman who cared deeply about the people around her. The twenty-some-things began calling her Momma behind her back. The handle swiftly spread through the office and before long it was out in the open. A fierce glare from the general was all that was needed to send a user of the moniker into swift retreat, but when Marshall himself began to use it Johnson relented. The nickname stuck. Truth be told, Carly was secretly proud of it.

"If the day had forty-eight hours, I'd be doing fine, Buford. But since it only has thirty-six, I'm already behind. Does that answer your question?" she grouched. "And don't tell me that someone created today with only twenty-four hours, because I'm not quite ready to accept that reality."

Jackson chuckled. "Do we need to get you more help?"

"No, I just consider it my sacred and inalienable right to complain. I'll make it, though I might relieve a few shoulders of their heads before the day is done. Why don't you order more body bags? I seem to be running low."

"Hang in there, Momma. We'll get there. Now, call everyone together in the conference room, please. I've got an announcement to make and I want everyone to hear it."

The Marshall campaign now occupied nearly twelve thousand square feet, the entire top floor of the office building at 1600 Jackson Street, in Golden. Jackson had already notified the property management company that if any of the lower floor tenants wanted out of their lease, the Marshall campaign would be glad to take their space. Every square inch of the headquarters was already crammed with desks, computers, telephones, and volunteers or paid staff.

"Good morning, everybody," Jackson greeted the fifty-seven gathered workers. "Thanks for taking a minute out of your busy day to meet, I won't keep you long. I've got some great news and wanted to share it with you. Henry would be here to tell you himself, but he's meeting with potential donors today in Austin, Texas. Late yesterday we heard from our organizations in Arizona, Oregon, Utah, both Carolinas, Florida, and Puerto Rico: their petitions have been accepted! We are now on the ballot in all fifty states and all the territories, people!"

The room erupted in shouts and applause. Staffers and volunteers were slapping each other on the back or hugging each other, and a few had tears streaming down their face. It was the first major milestone of the campaign and they had achieved it twenty days ahead of schedule.

The lawyer continued, "Josh Cummings would have been here to celebrate, but he's with Henry in Texas. They asked me to share the news with you, and to offer their warmest congratulations and appreciation. You all have worked long hours manning the phones, answering mail, fielding questions and comments on the blog, and performing a host of other jobs. You've done well. We owe this success to you and to our organizations in each state. Well done, people, well done! Are there any questions?"

One of the college students, a female volunteer who had been working with the campaign for several months, raised her hand. Jackson pointed to her and smiled, "What's your question, Mariah?"

"Are there any new endorsements, Mr. Jackson?"

"Oh! I'd forgotten about that, Mariah, thanks for the reminder. Yes, there are. Senator Elizabeth Montgomery, Republican senator from Texas, endorsed Hank over the weekend—some of you might have already heard that. But this morning, Governor James of Indiana held a news confer- ence and announced his endorsement. That makes seven heavyweights who have lined up behind Henry."

Applause broke out again.

"To celebrate this milestone, we've got a small surprise for everyone. We're ordering ice cream from Cold Stone Creamery, on the house! Should be here at 2:30. Be sure to place your order with Martha at the reception desk before eleven; she's got a menu if you need to see it. Okay, everyone, let's get back to work. There's much to do, and we want to spend the summer firing on all cylinders."

****

Three months later on a pleasant September day, Wayne Bushnell flashed his trademark grin as he headed for the Senate building. He waved to a small throng of reporters who'd gathered there to catch a word from the great man as he exited the limo that had picked him up at Reagan National. His chief of staff, Andrew Rapp, was with him and moved between the senator and the reporters. But when Bushnell spotted a television camera, he said, "It's okay, Andy, I've got five minutes I can spare."

The reporters crowded close, shouting questions. Bushnell pointed at a reporter from Fox.

"Mr. Bushnell, there are now fourteen Republican candidates in the campaign. How do you assess the race so far?"

"It's Paul Norris, right?"

The reporter nodded, pleased to have been recognized.

"Well, Paul, it's crowded." The reporters all laughed. Bushnell continued, "Other than that, I'm ahead in all the polls of Republican voters, and I'm the candidate that matches up most favorably with the likely Democrat nominee, so I think the race is going just fine! Wouldn't change a thing," he said with a chuckle.

"At the beginning of the summer I think I counted twenty Republicans in the race. Hopefully that was our high-water mark. Financial and political realities have reduced that number to fourteen, and I suspect we'll lose half of those before we get to the Iowa caucuses in February." Bushnell pointed to a reporter with CNN credentials.

"Thank you, sir, Ann Taylor, CNN. Senator, over the summer we've seen several important Republicans endorsing an independent candidate for the presidency. What's happening to your party, and why are these registered, elected Republicans not supporting you or one of the other Republican candidates?"

"Ann, that's an excellent question—one we've been asking each other on Capitol Hill. There is a small but noisy constituency in the Republican Party that is very—extremely—conservative. They want to drag the party back to the days of Goldwater and Joe McCarthy. Well, I have news for them: we ain't goin' back. History shows that the electorate will not vote for such conservative candidates; the voters clearly want a moderate."

"But what about Reagan?" Taylor asked. "He won two

terms."

"Reagan was an outlier, and besides, he was really more of a moderate anyway. But these modern-day rebels have coalesced around an unknown and convinced the poor guy to run for president. My heart goes out to him. They know he'd never make it inside the Republican Party, so they've evidently talked him into running as an independent. Write this down, Ann: it's September now, by December this independent—what's his name, Howard Mansfield?—will be out of the race and the people who endorsed him will probably never again win an elective office in the Republican Party."

"But, sir, he's already polling at ten percent nationally—" objected one reporter, who was cut off by Andrew Rapp.

"That's all we have time for, ladies and gentlemen, I'm sorry," claimed Rapp, holding out his hands to bar pursuit as Bushnell turned to enter the building. "The senator has an extremely busy day, I'm sure you understand." Rapp turned and hurried after his boss, ignoring the shouted questions.

Bushnell was striding down the hall, his face red with rage when Rapp caught up with him. The senator fired off a string of expletives, and then grouched, "That idiot Henry Marshall! Who does he think he is, running for the Office of the Presidency before he's even been elected dogcatcher? He's messing everything up, Andy!"

"But I thought you said he'd be out by December, Senator? Surely he can't be that much trouble, can he?"

Bushnell stopped and pulled his chief of staff into an empty office where they wouldn't be overheard. "Andy, listen to me," the politician said, keeping his voice low. "Marshall is already on the ballot in all fifty states. He's wealthy enough to fund his own campaign, so he's not going to have money problems. An independent candidate has no primary opponents to fight, so he's got a free ride until the general election campaign begins after the major party conventions. Somehow he managed to snag the best campaign manager in the business, Joshua Cummings. Marshall's not only going to make it past December, Andy, I have a feeling he'll go the distance."

"You think he'll win?" Rapp hissed, incredulity written all

over his face.

"No, no, no, nothing like that. Just that he'll be a factor all the way to Election Day. He's a spoiler, draining conservative votes away from the Republicans and throwing the election to the Democrats. He's a disaster for our party."

****

By mid-December the RealClearPolitics average of national polls showed Henry Marshall leading the pack with fifteen percent of the vote. Another thirty-three percent was split between the Republican candidates, and forty-five percent among the Democratic slate. Seven percent stubbornly lodged in the "Uncommitted" category.

"Hank, you're on top of the RCP national average again, third week in a row!" exulted Buford Jackson.

"Jacks, you know better than to pay any attention to that," Joshua Cummings chided. "While Hank is showing well nationally for this point in the campaign, it's only because the voters in the two major parties are splitting their votes among a broad field of candidates. The Republicans still have nine candidates in the race, the Dems seven. As the race narrows down you'll see those national averages shift significantly. Don't pay too much attention to the polls until after June 7 when California holds its primary."

"I know, Josh, but right now it is providing name recognition and media coverage. Everyone's gone out of their way to pretend they don't know who this independent upstart is. They're purposefully getting his name wrong and doing everything they can to virtually deny Hank's existence. But since he's climbed to the top of the polls they're no longer able to do that and remain credible."

"True, Jacks, but there is a downside. Once the field of candidates consolidates, it's going to look like Hank is losing support. Even though his overall percentage stays the same in the RCP averages, he'll move into the number three or four slot unless the number of voters committed to him grows."

"Well," Hank said, "getting that support number up is why we're meeting today, so let's get on with it."

"Henry, our volunteers across Iowa have been keeping an ear to the ground, watching the local papers and listening to their neighbors. We've identified the time and place of seventeen of Wayne Bushnell's campaign appearances between now and February 1. I've scheduled you in each of those locations just a few hours before his events. We're going to drain away his people and weaken his showing. The longer it takes for a Republican front-runner to develop, the better it is for us.

"I've also scheduled Marshall-for-President rallies on the night of the caucus in the quad-cities area, Iowa City and Des Moines. We've chartered an aircraft to get you from Iowa City to Des Moines, and back again, that night. Going head to head with the Republicans in Iowa will generate some media buzz we don't have to pay for."

Ashton Bancroft objected, "Josh, do you really think it's wise to be so aggressive this early in the campaign? You'll make an implacable enemy of Bushnell by shadowing him across the state, and the Republican machinery will be very unhappy with us for going head to head with them."

"I do, Abe, for several reasons. Though the major parties are stuck in primary season right now, the general election campaign is in full swing for Hank. He's got to go straight at the likely Republican front-runner to keep him from pulling too far ahead. This will be good preparation for the fall when things get really brutal. And Abe, the Republican machinery will try to crucify Hank and all the rest of us without mercy, no matter when we come out swinging."

Bancroft nodded. "Okay, those are good points. Then let's go for a full-court press and let Hank start highlighting his opposition to crop subsidies. If he can get away with it in Iowa, he can get away with it anywhere."

"I agree," Marshall affirmed. "We might as well get the difficult messages on the table early so I've got time to explain my positions before the fall. Besides, I'm not going to change my message to win a campaign. If I'm going to win it has to be on the basis of what I believe, not what the voters want to hear. In addition to the message on subsidies, I want to use the Iowa campaign stops to hammer on corporate welfare and the misuse of foreign aid."

"I like it," replied Trujillo. "You're developing a brand, Hank, an identity by which voters will know you. You're carving out a unique spot in the race with a message none of the other candidates have."

"Yes, indeed," Cummings said. "Let's make the most of it. Tru, work with your media people to come up with a catchy way to emphasize Hank's stance on the Tenth Amendment."

"You got it," Mike promised.

Carly Johnson tapped on the conference room door and entered. "Here are your tickets, gentlemen," she said, passing out folders to Marshall, Cummings, and Bancroft. "You are booked on Southwest, and your flight to Des Moines leaves at 10:10 tomorrow morning, landing at 12:30. Alastair Williams of our Des Moines headquarters will pick you up. Williams called a few minutes ago. He's got a small army of volunteers led by a staffer who will handle the all grunt work on the west side of the state. There's another crew in Iowa City who will cover the east side. Your briefing folders have all the names, phone numbers, and other arrangements and reservations."

****

Wayne Bushnell was beside himself. The Marshall campaign was stalking him across Iowa and beating him to the punch in nearly every location. The media had noticed and Marshall was getting priceless publicity without paying a dime for it. Marshall had not seen a bump in the polls, but more and more of the electorate was becoming aware of his presence in the race. Bushnell knew the first step of attracting a voter was simply letting him know there were alternatives. The Pennsylvania senator didn't want the voters to think of alternatives, he wanted to present himself as a fait accompli.

While there had been no direct confrontations on the campaign trail, the Marshall people were sucking up a lot of the oxygen. Bushnell was not getting clean media coverage; every news report on Bushnell included a brief summary of what had happened at the earlier Marshall event.

"The man's a parasite! I want this to stop NOW!" Bushnell shouted at his staff. He'd called a meeting of his top people and was unloading on them. His Iowa staff was seated on his left, the national campaign staff on his right.

"But what can we do, Senator?" asked the Iowa state campaign coordinator, John Wainright. "Marshall's people aren't breaking the law. They aren't interfering with our events, they're not even showing up at them."

"How does he know our schedule?" the senator demanded. "Everywhere I go I find he's been there just hours ahead of me! Is someone leaking this?"

"Our events aren't secret, Senator. We publicize them weeks in advance," Wainright pleaded. "And Marshall's got a good ground game, their people are everywhere even if not in great numbers. It would be a simple matter for them to learn our schedule of events."

Bushnell nodded and sat down heavily. He needed to be careful with his temper. It wasn't the Iowa man's fault. The senator knew if he didn't control his anger, sooner or later his own people would desert him. "Okay, John—look, I'm sorry for losing it. Of course you're right." He thought for a moment and then looked at his national staff. "I don't care how you do it," he said, his voice level. "But I want this stalking stopped."

No one else saw it, but his chief of opposition research, Bob Vanderveld, gave a slight nod of his head.

****

"You do realize that you're going to be a sacrificial lamb, Jerry, right? Bushnell will fire you if news of this leaks out. The campaign will disavow any knowledge of your activities," Bob Vanderveld said. The portly man was the head of the Bushnell campaign opposition research team, only sometimes the oppo team went a little beyond research—always without Bushnell's knowledge, of course. Bushnell liked the way Vanderveld handled business and he especially liked not knowing what Vanderveld was up to. Plausible deniability. The results were all that mattered.

"I'm good with that. But I was also told I'd have a golden parachute. So what's gonna make this worth my while?" Jerry Bolden asked. Bolden possessed what might best be described as unique talents. Accustomed to operating below the horizon, the diminutive, wiry man had known he was expendable when he signed on, but he wasn't going away cheaply.

"I figure five Gs will be adequate compensation," Vanderveld offered, knowing that the little man would not accept it. It was all part of the game.

"No, it's not." Bolden knew better than to accept the first offer. "Not even close."

Vanderveld didn't blink. He sighed, "Okay, I'll get Pickens to do this one. You can go back to research on your regular salary." He knew the operative hated research and preferred direct action. He expected Bolden to make a counteroffer.

"Fine. Thanks for thinking about me, Bob. Maybe the next job." Bolden picked a piece of imaginary lint off his cheap suit, turned and reached for the door handle. No counteroffer. Part of the game.

The manager sighed. "Okay, Jerry, seven, and that's my final offer."

Jerry didn't even turn around. "Ten," he said as he opened the door.

"Eight."

"Ten," he insisted, shaking his head.

"Eight and a half."

Bolden grinned, turned around and said in a fake Jersey accent, "Now you talking business, boss. Eight and a half oughtta do it." He shut the door and returned to his seat. "You want I should make Iowa an unfriendly place for pajama blogger?"

"Something like that."

"What's my budget?"

"Eight and a half for you. Ten thousand for the action," Vanderveld replied.

"Yeah, I can do that. How soon?

"Now. Yesterday."

****

Marshall paused and took a sip of water from the bottle in his hand. Then he continued his speech to a crowd of around five hundred gathered in the large conference room of the hotel.

"The federal government's attempt to control agriculture through quotas and subsidies and other mechanisms is an unwarranted and unconstitutional intrusion of federal power into private business. Hamilton assured us in *Federalist #17* that the control of matters such as agriculture was beneath the 'splendor' of the federal government, as he put it. Whenever Hamilton would talk about the supremacy of federal law, he'd always qualify it by using phrases like, 'pursuant to the powers entrusted to it by the Constitution.' In other words, although Hamilton was arguing for the creation of a strong federal government, he was arguing for one that would be limited by the constraints of the Constitution.

"In *Federalist #33*, Hamilton said this regarding the doctrine of the supremacy of federal law over state law:

> But it will not follow from this doctrine that acts of the large society which are NOT PURSUANT to its constitutional powers, but which are invasions of the residuary authorities of the smaller societies, will become the supreme law of the land. These will be merely acts of usurpation, and will deserve to be treated as such.

"Hamilton was saying that the laws of the large society, the federal government, would be supreme over the smaller societies—the states—so long as its laws are pursuant to the Constitution—in other words, constitutional. If they are not constitutional, they are usurpations of power and should be treated so.

"My friends, any federal government attempt to control agriculture is, as Hamilton insisted, an unlawful usurpation of power. This includes not only the regulation of agriculture but the subsidy of it as well. When I am sworn in as the chief executive of this great nation, I will do all I can to end the unlawful acts of the federal government. This includes the elimination of all corporate subsidies, whether through federal grants, tax credits, or any other means.

"If the individual states wish to subsidize agriculture within their own borders, they are free to do so. But our Constitution removes that option from the federal government.

"If I am elected and if I can gain the cooperation of Congress, by the time I leave office there will be no Department of Agriculture, no Department of Housing and Urban Development, and no Department of Education. The Department of Energy will be reduced to an agency of the Department of Commerce, whose sole function will be to regulate energy transmission between the states. The income tax will be abolished and replaced with a national sales tax, and the IRS will be shrunk to a tiny agency."

When Marshall concluded his speech he took questions from the audience. Some of the farmers in attendance were irate about his plan to end crop subsidies, but many were convinced by his arguments that the federal government had overstepped its bounds. Informal polls taken before and after the meeting found that seven percent who'd arrived curious departed with a negative impression. Another eleven percent were swayed by Marshall's arguments, and fully sixty-five percent left with a better impression of the candidate than they had when they arrived.

The media were in a feeding frenzy. Marshall's speech provided them with controversial soundbites that would play well on the evening news. Properly edited, Marshall could be made to look like a crazy zealot intent on destroying the government.

Two hours after Marshall's event was over, Bushnell

arrived at the University of Iowa, less than a quarter mile away. Marshall's event had already consumed much of the local political energy before Bushnell's rally started.

****

"So, how'd you sleep last night?" asked a bleary-eyed Ashton Bancroft.

"Hardly at all. There was some sort of drunken party going on in the hall outside our room. The police came three times. Each time things would quiet down for half an hour or so, and then it would get noisy again," Marshall said, picking at his breakfast. "This is the fifth night in a row something like this has happened. I don't understand—don't college students have anything else to do besides party?"

"I called Buford this morning. He's going to get right on it," said a weary Joshua Cummings.

"Buford? What can he do about it?"

"Hank, think about it. We've had these beer-blasts outside our rooms five nights in a row. Yesterday our venue stank so badly we had to cancel the event. Someone discovered a rotting raccoon in the ventilation system after we left. Eight days ago our tires were slashed—for the second time. So, what does this sound like to you?"

"Dirty tricks," said Bancroft. "I'd wondered about that myself."

"Sure," said Cummings. "I've seen it before. So I called Jackson. He's going to get that private investigator, Jim Stewart, to snoop around a little. We've got twelve days before the caucuses. If Stewart can come up with something it's going to give us some good press, and it will give someone else a black eye."

****

Tony Clarke was parked in a van with tinted windows in the hotel parking lot with an unrestricted view of the large

Suburban that had been rented by the Marshall campaign. Just after midnight, a pickup truck pulled next to the Suburban. A man exited the passenger side of the truck, his face covered by a ski mask. He swiftly slashed the tires of the car and reentered the truck, which then pulled away.

"Jim, it's a dark grey pickup, should be coming into your view about now."

"Got it, Tony. He's headed south."

"I'm on my way."

The two vehicles tailed the truck, alternating positions so the target would not know he was being followed. Eventually the vehicle pulled into a suburban driveway. The tail drove past and exited the development. Stewart and Clarke met in the parking lot of an all-night convenience store close by.

"Tony, set up surveillance on that house. Follow that guy in the morning and see where he goes, who he meets with. Get some good pictures. I'm headed back to the hotel. I'm hoping they do the party thing again tonight—I've got a few tricks up my sleeve. Tomorrow I'll run the plate numbers on the truck. I'm also gonna follow Bushnell around, getting some photos of his people. We'll see if anything matches up."

Jim Stewart returned to the hotel where he found the party in full swing on Marshall's hall. He walked up to a particularly tipsy young man and pulled out a one hundred dollar bill. "Hey man, this is yours if you can take me to the chief head party animal."

"Sure, dude. Follow me, man." The fellow staggered down the hall, and pointed through an open door at a man struggling to stay upright in his chair, a can of beer at his elbow. Stewart guessed the fellow was in his mid-twenties. His eyes were glassy and the former FBI agent surmised that there was more than just beer involved.

"Hey, party guy, can I have a word?"

The man immediately became belligerent. "You tryin' to shut ush down, dude?" He belched a long, loud one and everyone in the room giggled.

"No, no, nothing like that. I just want a little information." Stewart pulled a roll of hundred dollar bills out of his pocket and showed it to the drunken man.

"Information I got. Lotsh of it. Eshpeshishilly for you. I mean, for that. For them," he struggled, pointing at the money.

"Okay, but I want to talk to you alone. Can you ask your buddies to step out in the hall for a minute."

"Sure, dude. Hey everybody. Go out there. Give ush a minute, will ya?"

When the others had stumbled into the hall, Stewart shut the door, and turned to the man who finally gave up trying to stand and just slumped in his chair. He burped again and smiled.

"Someone is paying for this party," Stewart began.

"Yeah, me," the man said with a silly grin on his face. He giggled again.

Stewart smiled. "And someone is paying you to have this party, aren't they?"

"Thash right. Whatsh to you?"

"Well, I'm guessing he's going to give you the other half of the money tomorrow, right?"

"Yep. Money, money, money, beyoooootiful money!"

"Well, I have beautiful money, too, and I'll give you three hundred now and another seven hundred tomorrow if you tell me where and when you're going to meet your money buddy. But you have to keep this a secret, okay?"

And it was just that simple.

****

"It's the same guy," Stewart said, looking at the photos he'd taken and comparing them with Clarke's.

"Yeah. Here he is meeting the guy who drove the truck. Here he is paying your party animal. And here he is going into Bushnell's Iowa headquarters."

"Nailed him!" Stewart exulted.

"What now?" Clarke asked.

"Let's meet with the Marshall people and see what they

want to do with this."

Late that evening the two investigators met with Marshall, Cummings, and Bancroft.

"Henry, all these problems seem to be coming from the Bushnell campaign. We've got enough evidence to pin it on them in a court of law. I am guessing that we could probably even tie the dead raccoon incident to them, if you gave me enough time to investigate it."

"No, there's no need, Jim," answered Marshall.

"I know what we ought to do, Hank," volunteered Bancroft. "Let's turn all of this evidence over to that reporter, what's his name? The one who did the article about the porn thing."

"Adam MacKenzie?" asked Cummings.

"Yes, him. Rather than go to the police, offer MacKenzie a story and let the chips fall where they may."

Two days before the Iowa caucuses, the *Chicago Tribune*, the *Des Moines Register*, and the *Iowa City Press-Citizen* headlined a syndicated MacKenzie story, *Down and Dirty in Iowa*. The reporter had done additional investigative work and had tied the dirty tricks not only to Jerry Bolden but to Bob Vanderveld himself. Suddenly the Bushnell campaign was backpedaling, his Republican opponents were piling on, and Bolden and Vanderveld both found themselves unemployed. Mike Trujillo held the Marshall campaign to a disciplined *no comment* on the matter.

Bushnell lost the Iowa caucus, placing third among Republican candidates. The Marshall campaign went from fifteen to eighteen percent in the national polls.

****

Henry Marshall sat in his study working on his next speech, but his mind wasn't on what he was doing. He felt like a schoolboy about to play hooky—excited and impatient. He looked at his watch for the fifth time in ten minutes. It was almost four o'clock, Friday, May 6. Haley should be home anytime. He couldn't wait to surprise her.

Charlie and Conner had just wrapped up their junior year at the University of Colorado Boulder. They arrived home last night after a grueling schedule of exams. Both boys had found summer work. Conner was on the grounds crew at the Breckenridge Ski Resort, and would live in a crew bunkhouse at the resort for the summer. He planned to head for Breckenridge on Tuesday. Charlie would be living at home for the summer, working on a crew installing lawn sprinkler systems.

Finally Marshall heard the sound of the garage door going up. Even though he knew it would take his wife an hour or so to pack, and they didn't have to be at the airport until six, he shut his laptop and put it in his briefcase, setting it with the rest of his luggage at the foot of the steps. He was too excited to concentrate on work.

He heard the kitchen door open and called out, "Hey, babe. Welcome home."

"Hey, yourself, Hank. Whew, what a day!"

Hank walked into the kitchen and hugged his wife. "Why, what happened?"

"Oh, nothing much. Just a big brawl in the cafeteria. It started over a girl, I think, but by the time the police and the teachers got everyone separated no one could remember why they were fighting. Anyway, it caused a lot of excitement and the whole school was tense for the rest of the day." She dumped the remains of a thermos of coffee in the sink and set the thermos in the dishwasher.

"Well, would you like a little surprise? Maybe something fun?"

"Oh, I love surprises." She turned around and put her arms around his neck. "Tell me."

"I've been planning a little surprise for you for about two months," he said, grinning.

"Ooo, this is getting interesting. I'm all ears."

"Well, I've talked to your principal and she is complicit with me in this little undertaking. Apparently she can keep secrets if you haven't heard anything about it."

"What? About what? Tell me!"

He snickered, "Are you sure you don't want a few minutes to relax and decompress before I tell you?"

She reached up and grabbed his ears and pulled his face down to hers until their foreheads were touching. "Tell me now, buster!" Haley was a sucker for surprises. She loved getting them, but once she knew a surprise was coming she had to know what it was. It was one of the myriad little quirks between husbands and wives that endeared her to him. And he loved to tease her, dribbling out the information slowly.

"Oh, it's just a small thing. I didn't mean to get your hopes up."

"HANK!"

"We are taking a little five-day getaway to the Grand Canyon. If you get packed in a hurry, we might make our flight to Phoenix. We need to be at the airport by six."

The expression on her face was worth the planning all by itself. It was a mixture of joy and concern. "Really? But I have classes next week. And what about the campaign? The kids?"

"All taken care of," he said, smiling. "Your principal has already arranged for your replacement—I told her three weeks ago. The kids can fend for themselves, they're old enough. Buford has known for the last two months, so he kept my schedule free. It's just you, me, five days, and the Grand Canyon."

She hugged him fiercely, putting her head on his chest. After a moment she said quietly, "You have no idea how much I needed this. And you have no idea what it means to me, knowing that you planned all this for me."

He lifted her chin and gently kissed her on the lips. "Well, then, sweetie, what say you get packed and let's go!"

She brushed a tear out of her eye and laughed with excitement. "I'll be ready in a jiffy."

For the next five days they hiked and explored and enjoyed long chats as they watched sunrises and sunsets over the Grand Canyon. Experiencing a landmark of such astounding beauty became a spiritual experience for both, because it constantly displayed the glory and power of the Creator. Sometimes while hiking the rim they would stop and sit on the rocks and read the Psalms to one another, or sing hymns, or pray, all the while rejoicing in what God had made.

At the end of five days they returned to Denver spiritually, emotionally, and physically renewed, ready for a grueling summer of campaigning.

****

"My guest today is Henry Marshall, who is currently engaged in a vigorous campaign for the presidency. Welcome, Mr. Marshall." Marshall was sitting opposite the MSNBC interviewer, Patty Holmes, in front of a green screen. He knew the viewers would be seeing them both as though they were sitting in front of a large window overlooking the Capitol. Patty Holmes was wearing a black turtleneck sweater, black slacks, and a single strand of pearls. Her auburn hair was done in a medium-length bob cut.

"Thank you, Patty. I'm delighted to be here."

"It's not your first time on my show. Last time I interviewed you, as I recall, you were serving Congressman Ashton Bancroft as a senior domestic policy advisor."

"Correct."

"And he is now on your campaign staff as your foreign policy advisor? That's a bit of a switch for both of you, isn't it?"

"Yes, it is. Ashton has been a mentor to me for almost as long as we've known each other. I feel honored to have him serving on my campaign, and I deeply value his wisdom and experience."

"If there's one expression that seems to describe your campaign, Mr. Marshall, it seems to be the term *corporate raid*. You're running as an independent, but to the casual onlooker it seems that you have been cherry-picking the cream of the crop right out of the Republican Party. When we come back from our commercial break, I want to know why aren't you running as a Republican? That seems to be the question everyone is asking."

When the LIVE light extinguished, Patty turned to her guest and said, "You know, Mr. Marshall, I read those books on the Constitution that you recommended several years back, and it was an eye-opener. I was struck by the elegance, the finely-tuned checks and balances, and the simplicity of the document. It created a hunger in me to understand and appreciate our own history. I've probably picked up a pen to write you a thank-you note a dozen times, and never followed through."

"That's great, Patty! I'm glad to hear it. You're living right in the heart of our government, here in DC, and I expect knowing the Constitution better has helped you get a sense for all that happens in our Capital."

"Sort of. The older I get the more I see that has very little to do with the Constitution." She held her finger to her ear, pushing her earpiece in, and pointed to the camera. In a few seconds the LIVE light blinked on.

"With me in the studio is our guest, Henry Marshall, independent candidate for president." She turned to face Marshall. "We are now just one week from the California primary and everyone is beginning to think in terms of the major party conventions, a little over a month from now. It appears obvious that Bushnell will emerge victorious on the Republican side, Hastings on the Democratic side, and then there's you."

"Yep," Hank replied, laughing.

"There are only three independent candidates who have made the ballot in all fifty states, and of the three only you made the ballot in all the territories as well. Mr Marshall, the RealClearPolitics national averages have you at a solid twenty-one percent, Wayne Bushnell of Pennsylvania at twenty-eight percent, and Pamela Hastings, Democratic senator from Massachusetts at thirty-three percent. Their numbers will climb a few points once each has been anointed as the nominee by their respective conventions. You are already polling much stronger than most independents I can remember. Tell me, why didn't you run as a Republican?" she asked.

He chuckled again. "I get that question every day, usually just before or after I'm accused of being a traitor. But the answer is very simple: although there are many fine Republican politicians and voters, the Republican Party itself is committed to the wrong vision of the federal government. Most Republicans you talk to today believe the government has gotten too big but they don't really know why or how it happened, or how to correct it. Consequently, they mostly talk about *doing government better*—things like reducing waste, fraud, and abuse, or some such.

"Well, Patty, it is very clear to me what has happened to our government and how to correct it, but it is equally obvious neither major party has the stomach to do what must be done. So I decided to run as an independent. One of the advantages I have is that I can't be primaried."

"Meaning," Patty clarified, "you can't be eliminated from the race by failing to win enough primaries."

"Exactly. Of course there are many downsides. For example, the effort and money required to get on the ballot in all fifty states is huge. Setting up a campaign organization from scratch is difficult to say the least. Every time I turn around, we're having to reinvent the wheel in some way or another."

"So, Mr. Marshall, what is wrong with our federal government and how do you propose to fix it?"

"All three branches of the government, the executive, the judicial, and the legislative, have boxed out the Tenth Amendment, trying to evade its simple, direct prohibition. They have employed devices such as the Commerce Clause to shoehorn expansive federal intrusions in the economy, in land use, in the environment, energy, and even things as basic as religious freedom. In so doing they have applied a logic so tortured and convoluted that it would be humorous if it weren't causing such terrible damage to our country. The three branches are all complicit—they have given each other a pass for ignoring the Tenth."

"And what does the Tenth Amendment do, Mr. Marshall?"

"The Tenth Amendment limits the authority of the federal

government to those matters expressly assigned to it by the Constitution. And through documents such as *The Federalist Papers* we know that was the Founders' original intention. Hamilton stresses over and over again that the federal law is the supreme law of the land so long as it sticks to the Constitution. For example, in *Federalist #33*, Hamilton says this: *It will not, I presume, have escaped observation, that it—the Constitution—expressly confines this supremacy to laws made pursuant to the Constitution.* In the original, he puts the word 'expressly' and the clause 'pursuant to the Constitution' in all capital letters, indicating his emphasis that federal law, if it is to be supreme must be expressly constitutional."

"And your contention, Mr. Marshall, is that our modern government has gone way beyond what the Constitution permits."

"Correct. Article 1, section 8, gives an explicit list of what the federal government may do. Section 9 provides an explicit list of what it may not do. Section 10 describes what the states may and may not do. If we want to save our government, and our country, we should read those lists and reform the government from the ground up to follow the Constitution."

"That's very interesting, Mr Marshall. You must have found an audience for your message if you are polling as strongly as as you are. I know you have many bold opinions in other areas of government as well. One thing that we are seeing in exit polls is that your opinions on foreign aid are catching on with the electorate. Sixty-five percent of the voters are in favor of slashing foreign aid. Can you tell us what is behind your thinking on that?"

"Patty, I am all for the right kind of foreign aid, such as that which is purely humanitarian, but with one caveat. When any aid, be it humanitarian, military, or infrastructure, winds up in the pockets of warlords or corrupt administrators or dictators, that aid needs to be terminated immediately. I am strongly opposed to projects such as foreign regime change—I think our clandestine services have been way too involved in that sort of thing. It simply is not our business. But I'm not an isolationist and I don't want to dismantle the CIA. I believe in a muscular and unilateral foreign policy that pursues our own national interests—but they have to be legitimate interests."

Holmes looked down at her notes. "Adam MacKenzie wrote an article in the *Chicago Tribune* last week claiming that your views in this area have pushed both major parties in a more conservative direction, with legislators from both parties calling for foreign aid to be scaled back. MacKenzie called it 'the Marshall effect.' What do you say about that?"

"I think it's a good thing, Patty. Listen, we're not going to balance the budget simply by reducing discretionary spending —I understand that. We'll have to rein in entitlements to make a dent in our budget crisis. But it is a crime for our legislators to waste fifty million of the people's money simply because it's only fifty million and not fifty *billion*. We have to be serious about *all* of our spending."

****

Byron Gillespie, code-named Ares, sat in his darkened office at the State Department watching the interview on MSNBC, a glass of scotch in one hand. He shook his head. *Just another idiotic do-gooder, but this guy is beginning to eat my lunch. And he's pushing the whole idiotic field of blowhards in the direction of his idiotic notions. Gonna have to put a stop to this boy before he messes up my meal ticket with all this foreign aid babble.*

Chapter 13

Monday, June 13, 2016

An early-season thunderstorm raged over the Front Range of the Rockies. Twenty floors down, on the street, the air in Denver was uncharacteristically warm and humid, and felt electric. Jagged shards of lightning crisscrossed the sky, connecting snow-capped peaks and angry clouds with blinding flashes of light. An almost continuous mutter of distant thunder played counterpoint to thunderclaps so deafening they rattled the windows. Buford looked towards Fort

Collins. Far to the north, sunny blue sky smiled between scudding purple cumulus clouds. The lawyer shook his head. Like a young boy glued to the exciting activity around an excavation site, he could sit and watch the storm all afternoon.

He heard the conference room door open, and turned around. Sam Sebastian, Mike Trujillo, Joshua Cummings, Ashton Bancroft, and Carly Johnson filed in, followed by Henry Marshall. After everyone was seated and Marshall opened in prayer, Buford got right to business. "Before Josh gets started, I've got one item of business. I got a call from our liaison at the Secret Service yesterday. The Secretary of Homeland Security hasn't issued a decision yet as to whether this campaign qualifies for Secret Service protection, but they want to start preliminary discussions about providing a security detail for Hank and Haley so the agents can hit the ground running if clearance is given."

Marshall looked at Cummings, knowing he had dealt with this in his experience as a consultant. "Do we have a choice, Josh? If they offer do we have to accept?"

"No, we don't have to accept it. But if you win the election, that decision is taken out of your hands—you'll have immediate Secret Service protection," Cummings said.

"Why would we turn it down, Henry? I don't understand," said Bancroft.

"The overhead, Abe. Right now, we're able to be light on our feet—we can respond to opportunities immediately. When I go somewhere I'm not dragging an entourage with me. We don't have to worry about security planning and all the hassle that goes with it. But once we get Secret Service protection, all that changes. I really don't want it."

"Hank, I disagree with you," said Jackson. "We have no security here whatsoever. Not only is this headquarters defenseless, so are you and Haley. All it takes is one moonbat and someone gets hurt—or worse. And besides, I don't even have anyone on staff that the Secret Service can liaise with— who do I have them talk to, with all the questions they have?"

Cummings nodded. "Jacks is right, Henry. We've been really lucky so far. Security is an issue you want to talk about *before* something happens, not after. For your sake, as well as the entire headquarters staff, let's put together our own small security team."

"So, does everyone in this room but me think we need a security team?" Marshall asked, looking around at each one. They all nodded. He sighed and smiled. "Okay. I know when I'm beaten. Does anyone have any ideas about who we hire?"

Bancroft spoke up, "I still have some contacts in the special operations community. Let me make some calls. We ought to hire someone to be the head of security and then let him build his own team."

"How many people are we talking about, Abe?" Marshall asked.

With a crisp *SNAP!* a blinding flash lit up the room, followed immediately by an ear-splitting *BOOM!* that shook the building. The power went out for about five seconds, flickered, and then came back on. Rain mixed with hail started beating on the windows and made it difficult to hear one another.

"Wow! That was close," exclaimed Trujillo.

"It was more than close—I think it hit our building! Thank God for lightning rods," said Buford.

They took a break for several minutes and just watched the storm. Once the hail let up Hank repeated his question. "How large of a security team do we need, Ashton?"

"That's not a question anyone in this room answers—that's a question the head of security will answer. We need to let him do his job," Bancroft asserted.

"Agreed," Jackson said. "Let's do it. Abe, as soon as you have a prospect let's bring him in and you and I can interview him."

Bancroft nodded. Marshall spoke up again, "One caveat. Unless there are big objections, I'd like Jim Stewart on the team, if we can get him. Stewart is former FBI and he has served us well in the past. He should have some great contacts in the intelligence community. Everybody good with that?"

The group nodded. Marshall looked down at the list on his pad and said, "Now, Josh, how do you see the next five months unfolding?"

Joshua Cummings opened a manila folder and spread out its contents. "Henry, we need to run this race like an athlete who's saved his strength for an all-out sprint in the final lap. We should surge in October, preferably the last half, with massive targeted media buys in the states we must win."

"What's wrong with slow and steady, Josh? Aren't we gambling by throwing all the dice on the final month?" objected Buford.

"Yes, it is a bit of a gamble, but not as much as you think. As long as we're comfortably trailing Hastings and Bushnell, they won't be wasting much media ammunition on us because they view each other as the real competition. In this election, with the exception of a few core constituencies, the electorate is not showing much party loyalty—there's been a great deal of crossover. Which means that Hastings and Bushnell are fighting a knock-down-drag-out contest for the same segment of voters—they're both drawing liberals, left-of-center moderates, and the neocons.

"The people Hank is attracting are not folks that would be voting for either of the two major candidates in any case— movement conservatives, constitutionalists, paleoconservatives, and both fiscal and social conservatives. So not only is Hank comfortably behind, he's not eating their lunch anyway. Hence, they don't view him as a threat."

"What about the undecideds?" asked Bancroft.

"There's an unusually high percentage of swing voters in this election, and that's where our likely advantage will be. The two majors will be slugging it out in October with some pretty nasty advertising aimed at each other. They're liable to turn off many of the undecideds with negative ads. We are positioned to be the only campaign in October putting out a wholly positive message. Henry's main opponent really isn't either of the major candidates as much as it is the federal government itself. So he can distinguish himself in October with a very positive, upbeat message of his vision for the country, while the other two are grappling in the gutter. I think we ought to saturate the airwaves. Not only could we pick up many of the undecideds, I'd say we also have an even chance of flipping a few of the majors' loyalists, perhaps as many as a percentage point, maybe even two."

"I like it, Josh. It makes sense, it fits, and it lets me control the message as opposed to merely reacting to the other campaigns. It showcases our strengths," affirmed Marshall. The others around the table nodded.

"What about the veep announcement?" asked Sebastian.

Cummings looked at Henry. "You should delay your running mate announcement until the beginning of October, because we'll get a huge splash of free coverage in that press conference, and the media buzz will go on for as much as a week after. Withholding the announcement until then will be a great way for us to lead off the last month with the final push to Election Day."

Trujillo asked, "How do you assess our chances of pulling off a win, Josh?"

Cummings got up and walked over to the window. The first slivers of blue sky in the west appeared as the thunderstorm drifted to the east. He turned around and said, "Tru, when we started this campaign I put our chances at one in forty. I didn't say so at the time, but in this business you have to be a hard-nosed realist in your thinking and planning but a starry-eyed optimist in the things you say.

"How do I assess the race now? Humanly speaking we've got one chance in eight—maybe one in six. Obviously I have no idea what the Lord is going to do—but I know His will will prevail, whatever it is. Our job is to run the race faithfully and steward our resources for that final all-out sprint."

****

Carlos Estrada stood out in a crowd. Literally. At six foot four and 230 pounds, the tall, muscular former SEAL drew attention in any setting. Sporting a gold ring in his right ear and a scar on his left cheek, the bald man could have passed for a pirate. Even-tempered and always in complete control of himself, Carlos was a decorated warrior for exploits down-range that would probably remain classified for the next fifty years.

At forty-two he retired from the SEALs as a chief petty officer and accepted a contract from the NRA Whittington Center (WC), as a firearms trainer. Although he was certified to teach all the courses at WC, his specialty was the *School of 1000 Yards*, teaching the art of long-range shooting. He loved the work and the best part was that he could sleep at night without worrying that someone was going to stick a knife in his guts.

His current client had signed up for the *Precision Long Range III* course, bringing with him an old Savage .308 with a Zeiss Conquest Black Rapid scope. The client was an older man, perhaps seventy, tending a little to the heavy side yet very light on his feet. He seemed to be in good cardio condition, able to negotiate the rough terrain of the school without difficulty.

"Before we go into the training portion, I'd like you to take me up to one of the high-angle ranges. It will be fun to see how much I improve from start to finish," the old fellow requested.

Estrada was doubtful. "Are you sure? We've just got three days, and high-angle shooting is difficult. Might be better to have some instruction first."

"I know, but let's try it anyway. I'm looking forward to learning a lot, but let's give it a go."

According to the front office, the client had done well in the previous courses, so Estrada shrugged his shoulders, and up to the mountains they went. When they arrived at the shooting position Carlos tried to give the man some tips but he waved them off.

"What's the exact distance to the target?"

"Nine hundred eighty yards."

The man sited on the target and checked his angle cosine indicator. He did a quick calculation in his head and dialed the correction into the scope. Picking up his binoculars, the client studied the target, watching the sage brush as it bent to the slight breeze. Making a minor adjustment for windage, he lay prone and fired six quick shots.

Carlos examined the target with his binoculars. Every round penetrated the target within three inches of the center. *Unbelievable.* The old man loaded six more rounds into his rifle, then squeezed off all six in rapid succession. Same result.

Carlos looked at the old fellow with a grin, and said, "That is incredible shooting. *I* couldn't compete with you. Sir, I don't think you need this course. I'll talk to the front office, and we'll get your money back."

"Don't bother, Carlos. Just getting out here and popping a few caps is worth the money."

"Sir, where did you learn to shoot like that?"

"Marines. I was with the 1st Recon Battalion in Nam. Sniper." He squatted down and picked up his brass.

Estrada smiled and shook his head. "No wonder. What's your name, sir? I was told to call you Abe."

"Ashton Bancroft," Bancroft replied, grinning as he stood up.

"You're Ashton Bancroft? My word, what a privilege! They still talk about you in sniper school, sir. I never dreamed I'd get to meet you."

Bancroft chuckled, "Carlos, I set you up. I wanted a chance to talk to you and figured this was as good a way as any, especially since I'd get to do some shooting."

"Why do you want to talk to me, sir?"

"No more *sir*, Carlos. Just Abe, okay?" Bancroft insisted.

"Yes, sir—oh, good grief—I'm sorry, ah, Abe, it's pure military reflex."

"Listen, son, have you ever heard of Henry Marshall, the independent candidate for president?"

"I have. Planning on pulling the lever for him, too," Estrada affirmed.

"Good. I work on his staff as his senior foreign policy advisor." Abe glassed the target, inspecting his handiwork, and then turned back to the other man. "We are looking for someone to head up his security team, and we'd like to inter-view you. I've done some calling around, Carlos, and you've impressed a lot of people."

Ten days later Estrada moved to Golden, Colorado, having accepted an offer to be head of security for the Marshall campaign.

****

Ares stared at the TV angrily. Pamela Hastings had just held a news conference in which she took direct aim at foreign aid in general and programs like GSCF in particular, vowing to slash or eliminate them as ineffective from a foreign policy standpoint and extremely wasteful from a budgetary standpoint.

Byron Gillespie knew she'd been driven to that position by the Marshall campaign, whose positions on foreign aid were proving very popular. He knew that by the simple fact that Hastings was on the Senate Foreign Relations committee and had voted in favor of every single GSCF initiative, and had even sponsored several.

"Time to act, Byron, before they take your candy away," he muttered to himself.

Two days later Ares landed in Albuquerque with an assumed name and a pocketful of cash—he was definitely going to stay off the grid. He rented a car and drove to Denver. Spending the next three days holed up in a hotel room with a good Internet connection, he carefully researched the senior staff of the Marshall campaign, looking for the weak link. He found what he was looking for in Tim Hardy.

For the next five days Ares had Hardy under surveillance, watching his habits and patterns. Hardy's life was pretty monotonous. Monday through Friday the man began and ended his business day at the Starbucks across the street from the campaign headquarters. *Piece of cake*, Gillespie thought.

On Monday morning, July 11, Ares was sitting in the back of Starbucks sporting hair color that wasn't his, a beard that wasn't his, and contacts that changed his brown eyes to blue. He was togged out as a jogger, complete with running gloves that would eliminate the problem of finger prints. After a few minutes, Hardy showed up right on time for his twelve-ounce morning cup of java, his man bag hanging over his right shoulder as it always did. *At least he's changed his shirt and slacks from last week*, thought Ares derisively.

Ares got up and navigated through the crowded store, holding coffee in one hand and palming a cheap burner phone in the other. On the way out he accidentally bumped into Hardy, slipping the cellphone into the IT director's man bag. Two hours later Ares was headed south on I-25 for Albuquerque, mission accomplished.

****

Buford Jackson's iPhone vibrated in his pocket. He didn't recognize the number. Jackson, Henry Marshall, Joshua Cummings, and Mike Trujillo were traveling through Pennsylvania in a silver 2015 Toyota Sienna, crisscrossing the state, attending campaign events.

"Jackson," he said, crisply into the phone.

"Mr. Jackson, this is Andrew Rapp. I'm Senator Bushnell's chief of staff. The senator is wondering if he might meet with Mr. Marshall in the next day or two, while you're campaigning here in Pennsylvania."

"Hello, Mr. Rapp. What's the meeting about?" asked Buford, somewhat cautiously.

"I'm afraid I don't know. My boss didn't tell me, he just asked me to arrange it. He wants a meeting with Mr. Marshall alone, no one else from either staff present."

"Hang on." Buford muted the phone and looked at Hank. "Hank, this is Andrew Rapp, Wayne Bushnell's chief of staff. Says that Bushnell would like to meet with you, alone, while you're here in his stomping grounds. What do you say?"

Hank shrugged, "Sure. Be glad to. I'm planning on sending him back into the Senate on November 8. Might as well start with a good working relationship."

Buford unmuted his phone. "My boss says that he wants

to be on good working terms with your boss when he sends him back to the Senate on November 8, so he's glad to meet with him."

Rapp chuckled, "We'll see about that. I'll pass your boss's sentiments on to my boss. I'm sure he'll appreciate them. Now if I'm reading the papers right, you've got a rally at the naval depot in Mechanicsburg tomorrow at nine. Would Mr. Marshall be available for lunch after that?"

"That works. Where should they meet?"

"How about noon, at Chalit's Thai Bistro, 5103 Carlisle Pike, in Mechanicsburg?"

"Got it. Mr. Marshall will be there."

****

Tim Hardy scanned the system logs for the network servers in the Marshall campaign headquarters. One of the hard drives of the RAID 10 array was showing early signs of failure—a growing list of bad blocks. He broke out a spare drive, walked over to the server rack and hot-swapped the malfunctioning disk. The rebuild time would be negligible, the users probably wouldn't even notice.

He carried the bad drive over to his workbench, and connected it to a controller cable. Firing up his bench PC, he launched a disk-wipe application that would eliminate all data from the drive before he pitched it.

He heard a cellphone ring somewhere, and chuckled at the ringtone. It was the music of the Mozart's Ghost hack from the 1995 Sandra Bullock movie *The Net*, which was one of his favorite movies. The ringing continued and suddenly he realized it was coming from his own bag. He fished around in the bag for a moment and came up with a cheap flip phone he'd never seen before. *How did that get in my bag?*

It continued to ring, so he opened it and answered, "Hello?"

"Hi, Tim Hardy." The digitally processed voice was that of Cyberbob, also from the movie.

"Who is this?"

"Check your bank account, Tim, and keep this phone handy. I have a business deal for you, but you can't tell anyone. If you tell anyone, I'll know, and the deal is off."

"What? What on earth are you talking about? WHO IS THIS?" Hardy nearly shouted into the phone.

"Relax, dude. Check your bank account. I'll contact you tomorrow." The caller hung up.

Hardy flipped the phone shut and stared at it. He mentally retraced his steps on the way to work and then remembered. Someone had bumped into him in Starbucks, across the street, causing him to slosh some scalding coffee on his hand. It was still sore. He must have slipped the phone in his bag then. He put the burner phone down and signed into his bank account on his iPhone. His eyes widened—someone had deposited one thousand dollars in his account that morning.

He got up and shut the door to his small office and sat at his workbench. *What is this all about? Who is that guy?* With a chill he realized whoever these people were, they knew him pretty well. They knew his bank account number. They knew he liked Starbucks. They knew he liked *The Net.* And they knew he loved money. His conscience was warning him, sending up red flags. He looked at the deposit and decided to ignore his conscience. Heart racing, he logged out of his bank account, pocketed both phones, and tried to pretend like nothing happened.

****

Henry Marshall parked the Sienna and pulled a digital recorder out of his briefcase. He pushed RECORD, and then slid the on/off switch to the locked position, and dropped the recorder into his shirt pocket. A few minutes later he was being seated at Bushnell's table.

"So you are that famous blogger, Henry Marshall! I've been wanting to meet you," Bushnell said.

Bushnell's enthusiasm sounded genuine, Marshall decided.

"Indeed I am. Good to meet you, too, Senator. I'm surprised our tracks haven't crossed before in this campaign."

"Well, we came pretty close in Iowa, actually," Bushnell chuckled. "Many times. I think you cost me that state. Didn't matter, though, since I won most of the rest of the states. When the Republican convention meets next week I'll sew up the nomination."

"Congratulations, Senator. I'll look forward to going head-to-head this fall."

The two men ordered their meal and talked about politics, campaigning, and a host of other subjects. Marshall found Bushnell to be interesting, warm, and engaging; he'd heard about the man's legendary temper, but saw no sign of it as they ate.

"I actually want to talk business with you, Hank. Let's be realistic, okay? The way the polls look, you aren't going to win the presidency." He motioned to the server and asked for a cup of coffee, then continued. "Based on our polling data, and I'm sure Josh Cummings has told you this as well, you've hit your ceiling of support. Rising any higher in the polls is going to be like pulling hen's teeth.

"Listen, Hank, you've already made history—I can't think of any independent who has done as well as you have. I commend you for that, and for running a good, clean race."

"Thank you, Senator, I appreciate that." Hank waited for the 'but' he knew was coming.

"But, Hank, you've gone as far as you can. You're not going to do any better than your current twenty-eight percent, and that's not enough to win, not even close. Making matters worse, you're draining away several points of *my* support. Most of our voters walk in different worlds, I will agree with you about that. But there are probably enough that *would* vote for me—if you weren't in the race—to put me ahead of Hast-ings." The server brought Bushnell's coffee and the bill. "I've got this," Bushnell said, setting the bill next to his plate.

"Thank you. Senator, I'm not going to drop out, if that's what you're getting at."

"Actually, I have a better idea. Would you consider running

on my ticket as the Republican vice presidential candidate? If we combine our teams and our voters, we would clean Pamela Hastings' clock come November."

"Do you think I am angling for a vice presidential slot?" asked Marshall, surprised. "Do you think that's what my campaign is actually about—so I can be your running mate? Do you really think that's what's been on my mind?" He was caught off guard. Of all the things the senator might want to discuss, this option hadn't occurred to him.

Bushnell replied, "No, of course not! I don't *want* you as my vice-presidential running mate." He paused and grinned. "I *need* you to run with me. It's the only way we can beat Hastings."

Marshall thought for a minute. "Senator, this question may seem like an ambush, but I don't intend it that way. What is your opinion of the Tenth Amendment?"

"The Tenth Amendment?" Bushnell looked puzzled.

"Yes, the Tenth Amendment." Marshall sipped his water and watched the flustered politician.

The senator shrugged. "The Tenth Amendment has to do with the division of power between the federal government and the states. It's the last piece of the Bill of Rights."

Marshall nodded. "The Tenth Amendment states this: *The powers not delegated to the United States by the Constitution, nor prohibited by it to the States, are reserved to the States respectively, or to the people.*"

"Correct. So, what is your question?" Bushnell asked, eyes narrowing.

"What is your opinion of the Tenth as to how it applies to our present government?"

"Well, I think it applies, obviously," said Bushnell.

Marshall sensed the man was getting irritated, but he pressed on. "In what way, Senator? How will the Tenth Amendment affect your administration?"

"Well, we need to be careful that the federal government does not usurp the role and authority of the states," the politician affirmed warily.

"What about, say, the Department of Education? How will

you apply the Tenth Amendment to that department?"

"One way is that we will not force schools to accept any federally-mandated curriculum. We leave that in local hands. We leave the management of the schools to the local school boards, for the most part. We block-grant school money to the states, wherever possible, so they can decide how to spend it. Those are some of the ways we apply the Tenth." Bushnell sat back, studying his opponent.

Marshall took a sip of his water before continuing. "Senator, with all due respect, the US Constitution does not give to the federal government *any* role in education whatsoever. None. Which means—if we take the Tenth seriously— the feds should not be involved in it, period."

"Marshall, that's a very radical interpretation, one not shared by many jurists today," Bushnell rejoined, curtly.

"Not so, sir. That interpretation is exactly what the Founders were aiming at as revealed by their writings at the time, such as *The Federalist Papers*. And it is an interpretation shared by all constitutional scholars who see their job as interpreting what the document actually says, not what we might want it to mean.

"Senator Bushnell, your offer to me was very kind. But I cannot accept. It's my settled conviction that we must rein in the federal government using such tools as the Tenth Amendment. You obviously disagree. I could not serve as your running mate, and frankly I wouldn't be interested in that position anyway. I'm in this campaign for the long haul, whether I win or lose." He stood up and held out his hand, "I've got to be getting back. May the best man—or woman— win!"

Marshall walked out of the restaurant. Bushnell waited at the table until an aide walked in and confirmed, "He's gone." Then Bushnell pulled a digital recorder out of his pocket, and hit STOP. "Take this," he said, giving the recorder to his aide. "You know what to do with it."

****

Tim Hardy was diagnosing a network printing problem when he felt the burner phone in his pocket vibrate. He fixed the printer and then went into his small office and shut and locked the door. There was a text on the phone.

I need a favor.

What?

Marshall's schedule for the rest of July. It's worth another $1000.

Why?

I'm a journalist working on a book about Marshall's historic campaign. Flying under the radar. My publisher has given me a budget to get inside info.

Pro-Marshall or anti-Marshall?

Neither. Objective. Will give him a fair shake.

Tim thought about it for several moments. He could certainly use the money—the campaign was paying him well, but, as he frequently reminded himself, he could be making more in business or industry. And Marshall's schedule was not exactly secret—the whole thing could be cobbled together from advertised events, although collecting all the data would be daunting. So it wasn't like he was betraying his boss or anything. *In fact, I bet Mr. Marshall would encourage me to take this offer, since it would benefit me and does not hurt the campaign.*

Okay. How do you want it?

Excel format. Attach to text message, send via phone.

Who is your carrier?

No. You send it to this phone, then forward to me.

Okay. Give me ten minutes.

Hardy exported the data from the calendar program, and then emailed it to the burner phone as a multimedia message, and forwarded it to his anonymous contact.

Half an hour later, he got another text.

Check your bank acct. Keep the phone. I'll be wanting more info.

****

On Tuesday, August 9, the *Drudge Report* headlined a *New York Times* article claiming that Marshall was in the race only to secure a vice presidential slot. The article cited an unsourced audio recording that had been anonymously emailed to the newspaper. It had also been uploaded to YouTube with Marshall's picture on which were superimposed the words, "Political Opportunist?"

The YouTube piece went viral within twenty-four hours, and all fifty of the Marshall state headquarters were deluged with angry calls from voters and donors, as well as people who'd endorsed Marshall.

Cummings, Jackson, Trujillo, and Marshall sat in the Golden headquarters meeting room playing the YouTube piece:

> BUSHNELL: "Let's be realistic, okay? The way the polls look, you aren't going to win the presidency. Based on our polling data, and I'm sure Josh Cummings has told you this as well, you've hit your ceiling of support. Rising any higher in the polls is going to be like pulling hen's teeth. Listen, Hank, you've already made history—I can't think of any independent who has done as well as you have. I commend you for that, and for running a good, clean race."
>
> MARSHALL: "Thank you, Senator, I appreciate that."
>
> BUSHNELL: "But, Hank, you've gone as far as you can. You're not going to do any better than your current twenty-eight percent, and that's not enough to win.
>
> MARSHALL: "I am angling for a vice presi-

dential slot. That's what my campaign is actually about—so I can be your running mate. That's what's been on my mind."

BUSHNELL: "I don't want you as my vice presidential running mate."

"Oh, this is bad. Real bad," muttered Trujillo, holding his head in his hands.

"Hank, this thing is killing us! I thought you told me that Bushnell offered you the veep slot and you turned it down. When did this conversation take place?" asked Joshua Cummings.

"What I told you, Josh, is true. This is a very carefully edited set of excerpts. I can't believe Bushnell would do this," Hank said, shaking his head sadly.

"Well, then," Buford said in his gravelly voice. "Let me cure you of your naiveté. Some politicians would climb over their own mothers in order to secure the White House. Wayne Bushnell happens to be cut out of that particular cloth."

"You think I can't believe it because I'm naive?" asked Marshall, grinning. "No, Jacks, that's not it at all. I just can't believe he'd pull a trick that could be so easily refuted." Marshall dipped his hand into his suit coat and pulled out his digital recorder and placed it on the table. "The entire, unedited conversation is right here."

"Oh, thank the Lord! What possessed you to record that conversation, Hank?" asked Jackson, visibly relieved.

"Something didn't smell right from the start, Jacks, especially since he didn't want anyone else present. So I decided I'd record the meeting. He's not aware that I have this. He must have been counting on my naiveté," Hank chuckled.

"We need to get that to our people right away and kill this vicious lie," declared Trujillo.

"No. Not us," interjected Cummings.

"Why not?"

"Everyone expects us to defend ourselves. If we mount a defense, it's no better than a he-said-she-said. We need to give this to a third party," the campaign director said.

"Adam MacKenzie," said Marshall.

"Exactly. Let him follow up on it. He'll be able to dig in ways we cannot. He's undoubtedly got sources in all the campaigns."

"Great idea," agreed Jackson.

"In the meantime, let's do this," Marshall decided. "We don't want anyone to know we have this tape. Tru, issue a press release admitting that the meeting took place and provide the location and date. Say that the recording is not an accurate representation of the conversation, and affirm that I am in the race to win the presidency. But any questions beyond that, respond with a *no comment*."

Marshall smiled, a steely glint in his eyes, "We want to give Bushnell a chance to dig himself a hole he can't get out of. The more he takes advantage of this YouTube piece, the worse he will look when the exposé comes out. We will lose momentum temporarily, but the whole thing will boomerang on the Bushnell campaign and we'll probably pick up several points on him."

****

Jackson, Cummings, Trujillo, and Henry Marshall stood as Adam MacKenzie entered the conference room of Western Law Associates.

"Thanks for coming, Adam," said Marshall.

"Anytime I can get an exclusive, I'm available, Mr. Marshall. Thanks for the offer."

"Adam, I'm sure you've got questions about the latest YouTube video that's circulating, claiming that Hank is angling for a veep slot. If you don't mind, could you hold your questions on that matter until the end of the interview?" asked Trujillo.

"But the video is not off the table, is it?" asked MacKenzie, disappointed.

"No—in fact we have a great deal to say about it, and you're free to ask anything. But if we start with that I'm afraid we won't talk about anything else."

"Okay," the reporter nodded. "Let's start with your position on HUD, Mr. Marshall. Why are you wanting to shutter the Department of Housing and Urban Development?"

"Two reasons, at least, Adam. From a constitutional standpoint the federal government has absolutely no business dealing with housing or urban development—unless of course we are talking about the District of Columbia, but we don't need a cabinet-level position to deal with DC issues. Once again, this is an issue for the states. If the states want to create subsidized housing or enact other statutes dealing with urban development—fine. Let them. I have no problem with that. They'll probably do a much better job than the feds. But Uncle Sam has—once again—usurped authority belonging to the states.

"And from a practical standpoint, Adam, I don't recall anyone saying anything very positive about government housing. Like most things it attempts outside the realm of its constitutional grant of authority, the government has done an exceedingly poor job with this.

"It's time to roll back the applicable legislation, eliminate HUD and all of its regulatory agencies, sell all the buildings and assets, and terminate the employees," said Marshall.

The reporter grinned, shaking his head, "Wow. And this is on the record, sir?"

"Certainly Adam. It's all on our website, too. Look—I'm dead serious about dismantling every department and agency within the federal government that does not have a clear constitutional warrant. I realize that will require substantial legislative rollbacks. But if I have the support of enough Americans, I think I can get Congress to go along with me—their jobs, after all, will be at stake, too, if the voters speak with a loud enough voice. With adequate support, not only can I do it, I will do it."

The interview continued for thirty minutes and then Jackson looked at his watch. "Adam, you've got fifteen minutes left. You're welcome to ask your questions about the YouTube piece."

The reporter nodded and flipped back through his notebook. "Did you meet with Wayne Bushnell and discuss the vice presidential position."

Marshall nodded. "I did. I agreed to meet with him, but the purpose of the meeting was not disclosed at the time. It was my impression he just wanted to get to know me. When we met, Bushnell is the one who broached the topic of the veep slot. He asked me if I would consider being his running mate, saying that if we formed a combined ticket he'd be able to defeat Pamela Hastings."

"But that's not how it sounds on the recording."

"That's because someone edited the recording." Marshall produced a USB stick and slid it across to MacKenzie. "Bushnell is not aware of this, but I also recorded the meeting. That stick contains the raw, unedited audio from my digital recorder."

Buford Jackson said, "Adam, the law in Pennsylvania says that one of the parties to a conversation must consent to the recording. That means both Bushnell's and Marshall's recordings are legal, since each man consented to his own recording."

"So this would be admissible, say, in court?"

"Absolutely," Jackson nodded.

"And I'm guessing that what I'm going to hear on this USB stick is substantially different from what is on YouTube."

"Correct. The recording is as clear as a bell. You should have no difficulty picking out what is said, and who is saying it," affirmed Marshall.

"Why haven't you guys said anything about this? You're getting killed in the polls."

Marshall grinned. "Didn't want to steal your thunder. Bushnell knows this is a pack of lies, so he's morally responsible for it. We're letting him fall into his own pit. He is entrapping himself."

"Listen, Mr. Marshall, you're a great guy and everything, but I'm not a shill for your campaign. I'll be pulling the lever for Pamela Hastings, if you want to know."

"Trying to win you over to Marshall, Adam, is not why we contacted you," Buford Jackson replied. "Answer this, Adam:

what would a man of integrity do when party B is telling lies about party A, and party A is suffering significant harm as a result, and the man of integrity knows that party B is lying? What would a man of integrity do?" asked Jackson.

"He'd expose the lie," the reporter responded.

"That's all we're asking you to do. Clear up the lie. We're not asking you to endorse Marshall. The reason we are giving you a scoop most reporters would die for, MacKenzie, is because we believe you are in fact a man of integrity."

****

The news for the next two weeks was uniformly bad. Marshall was made out to be a craven opportunist by both opposing campaigns, and donations and endorsements dried up. Volunteers quit showing up at the headquarters, and throughout the nation the retail aspect of the campaign tanked as volunteers quit knocking on doors. The RCP average of national polls showed that Marshall had fallen to eighteen percent nationally, ten points down from his high point. The comments on Marshall's blog were furious—accusing him of being a sellout.

Nothing is more delicious for the media than to have a crusader, a moralist, exposed as a hypocritical opportunist. And they found their newest target in Henry Marshall, the man that was going to return the federal government to the Founders' vision, the man who would be impervious to the special interests and their money, the man who would sacrifice his political ambition for the sake of principle. There is something perverse, twisted, in human nature that rejoices when a good man falls, or even better, when a so-called good man is exposed as having never been the principled individual his reputation made him out to be. The media's response to the YouTube piece was brutal. The Marshall campaign dominated the news cycle for two weeks running, and the press was all bad.

The ridicule that Charity, Conner and Charlie were

exposed to at work and school was merciless. Henry Marshall, portrayed as a crusader, was nothing more than a self-serving political hack—or so their friends thought. Added to the pain was that the kids knew the inside story but were sworn to secrecy. They couldn't defend their dad.

Mike Trujillo did an outstanding job of enforcing media discipline. Other than a press conference that denied every allegation made by the video, the curt response to media inquiries about Henry Marshall's alleged attempt to ingratiate himself onto Wayne Bushnell's ticket was a firm *no comment*. Meanwhile, the campaign's inner circle agonized privately, wondering when Adam MacKenzie's exposé would break.

The man whose code name was Ares watched the news and the rapidly diminishing impact of Marshall's strict constitutionalist platform, and smiled. The direct action he contemplated against Henry Marshall no longer appeared to be necessary. The political movement against foreign aid, of the sort that was making Ares a rich man, would simply die on the vine—especially since Marshall had been the one to stir it up—and the status quo, the wonderful status quo, would continue.

Ares debated texting Tim Hardy and telling him that the "book deal" fell through, and instructing him to ditch the burner phone. In the end, he decided to hold off shutting down that operation, just in case. Hardy could keep the phone a little longer.

****

"Is he here yet?" asked Patty Holmes, the pretty MSNBC news anchor.

"Not yet. He texted me that his cab was tied up in traffic," responded Bob McKinney, the associate producer.

"We're on air in eight minutes," she complained. "That's the lead story. What should I do?"

"Go with your intro. If you can make it a little longer, do. When you're done with your intro, we'll cut to a commercial break and hope that he's here when you go live after the break. If he's not, give us a transition line and we'll cut to the weather. He's gotta be here by the time the weather is done. We'll skip makeup and just put him on as he is. And Patty, remember: if you feel flustered, he's going to feel even more flustered at being late for a live news show. You'll do fine. Hopefully, he will, too." Bob could be an inhumane slave driver at one moment and everyone's grandpa the next.

She was thankful he was doing the grandpa shtick at the moment. "Thanks, Bob. Sounds good—we can do this." Patty walked over to the set and went over her intro, finding a few places she could expand. She looked calm, but her stomach was churning. This was a breaking story and MSNBC would be the first to air it. It was probably one of the biggest moments of her career—and it could affect the course of a nation during a presidential election. *Breathe, girl, you can do this.*

When the LIVE light went on, there was still no guest. She pasted a smile on her face, and started her intro. "Good evening, this is *Special Report* with Patty Holmes. It's Sunday, August 28—we are now just seventy-two days from Election Day. This year's presidential campaign has been one of the most unusual in recent memory. The current Democratic administration is considered by many to be one of the more divisive and controversial administrations in the last sixty years. At the outset of primary season, the Democrats fielded a broad slate of presidential hopefuls who couldn't decide whether to run on, or away from, the current administration's legacy.

"On the Republican side, it seems that nearly every registered Republican in the country decided they wanted to run for President. It was felt by many that there would never be a better time to elect a Republican president, given the weakness of the current, lame-duck administration. The campaign cycle kicked off with no fewer than seventeen, *seventeen*, candidates.

"To add to the circus-like atmosphere, there are also many people running as independents. It's not unusual to have a large slate of—well—rather colorful characters running on platforms that range from the amusing to the outrageous. But this year there's a significant twist. Not only have three independents made the ballot in every state, but one of them—Henry Marshall—is mounting a credible challenge, at one point polling as high as twenty-eight percent nationally."

While she was speaking, McKinney's voice came through her earbuds. "He's here. Wrap up the intro, you'll have him immediately after the break."

She continued without missing a beat. "When the field was winnowed down to the two major party nominees, plus Marshall, it appeared that the campaign season would settle into a normal, if not predictable, chain of events leading to Election Day, a little more than two months away.

"But two weeks ago a political bombshell exploded when it became apparent through an audio recording posted to YouTube that Henry Marshall has been angling for a vice presidential spot on the Republican ticket, and that his sights have never been higher than that. Aftershocks from this damaging recording have included a free fall in the polls. Marshall is now down to sixteen percent. The revelation has thrown the campaign into an uproar. While the Marshall people have denied the allegations, their most frequent response to questions from the media about the meeting between Bushnell and Marshall has been a crisp *no comment*.

"Until today. This morning Adam MacKenzie, senior political reporter for the *Chicago Tribune*, published a devastating exposé in which he claims that it was Bushnell, not Marshall, who tried to create the joint ticket, and that Marshall flatly rejected the idea. MacKenzie further claims that the recording posted to YouTube has been heavily edited to give the impression that Marshall was seeking the vice presidential slot, when in fact he was rejecting Bushnell's offer.

"Adam MacKenzie is in the studio with me, and when we return we'll ask him directly about these shocking new revelations."

When the LIVE light was extinguished, she exhaled, "Whew, Bob, that was close."

Working swiftly, the makeup crew managed to make

MacKenzie presentable. His dark tan made the job a little easier. When the commercial break ended, everyone was in place and ready to go.

"With me in the studio today is Adam MacKenzie, senior political correspondent for the *Chicago Tribune*. Welcome, Adam, it's great to have you *here*." She couldn't help smiling at the double entendre.

"Thanks, Patty. I almost didn't make it. Northern Virginia traffic is horrendous."

"Tell me about it," she said dryly. "Adam, you've had a bit of experience exposing the dirty tricks that people have played on Henry Marshall."

"That's true, Patty. This is now my third story detailing the attacks Henry Marshall has experienced from political rivals."

"Yes. There was the pornography story back some years ago, and then the dirty tricks that were pulled on his campaign in Iowa this past January, and now this. Are you a Marshall fan, then?" she asked, raising her eyebrows.

"Well, yes and no, Patty. I don't line up with him politically, if that's what you're asking. I won't be voting for him. But personally, I like the man. I appreciate his integrity and character, and the genuine concern he has for our country. I just don't agree with his solutions."

"So tell us about the latest attack, and what you've discovered through your research."

"Several weeks ago a recording was uploaded to YouTube, in which Henry Marshall is heard virtually begging to be Wayne Bushnell's running mate. In this recording, Marshall can be heard saying that gaining the veep slot was the whole purpose behind his campaign."

"And that didn't go over well with Marshall's followers?" Holmes prompted.

"No. Several days after the recording appeared, the Marshall campaign provided me with a separate recording that they claimed was an unedited, raw recording of the meeting between Bushnell and Marshall. It was very different from the YouTube version, which, as it turns out, was created from carefully edited excerpts of the whole meeting. The recording provided by the Marshall campaign reveals that it was Bushnell asking Marshall to be his running mate, and claiming that only by combining their voters could they defeat Pamela Hastings.

"I gave both recordings to Audio Forensics, which is the premier lab used by the FBI to analyze recordings for signs of editing. The results were conclusive: the Marshall version was clean, the YouTube version was heavily edited."

Patty looked at her guest. "That's shocking! Someone is obviously trying to destroy the Marshall campaign. But who?"

"Well, that's the next question, isn't it? I started doing a little research. For starters, calling that YouTube piece a video is a bit of a stretch. It's an audio recording that plays while you're seeing a picture of Henry Marshall with the words, "political opportunist" floating around. The YouTube account that uploaded the video was created one day before the video was posted. YouTube won't tell me who owns that account, so that was a dead end. Then I looked at Twitter. The first tweet came only fifteen minutes after the video was posted, and the tweeter was Bob Vanderveld, who was on the Bushnell payroll up until the dustup in Iowa, back in January. The next ten tweets advertising the video all came from Bushnell operatives, some tweets being posted as little as thirty seconds after Vanderveld's. By comparison, I did not find any tweets from Hastings operatives until five days after the video was uploaded.

"I went to Vanderveld's home to interview him, and he slammed the door in my face. Wouldn't talk to me. Now all anyone can tell me is that he's gone to Florida on vacation and won't be back soon. The Bushnell campaign denies any knowledge of the video. They wouldn't let me interview the senator."

"Wow," responded Patty Holmes. "What conclusions do you draw from this, Adam?"

"I'm a journalist, not a judge, Patty. My job is to present the information, not draw conclusions from the data. But I can say this: it appears quite clear that there was a concerted, disingenuous effort—by *someone*—to falsely portray Henry

Marshall's intentions in this campaign. And while I'm not a Marshall voter, I deeply resent someone trying to corrupt the process."

****

If the week following the posting of the YouTube video was chaotic for the Marshall campaign, the week after Patty Holmes' interview of Adam MacKenzie on MSNBC was even more so. Voters, donors, and volunteers all seemed to respond with a collective sigh of relief. Donations, phone calls, offers of volunteer labor, and even some endorsements poured in. Americans don't like cheaters, and while Marshall's numbers recovered and climbed to thirty percent, Bushnell's dropped a few points to thirty-one.

Bushnell threatened to sue anyone who accused him or his campaign of the YouTube video. No one came right out and said it, but the evidence was very suggestive.

Marshall's platform of states' rights continued to poll well among voters of all stripes, and the major party candidates were forced to resume tacking to the right.

This fact was not lost on Ares. It was becoming apparent that if Marshall continued to influence the majors, Ares would lose a very lucrative position in the next federal budget cycle.

"That's not going to happen," he muttered to himself. He thought for a few minutes, and then pulled out his Boeing Black Smartphone and made a call. Viper was a fellow former SEAL who'd had trouble acclimating to civilian life and was now a black-ops mercenary, serving the highest bidder without regard to the morality of the thing.

"Hey, Vipe, what's going on?"

"Yo, Ares. Just cooling my heels on a Caribbean beach that shall remain unnamed, my friend. Lots of wine, women, and song. Well—mostly women and whiskey, actually. Haven't been doing any singing."

"Don't make me jealous. I might have to retire so I can join you. Listen, beach bum—you want a job?"

"Maybe. Tell me about it."

"It's all CONUS, probably all in Colorado. Gonna need to make some deliveries, make some pickups, and make someone disappear. Maybe some other stuff. Won't need you for more than a week, two at most."

"I'm not messin' with drugs, man, I'm staying out of that war. Those people are crazy bad."

"No, Viper, no drugs. The pickups and deliveries are things like cellphones and an IED."

"Okay, that works."

"What's your price, man?" Ares knew that Viper got top dollar—but he also knew that he had a track record of completing his jobs successfully.

"Ah, let's see. Expenses, plus ten Gs in advance for the hit, plus two grand for every day I'm on site."

"One grand per diem," Ares counteroffered. Couldn't hurt to try, he figured.

"Two."

"Uh-uh. One," Ares insisted, knowing that he was losing the battle.

"My goin' rate is two, Ares. Two, take it or leave it."

Ares shrugged. Getting Marshall out of the way was worth far more than this deal would cost him. "Two it is," he agreed.

"Deal. When do you want me there?"

"Let me do some figuring. I'll get back to you."

Chapter 14

"DO NOT BE DECEIVED, GOD IS NOT MOCKED; FOR
WHATEVER A MAN SOWS, THIS HE WILL ALSO REAP.
FOR THE ONE WHO SOWS TO HIS OWN FLESH WILL
FROM THE FLESH REAP CORRUPTION, BUT THE ONE
WHO SOWS TO THE SPIRIT WILL FROM THE SPIRIT
REAP ETERNAL LIFE."

Paul the Apostle, Galatians 6:7-8

Wednesday, September 21, 2016

Through the middle of September Bushnell and Marshall traded places in the polls, back and forth. Finally, by September 20, the race solidified with Bushnell leading Marshall by one point, thirty-one to thirty, while the Democratic candidate, Pamela Hastings, remained at a solid thirty-five percent. It was beginning to appear that Hastings would be elected by one of the lowest pluralities in modern American history.

Marshall returned from campaigning in California on Wednesday, September 21, and met with his senior staff late Wednesday afternoon as soon as he got back in the office. "This is one of those rare weekends, Hank, where your schedule was clear, but—" Cummings was saying when Marshall interrupted.

"Oh, good. I'm exhausted. It will be good to sleep in my own bed and go to my own church on Sunday," Marshall interjected, rubbing his face with his hands.

"You didn't let me finish. I was about to say that just an hour ago you received an invitation from the Illinois Education Association to speak this Friday evening on the same stage with the two major candidates, and I told them you'd be there.

"Besides that, Tru has written a great campaign ad about your intention to shut down HUD—he wants you to shoot it on site at a government housing project in Chicago on Saturday." Cummings looked at Hank and shrugged.

Marshall grinned weakly. "No rest for the weary," he sighed.

"Hang in there, Hank. I know both you and Haley are frazzled, but it's going to get worse before it gets better. The election is just forty-eight days out, and we need to push, push, push," Cummings said. "We need to finish strong—and you are so close, so close."

Hank nodded. "I'm good. We're good. Let's do it. There will be time for rest later."

"Okay, great. I'll have Carly book the tickets. It will be you, me, and Carlos going on this one."

****

Haley was in the kitchen pouring coffee and putting donuts on the table. She looked at the time as Hank walked in —it was quarter till six. "Your flight for Chicago leaves at ten. You've got time for a bit of breakfast. What else is on your schedule today, Hank?"

"Morning, babe. Got a strategy meeting this morning with senior staff, then I'm off to the airport. The Illinois Education Association is trying to decide who to endorse, and they invited both major-party candidates to speak to the membership this afternoon. Apparently Adam McKenzie of the *Chicago Tribune* shamed them into inviting me as well, so I'm going as the token loon. That's going to take up my afternoon and early evening. On Saturday morning I'm headed for the south side of Chicago where we'll shoot our final campaign ad in front of another failed HUD housing project. I fly home Saturday afternoon."

Hank and Haley treasured the precious few minutes they

had alone. They chatted about each others' schedules and the grueling pace of the campaign. They were both weary with the non-stop demands of campaigning, especially when the outcome was as obvious as it was inevitable: Hastings was sure to win. But Marshall was determined to fight to the end, if nothing else to honor his volunteers and to win a few more converts to his message of limited government.

All too soon it was time to head for work. Hank switched off the coffee pot and put the cups in the sink. He turned around and embraced his wife. "Listen, Haley, in six weeks it will be over. You and I can resume being Mr. and Mrs. Nobody, and life goes back to normal."

She shook her head. "No, it doesn't, Hank. It will never go back to normal. This *is* the new normal. You've become the spokesman for the opposition to the two political parties. The Dems are the party of big government. The Repubs are the party of slightly smaller big government. There are very few people out there who can mount a credible challenge to the status quo, but you are one of those who can. This isn't the end, Hank, it's just the beginning. It will go on for the rest of our lives, but it is a fight worth having. So let's saddle up our horses and do this. I've got your back."

****

Tim Hardy closed and locked the door leading from his kitchen to the garage and hit the switch to open the garage door. He put his briefcase in the back seat, then got in the car. As he was reaching for the ignition, he noticed a laptop battery on the passenger seat. It hadn't been there when he put the car in the garage the night before.

A cold chill swept through him. *How does he know where I live? I never told him!* And then he wondered, *How did he get in? My garage is locked.* The hackles on the back of his neck rose, and he felt goosebumps. It was one thing for the stranger to communicate with him via a strange cellphone, but it was another thing entirely to invade his personal space, and it frightened him.

His conscience was screaming warnings to him. *Don't do it! Don't go through with it!* Something about the whole deal stank, and he knew it. Hardy wasn't stupid, but he was greedy. And despite his discomfort and the voice of his conscience, he couldn't bring himself to back out of it. Half the twenty thousand had hit his bank account that morning—he knew because he'd checked. He'd already spent the whole thing in his imagination.

The anonymous "journalist" had assured him that the battery was harmless, that all it would do once installed in Marshall's laptop was provide the journalist with access to Marshall's keystrokes, camera, and microphone. It was a chance, he'd said in a text message, to get the ultimate inside story on Marshall's campaign from Marshall's own communications. As part of the package deal—twenty grand to install the battery—Hardy had needed to provide the journalist with Marshall's schedule for the day, especially verifying the time that Marshall would be skyping with his chief of staff—9:00 p.m. Chicago time.

But you are a Christian! Christians don't do this sort of thing. On the other hand, it's easy money and it won't hurt anyone. It will help someone who is writing a book about Mr. Marshall's amazing accomplishment and his historic campaign. It will be good for Mr. Marshall.

He was lying to himself and he knew it. And he also had an idea something more sinister was going on. But he didn't have the courage to back out. If he tried to he was afraid the "journalist" would expose the fact that he'd already betrayed the campaign. Sure, the information he'd sold—*sold? really?* —*yes, sold*—had been minor stuff, but it had gotten him on the hook and by itself constituted a betrayal at some level. He couldn't bear the shame of exposure. *Why, oh, why did I get involved in this?*

He remembered his pastor's sermon from Sunday: "If you're in doubt about the propriety of an activity, whether it's something you can be involved with as a believer, just ask yourself one question: will it glorify Christ? Can you lift it up before the Throne with the voice of praise and thanksgiving?" *No. I can't.*

Pastor Joe had begun his message on Sunday by reading from Galatians 6:7-8, and in his mind Hardy could still hear his pastor's Texas twang as he read the Scripture: "*Do not be deceived, God is not mocked; for whatever a man sows, this he will also reap. For the one who sows to his own flesh will from the flesh reap corruption, but the one who sows to the Spirit will from the Spirit reap eternal life.*"

The text was like a sharp sword, slicing to the depth of his heart. In that instant the evil of his actions and his motives were clearly exposed to him. He knew God was giving him an opportunity to stop, a way of escape, what Pastor Joe had called "door number two." He wavered for a full five minutes arguing with himself. But in the end he knew he wasn't going to take door number two. His shoulders slumped and he dropped his hands to his sides, hanging his head. *Am I really going through with this? Am I really going to do it?* he asked himself.

And then he thought again about how he was going to spend all that wonderful money, how much he would enjoy it, how much he *deserved* it for serving Marshall at less than the going rate for information technology managers. "SHUT UP!" he screamed at his conscience, "JUST SHUT UP!" And instantly it was silenced.

With a start, Tim realized that he'd shouted it out loud. He looked around, hoping no one in the neighborhood had heard his outburst. The coast was clear. He put the car in gear and backed out of the garage.

****

Henry Marshall surveyed the crowd of over two hundred officers, board members, delegates, teachers' union reps, and other notables connected with the Illinois Education Association. Many in the crowd were sporting blue-themed campaign buttons promoting Hastings and a few brave souls had red

Bushnell campaign buttons. He didn't see any of his own.

The three candidates were seated on the dais, with the podium in front of them and a teleprompter below that. His speech was scheduled to be first, the Republican was next and Hastings had the anchor position, which meant that her words were the ones the delegates would most remember. His own speech would be forgotten, dismissed without serious reflection. He smiled, appreciating the tactics and knowing the union was ensuring an inevitable outcome. Marshall sighed. *You knew this was going to be a hostile crowd, Hank, so don't whine about it now.*

The president of the IEA, Robin Goldberg, strode to the microphone and opened the meeting. After running through various housekeeping matters on the agenda, she intoned, "Let's move on to today's big event. You know that it has been the history of the IEA to endorse the Democratic candidate for president every four years on the simple grounds that the Democratic Party is the best friend to education this country has." Uproarious cheers and applause interrupted her, and she smiled and waited for the ruckus to subside. "However, after both parties held their conventions this summer and the candidates and platforms were set, many of our members also found the proposals of the Republican candidate, Wayne Bushnell, to be intriguing and worth investigating. He is advocating a fifty-percent increase to the budget of the US Department of Education, the denial of federal funding to states which use vouchers, and making union membership a compulsory component of teacher certification.

"I must admit that many of us find these positions to be innovative, forward-thinking, and very persuasive. Both our executive board and our membership are divided on this matter, so we decided to host this forum today and allow both parties an opportunity to make their case. In light of the fact that the independent candidate, Mr. Marshall, is also polling thirty percent of the electorate the executive board decided to issue an invitation to him as well. Mr. Marshall has ten minutes, followed by thirty minutes for Senator Bushnell. We will then take a fifteen-minute break, and then allow thirty minutes for Senator Hastings. After a question and answer time, we will dismiss for supper and then regather at seven to vote on an endorsement." She paused and gathered her notes from the podium, then looked at Marshall with a frigid smile.

"I know that very few of us in this room will pull the lever for Henry Marshall in November. But we are academics, after all. Let's send Mr. Marshall home with a favorable impression of Chicago and the IEA. Even though you will not agree with what he has to say, I ask you to give Mr. Marshall a fair and respectful hearing. Mr. Marshall, I welcome you to the podium."

The hall filled with polite, scattered applause as Marshall stepped to the podium. He waited briefly for the teleprompter to display his prepared notes, but it remained blank. He had been expecting something like that to happen. He pulled a few notecards out of his pocket and arranged them on the podium, then looked up with a big grin. "Madam *President*— may I call you that?" When Goldberg smiled and shrugged, he continued, "Madam President, board members, IEA members and educators, thank you for this gracious opportunity. You'll pardon me if I say that I think I know how Daniel in the lion's den might have felt." Light laughter echoed around the hall.

"And being a Christian, Madam President, I believe in miracles. I find myself in dire need of one, sometime in the next six weeks." More laughter. "I've been getting a lot of invitations to speak lately, and the introductions have sounded very much like Dr. Goldberg's a moment ago: 'We're not going to vote for you, but would you mind speaking to our group?' My twin sons, Conner and Charlie, came to me a week ago with a problem and said, 'Dad, we're not going to vote for you, but would you mind giving us your opinion on this?' I was able to handle that somewhat equitably, but when my wife called the other day and said, 'Hank, I'm not going to vote for you, but—'" At that point the hall erupted in laughter. The tension he felt when he climbed the dais had eased somewhat, and he knew the self-deprecating humor had disarmed his audience.

"But enough about my upcoming victory. I'd like to ask

you to consider a simple question: *why is the federal government involved in education?* What do they bring to the table —besides money—that you don't have in this room and scattered across the state? The Illinois Education Association has no lack of rank-and-file members with advanced degrees in physics, chemistry, mathematics, English literature, government, history, and a handful of other disciplines. The state of Illinois is burgeoning with scientists and scholars in all disciplines. You have excellent universities and colleges.

"So tell me: what does the federal government bring that you don't already have on the state and local level? I've visited all fifty states in the last eighteen months, and I have a team of researchers wholly devoted to the study of education policy. I can tell you that the only thing we've come up with is this: the federal government brings money and national standards, at the expense of local control and stifling regulations and mandates." Several dozen heads nodded in agreement.

"You say, *well, we need standards.* Of course we do. We *do* need standards. We need excellence. But on what grounds do you think the only people concerned about standards and excellence live in Washington, DC? I say that there are skilled, trained, gifted people in Illinois, like the people gathered here today, who care about standards and excellence." Applause filtered through the room, with some looking nervously about them as though they were afraid to be seen clapping.

"Gifted people like you exist in all fifty states. And may I propose this: isn't there a possibility that the educational needs of Arizona might not be identical to those in Wisconsin? Might there be some needs in West Virginia that don't exist in, say, Indiana? Is it possible that children in Georgia and those in California, perhaps Silicon Valley, will require different skill sets for their future?

"In 1983, the report *A Nation at Risk* fell like a bombshell on Washington. It detailed ways in which the country's educational structure was failing. It revealed how we were falling behind the other educated countries in the world. Although Ronald Reagan's original intention was to do away with the Department of Education he was overtaken by events.

Instead of abolishing the Department he tasked them with the goal of reforming how America does education. But thirty-three years after the fact we are still struggling mightily in this area, and we still have falling achievement across the nation.

"I'd like to suggest that the federal government's increasing involvement is part of the problem, not the solution. There are two significant statements in *A Nation at Risk* that point to the real solution. First, the authors of the report state:

> All, regardless of race or class or economic status, are entitled to a fair chance and to the tools for developing their individual powers of mind and spirit to the utmost. This promise means that all children by virtue of their own efforts, competently guided, can hope to attain the mature and informed judgment needed to secure gainful employment, and to manage their own lives, thereby serving not only their own interests but also the progress of society itself.

"Children advance, the authors say, by their own efforts, competently guided. The authors recognize the role of the children themselves, combined with the role of the parents and teachers who guide them. The goal is to advance them to the point where they can manage their own lives. The problem today is that government has usurped parental and teacher responsibilities in a most intrusive fashion with the result that Uncle Sam is attempting to manage their private lives.

"The vision on which I am running for president is to radically roll back the federal government. In my opinion— and the opinion of the Founders of this country, I might add —the federal leviathan has become unmanageable and intrusive, and it's time to reduce its role to that mandated by the Constitution. It's time for the federal government to get out of education and turn the management and reform of education over to the several states.

"You might object, *but the states weren't doing the job so the feds had to take it away from them*. That brings up the second great statement from *A Nation at Risk*. The authors quoted Thomas Jefferson, and I believe that wise man was right on the money when he said,

> I know no safe depository of the ultimate powers of the society but the people themselves; and if we think them not enlightened enough to exercise their control with a wholesome discretion, the remedy is not to take it from them but to inform their discretion.

"In Jefferson's opinion, the remedy is not to usurp the power, but to inform the people. Certainly the states should be informed as to how their educational processes are failing, but it should be up to the states and localities themselves to figure out how to fix it, not the federal government. To put it another way, I'd rather trust the people in this hall to fix Illinois' educational problems, than a bunch of bureaucrats in Washington, DC!"

Marshall's audience had remained quietly respectful throughout but broke into loud applause at this point. He concluded his remarks to polite applause, and then watched as the Republican and Democratic candidates spun dozens of promises of increased spending and new programs without saying a word about how it would be paid for. Senator Hastings received a sustained standing ovation, the only one of the day.

When all the candidates were done, Dr. Goldberg opened the floor for questions, asking the the questioners to introduce themselves.

"Mr. Marshall, my name is Dr. Edith Pennel. I'm a high school social sciences teacher in Gary. I've followed your campaign closely, sir, and I am sorry to say that your message is the same in almost every policy area, and I cannot agree with you. To argue that there is no role for the federal government is basically to argue that there should *be* no federal government. You've done that, sir, not only in the area of education but also the environment, commerce, finance, and on and on. Your stump speech sounds good, sir, but I think it's all smoke and mirrors." Scattered applause rippled through the hall, with many delegates nodding their heads in agreement.

"Dr. Pennel, is there a question in that statement?" Marshall responded.

"Well, yes, of course. How do you support the idea that there should be no role for the federal government in modern society?"

"Dr. Pennel, I must respond by rejecting your premise. One of the difficulties a conservative has in debate is that he is frequently faced with a logical fallacy dressed up as an argument."

"And what fallacy is there in my question, sir?"

"The fallacy of the excluded middle, Dr. Pennel. Your question implies that the only possible positions in this debate exist at the two poles, the two extremes. In other words, that our only two options are either the current intrusive level of federal involvement, or no federal involvement at all. Because I am not in favor of the current intrusive level of federal involvement, you are charging me with saying there is no role *at all* for the federal government. But that's not a fair representation of my policy positions. What I argue for is a much *lesser* role for the feds, not their elimination. There is legitimate middle ground in this debate."

"So what is the role of the federal government?" she asked.

"My position is that the role of the federal government is well defined by the US Constitution. I believe we need to return to a stricter reading of the Constitution as intended by the Founders. The Constitution does not have anything to say about a federal role in education, which means education is one of those matters reserved for the states. Education, therefore, is one of the areas in which I would eliminate most of what the federal government does, with several exceptions. And where the states have abdicated their role in education, the voters in those states need to call their state legislators to account. " He pointed to the next questioner, and nodded.

"Mr. Marshall, my name is Randall Carter and I teach various classes of high school history in Chicago. What you say is all well and good, but if it were not for the federal government our society would not be integrated today. The mandate for integration was top-down, and numerous states resisted it. What do you have to say to that?"

"I think that's an excellent question, Mr. Carter. Integration is one of the few areas in which the federal government *should* take a role in education. While no law can change the heart, the law can certainly mandate behavior. In my opinion, racial discrimination should not be tolerated in any form, whether we are talking about discrimination that denies opportunity or discrimination that sets quotas. Both are repugnant. Neither should be permitted. Discrimination in these areas should be a violation of *both* federal and state laws, in my opinion." Hank took a sip of water as the questioner followed up.

"But, Mr. Marshall, how is that consistent with your view of the Founders and the Constitution? Many of them did, after all, have slaves. And Article IV of the Constitution, Section 2, in its original language supported slavery. Your website says that you are a strict constitutionalist. How can you defend *both* a document that originally supported slavery, and the federal involvement necessary to end slavery and discrimination?" More applause and nodding around the hall. Carter wore a thin smile that telegraphed *gotcha!*

Marshall waited until the hall was silent again before he answered the question. "As a teacher of history, Mr. Carter, I'm sure you are aware that one of the greatest errors one can make in the study of history is to judge the past by the mores of the present. The Founders were brought up in an age in which slavery was widely practiced. In order to obtain a Constitution that would be acceptable to the southern states, the Founders compromised and included a provision for slavery. This created a fatal contradiction in our founding documents. The Declaration pronounced all men equal; the Constitution permitted the abomination of slavery until the Thirteenth Amendment was added. Such a contradiction was doomed to cause heartache and trouble to our nation and its people. And so it did: the dual tragedies of slavery itself and the bloody war that ended slavery within our borders.

"I think the important point to note, Mr. Carter, is not so much the original inconsistency—people are, after all, a product of their times—but the fact that *the Constitution and the nation it nurtured were sufficiently robust to correct the problem*, such that today our Declaration and our Constitution as amended do agree.

"So this is an area in which I *do* find a vital role for our federal government, that of defending the basic premise of equality regardless of one's ethnic or national heritage."

The question and answer period lasted another thirty minutes. When the meeting broke up Marshall felt as if he had a contagious disease. People gathered around Senators Bushnell and Hastings, shaking hands, getting photos, asking questions, but no one came within ten feet of him. After a few minutes he gathered his things and left the convention hall.

"Mr. Marshall! Mr. Marshall! A moment, please!"

Hank turned around and saw Adam McKenzie of the *Chicago Tribune* sprinting after him. "Hello, Adam. What can I do for you?"

The reporter fished in his pocket and found his digital recorder. Pressing RECORD he held it where it would capture the conversation. "I have a couple of questions for you, sir, on the record. Do you have a minute?"

"Sure. Fire away."

"What do you think of your reception here this afternoon?"

"Well, I certainly was not the crowd favorite but I found them to be polite and attentive," Marshall answered, setting his briefcase down.

"No complaints?"

"No, none."

The journalist shrugged, evidently surprised by Marshall's response. Then he changed tacks. "Sir, Ronald Reagan intended to abolish the Education Department. Is that really in your plans, should you become President?"

"Yes, Adam, it is. And you can find that on my website, as I think you know. We need to maintain a small agency that gathers statistics, but I do not believe a cabinet-level department is necessary for the task."

"What about student loans? Who will process them?"

"If I become president, Adam, I'm going to push for legislation that puts an end to federal student loans and grants. We will honor all current commitments, but that will be it. By eliminating these programs alone we can save around twenty-five billion dollars a year."

MacKenzie glanced at his recorder to make sure it was still functioning, then asked, "What impact will that have on post-secondary education?"

"That's difficult to gauge in the short-term, Adam. Federal loans and grants amount to a subsidy of Big Education. It is an eternal truth that whatever the government subsidizes becomes more expensive. I realize it's going to be more difficult for the average student to pay for college, at least at first. Certainly, the states are free to step in with their own loan or grant programs, and I am not opposed to that. But in the long run market forces will bring down the cost of post-secondary education. Eliminating the subsidy will create short-term pain for long-term gain."

"But what about the economy of scale? Instead of one federal Department of Education, you're now talking about fifty smaller state departments. Isn't that inefficient?" the reporter asked.

Marshall laughed. "Adam, there is no economy of scale when it comes to the federal government, just massive waste, fraud, and abuse. Anyone who's ever been involved with government procurement knows that. The regulatory burden is so massive, the rules so complex, arcane, and daunting that the feds wind up buying obsolete technology at greatly inflated prices. Federal procurement promotes the very worst of crony capitalism. Trust me on this Adam, I once had a technology company that dealt with the federal government. There is no economy of scale when it comes to the federal government."

MacKenzie pressed **STOP** on his recorder and dropped it in his pocket. "Thank you, Mr. Marshall, for your time."

"Any time, Adam, any time."

****

Marshall's plans for the evening and the next day fell apart almost as soon as he'd gotten back to the hotel. Two phone calls changed everything. The first was a notification from the Golden Police Department that Tim Hardy had been hit by a car while crossing Jackson Street, and was in the ICU at St. Anthony's Hospital in Lakewood, Colorado. The second call was from Conner: Haley had fallen down the stairs and struck her head. She, too, was there in the ICU. Hank decided he had to return home immediately with Estrada, leaving Joshua Cummings in Chicago to shoot the HUD ad.

Because the Golden PD was concerned that Hardy's accident might not have been an accident at all, the men decided to seek Secret Service protection for the campaign. While Hank packed his suitcase, Carlos Estrada got on the phone with their Secret Service liaison, asking for immediate coverage. Cummings called Carly Johnson and asked her to book Marshall and Estrada on the first flight back to Denver.

In a few moments, Carly called back. "Josh, they're booked on an 8:50 p.m. flight out of Midway. I'm sending the boarding passes to their phones now."

****

"May I have your attention, please. This is the final boarding call for Southwest Airlines flight 1356, non-stop to Denver, boarding at gate B15."

The line in the jetway backed up as passengers clogged the aisle of the crowded Boeing 737-800, stuffing their carry-ons into the overhead compartments and maneuvering into their seats. When he got to his seat, Marshall found that he was unable to fit his laptop into the crowded overhead compartment.

"Mr. Marshall, I'd be glad to put that bag in the forward

closet, if you like." The flight attendant smiled at him.

"Thanks so much. I'm not going to use it during the flight and I'd love to have it out of my way."

He sat down in the middle seat and buckled in, and Carlos took the aisle seat. Laying his head back, Marshall shut his eyes and ignored the chaos around him, praying silently for his wife and for Tim Hardy.

"Excuse me, sir. That's my seat by the window."

Marshall looked up. An attractive young woman, perhaps in her early mid-twenties, was standing in the aisle and pointing at the window seat next to him. She smiled apologetically and asked, "Can I get by you guys?"

Estrada frowned and stood, maneuvering his muscular bulk out of the way, and then Marshall also moved into the aisle to let the woman pass. His security chief growled quietly to him as they stood in the aisle, "I don't know how many times I've told Carly to book all three seats, and she still doesn't do it."

"It's okay, Carlos. She's just trying to save the campaign money," Marshall whispered back, as the young lady arranged herself in her seat.

"I understand that. But I'm trying to protect you, sir, and that's higher priority. It's hard to do when you've got an unknown sitting next to you."

As Marshall squeezed back into his own seat he winked at his bodyguard, "Relax, Carlos. She doesn't look dangerous."

Estrada raised his eyebrows. "They never do, sir."

Once the girl had settled in she studied Marshall. "I'm not trying to be forward, sir, but I feel like I've seen you before. What is your name?"

"Henry Marshall," he answered with a warm smile. "And what is yours?"

"I'm Lucy Gillespie. Oh! Of course! I know you! You're running for president, aren't you?" she said, wide-eyed.

He nodded. "That's what my campaign manager keeps telling me."

"Oh, wow. This is awesome! I can't believe I'm sitting next to you. Can I—I mean, is it okay if I talk to you?"

"You mean kind of like we're doing now?" he asked with a twinkle in his eye.

She flushed. "I guess that sounded sort of stupid, didn't it? I mean, are you too busy or too tired for conversation?"

"Not at all. But let's talk about you first," he said with genuine interest. "So who is Lucy Gillespie?"

"Oh, well, I graduated in May from the University of Michigan—go Wolverines!—with a degree in Marketing and Communications. I am on my way to Denver to interview tomorrow with the Denver Broncos."

"Good for you! And what position were you hoping to play?" he asked, amused with the perky young woman. "You're a little small for the offensive line. Maybe wide receiver?"

She laughed and said, "Marketing assistant—bottom of the rung."

"Tell me about your family," he prompted. Marshall loved talking to young people, and knew that he could put this girl at ease by getting her to talk about herself.

"Well, my dad works in DC for the State Department doing some sort of super-secret stuff. My mom died eight years ago from cancer."

"Oh, my. I'm sorry to hear that. I expect it's really tough for a young lady to grow up without her mother."

"Yeah. It really, really hurt to lose her. She was an awesome mom and I still miss her so much. I wish she could have seen me graduate." Her voice quivered a bit and her chin trembled, then she went on. "Dad tries to make up for it. He spoils me. He's a great dad. Oh! That reminds me, I promised to call him before I left Chicago. Will you excuse me? This will just take a minute. There's so much I want to ask about your platform and your campaign."

She pulled out her phone. "Rats! Darn phone is going to die any moment—battery is almost dead."

As she called her dad the flight attendants closed the aircraft door and a ground tug pushed the airliner away from the gate. Lucy's phone died as she was leaving a message on her dad's voice mail.

"Now, can we talk about you, Candidate Marshall?" she asked. Her eyes were bright and expectant, full of hope for the future.

"Is this on the record, or off, Voter Lucy?" he asked, teasing.

"Strictly off the record, sir. I just love your emphasis on states' rights, Mr. Marshall. I think that's the only way the citizens can regain control of the government. Washington has gotten too big and the budget process has become like something out of Carroll's *Alice in Wonderland*. They're spending imaginary money."

He grinned at her, "Now that's my kind of voter! We share the same opinion, at least on that matter."

A lively conversation followed as the aircraft taxied to the runway. The 737 got in line with four other aircraft, awaiting its turn. Finally the airship was cleared for takeoff, and the pilot stood on the brakes as the two powerful CFM turbofan engines spun up. The pilot released the brakes and the aircraft accelerated down the runway.

Just as the pilot rotated the nose, the tiny microprocessor in the replacement battery in Marshall's laptop sensed its embedded timer tick over to 9:00 p.m. A signal, gated from its peripheral interface circuitry, energized a semiconductor switch and a surge of electricity pulsed into two detonators. The C4 explosive packed into the two fake cells exploded with catastrophic violence, creating a shock wave that blew the side door off the aircraft, pulverized the interior of the first class section, and crushed the flight deck bulkhead, stunning both pilots. Debris from the door and forward closet was ingested by the left-hand engine, which promptly flamed out.

The jet immediately yawed, going left of the center line into the grass. The engine on the right wing continued to provide maximum thrust, pivoting the aircraft to the left and putting it into a lazy counterclockwise pirouette. As the plane spun, the wings lost their aerodynamic lift with the result that the nose slammed down, collapsing the nose gear. Skating sideways down the grassy concourse between runways 31C and 31L stressed the main gear, causing it to tear off and rip great holes in the underbelly of the fuselage, leaving a trail of tumbling baggage. The copilot, struggling for consciousness, yanked the throttles back and killed the remaining engine, but by now he was little more than a passenger on a crazy, madhouse ride.

After the aircraft had done two complete spins the right wing dug into the ground and the plane nearly pitch-poled on it, rising to a fifty degree angle. But the momentum was no longer adequate to flip the plane all the way over, and as the wing crumpled the jet slammed back to the ground, coming to rest on its belly. The right wing tanks split, and Jet-A fuel gushed out, puddling under the wing. Damaged power cabling to the engine in the crushed wing was sparking, and it ignited the fuel. At first it began burning very slowly, but as the flames raised the temperature of the growing puddle of fuel to the flash point, the fire spread until with a throaty *whoosh!* the whole puddle ignited.

The scene inside the passenger compartment was absolute bedlam. Screams, groans, and crying filled the confined space. Some passengers sustained back injuries when the plane slammed down and were unable to move. Everyone had been yanked about as the aircraft spun, most sustaining concussions as their heads collided alternately with one another, the side of the aircraft, and the luggage that came cascading out of the overhead bins.

For a brief pause after the aircraft stopped, no one moved. Then more chaos ensued. Passengers began wrestling with the emergency exits on the left side of the jet. Then came the gruesome discovery that everyone in First Class had been killed by the explosion. Terrified passengers began climbing over one another, struggling through the debris and carnage in the forward sections and spilling out of the jagged hole where the door had been, dropping six feet to the grass below.

Carlos Estrada took a brief inventory and found himself virtually undamaged. Marshall was unconscious and bleeding profusely from a deep gash on the left side of his face. The young lady, Lucy, was in shock. Her face was also bleeding, and her eyes were squeezed shut as she tried to close out the horror that surrounded her. She was crying softly, cradling her right wrist which was obviously broken.

Carlos assessed the situation rapidly. The fire under the right wing of the aircraft was blazing but it had not yet penetrated the fuselage. There was time to act if people avoided panic. The only flight attendant he could see appeared to be dead, so he took control of the situation.

"EVERYBODY, CALM DOWN! CALM DOWN! We'll get you all out of here. If you are injured and unable to walk, please remain in your seats. We'll get you out. Now listen! Do not open any of the right-side exits because of the fire. If you are able to walk, please leave by the exits on the left side. Do not look for your carry-ons—we need you out of the aircraft immediately so we have enough room to help the injured. Please calmly line up and leave the plane by the nearest left-side exit."

The sight of someone taking control of the chaos had an immediate, calming effect on the passengers. They began queuing for the exits in an orderly manner, and the plane rapidly emptied of the uninjured and the walking wounded. But by the time there was enough room in the cabin to help those who could not move on their own, the right side of the cabin interior was beginning to smoke. Estrada heard sirens in the distance but knew he was out of time. He'd have to risk moving his boss immediately, injured or not. Picking Marshall up carefully, he turned to Lucy and commanded, "Stay put. I'll be right back for you." She nodded, tears streaming down her face.

He carried Marshall to the nose of the aircraft and lowered him to an uninjured passenger, an athletic-looking man who'd taken charge of the situation on the ground. Carlos dashed back through the plane and picked up Lucy, who clung to him like a tiger. After navigating the debris in the ruined first-class section, he arrived at the gaping hole and tried to lower her to an emergency responder who'd just arrived, but she would not let go. He tried to peel her off but she clung to him, crying, broken wrist and all. "Miss? Miss? You have to let me go, ma'am. These people will help you."

The cabin was rapidly filling with smoke. Estrada made two more trips for the injured. By then emergency personnel wearing breathing apparatus took over. He jumped out of the nose section, coughing and gagging, and trotted over the triage area to locate his boss.

****

"Breaking news! CNN has just learned that—minutes ago—an aircraft crashed during takeoff at Midway International Airport in Chicago. All runways are shut down, and traffic is being diverted to O' Hare International." The screen filled with a live picture taken from a local news helicopter. A passenger airliner, right wing destroyed, was in flames on the ground between two runways and at the intersection of a third. Emergency crews could be seen spraying foam over the fire.

Ares picked up his Colt, racked the slide, and placed the barrel into his mouth. As he flipped the thumb safety, the CNN report continued.

"Of one hundred twenty-two passengers on the manifest of Southwest Flight 1356, nonstop to Denver, we have been told that there are seventeen confirmed deaths and at least sixty-seven survivors, most with injuries ranging from minor to critical. Southwest is not releasing names of the deceased or the survivors until all the information has been confirmed and next of kin have been notified."

He pulled the gun out of his mouth and put it back on the desk. "Oh, dear God," he prayed to the God in whom he did not believe, "please let Lucy be one of the survivors."

****

Estrada sat on the ground next to Marshall's litter. The triage crew had red-tagged Marshall due to significant blood loss, a weak pulse, and his persistent unconscious state. Finally an ambulance was available. A crew of paramedics ran to

Marshall's litter and picked him up. Estrada followed and got in the front passenger side of the ambulance as the crew strapped the litter down in the back.

An EMT came around the side, saw him buckled in, and said, "I'm sorry, sir, you're not allowed to ride in the ambulance. A bus will be here soon to take you to the terminal. You can arrange ground transportation from there."

Carlos shook his head. "Sorry, ma'am, but I'm his bodyguard and I'm not leaving him."

She insisted. "Sir, I am very sorry, but that's against regula —"

"Listen, lady! That man in your ambulance is Henry Marshall, a candidate for the presidency of the United States of America. As of 7:00 p.m. tonight he received Secret Service protection, which was supposed to catch up with us in Denver. I am his chief of security, and I am *not* going to leave his side. So you're welcome to ride on my lap if there's no room in the back, but I'm staying right where I am."

The driver had gotten behind the wheel and witnessed the confrontation. He said, "It's okay, Stephanie. We'll make an exception this time and I'll take responsibility for it. Why don't you ride in the back?"

****

Ares was glued to the television set. He'd been dialing every Southwest number he could find, trying to get news on Lucy, but to no avail. The crash was less than twenty minutes old and the media had not yet published Southwest's Family Support telephone number, but he had been able to contact a Southwest representative who entered his cell number into a database as a family member of passenger Lucy Gillespie.

The Boeing Black smartphone vibrated in his pocket. The incoming call was from Viper, his asset in Denver who was tasked to eliminate Tim Hardy.

"Yeah?"

"The contract has not expired after all."

"What? Why? What happened?" Ares was angry. This day was going from bad to worse.

"We obtained a good solid connection, it just proved inadequate to seal the deal. What do you want me to do?"

"I want you to contact the client and *kill the deal*," Ares growled, trying to control his anger. "I want to move on to new business opportunities and not have old news around my neck, right? So I want that contract to die a natural, repeat, *natural* death, understand?"

"That's going to be difficult," Viper replied.

"Maybe. But that's why you get paid the big bucks, Viper. Now fix it," he demanded hotly. He terminated the call. *If Lucy's dead, it frankly won't matter because I'll be dead, too. But I'm not pulling the trigger so long as there's a chance she's alive.*

****

Carlos Estrada stood next to Henry Marshall's gurney in the ER at the Loyola University Trauma Center, as blue-robed doctors and nurses struggled to keep up with the influx of victims from the crash of Southwest Flight 1356. Soon the ER staff was repeating the triage process on incoming patients, dividing their limited resources among the most critical.

"Who are you?" the attending physician barked at Carlos as he walked into the cubicle.

"Carlos Estrada. I'm his chief of security, right now serving as his bodyguard," he barked back, matching the doctor's brusqueness. "Your patient is Henry Marshall, candidate for president. He just came under Secret Service protection this afternoon, but we were supposed to meet the Secret Service team in Denver. Right now I'm all the security he's got, and I'm sticking with him like white on rice. I'll stay out of your way, but you can forget about asking me to leave." Carlos glared fiercely at the doctor, not about to take any more hassle from anyone.

For a moment the doctor glared back, unaccustomed to being challenged on his home turf. He sized up the powerful man standing by the gurney and decided arguing the point was not going to be productive. "Very well," he said, relenting. "Sit over there. If any of the nurses ask you to leave you just tell them that Dr. Andrews said you could stay."

"Thanks, Doc," breathed Carlos gratefully. "There's one more thing, Doctor. The reason we were on that flight is because Mr. Marshall learned this evening that an accident has put his wife in the ICU of a Denver hospital. As of this moment I'm the only one available to consult on his condition. Please, sir, don't get hung up on HIPAA—I've got to notify his family, his campaign team, and the Secret Service about his status, so I'll need to be fully informed."

"Never did like that stupid HIPAA law to begin with," groused the physician, "pain in the butt and vastly unfair to loved ones. Mark my words, son, that's what happens when lawyers get involved. Look, whatever-your-name-is, I'll keep you informed. But you never heard it from me. Got it?"

"Got it. Thanks, Doc." Carlos sagged a little, then caught himself. He was suddenly desperately tired, and was beginning to ache all over his body.

"You're welcome. Now, sit down over there before you fall down. I'm not gonna hurt your boss," he said dryly. "And since you've insisted on staying, I'm going to have you checked out too, to make sure you didn't sustain internal injuries."

The doctor checked the monitors wired to Marshall and studied the brief report filled out by the paramedics who brought him in. Gently pulling back the eyelids, he examined the reaction of Marshall's pupils to light. He grunted and scribbled on the chart.

"I'm ordering a CAT scan. He's probably okay, but 'probably' is not an adequate medical diagnosis. I want to make sure nothing bad is going on in his cranial cavity. Assuming that scan comes back okay, once we replace the blood he's lost we should see improvement fairly quickly. I'll have more to tell you when I see the results of the CAT scan." Without waiting for a response the doctor strode out of the room.

Estrada pulled out his cellphone and started dialing. He called Josh Cummings first. "Mr. Cummings? This is Carlos. Have you got the news on, sir?"

"No, I don't, Carlos. What's up?"

"Our plane crashed on takeoff. I'm at the Loyola Trauma Center with Mr. Marshall."

"Oh, that's terrible! Is Hank okay? Are you injured?"

"No, sir. Other than bumps and bruises I haven't a scratch, but Mr. Marshall got clobbered by something when the plane went down and he's been unconscious since. He's got a pretty nasty gash on his face and he's lost a good deal of blood. They've ordered a CAT scan on him. The doctor was just in —said the preliminary assessment wasn't too bad, but he wouldn't know for sure until he'd gotten a look at the scan."

"I'll be right over. Do you feel up to calling Charlie, Conner, and Charity and giving them the news? I'd hate for them to see it on television and not know whether their dad survived."

"Yes, sir, I'll call them right now. Is there anyone else you want me to call?"

"Yes, please call Carly and give her a heads-up. Have her notify everyone else. Tell her that no one speaks to the press but Trujillo. I'll call him as soon as I get a look at Hank. Understand?"

"Yes, sir. I'm on it."

Carlos hung up, then dialed Conner. "Hey, Conner, this is Carlos. How's your mom doing?"

"Hi, Carlos. I was just about to call Dad and tell him. She is just now going into emergency surgery to relieve pressure on her brain. When we got to the hospital she had begun bleeding from the eyes." At this the young man's voice caught, and became husky. "She looked awful. They gave her a CAT scan and it showed what the doctor called a 'subarachnoid hemorrhage.' She's bleeding inside her skull. We don't know yet what's going to happen or what this means for her condition. The surgeon warned us it that it might be several days before we know anything for sure, as far as how she's going to do. When's Dad going to get home? We really need him here."

"Conner, there's been a problem. Your dad booked the first available flight back to Denver, trying to get back to your mom. But there was an accident, and your dad is in the hospital. I think he's going to be okay, but I am waiting for a report from the doctor. It's liable to be several days before he can return to Denver."

"Dad's been in an accident? What happened?" Conner asked fearfully.

"Our plane crashed on takeoff, Conner. It's all over the news. When you see the pictures on TV it's going to look really bad but don't let that scare you," the security chief reassured him. "We didn't actually get off the ground, Conner. Most of the people on the airplane survived with cuts and bruises. We are all very fortunate to be alive."

"How bad is my dad, Carlos? Please just tell me the truth —I don't want to wonder and worry."

Carlos glanced at the unconscious figure on the gurney. "He's going to have a lot of bruises, maybe a broken bone here or there, but the worst thing is that he took a nasty knock on the head. I have no clue as to what hit him, but it put a deep gash from his temple down to his jaw on the left side. He lost a lot of blood and he's still unconscious. They are wheeling him out right now to get a CAT scan—I should know something more in a couple of hours. But, Conner, the doctor was pretty optimistic about his condition. Don't worry about your dad. I think he's going to be fine—we'll find out for sure soon."

There was silence for a minute. Then Conner said with a trembling voice, obviously struggling for control, "Okay, Carlos. You keep me up with what's going on with Dad, and I'll make sure to keep you up to date with news on Mom."

"You got it, son. Now—two more things. Conner, don't you or Charlie speak to the press at all, okay? This whole complicated situation is made more complex because your dad is a public figure running for president. So make sure that neither of you talk to the press at all, okay? Let Mike Trujillo handle all that."

"Fine with me. What's the other thing?"

"This afternoon we decided that it was time for Secret Service protection—right after we heard about your mom's accident. I expect in the next hour or two they will show up at the hospital. I want you and Charlie to cooperate with them just like you do with me, understand? It's going to make everyone's life a little more complicated, but it's a necessary evil." Carlos stifled a groan. He was beginning to feel his bruises.

"Will do."

The bodyguard next called Charity, then Carly Johnson, and then dialed his Secret Service contact to bring him up to date.

Chapter 15

THE FIRST QUESTION THAT OFFERS ITSELF IS,
WHETHER THE GENERAL FORM AND ASPECT OF THE
GOVERNMENT BE STRICTLY REPUBLICAN. IT IS
EVIDENT THAT NO OTHER FORM WOULD BE
RECONCILABLE WITH THE GENIUS OF THE PEOPLE OF
AMERICA; WITH THE FUNDAMENTAL PRINCIPLES OF
THE REVOLUTION; OR WITH THAT HONORABLE
DETERMINATION WHICH ANIMATES EVERY VOTARY OF
FREEDOM, TO REST ALL OUR POLITICAL
EXPERIMENTS ON THE CAPACITY OF MANKIND FOR
SELF-GOVERNMENT. IF THE PLAN OF THE
CONVENTION, THEREFORE, BE FOUND TO DEPART
FROM THE REPUBLICAN CHARACTER, ITS ADVOCATES
MUST ABANDON IT AS NO LONGER DEFENSIBLE.

James Madison, Federalist #39

Friday, September 23, 2016

Roland Yates was at a birthday party—his own. His wife Phyllis and their four adult children had thrown a surprise party, inviting friends and neighbors to celebrate his sixtieth year on the planet. Rollie's wife was a breast cancer survivor and the family had decided that none of the important moments of life should ever again be taken for granted—every landmark should be celebrated.

"Shareen, do you remember when Momma was taking you to check out CSU, and she got on I-25 and turned south instead of north? You guys drove all the way to Colorado Springs before you realized you were headed the wrong way." Yates chortled, enjoying the favorite family pastime of "remember when."

Roland Jr. shot back, "I remember hearing about that. But I also seem to remember that *you* were supposed to drive *me* to the Air Force Academy to apply for admission and you forgot to check the gas. Halfway there we ran out, missed our appointment—and I almost lost the chance to go to the Academy because of it. You had to call in some favors from General Franks to get me rescheduled. Did you ever forget to gas up the plane when you were a pilot?"

"If I had neither you nor I would be here right now," his dad laughed. Roland Yates retired as a full colonel after a distinguished career spanning thirty years. His final tour with the Air Force was spent in the left-hand seat of the B1 bomber. When he retired he'd signed on with the National Transportation and Safety Board (NTSB). Eight years later he was the Investigator-In-Charge (IIC) for the Midwest regional office, based in Denver.

At 8:40 p.m. (9:40, Chicago time), in the middle of a board game which he was decidedly losing, his cellphone vibrated. "Excuse me, gang, I've got to take this call." It was the NTSB Communications Center. They sketched out the sparse details of a crash at Chicago's Midway Airport. They did not yet know the cause of the accident. Yates quickly selected his Go Team of specialists and left it to the Communications Center to make the contacts.

By ten p.m. he was on a flight to O'Hare International, where a Midway International Airport security representative was waiting to pick him up and drive him to the scene of the crash.

****

A lean, muscular man, dressed in blue scrubs and wearing a stethoscope around his neck, lingered outside the St. Anthony's ICU doors, studying a chart on a clipboard. A nurse headed into the unit passed him by and he fell in behind her as the hall doors opened to admit her. No one paid him the slightest attention. He walked through the unit slowly, pretending to study the clipboard, until he arrived at Tim Hardy's room. A sleepy-looking policeman was standing outside the door.

"Officer," the man acknowledged, nodding his head as he entered the room. He drew the curtains around the bed, shutting off the view from the nurses' station and the officer. Working rapidly, he produced a syringe full of morphine and injected it into Hardy's IV drip bag. He pulled a bottle of morphine from his pocket, refilled the syringe and then emptied it into the drip bag again. Twice more he repeated the process. As he was withdrawing the syringe from the IV bag port, the curtains swept back and an ICU nurse stood looking at him.

"Who are you, and what are you doing?" she demanded.

"I'm his attending physician, and . . ." he trailed off, suddenly realizing how implausible he sounded—doctors don't mess around with IV bags, nurses do that. He backhanded her, knocking the nurse over a chair, and darted from the room. Blood streaming from her mouth, she leapt up and yanked the IV from Hardy's arm.

The ruckus alerted the lethargic policeman in time for the fleeing assailant to bowl into him, and they both sprawled to the floor. Viper was quicker to regain his feet. He kicked the cop in the jaw, then raced down the hall, crashing through the ICU doors and sprinting for the stairwell. Ignoring the agony of a broken jaw, the policeman ran after him, radioing for assistance.

Taking the steps four at a time, Viper dropped down two flights, exited the stairwell and raced through the hall to the stairwell on the other side of the building, shoving surprised doctors and nurses out of his way. Glancing over his shoulder as he ran, Viper didn't see the medical technician roll a cart of blood samples out of a room. He stumbled over the cart and went flying, colliding headfirst with the open door of a maintenance closet, knocking himself out cold.

****

Grady Wilson was home watching the late news when he got the phone call.

"Grady, this is Dispatch. I just got a call from Officer Belden at St. Anthony's. Belden was standing guard outside Timothy Hardy's room this evening when a man posing as a doctor made an attempt on Hardy's life. He was discovered by a nurse and attempted to flee the scene but was apprehended when he tripped over some medical equipment. The suspect is in custody, and en route to the station. Belden thought you'd want to know."

"Yeah, I do. I'll be right down, thanks." Grady terminated the call and slipped his phone in his pocket.

The detective stared at the television, deep in thought. Just before the phone call he'd seen a news piece on an airline crash at Midway, in Chicago. The reporter had verified that Henry Marshall was a passenger. Speculation was already rampant that the plane could have been brought down by a bomb. "There are no coincidences," Wilson muttered to himself. *First Hardy, now Marshall*, he thought. *It's got to be connected somehow.* After talking with the chief of police, he called the FBI. The case had just expanded beyond the resources and jurisdiction of the Golden PD.

Grady drove to the station and set up the interrogation room. He was joined by Detective John Barna, and Agent Samuel Bergman, Jr., who was with the Denver field office of the FBI.

"Hi, John," Grady said as the detective walked in. "Sorry to call you in so late, but this case is developing into something very serious and I need you in the interrogation room."

John Barna was a clothes horse. As a detective he didn't wear his uniform, except for special occasions, but he was always dressed to a tee. On this particular night he was wearing a maroon turtleneck, black slacks and wingtips, with a grey jacket. His fellow officers called him "Dandy John," and he enjoyed both the nickname and the notoriety.

"No problemo, Grady. I was just sleeping. Nothing important," John responded with light-hearted sarcasm. "Why can't these thugs learn to do their thing during business hours?"

"Yeah, really. John, this is Special Agent Samuel Bergman of the local field office," Grady said, motioning to the FBI agent.

"Always pleased to meet the local G-man, Agent Bergman," Barna said. "Are these your normal working hours or did Grady interrupt your repose as well?"

"Pleased to meet you, John. Please call me SJ, everyone else does. And, no, these are not my favorite working hours. When the call came, I was enjoying a detailed study of the backside of my eyelids," Bergman replied with a smile. He was dressed in a pair of jeans and a Denver Broncos sweatshirt. His identification was hanging from a lanyard around his neck.

"SJ? What's that stand for?" asked Wilson.

"Samuel, Jr."

Grady nodded, and turned to Barna. "SJ and I have already agreed that he'll watch through the one-way while you and I conduct the interrogation. We don't want the suspect to know that the FBI is involved, not yet anyway."

"Sounds good. So who's the perp and what's the story?" asked Barna.

"He won't tell us his name. We're running his prints now. He's definitely ex-military, has a SEAL Budweiser tattooed to his right bicep. He was picked up at St. Anthony's. He was impersonating a doctor and tried to load up a patient's IV bag with morphine. At least, we think it's morphine—that's what was on the label of the bottles—we should hear a verification back from the lab later today. Anyway, he was caught by a nurse and clocked her, clocked the duty cop stationed outside the door, and while he was fleeing managed to do a Laurel and Hardy over a medicine cart, got knocked out cold.

"But the part that's really interesting is this: the patient he was trying to bump off, fellow by the name of Tim Hardy, was the victim of a hit-and-run accident on Jackson Street last evening. Statements from witnesses say that it appeared Hardy was targeted. My current theory is that the bad guy came back to finish the job.

"Now, here's why Sam and the feds are involved. Hardy works for Henry Marshall, the independent candidate for president. And earlier this evening, Marshall's plane crashed while taking off from Midway in Chicago."

"And you think there's a connection between our bad boy and that plane going down?" Barna surmised.

"I think it's a possibility we need to keep in mind," Grady replied.

Barna nodded. "Okay. Let's get started."

Wilson verified that the video recorder was running while Sam Bergman took a seat close to the observation window. Then the two detectives walked into the interrogation room.

"My name is Detective Wilson, this is Detective Barna, and we'd like to ask you a few questions."

"You can ask all you want, boys, but I'm not saying anything without my legal counsel present. I demand an attorney. This interview is over until I have one." Viper sat back calmly and looked at the two cops with soulless eyes. He'd said all he was going to say until his lawyer was present.

****

When Roland Yates landed at O'Hare he was met at the jetway by a representative of Midway International Airport. "Mr. Yates, I'm Phil Santos, assistant director of security at Midway. I understand you're the Investigator-In-Charge. Come with me, please, sir." An O'Hare security officer escorted them down some stairs to the tarmac, where an airport security vehicle was waiting.

Once in the car, Santos briefed Yates as they drove to Midway. "I'll be your liaison to the airport. I've been instructed to provide you with whatever you need. A Southwest representative is flying in, should be landing at O'Hare around two in the morning. Boeing's rep lands at 5:00 a.m. I've already assigned people to pick them up and bring them to Midway."

"Excellent," acknowledged Yates. "My Go Team will be landing at O'Hare between five-thirty and seven in the morning."

"I'll detail someone to pick them up as well."

"Great. Can I call you Phil? Good, thanks. Please call me Roland. What can you spare to help us secure the scene?"

"I've only got five men available for that. They've already established a security perimeter around the scene. If that's insufficient I can call on the Chicago PD."

"Okay, good. What sort of arrangements can the airport provide for my Go Team? There will be eight of us, including me."

"FedEx has just completed a new hangar facility and they are offering the old one to the NTSB for this investigation. It's plenty big enough for the wreckage and it's got a glassed-in conference area with thirty seats on the mezzanine above the floor. There's a separate section you can use for briefing the press."

Yates phone vibrated. It was a text from the NTSB Communications Center notifying him that a shipment of twelve preconfigured laptops, an ion mobility spectrometer (IMS), and other equipment would arrive at 5 AM. The hardware would be used by his Go Team and other parties to the investigation.

"Is there any tower video available?" asked Yates as he texted a confirmation back to the Communications Center.

"Should be," Santos affirmed. "I've got someone setting up a terminal in the hangar and isolating all available video. Should be online when we get to Midway."

"Excellent. I appreciate all the work you've done so far, Phil. What's the latest on casualties?"

"Thirty-five confirmed dead, eighty-two with injuries ranging from critical to cuts and bruises, and thirteen lucky ones who got out of it with nothing more than a big scare. Southwest has not released this information yet, but all passengers and crew have been accounted for. I imagine that some of the survivors could still succumb to their injuries, but that's just my guess.

"Roland, there's a piece to this puzzle that could raise the stakes significantly: one of the passengers on the manifest was Henry Marshall."

"Not *that* Henry Marshall?"

"Oh, yeah. That one. He's on the preliminary list of survivors but that list was done by the triage people about three hours ago, so I haven't a clue about his present status."

Yates chewed on that for a moment. "Okay, Phil, as soon as we get to Midway call the Chicago PD. I want the entire site locked down."

Several minutes later Santos pulled up to an unmanned security gate at Midway and inserted his badge. The gate trundled open and the men drove through. As the gate closed, Phil stopped the car and made the call to the Chicago Police Department. Then he started driving toward the old FedEx hangar.

"I want to see the site and the wreckage before we head for the hangar," requested Yates.

"Okay," Phil replied. Santos contacted the tower to let them know. He drove the route that Flight 1356 had taken from the terminal to the runway apron, and then traveled down the runway to the site of the crash. Parking behind a light truck, Santos and Yates got out of the car carrying powerful flashlights. Other than a few security officers, and several firemen making sure the wreckage did not rekindle, the site was deserted.

Yates circled the wreck several times, playing his flashlight over the torn, smoking fuselage and the surrounding ground. He was careful not to touch any of the wreckage or baggage strewn across the area. Finally he climbed a ladder and entered the aircraft through the hole where the door had been and inspected the interior, walking to the back of the aircraft and working his way back toward the front. After eight years serving with the NTSB he'd seen his share of aircraft accidents. Equipment failures, pilot error, collisions, terrorist actions, he'd seen it all and he knew what to look for.

Santos accompanied him, watching the older man but not interrupting his thinking with unnecessary chatter. The front end of the passenger compartment and the adjoining flight deck took most of Yates' attention.

"How about the pilots?" Yates asked.

"Amazingly, they're both alive. Among other injuries they both sustained broken backs, but they are expected to survive."

"I'll need to interview them."

Yates spent another ten minutes examining the scene, and then said, "Let's go check out the tower video."

Santos drove him to the hangar and they sat down in front of the computer connected to the tower and taxiway camera system. They noted how the 737-800 picked its way through the taxiways and intersections, then turned on to Runway 31C and began accelerating. Faster and faster the plane raced down the runway in an apparently normal takeoff. As the nose wheel lifted off the ground there was a flash from the left side of the aircraft, ahead of the wing, and the plane began to spin counter-clockwise. The nose slammed back down as the plane —continuing to rotate—slewed sideways off the runway. The tower camera did not have sufficient resolution to zoom in, but it was clear that debris was flying off—or out of—the airplane and that its gear had collapsed. The right wing dug in and the aircraft nearly flipped, but slammed down to rest on its belly, fire springing up on the right side of the fuselage.

"Rewind it, please," requested Yates. Santos complied and they watched the tape again. "Stop! Now advance frame by frame." They watched until they got to the bright flash Roland had seen. "Stop there. Now check out the time, Phil."

Phil Santos noted the timestamp on the video and replied, "It's one second after 9:00 p.m."

"Right. When the Boeing rep gets here he can help us on this, but as far as I know there is no aircraft system in that section of the fuselage that could explode. But we clearly have an explosion. I'd bet next year's salary it was a bomb set off by a timer," Yates declared.

"Why do you say that, Roland?"

"It was an explosion of some sort—the video makes that much clear. But there's nothing in that part of the plane which could explode with that kind of violence; hence, a bomb. It was probably not manually triggered, because it went off while the plane was still on terra firma. If a terrorist was triggering a bomb they just missed a great opportunity for death and destruction by setting it off about twenty seconds too soon. They would not make that mistake; hence, a bomb on a timer.

"So how does a bomber decide what time his bomb is going to go off? Usually it's going to be set for a time that will do the most damage. Obviously that was not the case here. The next possibility is that the detonation time represents an event in history that's somehow important to the bomber—he's making some sort of political statement. I don't think that applies to this bombing. The remaining possibility is that the time does not really matter. In that case, the natural human impulse is to set the bomb for a natural mark, such as the hour, the half-hour, or the quarter-hour. Clearly that's what we have here. The important thing to remember is that the time is almost never random."

"Makes sense now that you explain it," agreed Santos.

"In view of the fact that Henry Marshall was on this flight and the explosion happened at precisely 9:00 p.m., I'm going to proceed on the assumption that a crime has been committed. I'm getting an FBI Evidence Response Team on this immediately. Based on the limited extent of the debris field, they should be able to photograph, tag, and bag everything by the end of the day. If everything goes well, by tomorrow morning you should be able to reopen Runway 4L and R, and probably 31R. By tomorrow afternoon we should be able to relocate the fuselage to the hangar, and you can reopen 31C and 31L."

Santos nodded. "I'll give the airport manager an update, and tell him your estimates are tentative."

"Sounds good. Be sure not to tell him—or anyone else—my suspicions."

****

By 6:00 a.m. Denver time, the Denver and Chicago offices of the FBI as well as the Golden Police Department and the

NTSB were coordinating their investigations, due mostly to the fact that Jim Stewart spent a good part of the night on the telephone helping the various organizations connect the data. It was now believed that the attempt on Hardy's life as well as the bombing of Southwest Flight 1356 were related.

Enforcing a news blackout was an exercise in futility. By nine the nation knew that Henry Marshall was on the passenger list of Flight 1356 and was in stable condition in a hospital in Chicago, and that Haley Marshall was in an ICU unit in Denver, and that an attempt had been made on the life of the Marshall campaign's IT director. Mike Trujillo scheduled a news conference for 10:00 a.m. at the Marshall campaign headquarters.

"Ladies and gentlemen, if you'll take your seats we'll get started. I'll make a brief statement, and then open it up for questions." Mike Trujillo waited as reporters jockeyed for seats near the front. The press conference was taking place in the parking lot of 1600 Jackson Street since the conference room wasn't large enough to hold the turnout. At the last minute campaign workers moved their cars and set up fifty folding chairs. Half a dozen television crews were on the scene, and cables snaked everywhere. It was a beautiful, late September morning, the atmosphere was clear and dry, and the Front Range of the Rockies towered majestically in the background. *If Hank were here*, Trujillo thought, *this would have made a great photo op.*

"In the last twenty-four hours the Marshall campaign has experienced three tragedies. Our information technology director was hit by a car yesterday afternoon shortly after leaving this building. Last evening Haley Marshall had an accident at home, falling down a flight of stairs and hitting her head. Both Tim Hardy and Mrs. Marshall are now patients in the Intensive Care ward of St. Anthony's in Lakewood. And late last night the aircraft on which Henry Marshall was trying to return to Denver crashed on takeoff. Mr. Marshall was attempting to get to his wife's bedside, but now he himself is also in the hospital in Chicago.

"The Marshall campaign would like to extend its heartfelt

sympathy to the families of the passengers on Southwest Flight 1356 who perished or were severely injured. Our hearts go out to them and our prayers are with them. We also want to extend our gratitude to the first responders and the medical community who have performed so admirably in each of these situations.

"I want to stress that Henry Marshall is not, I repeat, not suspending his campaign at the present time. All of our staff and volunteers continue to work hard to see that Henry Marshall is the next President of the United States. Thank you."

Mike folded the paper he'd been reading from and put it in his breast pocket. "Your questions?" He pointed to a CNN reporter in the front row.

"Cindy Sanchez, CNN. What is Mr. Marshall's condition at the moment, sir?"

"Hank has a deep cut on one side of his face, and he sustained a mild concussion. He's also got a myriad bumps and bruises. Other than that, he's fine. I should add that our chief of security, Carlos Estrada, was also on the flight. Thankfully, Carlos walked away with nothing more than some bruises."

Cindy continued. "I understand from our Chicago bureau that he was in a persistent unconscious state from the time he was removed from the aircraft until he arrived at the hospital. Can you comment on that?"

"Yes, Cindy. I've been told it was a combination of blood loss and the concussion. But I can assure you that he is conscious now. In fact, I spoke to him on the telephone this morning."

"What did he say?"

Trujillo chuckled. "Nice try, Cindy. One more question before I give someone else a shot."

She nodded. "Sir, you said that the campaign is not being suspended *at the present time*. Are you leaving that open as a future possibility?"

Trujillo nodded. "Under the circumstances we have to admit that as a possibility. The last word I received from Hank is that we are not suspending the campaign, pending his discussions with Haley, which we hope will happen by the middle of this coming week."

Sanchez followed up quickly, before Trujillo could turn to another reporter, "Is Mrs. Marshall conscious?"

"I'm sorry, but I'm not going to discuss her condition at the present time."

Mike pointed to another reporter.

"Arthur Mitchell, *Denver Post*. Was Mrs. Marshall's accident alcohol-related?"

"No. Neither of the Marshalls use alcohol at all, with the exception of a glass of wine on special occasions. According to the family she tripped on a step and was unable to catch herself. It was just a common, household accident that resulted in a serious injury.

"Next question, yes, you there in the back row."

"Cletus Richards, *Fort Collins Coloradoan*. Can you comment on the rumors that Tim Hardy was targeted by the automobile that hit him yesterday?"

"No, I'm afraid I cannot. Next quest—oh, do you have a follow-up, Cletus?"

"Yes, sir. Is it true that there are police officers stationed outside both Mrs. Marshall's and Tim Hardy's hospital rooms, and can you say why?"

"I can verify that there are officers stationed outside all three of their rooms. And no, I can't say why other than I assume it reflects an abundance of caution. Next question. Yes, Adam MacKenzie."

"Adam MacKenzie, *Chicago Tribune*. Mr. Trujillo, my sources confirm that the US Secret Service is now protecting the candidate and his wife. Mr. Marshall's campaign rejected an earlier offer from the Secret Service. Is this change of heart related to yesterday's events?"

Trujillo looked exasperated. "Ladies and gentlemen, I am not going to discuss the whys and wherefores of the security arrangements that are presently in place—I'm sure you understand. Adam, I can confirm that yesterday we did request Secret Service protection for the campaign. But I cannot comment on whether or not that request was related to yesterday's events. Do you have a follow-up?"

"Yes, sir. My sources are also claiming that the NTSB investigators working on the crash of Southwest Flight 1356 are currently pursuing the theory that a bomb brought the flight down just before it took off. The presence of FBI agents on the scene tends to corroborate that theory. Can you comment on that?"

"No, Adam, I cannot comment on it because I have not been briefed on any aspect of the crash investigation. I know that the NTSB is on the scene, and doubtless they are examining all possibilities. The NTSB plays very close to the vest on its accident investigations—for good reasons—and it might be months before we know anything for sure. It is quite likely that with your sources you will know before I do."

The press conference lasted another twenty minutes. Most of the reporters asked variations of the same questions previously asked, hoping to squeeze additional information out of Mike Trujillo.

Chapter 16

> THE SOBER PEOPLE OF AMERICA ARE WEARY OF THE FLUCTUATING POLICY WHICH HAS DIRECTED THE PUBLIC COUNCILS. THEY HAVE SEEN WITH REGRET AND INDIGNATION THAT SUDDEN CHANGES AND LEGISLATIVE INTERFERENCES, IN CASES AFFECTING PERSONAL RIGHTS, BECOME JOBS IN THE HANDS OF ENTERPRISING AND INFLUENTIAL SPECULATORS, AND SNARES TO THE MORE-INDUSTRIOUS AND LESS-INFORMED PART OF THE COMMUNITY. THEY HAVE SEEN, TOO, THAT ONE LEGISLATIVE INTERFERENCE IS BUT THE FIRST LINK OF A LONG CHAIN OF REPETITIONS, EVERY SUBSEQUENT INTERFERENCE BEING NATURALLY PRODUCED BY THE EFFECTS OF THE PRECEDING. THEY VERY RIGHTLY INFER, THEREFORE, THAT SOME THOROUGH REFORM IS WANTING, WHICH WILL BANISH SPECULATIONS ON PUBLIC MEASURES, INSPIRE A GENERAL PRUDENCE AND INDUSTRY, AND GIVE A REGULAR COURSE TO THE BUSINESS OF SOCIETY.
>
> *James Madison, Federalist #44*

Late Saturday morning, September 24, 2016

Joshua Cummings stepped into Marshall's hospital room. His boss was trussed up in a rat's nest of tubes, wires, and bandages. Carlos Estrada was seated next to the bed, the bulge under his suit coat giving away the fact that he was armed. Two Secret Service agents stood outside the door.

Marshall grinned a lopsided smile, as the left side of his face was stiff with stitches and bandages. Cummings evaluated the scene and said dryly, "Next time you two need to switch seats before the plane takes off. You," he said, pointing at Estrada, "are supposed to be protecting him. How did you get out of this without a scratch, while your boss looks like Frankenstein?"

"Just lucky, I guess," Estrada replied, grinning at Cummings.

Cummings snorted, and sat down next to the bed. "How are you feeling, Hank?"

"Folded, spindled, and mutilated. Other than that, fine. And very thankful. Does anyone know what happened to the aircraft?"

"The media has the rumor mill grinding out everything from reasonable ideas to wild-eyed conspiracy theories: a tire blew, the left-side gear collapsed, a bomb did it, the pilot cried *Allahu Akbar* shortly before whipping the plane to the left—pick your poison. One moonbat is actually claiming the Republican Party wanted you out of the race, as though the Repubs would sacrifice an entire jetliner and all its passengers just to win an election—it's a ridiculous slander. Most of the reporting would read like tabloid journalism if it weren't for the fact the plane actually did crash. It will probably be quite some time before it's all sorted out," speculated Cummings.

"I know I heard an explosion before we started pirouetting around the airport," Estrada asserted. "I've been around enough ordnance popping off to recognize the sound of explosives. In my opinion it was a bomb."

"NTSB interview you?" Cummings asked.

"Not yet."

"They will be soon, I'm sure." Cummings turned back to his boss. "Have you heard the news from Denver, Hank?" he asked.

"Yeah. Talked to Conner about an hour ago. Sounds like Haley is improving but not yet conscious. Thank God, at least her condition is going in the right direction," he sighed, his voice cracking slightly.

"We're all thankful this morning—for you, Haley, Carlos, and Tim," Josh Cummings affirmed. "We could have lost all of you on the same day but the Lord spared us that. I've got some news on Tim but we can talk about that in a minute, other than to say he's still in ICU but the prognosis looks positive for him.

"I hate to bring this up now, sir, with all that has happened, but you are still in a campaign to win the presidency and the calendar won't stop advancing simply because we've been dealt a difficult hand. What do you want to do?"

"I know, Josh. Been thinking about the same thing this morning. But I'm not going to decide unilaterally. Haley and I will make that decision together in consultation with you, Buford, and the other senior staff. I talked to Mike Trujillo earlier this morning and told him to hold a press conference announcing that we're not suspending the campaign at the present time. For now we continue as though nothing has happened—full steam ahead. Did you complete the ad shoot this morning?"

"I did. If you decide to keep going the ad will be ready on schedule."

"Book it and roll with it. Even if we pull out of the race, the ad's got a good message."

Josh tapped an entry into the to-do list he kept on his iPhone. "Okay. But we've got to get ahead of the media and make sure that all statements from the campaign are coordinated. If you and Haley decide to stay in it, we should announce your VP pick soon and keep you in the news cycle."

"Josh, I don't want to make political hay out of this tragedy," Marshall said sharply.

"Nor do I, sir. You didn't engineer this and you were very nearly a victim of it. You and Carlos could have been killed. But it is what it is—we're in a political campaign, Hank, and one of the goals of the campaign is to stay on page one above the fold. We strategized a couple of months ago to make the big push in October. For good or ill you've been handed a legitimate opportunity to do that. If you still believe in your agenda for America, then I respectfully submit that if you fail to use this opportunity you're working at cross-purposes with yourself."

"Mr. Marshall, may I offer an opinion?" asked Carlos carefully. The burly security chief hesitated to offer a political opinion when his assigned role was protection.

"Certainly, Carlos. I'd value your opinion in this matter," replied Marshall.

"Well, sir, if this turns out to be a bomb—and I'm confident it will—then you were probably the primary target. Someone wants you out of this race bad enough to kill you. Proverbs 26:27 says, *He who digs a pit will fall into it, and he who rolls a stone, it will come back on him*. Someone dug a pit for you, sir, but if this keeps you in the news during October then they will have fallen into their own pit. You didn't make this thing happen, sir, but you can turn it to good."

"Carlos, I can't believe someone would be willing to bring down an entire airliner carrying more than one hundred souls, just to kill me. I can't agree with your theory because you and I weren't even supposed to *be* on that flight," Marshall insisted. "The only reason we were is because Haley had a bad accident."

Carlos shrugged. "True—I had not thought of that. But I still believe that this is a legitimate opportunity for you to get your message out to a wider audience."

Marshall turned back to his campaign manager. "I'm not turning this into a campaign event and I don't want anyone else to, either. I want a news lock-down. However, we will continue with our plans for the October push and the veep announcement. We'll try to hold the media news cycle based on our original plans. But no one speaks to the press except Trujillo, you, or me. No one! Have Mike gather the headquarters group and emphasize that." Marshall grimaced with pain as he shifted his position on his bed.

"Done." Cummings tapped a few more things into his iPhone, and then asked, "What about your schedule?"

"Cancel everything through Wednesday. I want to get back to Haley, and I don't want to be dragging an IV bag around. Now, Josh, you said you had some news on Tim."

"Oh, yeah," Cummings remembered as he slipped his phone into his pocket. "Tim is, of course, still in St. Anthony's

ICU and thankfully his condition continues to improve. But Carlos got a call this morning from the Golden PD—someone tried to murder Tim last night. Carlos and I decided it would be best if you didn't learn of this until the three of us could discuss it together."

"Murder him? Poor Tim—it just goes from bad to worse! What happened?"

"Last night a man posing as a doctor got into Tim's room and loaded his IV bag with enough morphine to kill an elephant. A nurse walked in on him just as he was finishing. The guy took off but the cops caught him and took him into custody. He's completely clammed up—won't even give them his name. He was carrying a Boeing Black cellphone. The police are trying to get a court order to hack his phone, hoping it will provide clues about why Tim was a target."

"Good luck with that," Estrada said.

"Why do you say that?" Cummings asked.

"The Boeing Black employs state of the art encryption and biometric authentication. They'll still be trying to break into that thing long after this election is over."

****

"Daddy!" Lucy cried as Byron Gillespie walked into her room at the Loyola University Trauma Center. She broke into tears and hugged her dad tightly. "I am so glad to see you. Oh, Daddy, it was terrifying. I can't believe I survived the crash."

"Baby, I'm so glad you're okay. I was so worried about you. I couldn't believe the news when I heard your flight went down. I was afraid I'd lost you—after losing your mother I wouldn't be able to handle it. When Southwest called to say you'd survived—well, I confess, sweetie, I bawled like a baby I was so relieved. How are you, Lucy, really?"

"I'm okay, Daddy. I've got this broken arm and I'll be wearing a cast for six weeks or so, but they said it was a clean break and should heal just fine. They tested me last night for internal injuries, but I guess I passed because the doctor came in about ten minutes ago and said they're going to release me. I've got bruises everywhere and I'm really sore, but other than that I'm fine. I feel so lucky just to be alive."

A nurse's assistant came into the room with a bag of clothes and the few personal items she'd had when carried off the airplane. "Here, honey, you can get dressed. Sign these release papers, and then I'll be back in a few minutes with a wheelchair to take you down."

"A wheelchair? There's no need, ma'am, I can walk just fine," Lucy protested.

"Hospital policy, dearie. I don't make the rules, I just have to live with 'em, and so do you. I'll be back in ten minutes."

Gillespie stepped out of the room while his daughter dressed. A few minutes later the woman returned with a wheelchair.

Lucy complained, "Please, ma'am, I feel silly. I can walk just fine."

The lady merely looked from Lucy to the wheelchair with raised eyebrows. Lucy rolled her eyes and muttered, "Okaaaay."

Gillespie asked the woman, "Is there anything that says I can't roll her down?"

"No, that would be fine. Just don't let her out of the wheelchair until you get to the front door," the nurse's assistant said firmly.

Gillespie winked and saluted, "Got it."

As they were rolling to the elevator, Lucy said, "Oh, wait, Daddy! We can't leave yet. I need to see if Mr. Marshall is okay. He's the man I told you about on the phone. His bodyguard probably saved my life. I was so frightened I couldn't move and there was this fire and everything, and his bodyguard carried me out of the airplane."

"Sweetie, if he's a candidate for president they won't let us get within fifty feet of him," objected Gillespie. The last person he wanted to see was Henry Marshall.

"Maybe not, but he was really nice. Can't we please just try?" she pleaded.

Saying no to his daughter was not something Gillespie ever

had much luck doing, so he wheeled her over to a nurses' station.

"Ma'am," said Lucy, "I was one of the passengers on Southwest Flight 1356. I was seated next to Henry Marshall when we crashed. I'd like to check on him before I leave the hospital. Could you give me his room number?"

The busy nurse brought up the record on her terminal but didn't notice it was flagged with a "no visitors" indicator. She said, "He was moved out of Critical Care this morning. You can find him in Room 4385 in the Intermediate Care Unit. Take the east elevators to the fourth floor, and follow the signs."

As the two approached the room, the Secret Service agents outside the door tensed and moved to stop them. One agent put up his hands, "I'm sorry folks, no visitors allowed."

"Oh, please," begged Lucy. "I was seated right next to Mr. Marshall on the flight, and his bodyguard saved my life. I just wanted to check on him and thank him."

"Sorry, ma'am. We can't allow it."

Lucy and Gillespie were turning away when Carlos Estrada emerged from the room. Hank had heard the request and recognized the young girl's voice, and dispatched Estrada to get her past the Secret Service.

"It's okay, gentlemen," Carlos said, smiling at the young woman. "She doesn't look too dangerous," he added, chuckling and remembering what Hank had said to him the day before.

"They never do, sir," murmured one of the agents as they stood down.

"Lucy, I'm glad to see you up and around. Yesterday was a little harrowing, wasn't it?" Carlos stooped and gave the young lady a hug. "And this must be your dad?" he asked, turning to Gillespie. Up until that moment he'd ignored the man standing next to the girl, but immediately recognized the fellow when he faced him.

"BG! How are you, man? Great to see you!" Carlos grasped Gillespie in a bear hug that would have crushed a normal man.

"Mex!" Gillespie cried, using the nickname Estrada had been given as a SEAL. "What on earth are you doing here? Last time I saw you was at Little Creek when you left the team. Thought you were down in New Mexico trying to teach civvies how to shoot straight."

"Yeah, I was. Now I'm chief of security for the Marshall campaign. So what are you doing, BG? I heard you got out a couple of years ago."

"He's doing secret things at the State Department, aren't you, Daddy?" chirped Lucy. She was proud of her father and his accomplishments. Of Gillespie's identity as Ares, Lucy knew nothing.

"Sounds like you're still in the thick of it, Byron," said Carlos. Gillespie just grinned and shrugged, but said nothing.

"Bring 'em in here, Carlos," Henry Marshall hollered from his room. He'd heard the reunion and wanted to know what it was all about. "I want to see Lucy and meet her dad!"

"It's okay, guys. Gillespie and I served in the SEALs together," Carlos said to the agents. "He's one of us."

As they entered the room together, Carlos noticed Gillespie's left cheek twitching. The nervous tic was a characteristic Gillespie's platoon on SEAL Team 8 had observed. Right before going into action, Byron's left cheek would start to twitch. It was so predictable some of his fellow operators started calling him *Twitchy*, a nickname Gillespie despised. Very few had the courage to say it to his face.

Gillespie rolled Lucy into the hospital room. It was the first time Lucy had seen Marshall since the crash. She gasped when she saw the stitches and bandages on his head, and all the tubes and wires disappearing under the sheet.

"Mr. Marshall, what happened to you?" she asked before thinking about it.

His face was discolored by a combination of bruises and the antiseptic they'd painted on his cheek shortly before stitching up the laceration. The black stitches following the cut up the left side of his face looked like a big black zipper. Cummings' characterization of him as Frankenstein was not too far from the truth. "Darned if I know," Marshall replied.

"One minute I'm talking to this gorgeous young thing seated next to me, and the next thing I know I'm in this hospital bed. I thought you'd slugged me, like maybe I'd said something offensive. Figured you must have a mighty mean right hook," Marshall chuckled.

She rolled her eyes, "Oh, Mr. Marshall, quit teasing me! But really, sir, you do look terrible. How do you feel?" Lucy inquired, youthful concern written on her face.

"A little knocked around, I guess, but I must feel better than I look," he said with a wink.

"Oh! I'm so sorry! I didn't mean—" she exclaimed, flushing.

"Never mind, Lucy. Now tell me how you're feeling, young lady. What are you doing in that wheelchair? I hope you didn't injure your legs," he said kindly.

"I'm feeling fine. I have a broken arm and I'm a little bruised, but otherwise fine. They're discharging me and won't let me walk out under my own steam. There's nothing at all wrong with my legs. It's really kind of embarrassing."

"I'm so glad you're okay. What are you going to do about your interview?"

"Oh, gosh, I'd forgotten all about it. I'll call them and reschedule. Perhaps they can see me on Monday."

"I hope so. Maybe you can come see Haley and me if you move to Denver. We have a daughter and a couple of sons your age. Here," he said, scribbling on a piece of paper, "this is our family email address—both Haley and I check that address regularly. Please do keep in contact, but don't share that address. Now, why don't you introduce me to your dad?"

"Dad, this is Henry Marshall. Mr. Marshall, this is my dad, Byron Gillespie."

As Carlos watched the two men talk, he observed two things that perplexed him. One was that—in contrast to his daughter—Byron was remarkably reserved as he conversed with Marshall. Civil, but nothing more than civil. The other was that the former SEAL's cheek continued to twitch. It bothered Carlos, but he didn't know what it might mean.

****

It had been a long night and a longer day. Roland Yates had not slept in over thirty hours. Late Saturday afternoon he gathered his Go Team in the conference room of the old FedEx hangar, along with the FBI's Evidence Response Team (ERT), and the Boeing and Southwest representatives.

"Okay, ladies and gentlemen. I want to remind you that the clock is ticking," Yates said to the gathered group. "We have a crash investigation that has become an FBI criminal investigation. They need good data and analysis as soon as we can provide it, because we don't want that trail to grow cold. We also have an airport manager who is caught between us, a Board of Directors, the airlines, and thousands of passengers who want to fly in and out of Midway—we've got to get this airport back in action as soon as we reasonably can. And then we've got grieving families, some of whom have already lawyered up, who are wanting answers. And that's not even to mention the insurance companies.

"You've probably all heard by now that it's been verified that a bomb brought the plane down. The ion mobility spectrometer detected trace amounts of RDX, probably some form of Composition C, most likely C4. We've already sent some materials to the FBI Explosive's Unit for more in-depth analysis. I'm hoping to hear back from them sometime on Monday.

"Let's go around the table and share what else we've got so far. Sarah, what's the status of bagging and tagging?"

Sarah Dalton, the FBI ERT team leader, pushed her glasses higher on the bridge of her nose and studied a few scribbled notes on her legal pad. "Rollie, we're almost done. The entire site was photographed in high-res from multiple angles before anything was touched. After we laid out the grid, each grid square was extensively photographed before we began cataloging. As of right now, all debris farther than thirty meters from the aircraft has been recovered. The final grids are in a thirty-meter square around the fuselage itself, and my people are working on them now. We've got some equipment on site to remove the larger pieces. I think we'll be ready to move the fuselage to the hangar by midnight."

"Great work, Sarah, your people are very efficient. Have we found anything that amounts to a smoking gun?" Yates asked.

"Well, the short answer to your question is no, not among the evidence that's been recovered. But we really haven't had a chance to analyze the data yet. The debris is being reassembled in the hangar in the relative positions in which we found it, tagged with the bearing and distance from the fuselage. By tomorrow evening we'll have something more solid for you."

Yates turned to Pete Allander. Allander was the Go Team's black-box specialist. He'd been working with the Boeing engineer and the Southwest rep, who was himself pilot-certified for the left-hand seat of the Boeing 737-800. The three had been working to create a computer animation detailing the aircraft's movements from the take-off roll through the crash, along with the flight crew's actions and responses. "Pete, what's your progress?"

"The black box is in great shape. Preliminary indications show a textbook take-off roll. Pilot conversation is strictly by the book, there's no sign of any problem until a loud bang can be heard on the cockpit voice recorder. At that point, pilot interaction with the controls ceases until about ten seconds later when the copilot kills the right-hand engine. We don't know why the pilots are essentially hands-off during that ten-second gap. There's no evidence that the pilot in command interacts with any of the flight controls after the explosion is heard."

"I've been told he was unconscious when removed from the plane," Yates said.

"Well, that would explain it. Anyway, we should have completed our initial analysis of the data by Monday. As it stands right now, there is no indication of any problem in the cockpit. Both men were flying by the book, very professional."

"Cass," Yates asked, addressing his question to the Boeing engineer, "although the IMS has probably rendered this question irrelevant, I'm going to ask it anyway: is there any aircraft system or part, forward of the wing but aft of the flight deck, that could explode or detonate under the right circumstances?"

Cass Simpson was a forty-year veteran with Boeing. His knowledge of Boeing commercial aircraft was legendary. Balding in front, he somehow managed to grow enough hair to sport a long gray ponytail. Intense, bright blue eyes set on either side of a hook nose gave him an aquiline appearance. "No, Roland, there's nothing in that part of the aircraft that could produce an explosion like what we've seen on the control tower video. I've examined the fuselage closely. The bulkhead separating the flight deck from the passenger compartment is completely deformed, bowing into the cockpit. The entire left side of the fuselage around the door was breached. We're clearly looking at bomb damage, Roland."

"I have to agree with Cass, Rollie. I examined the jagged hole where the door was supposed to be. The shards of metal are all bent outward, consistent with a blast inside the aircraft. Everything I've seen says bomb." Marty Baxter was the Go Team's airframe specialist.

Sarah spoke up again. "I've also inspected the fuselage around the door, Rollie, and I've got to agree with everyone else. I know we can't announce our findings until the NTSB investigation is done, but it *was* a bomb. I talked to the agent in charge of the field office several hours ago, and he has initiated an investigation on the premise that a criminal act doomed Flight 1356. We just can't afford to let the trail grow cold. We'll try not to get in your way because I know that the NTSB has a job to do, too, just like we do."

"The FBI can expect full cooperation from us, Sarah. We're all on the same page: it was definitely a bomb. Once the lab gets the forensic analysis back to us we'll have more to go on.

"Okay, good work, people. Let's finish the evidence recovery phase, and get that wreck moved inside the hangar," said Yates, closing the meeting.

****

Charity sat in her mother's hospital room, praying. She'd been to the early service at church and when the service let out she raced to the hospital and exchanged places with the twins so they could attend the late service.

Haley had not regained consciousness since the accident but her vital signs had been steadily strengthening since the day before when the doctors had relieved the pressure on her brain caused by hemorrhaging. The brain scan they had done earlier in the morning revealed increasing levels of activity, and the medical staff was at a loss as to why she'd not emerged from the coma. They feared that there might be more extensive damage than they had so far detected.

A subdued alarm on the IV stand sounded, signaling the need to change bags. After a moment a nurse entered, silenced the alarm, and replaced the bag. She looked at the girl and asked gently, "How are you doing, honey?" It was not a rote question, but came from a heart both tenderized and toughened by watching years of healing and death up close.

Charity smiled wanly. "Okay, I guess. I'm a little scared."

The nurse nodded. "That's understandable. I've been praying for your mom. I know the Lord will do what's best for her—and for you."

"He will," Charity agreed. "And thanks for praying. It's the waiting I'm having trouble with. I know God will do what's best. I just don't know yet what 'best' looks like."

The nurse wrote something on the chart and then turned back to Charity. "I know what you mean. Sometimes my idea of what's best and God's idea are two entirely different things."

"That's what I fear," Charity said, voice trembling. She wiped a lone tear from the corner of her eye.

The nurse sat on the window sill. "Charity, have you ever been to the Governor's Palace in Colonial Williamsburg?"

The girl brightened up. "Yes, I have. Our whole family went four or five years ago when we took a vacation to Virginia."

"Did you get to do the hedge maze in the palace gardens?"

"It was wonderful," Charity said, remembering. "We had a lot of fun trying to get to the center. It was harder than I thought it would be."

"Sometimes life is like that maze, Charity. We're confronted with left and right turns and blind alleys. We might think we're headed toward our goals, only to find we've been going the wrong way all along. But the Lord has a bird's eye view—looking down on the maze from above, so to speak. And He is the designer of the maze. He knows the end from the beginning, and His ways are perfect. He knows exactly what it will take to accomplish His good purposes in our lives. We just have to trust His goodness and His sovereign control. He always does right."

Charity wiped away another tear. "Thank you," she said. "That was exactly what I needed to hear."

****

On Sunday afternoon, Grady Wilson turned on the lights of the large conference room at the Golden PD headquarters and started the coffee pot perking. Ten minutes later people started arriving for a briefing on the Hardy case.

Jim Stewart arrived first, along with one of the Secret Service agents assigned to the campaign. "Detective Wilson, pleased to meet you. I'm Jim Stewart from the Marshall campaign security staff and this is Avery Yoder, Secret Service. Carlos Estrada is still in Chicago, so he sent me."

"Stewart, Yoder," Wilson acknowledged, shaking their hands. "Coffee's ready if you want some. Help yourself, and find a seat."

SJ Bergman came in next, and nodded at Wilson. He walked over to Stewart and Yoder and introduced himself.

"Samuel Bergman, Jr., did you say?" asked Stewart, his eyes narrowing. "Who did your daddy work for, son?"

"CIA. He's retired now. He was an analyst specializing in the Soviet Union."

Stewart grinned. "You've got to be kidding me," he laughed, shaking his head. "That means your momma is named Evelyn, her maiden name was Stinson, and she worked for the NSA."

"How could you possibly know that?" asked SJ, surprised.

"Oh, your dad and I worked together on an unusual case about thirty years ago, a little dust-up with the Sovs that never made the papers. It was your mom that provided the information that finally broke the case. In fact, that was how your dad and mom met. Son of a gun! Small world! Pleased to work with you, SJ, and pass my regards on to your mom and dad."

After a few more people came in, Wilson started the meeting.

"Gentlemen, on this past Friday afternoon, there was a hit-and-run accident on Jackson Street. Multiple witnesses claim that the victim, Tim Hardy, appeared to be targeted by someone driving a white Escalade, and we believe those witnesses are credible. Hardy was taken to St. Anthony's where he is now, in critical condition. Later on Friday evening another attempt was made on his life at the hospital, by an assailant posing as a doctor. We have the suspect in custody, but he's not cooperating at all. We had to book him as John Doe because he refused to give us his name. We tried to interrogate him, but he asked for a lawyer as soon as we started, so that went nowhere.

"The FBI's Next Generation Identification services link was down Friday night when he was arrested, but I was finally able to run his prints yesterday and it found him on the civil side. His name is Mark Atkinson, he's an American citizen with no prior criminal record. Atkinson retired from the US Navy SEALs in 2009, and is believed to have been working as a paramilitary mercenary since then, based out of the Cayman Islands. So far we've had no luck getting Cayman officials to cooperate with us, but we expect they will, eventually.

"On Friday, a white Escalade was reported stolen. We believe that it might be the car used in the hit-and-run. As of yet, we haven't located it. However, this morning we did find an abandoned rental car three blocks from St. Anthony's.

Fingerprints have conclusively tied the car to Atkinson. It contained a carry-on bag with clothes, toiletries, and various other items, including a round-trip ticket from the Caymans to Denver. He arrived on the 20th, the flight back is an open date. We're submitting several items for DNA testing. I believe when that Escalade shows up we'll be able to tie it to him as well, or at least to someone working with him.

"The complicating factor in all of this, which explains why we've got FBI, Secret Service, and representatives from the Marshall campaign all here is that the victim, Hardy, works for the Marshall campaign—he's their IT director. If in fact he was targeted by the driver of that Escalade, then the assassination attempt on him at the hospital might mean that he knows something that someone else wants to keep secret."

Detective Barna spoke up. "There's another equally plausible, much simpler explanation that has nothing to do with the Marshall campaign. Perhaps the hit-and-run was a simple revenge killing for, I don't know, a drug deal gone bad? The assailant realizes that at the last second before impact, Hardy recognizes him. So he tracks him down to the hospital and tries to finish the job because he doesn't want Hardy to finger him as the driver of the hit-and-run if he survives."

"No," Jim Stewart and SJ said in unison. They looked at each other and chuckled. Stewart motioned to SJ. "You first."

SJ grinned, "Thanks." He turned to Barna, "First of all, guys like Atkinson never do work like this for themselves, because there's no money in it. They go for top dollar and they never take risks without the promise of a big payoff. So you can be sure Atkinson is working for someone else."

"Bingo," Stewart muttered under his breath, nodding at the young FBI agent.

SJ continued. "Second, you know the stakes have to be really big. If a crook wanted to hire someone to kill Hardy, he'd just find a local thug. Atkinson is probably pulling down something in the five-figure range for this killing, which means whoever is writing the checks has really big reasons to see that the job is done. No, I've got to agree with Detective Wilson, it probably is somehow connected to the Marshall campaign."

"I agree with SJ," Stewart affirmed. "Atkinson is someone's asset, he's not an independent actor. He's not going to fly here from the Cayman Islands to do a job like this unless someone is paying him big bucks. Former SEALs who are selling their services are much too expensive for a simple hit."

Yoder asked, "Detective Wilson, would you include Mrs. Marshall's accident in your theory about a possible assault on the Marshall campaign?"

"No, not at the present time. Both the Marshall boys have been interviewed, and it appears that what happened to Mrs. Marshall was purely accidental. It almost seems more a case of the folk proverb that trouble comes in threes."

****

Charity stood looking out the window. It was nearing dusk late Sunday afternoon. In the distant southwest, Mt. Evans was wreathed in dark clouds. As a Colorado girl who'd spent a lot of time in the mountains, she knew there'd be snow squalls at the summit. The clouds parted momentarily, and the setting sun turned the mountain top into a silvery orange pastel. "The glory of God on display," she murmured, using an expression she'd often heard her father say. It was one of her favorites.

Buford and Sandy Jackson were sitting on the other side of the bed, each with their nose in a book. They'd been with Haley almost continuously since being informed of her accident. It was a great comfort to the kids—the Jacksons were more like grandparents than family friends.

"Baby?"

Charity whirled around. Her mom was looking at her and smiling. "Mom! Oh, Mom, you're awake!" She ran to Haley's bed and grasped her hand. "Oh, Momma," she cried, and began to sob. Sandy came around the bed and hugged the young woman until she had regained control. Haley continued to smile but was unable to say anything else. A tear trickled down her cheek.

Buford ran for a nurse, as they were under strict instructions to notify the staff at the first sign of consciousness. Soon Charity and the Jacksons were sent to the waiting room as the medical team evaluated Haley's condition.

Chapter 17

THE POWERS DELEGATED BY THE PROPOSED
CONSTITUTION TO THE FEDERAL GOVERNMENT ARE
FEW AND DEFINED. THOSE WHICH ARE TO REMAIN IN
THE STATE GOVERNMENTS ARE NUMEROUS AND
INDEFINITE. THE FORMER WILL BE EXERCISED
PRINCIPALLY ON EXTERNAL OBJECTS, AS WAR,
PEACE, NEGOTIATION, AND FOREIGN COMMERCE;
WITH WHICH LAST THE POWER OF TAXATION WILL,
FOR THE MOST PART, BE CONNECTED. THE POWERS
RESERVED TO THE SEVERAL STATES WILL EXTEND
TO ALL THE OBJECTS WHICH, IN THE ORDINARY
COURSE OF AFFAIRS, CONCERN THE LIVES,
LIBERTIES, AND PROPERTIES OF THE PEOPLE, AND
THE INTERNAL ORDER, IMPROVEMENT, AND
PROSPERITY OF THE STATE.

James Madison, Federalist #45

Monday morning, September 26, 2016

Susan Wyatt arranged her notes and then glanced at camera number one as the digital countdown timer on the back wall ticked under fifteen seconds. She was the anchor of ABC's *World News Tonight* and host of the network's popular feature *Campaign 2016 Special Report*, which was just seconds from going live. The timer hit zero and the red ON AIR light blinked on. Susan smiled at the camera.

"Good morning. I'm Susan Wyatt and this is *Campaign 2016 Special Report*. In the studio with me is our usual panel of experts: Rosalyn Jansen-Canford, Democratic political consultant; Thomas Bayfeld, Republican strategist; and Adam MacKenzie, the senior political reporter for the *Chicago*

Tribune. Welcome, panel.

"The news cycle over the weekend has been dominated by a series of shocking tragedies impacting the Marshall campaign. Henry Marshall was going into the weekend with a very solid thirty percent in the RCP national averages, just one point behind Republican Wayne Bushnell. There were rumors of several pending endorsements by high-profile Republicans, and some of those endorsements were expected this very week.

"But on Friday three catastrophes struck what might be a fatal blow to the Marshall campaign. It began with a hit-and-run accident on Friday afternoon in Denver. Tim Hardy, Marshall's IT director, was crossing the street in front of the campaign headquarters when he was struck by a vehicle traveling at high speed. Sources say it appeared the driver of the vehicle was intentionally targeting Hardy. The victim was rushed to the hospital, where he is now in Intensive Care. Not an hour later, Haley Marshall, the candidate's wife, fell down the steps in her home, striking her head. She, too, was rushed to the hospital where she remains in Intensive Care. And finally, while Marshall was returning from Chicago to his family in Denver, his flight crashed during takeoff, resulting in thirty-five fatalities and numerous serious injuries, including a head injury to Marshall himself." Wyatt looked down at her papers and then straight into camera number two. The director smoothly transitioned the feed to the new angle.

"On behalf of the entire ABC news family I want to pause and wish Mr. and Mrs. Marshall and Tim Hardy each a speedy and full recovery. Regardless of where we line up personally on the political spectrum, our hearts and prayers are with you and with the families of those who perished on Flight 1356."

Wyatt turned and looked at her panel. "I cannot think of another campaign in my lifetime that had such a terrible run of bad luck. Have any of you heard of something like this happening in recent memory?"

Jansen-Canford replied, "Well, what immediately springs to my mind is the assassination of Robert Kennedy in 1968 immediately after winning the California Democratic primary.

That was utterly horrific. It robbed the country of a man who was certainly going to be elected president, in my opinion. Of course, none of what has happened to the Marshalls appears to be anything more than an incredible string of bad luck."

"That's not necessarily true, Rosalyn," Adam MacKenzie offered. "My sources indicate that both the NTSB and the FBI have concluded that a bomb caused the crash of Flight 1356. If that is in fact the case it provides a much more sinister interpretation on the events of this weekend."

"Interesting," remarked Wyatt. "What does this mean for the race? Thomas, you first."

Bayfeld removed his glasses, placed them on the table, and looked directly at the anchor. "Susan, I don't see how Marshall continues. In a presidential election year, October is like the last mile of a marathon—everyone goes into the final mile exhausted, but it's in that last mile that the best runners dig deep and pick up the pace. Whatever strength Marshall might have reserved for the final lap has been stolen from him now. His wife is in ICU, he just got out of ICU yesterday, his data-wizard is in ICU—I think he's finished. I think he's got to throw in the towel."

"I agree with Thomas," nodded Rosalyn Jansen-Canford. "It's a tragedy. He mounted a historic campaign, a very solid campaign. Thirty percent of the electorate is taking him very seriously. But he's finished. He can't climb back from this— and it's not his fault. I really don't think he or his family will be able to absorb the rigors of October. He's done."

"You sound almost disappointed, Rosalyn," observed the anchor.

"I am disappointed. Look, you've heard the saying that 'politics stops at the water's edge?' Well, I also believe that politics stops at the Emergency Room. I admit it: Marshall never was a threat to my candidate. But anyone who rejoices at such misfortunes simply for political gain has abandoned some portion of their humanity."

"That was well said, Rosalyn," Bayfeld affirmed. "Couldn't agree more."

"Adam," Susan queried, "what do you think?"

"This has the potential to turn the race upside down, Susan, especially if Marshall drops out. The last RealClearPolitics national poll average puts Hastings at thirty-five percent, Bushnell at thirty-one, and Marshall at thirty, with a small handful of undecideds. You've got to ask the question: who stands to pick up the most voters from Marshall's crowd if he drops out? In my book the answer is clearly Bushnell. If Marshall suspends his campaign I would not be surprised to see those numbers flip, say, within two weeks. We might be looking at RCP averages that place Bushnell in the high forties, maybe even low fifties, Hastings in the low forties, and a large contingent of newly undecided voters."

Rosalyn nodded. "That's true. I think Pamela Hastings has to find a way to woo Marshall voters, or she'll be in deep trouble. Even traditionally blue states could shift red in November. But there is a wild card in this. Marshall is sooo far over to the right that his voters might go Libertarian, or to some other third party. If that's how it falls out we'll see the race between Bushnell and Hastings tighten, but it might not flip."

"And if he doesn't drop out?" Susan asked.

"He will. He's got to," answered Bayfeld. "He's done."

Rosalyn Jansen-Canford nodded. "I agree. He's done."

The anchor looked at Adam. "You agree?"

"Probably," MacKenzie responded carefully. "Probably. But I've covered Marshall for a long time. He's got tremendous strength of character, maybe more than anyone I've ever met. In his lifetime he's already endured quite a bit of suffering and he's come out stronger for it. And politically, for the last several years he's become pretty adept at pulling rabbits out of hats. Dallas Chamberlain learned that, much to his chagrin, and so has Wayne Bushnell. Let's just say that I think he's probably done, but it won't surprise me in the least if he stays in the ring. And if he does—look out. This race could become even closer than it is now."

****

Detective Grady Wilson and Special Agent SJ Bergman stopped at the nurses' station in the ICU unit and displayed their credentials.

"We'd like to ask Timothy Hardy a few questions. Is this a good time to do that?" asked Wilson.

The nurse at the desk frowned. "Is it really necessary right now? In another three days or so he might be doing much better, we might even be able to move him out of ICU."

"Yes, ma'am, it really is," insisted Wilson.

She sighed. "Five minutes?"

"Ten," replied the detective.

"Okay," she said, capitulating. "But no more than ten minutes. I'll be monitoring him from out here. If he begins to look like he's under stress, I'll have to ask you to leave."

Wilson and Bergman walked into the room. Tim Hardy's eyes were shut and he was festooned with an assortment of wires and tubes. Periodic soft beeps sounded from instruments monitoring his heart rate, respiration, and other vital signs.

"Mr. Hardy? Tim?" Grady asked.

Tim's eyelids fluttered briefly, and then his eyes opened. His neck was in a brace, so he was unable to turn his head. His eyes searched the room and then fixed on Wilson.

"Water," he croaked. The detective held the water container to his mouth and put the straw in his lips. Tim sucked on the straw and swallowed a few mouthfuls of water. "Thank you," he said in a stronger voice. "Who are you?"

"I'm Detective Grady Wilson from the Golden PD. This is SJ Bergman from the FBI. We'd like to ask you a few questions."

Tim shut his eyes and said, "Okay. Shoot." *Here it comes,* he thought to himself. *They're going to ask about that stupid battery. Why did I ever get involved in that?*

"Are you aware of how you wound up in the hospital, Mr Hardy?" Grady inquired. He glanced at the monitors—Hardy's heart rate had increased significantly.

"I know I was crossing Jackson Street and was hit by a car," he replied, eyes still shut.

"That's correct. Are you also aware that there was an attempt on your life here in the hospital." Wilson studied the man, looking for a reaction.

Tim's eyes popped open. "What?"

"Someone tried to kill you right here in this room. Were you aware of that?"

"No, I was not."

Grady observed perspiration on Hardy's forehead. "Do you know of any reason why someone would want to kill you, Mr. Hardy?"

Tim shut his eyes and didn't answer. Grady looked at Bergman and raised his eyebrows. He turned back to Hardy. "Mr. Hardy, we're trying to help you. Is there a reason why someone would want you dead?"

Hardy compressed his lips and kept his eyes tightly shut.

"You leave us no choice, sir. When I leave this hospital I'm headed for the District Attorney's office. We're going to seek a court order to search your house and place of business, and a subpoena to examine your banking records. And I'll obtain both, Mr. Hardy, because the average law-abiding citizen does not have people lined up to murder him, as you seem to. We'll get our answers, Mr. Hardy, but it's going to look bad that you refused to cooperate."

Wilson motioned with his head and Bergman turned to walk out of the room.

"It was a battery," Tim said weakly.

Both men turned around. "What?" asked Wilson.

"A stupid battery. Oh, dear God, why did I do it?" Tim said hoarsely.

Wilson made sure his pocket recorder was still going, and asked gently, "Help us out, Tim. What are you talking about?"

Hardy began to cry. "I replaced Mr. Marshall's laptop battery. I think they were trying to get rid of me because I replaced his battery. I did it for the money. Oh, God, I should have known better." He began sobbing so violently the bed shook. A nurse rushed in and shooed the law officers out of the room, closing the door behind them.

Wilson and Bergman walked out of the ICU unit and

stepped into an empty waiting room.

"What was that all about?" Bergman asked.

"That was the break we needed," asserted Wilson. "And it adds up. When the paramedics were scraping Hardy off of Jackson Street they said he kept babbling about a battery. Apparently somebody paid him to replace the battery in Marshall's laptop with a substitute they provided."

"Ah. And what if that battery was not just a battery?" asked Bergman rhetorically.

"Exactly. Call your counterpart in Chicago. Ask if they've found Marshall's laptop. Alert them to the possibility the bomb was in the laptop. Then let's go talk to the DA. We need to get that court order and that subpoena."

****

Later that morning the white Escalade was found. An alert Sam's Club employee who worked on the loading dock had noticed it parked behind the Arvada store since Friday night, and had mentioned it to his supervisor, whose wife worked for the Arvada PD. Damage to the grill and the windshield wipers verified that it was the vehicle used in the hit-and-run. Brown hairs matching Mark Atkinson's hair color were found on the driver's side headrest, and were sent for DNA testing.

****

Special Agent Sarah Dalton interviewed Carlos Estrada for fifteen minutes in one of the hospital's private consultation rooms. After she wrapped up the interview her phone vibrated.

"Special Agent Dalton."

"Dalton, this is Bergman in Denver. I just got some solid information that might affect your investigation. Henry Marshall's IT director survived two assassination attempts on Friday, one of which put him in the hospital. There's a strong chance that the attempts on his life mean someone is trying to cover their tracks. We were finally able to interview him a few minutes ago. Apparently someone bribed him to replace the battery in Marshall's laptop with a substitute they provided. There might be a connection with the bombing of Flight 1356. For instance—what if the bomb was in the laptop battery?"

Sarah thought for a moment. "That's an interesting theory, SJ. I'll tell my ERT to locate Marshall's laptop—or what's left of it. Thanks for the tip." She terminated the call and entered Marshall's room, showing her credentials to the Secret Service agents at the door.

After some initial questions, Sarah asked, "Mr. Marshall, have there been any threats directed at you or your campaign?"

"Other than a grab bag of dirty tricks, no. Why do you ask, Agent Dalton?" Marshall asked.

"Flight 1356 was brought down with a bomb, Mr. Marshall —we now know that. We're following up leads trying to establish a motive for the bombing. Of everyone on the manifest you are the highest profile passenger. We're trying to ascertain whether you were the primary target."

"I couldn't have been the primary target, Agent Dalton. I wasn't even supposed to be on that flight," Marshall insisted.

"Oh?" she asked, raising her eyebrows. "Please explain."

"I was not supposed to return to Denver until Saturday evening. I was scheduled for a campaign ad shoot on Saturday morning here in Chicago. The only reason I was on Flight 1356 at all is because my wife had a serious accident at home —I was rushing back to Denver to be with her in the hospital. No one could have known in advance that I'd be on the plane."

Dalton scribbled in her notebook. She looked up when she was done. "Makes sense," she admitted. "Where were you supposed to be at 9:00 p.m.?"

"In my hotel room skyping with Buford Jackson, my chief of staff. That was put on my schedule the same day the whole trip to Chicago was scheduled—several weeks in advance."

Dalton paused while a nurse entered and checked

Marshall's IV. After the nurse left, the agent continued. "So you were supposed to be in your hotel room at 9:00 p.m., and the only reason you were on that plane was because of your wife's accident?"

"Correct."

"Where is your laptop, sir? May I see it?" asked Dalton.

"I don't have it. I didn't come off the plane with it. I assume it's still at the airport."

"Did you check it as baggage?"

"No, it was one of my carry-ons." Hank took a sip of his water.

"So was it in the overhead bin?"

"Yes, I must have put it in there. I wasn't planning to use it on the flight home," Hank affirmed.

"Why not?" the agent asked, pen poised over her notebook.

"I was exhausted and worried about my wife. I just didn't ha—wait, no, it *wasn't* in the overhead bin. Now I remember —I tried to put it in there but it wouldn't fit. A flight attendant took it for me and put it in the closet up by the door of the airplane."

Dalton raised her eyebrows again and scribbled more in her notebook. "Had you used your laptop earlier in the evening? Was it working?"

"Yes. I was using it in the hotel. Why are you interested in my laptop?" Marshall asked, puzzled.

She ignored the question. "Do you know anything about a battery being replaced in your laptop before the trip to Chicago?"

"No, I don't. Oh, wait, yes, I do. When I entered my office on Friday morning my IT director was replacing the battery in my laptop."

"Did he say why?" Dalton asked.

"He said that the network management client had indicated the battery was about to fail."

Dalton wrote that down and made a mental note to call Bergman and have him check the logs on Marshall's network.

"Why are you asking about my laptop, Agent Dalton?"

asked Marshall, eyes narrowing.

She ignored the question again and asked, "Who knew your schedule?"

"No. No more questions until you answer mine. Why are you asking about my laptop?"

Marshall's steely stare and the set of his chin made it obvious to Dalton that he wouldn't back down easily. She set her notebook and pen down and looked directly at Marshall. "Did you set up the network at your campaign headquarters? Did you write the code for your website? Do you order the office supplies for your headquarters? No, of course not. You have hired others to do those jobs: a computer guy, a web developer, an office coordinator, right?"

Marshall nodded, "Sure. That's right," he acknowledged, puzzled.

"So did you tell the computer guy how to do his job—like how to set up his backup software or how to install the database software? Did you tell your office coordinator what office supply store he or she was to get supplies from, or did you simply get out of the way and let them do their job?" she asked, obviously irritated.

"I let them do their job," he acknowledged contritely, knowing where this was going. "I didn't tell them how."

"Well, sir, no disrespect intended, but will you please get the devil out of the way and let me do my job? There is only one FBI Special Agent in this room, and as far as I know she is not you. I cannot answer your questions at this point lest it jeopardize our investigation. I can assure you that you are not a suspect. You are, however, a person of interest simply because you might know things that will help us solve this crime. That's all I can say. Now can we please get on with it? Answer my questions: who knew your schedule?"

He shrugged. "Sorry. I guess I am used to being in command and having others answer my questions. Didn't mean to obstruct the process." He paused, and then repeated the question: "Who knew my schedule? All my senior people can see my schedule on their computers."

"Does that include Hardy?"

"Yes."

"Thank you, sir, I have no further questions at the present time."

****

Late Monday afternoon Marshall was released from Loyola. In the end his injuries amounted to bruises, a concussion, and a deep contusion on the left side of his face from which he'd lost a great deal of blood. But he had no internal injuries and no broken bones.

Carly Johnson booked the three men, Marshall, Estrada, and Cummings, on the first available flight out of Midway, which had reopened at noon on Sunday. Cummings firmly informed the penny-pinching Johnson that it was to be a first-class booking for all three plus the two Secret Service agents.

The airline was providing a restricted VIP lounge for all victims of Flight 1356 and their families where they could wait for boarding and not be subjected to stares and questions. When the boarding call came they filed out of the lounge and entered the first-class line. Someone cried out, "Look, there's Henry Marshall!" The boarding area erupted in spontaneous applause and cheers but the ovation wasn't about politics—it was about survival.

Marshall smiled and waved, and called out, "Thank you! God bless you!" and then disappeared down the jetway. News traveled fast, however, and when the five landed in Denver there was a mob of reporters and cameras just beyond the TSA security cordon.

"Oh no," Cummings groaned when he saw the assembled group of journalists.

"It's okay, Josh. I have to face them sometime and this is as good a time as any. I'll give them ten or fifteen minutes."

With Cummings on one side, Estrada on the other, and the two agents taking up positions on either flank, Hank stopped when he got to the crowd.

"Good evening, ladies and gentlemen. I'll make a brief

statement and then I'll take questions. First, let me thank the good people of Chicago, and especially the emergency responders, firemen, medical personnel, police, and security for their excellence and professionalism in handling a difficult situation. I also appreciate the great job Southwest is doing in trying to accommodate the needs of the victims and their families. To the families who lost loved ones, I want to express my heartfelt sorrow and sadness. Our prayers are with you. God always does what is good and right, even though we are usually not privileged to understand His purposes.

"It's good to be home. I'll take a few questions now."

A clamor arose immediately, with shouted questions coming from every direction. Hank held up his hands until the group quieted and then pointed at a reporter.

"Are you suspending your campaign, Mr. Marshall?" the journalist asked.

"No, not at the present time," Hank said. "Next question." He pointed to another.

"How do you feel, sir?" inquired the reporter.

"Bruised and sore, but thankful to be alive, and ready for the final push in October," he responded with a smile. He saw Arthur Mitchell with the *Denver Post* and pointed to him.

"Mr. Marshall, welcome back to Denver. We're glad to see you in one piece. How is your wife, sir?"

"Thanks, Art. Haley is improving. It's liable to be a slow process, and I won't know more until I talk to her doctors. But she is awake now, she is talking, and I'm very thankful she survived her accident.

"Okay, last question. You," he said, pointing at a woman off to the side. "You're Cindy Sanchez with CNN, right?"

"Yes, sir. Thank you for taking my question. In your state-ment a moment ago you made many references to God. We are a nation of many religious faiths, sir, including many who don't have any faith. If you win this election, are you going to set your faith aside and govern neutrally?"

"Well, first of all Cindy, thank you for taking me seriously when I say I'm not suspending my campaign," he said. Many of the reporters chuckled. "But no indeed, Cindy, I will not set aside my faith. Rather, I will govern as my faith informs me about every topic, such as sexual morality, business practices, social justice, the environment, abortion, homosexuality —everything. My faith impacts every aspect of my life. That's not going to stop if I am elected president." He could see that she wanted to ask a follow up, so he nodded at her to go ahead.

"But, sir, is that fair, governing without neutrality?" she asked, tilting her head. "How about those who believe differently than you do?"

"Cindy, I affirm the First Amendment regarding freedom of religion. I believe Americans should be able to believe and practice their religion, publicly and privately, so long as they break no constitutional law in doing so.

"Having said that, however, I want to take issue with your assumption of neutrality. There is no true neutrality. Anyone who believes there is, is a potential danger in public office because he is ignorant of his own biases. The secularist is not neutral. He insists the world is to be governed according to his own secular beliefs, which he considers to be right and true. He is convinced his convictions are neutral with respect to religious faith. But they are not neutral. His beliefs tell him that God either does not exist or is irrelevant if He does. That's not a neutral position. If he then governs according to his assumptions, he governs in a manner hostile to those who believe in God." Marshall could see that he had their attention. He knew what he was asserting was in absolute opposition to what most reporters believed, and that he was providing soundbites that would doom his campaign. *If the crash didn't torpedo my campaign, this news conference certainly will. Ah, well, fools go where angels fear to tread.*

"But how can you say that?" she objected. "Secularists are not hostile to people of faith."

"They certainly don't think of themselves that way, do they? They think of themselves as neutral, don't they? But they are anything but neutral. For example, Cindy, if a secularist adjudicates a dispute between two parties who believe differently about God by prohibiting either of them from speaking publicly about God—which is exactly what our government does when it suppresses public displays of religious faith—then whose religion is the secularist promoting if not his own?"

"Well, yes, if you look at it that way then genuine neutrality would be impossible."

"Thank you. That's my point," Marshall said, smiling.

"No, Ms. Sanchez, if elected I will govern according to my Christian faith. And though it might surprise you, I encourage all elected public officials, *within the bounds of the Constitution and constitutional law,* to govern by allowing their religious faith—*whatever it is*—to inform their public service; whether those officials are Christian, Jewish, Mormon, Islamic, atheist, agnostic, or what-have-you. Someone who doesn't govern according to their beliefs doesn't really believe what they profess to.

"That's all we have time for right now. The campaign will be releasing a major statement later this week. Thank you for your questions."

Estrada and the Secret Service agents formed a wedge in front of him, and he and Cummings walked through the crowd. He could see Buford waiting for him on the other side of the mob.

****

By mid-afternoon Monday Haley had been moved from the ICU to a room in the neurology center. There had been no bleeding in the brain for thirty-six hours and the pressure in her cranial cavity was normal. Her vital signs were now rock-solid. Her vision had improved, and while speech was at times difficult there was no question of her lucidity or situational awareness. She still bore an IV port in her arm just in case it was needed, but she was no longer connected to an IV stand.

The biggest problem had to do with her legs. Haley had neither feeling nor strength in her lower body. The neurologist was hopeful that might improve, especially since her speech had improved significantly in the last twenty-four hours. Nonetheless, he couldn't guarantee that she would regain the use of her legs. With the improvements in her condition the restriction on visitors was lifted; the doctor actually encouraged visitors, hoping the mental stimulation would have a positive impact on her recovery.

Marshall stopped at the door of his wife's room before entering. He looked at Buford, who'd stood with him in some of the most difficult times in the last twelve years.

"Jacks, give me an hour alone with her and the kids. Then I want you and Sandy, Josh, and Tru to meet with us. We've got some decisions to make. Talk to one of the nurses, see if you can locate a private conference room big enough for our group."

Buford asked, "If they'll let us, you want me to rustle up some supper for everybody?"

"That would be great. Haley will eat whatever the hospital gives her, but if you can get something for the rest of us I'd really appreciate it."

Buford nodded and went off to make the arrangements.

Hank walked into the room and shut the door behind him. Haley was sitting in a wheelchair. Tears began running down her cheeks. "I . . . nearly lost you, Hank," she said haltingly.

He knelt beside the wheelchair and hugged her tightly, unable to speak, tears running freely down his own face. Finally he was able to whisper, "I thought I had lost *you*, babe."

He squeezed her tightly again and kissed her on the lips, then sat down on the bed. For the next twenty minutes they related their experiences of the last four days and marveled together that the Lord had spared them worse outcomes. Then Hank called Charity, Conner, and Charlie into the room. The questions and concerns came fast and furious. It was their first opportunity as a family to share together what their thoughts and fears had been since the sequence of tragedies began. Many tears were shed, but when the hour was up they felt stronger and more bonded as a family than ever before.

Hank led them in a prayer of worship and thanksgiving, thanking the Lord for preserving his and Haley's lives, and he thanked God for the genuine faith of his children. Their family was strong, their faith stronger. The time for tears was past and it was time to move forward toward whatever the Lord had next.

At the end of the hour, Buford Jackson tapped on the door.

"Come in," Hank called.

Jackson stuck his head in the door, winked at Charlie, and asked, "Hungry?"

"Yeah, starved," Charlie replied, "my stomach's wondering if my throat's been cut."

Buford chuckled, "Well come on, then. Soup's on."

In a few minutes the whole crew was seated around a conference table in a private room down the hall. Jackson had ordered enough Chinese carry-out to feed the entire neurological wing, but with Conner and Charlie in attendance it might be barely enough for the group in the conference room.

While they ate there was much chatting and swapping of stories about the events of the last four days. After supper Marshall began the meeting.

"We've got a decision to make. Does this campaign keep going, or has the Lord put a stop to it? The decision is Haley's and mine to make together, but first I want the honest opinion of everyone in this room, starting with my children. Charity, we'll start with you."

Charity shut her eyes for a moment, thinking. Then she looked at her dad and asked, "Dad, back when you first decided to run, did you think God was leading you to do it?"

"Yes, babe, I did."

"So did I. I still do. So what's changed for you? With all due respect, Dad, and please don't take offense, but why are we revisiting this question?"

Hank smiled, in spite of himself. Charity might be a brilliant twenty-two-year-old software engineer, but she still had the uncompromising, black-and-white idealism of youth. "Well, Charity, your mom's condition is what has changed, sweetheart. She's liable to require more care, and I'm the person committed to see that she gets it. If it's a question between being president and caring for my wife, my wife comes first. Always."

"But if you thought God was leading you to run for president, wouldn't that still be true?" she argued.

"Charity, here is what we *know* is true. When I married Haley I made a covenant to love and care for her for better or for worse—a biblical commitment to love my wife as Christ loved the church and gave Himself up for her. I cannot allow subjective feelings about being led this way or that way trump Scripture. I'm not going to read tea leaves or try to interpret situations—instead I need to live according to clear biblical principles. So the question tonight is, will I be able to care for my wife if I continue to run for president?"

Charity nodded. "Okay. I see what you're saying."

"So what's your opinion?"

"Stay in the race, Dad. If need be, I'll quit my job tomorrow to help take care of Mom. I mean it, Daddy." Her eyes filled, and her lip quivered.

Hank got up and walked around the table and hugged his daughter. He couldn't have been prouder of her than he was at that moment.

He sat down again and looked at the twins. "Charlie? Your thoughts?"

"Dad, Conner and I knew we were going to have this discussion, so he and I have already talked. I'm speaking for both of us." Conner nodded. Charlie continued, "Let's go to the worst possible case, okay? Let's say you win—"

"That's the worst possible case, Charlie?" asked Buford, his eyebrows raised.

"Not quite, but almost. It gets a little worse yet."

"Thanks a heap, boys," Hank muttered, winking at Josh Cummings.

"Well, I'm talking worst possible case for this scenario, Dad, okay? Let me finish. So you win, and four years later you get reelected. So we have a total of eight years. That's the worst of the worst. So, anyway, Conner and I would only have to give up eight years of our lives to help you and Mom. After that, you'd be on your own and we'd be able to, you know, move on with our own lives."

"This sounds like the empty-nest syndrome in reverse," Jackson chuckled in his gravelly voice. "The twins would be pushing you two out of the nest," he observed.

Hank looked puzzled, "So, are you two saying you want me to stay in the race?"

"Yup," said Conner without hesitating.

"And you're saying you'd be willing to help, even if it meant putting your life on hold for eight years?"

"Absolutely. It helps, of course, knowing we'd be flying on Air Force One, going to Camp David, seeing the White House Situation Room, and getting our own private cook. But yeah, we're both willing," affirmed Conner.

"Haley, what do you think?" Hank asked his wife.

She smiled at him. "My . . . opinion . . . has not changed," she said, struggling with her words. "Let's saddle . . . up our horses . . . buster."

He looked at her and was unable to suppress a sob that rose up in his throat. It killed him to see his beautiful wife, so intelligent, so vibrant, now in a wheelchair struggling with normal conversation. He gazed at her and wiped the tears from his eyes. After Christ, she was his strength and backbone, and the love of his life.

He cleared his throat, and said hoarsely, "And what do my friends, my political advisors, say?"

Buford Jackson spoke up. "We also had this discussion earlier today. We're with you until the end, Hank. We're all agreed: you're the right man for this country, and this is the right time. It's now or never. We want you to stay in it, and we want to put you over the top."

Hank nodded, trying to swallow the lump in his throat. "How can I ever thank you guys?"

Trujillo grinned. "Well, winning would help."

****

"Tim, what you did was terrible," Pastor Joseph Johnson asserted. He was on Hardy's list of allowed visitors, and came by the hospital to encourage Tim. When he sat down to talk, Hardy opened up and spilled the whole story. Johnson wanted to be gentle, but it wasn't compassionate to sugarcoat Hardy's actions.

"I know. I can't believe I did it," replied the man miserably.

"That might be the best explanation of why you did do it," Johnson observed.

"What do you mean, Pastor Joe?" Hardy asked, surprised.

"Tim, Christians are capable of committing any sin in the book. We have to be constantly on guard against the evil in our own hearts. Proverbs says that the man who trusts in his own heart is a fool. Jeremiah says that our hearts are so deceitful we can't even reliably know them. If you are shocked by your behavior then you're not paying close enough attention to what God is telling you in His Word."

"That's true of people who don't know Christ, Pastor, but I do know Him," Hardy objected. "I thought all that would go away when I got saved."

Johnson took off his glasses and wiped the lenses with a tissue while he thought about how best to answer Hardy's confusion. "Tim, we Christians are caught between two worlds. Theologians refer to it as the 'already, not yet' problem. We're stuck between the reality of what God has *already* accomplished for us—such as deliverance from sin's bondage—and the reality that His work in us is *not yet* complete. For example, Romans 6 says Christ has *already* freed us from slavery to sin so that we can present ourselves to God as servants of righteousness. But Romans 7 indicates we have *not yet* been freed from sin's presence or temptations. Paul laments his own tendency to sin. We find the same thing to be true in our own experience: we're still doing battle with our own disobedience to God."

"I've heard you use that 'not yet, already' expression, Pastor, but somehow I never really understood how it applied to me," Hardy admitted.

"Philippians 1:6 is a good place to see it in a single verse,

Tim. Paul says, *For I am confident of this very thing, that He who began a good work in you will perfect it until the day of Christ Jesus.* God's good work in the believer, Tim, has *already* begun but it's *not yet* completed."

"Yeah, now I see it. Don't know why I didn't realize it before," Tim said. "But what about guilt? I thought that since Christ paid for our sins, the guilt was removed. But I feel so guilty—what I've done is awful and I can't undo it. If that laptop battery really contained a bomb, I've got the blood of thirty-five people on my hands." Hardy began to weep.

Johnson hesitated, knowing what he was about to say would hurt. But soul care is like surgery—the pain comes before the healing. He looked at Tim and said, "Feeling guilty is appropriate, Tim, because you *are* guilty. I'd be concerned if you didn't feel guilty. Your greed and selfishness has had cata-strophic results. The Holy Spirit is doing His gracious work of conviction in your heart."

"But what can I do, Pastor?" cried Tim.

"You can do what all of us must do every day, Tim. You can remember the Gospel. Look, let's take it from the top. The Bible is very clear. Every human being—with the excep-tion of Jesus—is a sinner in God's sight. We've all disobeyed and dishonored Him in more ways than we could count. And there is a penalty for sin—death, eternal, conscious separation from God. The Bible is unambiguous on this point.

"But this is where the Gospel comes in play, Tim. The writers of the New Testament tell us that God sent His Son into the world to die for our sins, in our place. Instead of God pouring His wrathful judgment on sinners, He poured it on His Son. Paul says in 2 Corinthians 5:21 that God made Jesus —who was sinless—to be sin for us. We deserved God's judg-ment but it fell on Christ instead. Jesus rose from the dead three days later demonstrating that God accepted His sacrifice on our behalf. Paul says in Romans 4:25 that *He was delivered over because of our transgressions, and was raised because of our justification.*"

"I know these things, Pastor. I hear them each week at church. I read of them in my Bible," Hardy objected.

"Yes, but have you acted on them? The forgiveness of sins does not apply to everyone, but only to those who repent and believe that Jesus died and rose again for their sins. So Tim, have you come to the point in your life where you've definitively repented of your sins and placed your faith in Christ?" asked Pastor Johnson, fixing his eyes on Hardy.

"I have, Pastor Joe. Shortly after I graduated from college I committed my life to Christ. I've made a royal mess of things since, but I truly know Him. I love His Word, I love His people, I love to worship Him. My problem is that all too often I love my sin."

"Don't we all?" asked Johnson, shaking his head. He knew of the sin that raged in his own heart. "This is why we must remember the Gospel daily, Tim. Not only did Christ purchase our forgiveness on the cross, He also *became* our righteousness. The second half of 2 Corinthians 5:21 indicates that God has gifted to us the record of Christ's perfect righteousness. When we trusted Christ, God placed us 'in Christ.' Paul says in Colossians 3:2 that *you have died and your life is hidden with Christ in God.* God graciously looks at us in His Son. He sees us clothed in the righteousness of Christ. We don't deserve it, we haven't earned it, but nonetheless it's true.

"That's how you deal with guilt, Tim. You remember and believe the Gospel. Repent of your sin, confess it to God, and remember that Christ carried your sin to the cross. Remember that you are clothed with a righteousness not your own, and God looks on you as a beloved son.

"You truly are guilty, but you're also truly forgiven. God promises in Jeremiah 31:34, *I will forgive their iniquity, and their sin I will remember no more.* So every day, Tim, whether it's a good day or a bad day, full of success, full of failure, or maybe some of each, we remember the Gospel."

Tim was silent, pondering what Pastor Joe had said. Pieces of the puzzle were falling into place. He'd known the Gospel but had never realized its richness. He'd always viewed it as the doorway into a relationship with God; he'd never understood the Gospel as the critical principle for his daily life.

While there was still great remorse for what he had done and the realization that legal consequences would probably impact him for the rest of his life, he was flooded with a sense of forgiveness and acceptance before God. For the first time in many months his heart was at peace.

"Thank you, Pastor Joe. Now I do understand, and it really helps."

"You're welcome." Johnson smiled at him sadly. "You know what this means for your future, Tim, right?"

"Yes. I'll be transferred from this hospital to jail, and that's where I'll probably spend the rest of my life. I certainly deserve it. But whenever my life is over I'm going to be with Jesus for eternity, and I certainly *don't* deserve that. But it's what I'll cling to."

Johnson nodded, "Good. That's the power of the Gospel, Tim."

"Pastor, on my stand there's a business card. Do you see it?"

Johnson picked up the card. "Uh-huh. It's for Detective Grady Wilson, Golden PD."

"Yes, that's the one. I can't manage the phone yet. Would you call him and tell him I'm ready to cooperate?"

Johnson fought down a lump in his throat, knowing what this would mean for Hardy. "Sure, Tim. I'll give him a call."

****

An hour later, Henry Marshall came in. "Tim, I heard that you were hit by a car! How are you doing, man?"

"Hi, Mr. Marshall. They tell me that my neck is broken, but that my spinal cord is not damaged. I have feeling in my hands and feet. I have a concussion, and both legs are broken. My left arm is broken. I had some internal bleeding, but they've fixed that. And I've got plenty of cuts, scrapes, and bruises."

"I've been praying for you, Tim. You could have been killed."

"Thank you, sir." Tim shut his eyes and took a deep breath. *Here goes. Lord, help me to honor You.*

"Mr Marshall, I've done something terrible. I've sinned against the Lord and against you, sir, and my actions may have caused the crash of that airplane."

Marshall's eyes narrowed. "What have you done, Tim?"

With shaking hands, Tim wiped his face. "About a month ago, I started getting anonymous texts. Whoever was sending them claimed to be a journalist writing a book about your campaign, and he wanted some inside information. Said that his publisher had given him a budget, and he was willing to pay.

"So I started selling him information. It was small stuff at first—your schedule of upcoming campaign events, that sort of thing—"

"Wait a minute," Marshall interrupted angrily. "You were *selling* information about my campaign and my plans? Tim, that wasn't yours to sell!"

"Yes, sir, I know. It was wrong, it was—sinful. I justified my actions by telling myself that it would help your cause, figured that a book written about you might raise your name recognition and get a wider distribution for your ideas. But the real reason, Mr. Marshall, was that I wanted the money."

The man's evident misery, coupled with his ready admission that his actions were sinful, stalled Marshall's rising outrage. With sudden insight, Marshall realized he was being given an opportunity to exercise the grace of Christ. He struggled with his temper and mastered it. "Go on, Tim," he said. "What happened next?"

"A week ago my anonymous contact told me that I'd find a replacement battery for your laptop on the seat of my car, and that I should install it. Supposedly it contained software that would bypass the battery monitoring circuit and provide remote access to your computer. By then they had me on the hook, and they were offering twenty grand for the battery swap.

"When you came in on Friday and found me in your office, that's what I was doing. I lied to you about the network management client warning that your battery was failing. I betrayed you, sir. I betrayed the campaign. Worst of all, I dishonored Christ. Please forgive me, sir. What I did was so, so wrong."

Marshall studied the man, his face stern. "Tim, what if the bomb that brought down the airplane was in that replacement battery? Have you thought about that? Thirty-five people died in that crash! You could have killed Carlos and me."

"To tell the truth, sir, that's all I've been thinking about. All I can plead, Mr. Marshall, is ignorance. I thought the battery was providing a simple hack into your computer. I'd never have knowingly endangered your life, or anyone else's."

Marshall stared at him, considering. Finally he responded, "Tim, I really don't believe you would intentionally harm someone. Nonetheless, it's likely that your greed and selfishness have contributed to the deaths of thirty-five people. If you are truly repentant you have to go to the police with this —even if it winds up putting you away for life."

"I know. I've asked Pastor Joe to call the police and let them know I'm ready to cooperate. Mr. Marshall, I sinned against you, terribly. Please sir, will you forgive me?"

Marshall looked down at the man. Hardy was both physically and spiritually broken. Hank battled his anger, disappointment, and disgust at what Hardy had done. But slowly he realized that what he was really fighting with was his own proud self-righteousness, and then he remembered, *there, but for the grace of God, go I.*

The statement of Paul in Ephesians 4:32 decided the matter: *forgiving each other, just as God in Christ has also forgiven you.* Christ didn't give him a choice—Marshall realized he was commanded to forgive.

He reached down and squeezed Hardy's right shoulder, which seemed to be the only uninjured spot on the man's body. "Yes, Tim. I forgive you. And I will stand by you as a brother in Christ as you face the consequences of your actions. But I'm sure you realize, there will be consequences."

"Thank you. Yes, sir, I do realize that. I'm ready to face them."

Chapter 18

> JUSTICE IS THE END OF GOVERNMENT. IT IS THE END OF CIVIL SOCIETY. IT EVER HAS BEEN AND EVER WILL BE PURSUED UNTIL IT BE OBTAINED, OR UNTIL LIBERTY BE LOST IN THE PURSUIT. IN A SOCIETY UNDER THE FORMS OF WHICH THE STRONGER FACTION CAN READILY UNITE AND OPPRESS THE WEAKER, ANARCHY MAY AS TRULY BE SAID TO REIGN AS IN A STATE OF NATURE, WHERE THE WEAKER INDIVIDUAL IS NOT SECURED AGAINST THE VIOLENCE OF THE STRONGER; . . . .
>
> *James Madison, Federalist #51*

Tuesday morning, September 27, 2016

Grady Wilson tapped on the door of Tim Hardy's room, and then entered. "I got a call from your pastor last night, Joseph Johnson. He said you're ready to talk to me."

"I am," Tim replied. *And so it begins*, he thought. *Lord, I'm trusting you.*

"You know I need to arrest you," Wilson said.

"Yes, I understand. Let's get it over with."

"Timothy Hardy, I am placing you under arrest for your actions connected with the bombing of Southwest Flight 1356 on September 23, 2016. You have the right to remain silent. Anything you say can and will be used against you in a court of law. You have the right to speak to an attorney, and to have an attorney present during any questioning. If you cannot afford a lawyer, one will be provided for you at government expense. Do you understand your rights?"

"Yes, I do." Hardy's voice was strong and clear.

"The police officer posted outside your room will not interfere with the medical duties of the hospital staff, but he will not allow you to leave this hospital. When you are discharged, unless the judge grants bail and you post it, you'll be moved from the hospital to the jail. Do you understand?"

"Yes, Detective Wilson," he acknowledged.

"I'd like to ask you some questions, sir."

"I'm quite willing to answer your questions, Detective, but if you would allow me to make a full statement first, it might save you quite a bit of time. Do you have a digital recorder?"

"I do."

"Good. You'll need it."

For the next hour Hardy recounted the complete story with all the details he could remember. When Wilson returned to his office he was satisfied that Hardy had been honest and open with him. It would save his investigation a great deal of time.

****

"Here's what we know so far," SJ Bergman said. He was teleconferencing from the Denver FBI office to a combined meeting of Roland Yates and his NTSB Go Team and Sarah Dalton and her FBI ERT agents in Chicago. "Over the last month Mark Atkinson, or someone working with him, was grooming Tim Hardy. It began with someone slipping a burner phone into Hardy's man bag, which they then used to communicate with him anonymously. They started by bribing him for campaign information, trivial stuff. The money was direct-deposited into his checking account. The bribery gradually ramped up until he was willing, for twenty thousand dollars, to replace the battery in Marshall's laptop. Hardy thought that the replacement battery contained a software hack that would give his anonymous handlers remote access to Marshall's computer.

"Two weeks ago they obtained Henry Marshall's schedule from Hardy and learned that he was slated to be in his hotel room in Chicago on Friday night, September 23 at 2100 hours, Chicago time. When I spoke to him early this morning, Hardy was emphatic—several times they texted him to verify that point, especially that Marshall would be alone in his hotel room at 2100 hours. When Hardy left for work on Friday morning a replacement laptop battery was sitting on the passenger seat. Both his vehicle and the garage had been locked and neither showed any signs of entry, not even a scratch—so we're dealing with some sort of professional.

"Hardy made the battery swap when he got to work and lied to Marshall about why he was doing it. He texted his handler to report the job was done, and was instructed to leave the burner phone in a bagel bag across the street at Starbucks, which he did.

"Friday evening as he was leaving work an unknown assailant—we believe it was Mark Atkinson—attempted to kill Hardy by running over him with an automobile. Hardy was taken to the ICU unit of St. Anthony's, where a little later on Friday evening Mark Atkinson made a second attempt to murder him. Fortunately a nurse walked in on him and raised a ruckus, scaring him off. He was apprehended before he could get away. He's currently in custody, refusing to say anything until his legal counsel is present. The lawyer Atkinson retained is just finishing up a big case and has not been available—so we've gotten nowhere with Atkinson. We expect to see his lawyer here shortly, and then we'll be able to interrogate him." SJ paused momentarily to look at his notes.

"From our end, it appears that the people running this operation had targeted Marshall and Marshall alone. Their multiple efforts to verify where Marshall was scheduled to be at 2100 hours on Friday night suggest that. By sheer coincidence Mrs. Marshall had an accident on Friday afternoon that forced a change of plans for Mr. Marshall. In conclusion, I'm suggesting that the bombing of Flight 1356 was wholly unintended, an unhappy synthesis of Murphy's law and the law of unintended consequences."

Sarah Dalton responded. "SJ, our investigation is tracking with what you have learned. We were able to interview the flight attendant who took Marshall's laptop. She verified that she put it in the forward closet. Our NTSB airframe specialist verifies that the explosion originated from within the forward closet. The evidence team located fragments of a laptop. Microscopic analysis of the pieces shows that they were at or near the center of an explosion. The ion mobility spectrometer found conclusive evidence of C4 explosive. The tower video shows the explosion happening at one second past 2100 hours. All of these data points suggest that your theory is correct—that the bomb was located in Marshall's laptop and was set to detonate at 2100 hours when Marshall would be isolated in his hotel room.

"We are expecting the report back from the lab in the next several hours. They should have an analysis that will identify the exact explosive. I'll call you as soon as it arrives."

"Thanks, Sarah. I'll send you a transcript of our chat with Mr. Atkinson."

****

Patrick Cavenaugh was a very successful criminal defense attorney. He had a love-hate relationship with his career: he loved the money and hated the clients. Nine times out of ten Cavenaugh was convinced that the thugs he defended were guilty as charged. But it didn't matter to him, not one bit, as long as they paid well. As he saw it, his job was to win at any cost. Justice did not motivate him; conquest and its rewards motivated him.

As a consequence, Patrick Cavenaugh was accomplished at making sure his clients beat the rap sheet whether by a legal technicality or a total fabrication. Judicial ethics had to do with what he could get away with, not what was just.

Cavenaugh read the brief one of his paralegals had prepared on his latest potential client. He shook his head—this was not a case he could win. He scanned the charges that the Grand Jury had handed down the day before: two counts of attempted murder, striking a police officer, assault and battery, criminal impersonation, grand theft auto, and a garden variety of other felonies and misdemeanors. He might be able to slip a couple of charges, but for the big stuff—attempted murder—the evidence was too solid.

On the other hand, the perp was bound to be well heeled. He was a former SEAL who'd established a second career as a mercenary—a gun for hire. Guys like that lived like kings on those little southern Caribbean islands. The man probably had his own private army protecting a luxurious villa.

Hmm. If he could stretch the case out with a bunch of pointless motions, it would delay ultimate justice for his client and would put some big bucks in his own pocket. He might even be able to get the man out on bail—*no, probably not.* Even a judge on the take could see that Atkinson would be a flight risk.

There was another possibility. Remote, but possible. If Atkinson was being used as an asset by someone else, he might be able to negotiate a plea deal—maybe even immunity —if Atkinson cooperated and agreed to testify.

Yes, that's a good possibility, the lawyer thought. *Maybe I will take the case. Even if I do lose, this client will be able to afford to pay me. No skin off my back.*

****

Grady Wilson set up the interrogation room, but this time he included a chair for Atkinson's legal counsel. A few minutes later Atkinson, hands and feet shackled, was escorted in accompanied by his lawyer. After some preliminary harass-ment from Cavenaugh respecting the accommodations in the jail, Wilson was able to get started.

"Mr. Atkinson, here's what we know so far. You attempted to murder Tim Hardy twice last Friday night. We've tied you to the white Escalade by DNA samples, we know you were driving it. We know that you attempted to murder him in his room at St. Anthony's—we have witnesses of that." Wilson looked up from his clipboard and stared at Atkinson.

"No, Detective Wilson, you do not. That charge is based on circumstantial evidence. No one observed my client tampering with Mr. Hardy's IV bag. All you know is that he was on the scene. It could have as easily been done by the nurse," objected Cavenaugh.

Wilson chuckled. "Counselor, I'd be very happy to go to trial tomorrow if the second count of attempted murder was the only charge against Mr. Atkinson, and the current evidence was all that we had."

He turned back to Atkinson. "We also know you bribed Hardy to plant a bomb in Henry Marshall's laptop, and that bomb brought down Southwest Airlines Flight 1356, causing thirty-five deaths. Tomorrow I'm going back to the Grand Jury with new evidence, and the Cook County DA in Chicago is convening a Grand Jury up there. When you and I next talk, Mr. Atkinson, you'll be facing thirty-five counts of murder one, and a whole raft of additional federal charges."

"Whoa, wait a minute! You can't pin that on me," shouted Atkinson. "I had nothing to do with that. I had no idea Marshall would be on that—"

"STOP!" Cavenaugh shouted at his client. He turned to Wilson and snapped, "My client is refusing to answer that question."

"Actually, Counselor, I was not asking a question, I was stating a fact. And I will point out here and in court that your client, with legal counsel present, freely volunteered information incriminating himself, protesting that the bomb was not intended to detonate on an aircraft."

Cavenaugh turned to his client and hissed under his breath, "*Don't say anything!*"

"I might also remind you, Mr. Atkinson, that conviction on any count involving that bombing renders you liable to civil suits from the survivors and families of the victims, as well as Southwest Airlines, their insurance company, and Midway International Airport. That little nest-egg you think you have in the Cayman Islands isn't going to last long when a flood of civil suits begins to clog your mailbox."

He turned to Cavenaugh and smiled, "You'll be lucky to

get paid, Counselor."

****

"SJ, we hit the jackpot on the lab analysis of the explosive," Dalton exulted.

"What did you find?" asked Bergman.

"Well, the explosive was definitely C4, but it was loaded with microtaggants."

"Really? Microtaggants? Hmm, then it was probably manufactured in Switzerland. Explosives manufacturers in the US don't use microtaggants."

"The lab was able to isolate the tag code. I'm sending you the complete report in PDF form," said Dalton.

Bergman studied the lab report carefully when it hit his email inbox. After a few minutes of reading he picked up his phone and speed-dialed Bill Sylvester, a friend of his who worked in a department of the FBI's Investigations and Operations Support Section (IOSS).

"Sylvester."

"Hey, Bill, it's SJ. What's goin' on at Quantico?"

"Oh, we're just up to our usual awesomeness, solving the crimes that are too hard for you poor dumb ground-pounders," Bill Sylvester replied cheerfully.

"Is that so?" said Bergman, "I thought they stuck IOSS with you guys who couldn't pass the physical requirements for field work."

"Somebody's been lyin' to ya, pal. IOSS is stocked with both the brains and the brawn."

"Meh. So you say. Listen, buddy, I do happen to need a little of your awesomeness."

"Shoot."

"You heard about the Southwest 737 that went down at Midway?"

"That's the one that had a presidential candidate on it, right?"

"The very same. Anyway, the bomber used C4 that just

happened to have identification microtaggants. I want to know everything about that batch of C4—who made it, who bought it—a complete chain of custody."

"Piece. Of. Cake. Did you want this yesterday or would you prefer it the day before?"

Bergman chuckled. "If I could have it by Friday, that would do. I'll email you the lab analysis right away."

****

Ares sat at his desk in the bowels of the State Department. His attempt to get rid of Marshall had not only failed, it had been a complete disaster, nearly killing his own daughter. He was shaken to the core, and ever since the crash he'd been an emotional wreck. He was not sleeping, he was finding it hard to concentrate, and a voice in his head kept reminding him that he'd almost murdered his beloved daughter.

Normally a news hound—a requirement for his line of work—he'd had neither the time nor the interest to keep up with the news. It was to prove his undoing.

Gillespie was irritated to the point of rage. He'd been waiting on Viper's call to assure him that Tim Hardy had been terminated. But the man had not called, and Byron was ready to shut the operation down. He didn't like loose ends.

He swore, and slammed his hand on his desk. Pulling out his Boeing Black, he dialed Viper. No answer. When it went to voice mail, he growled, "Viper, call me NOW!"

Fifteen hundred miles away, SJ Bergman was sitting at his desk in the FBI field office in Denver. Mark Atkinson's Boeing Black just happened to be sitting on his desk. When the call came through SJ was unable to answer it because of the biometric security devices in the phone. But he immediately grabbed a pen and wrote down the exact time on a notepad. If there was a way he could access the NSA's telephone metadata, he might be able to identify where the call originated. But that would require permission from a FISA court, and at the moment nothing about the case qualified it for that.

Several hours later Ares called again, and again the call went to voice mail. Fearing the worst, Gillespie went online and began searching for news that might indicate why Viper was not returning his call. Within five minutes he had his answer. Page one of the Saturday edition of the *Denver Post* had the mug shot of a John Doe who'd allegedly attempted to murder Tim Hardy in his hospital room. He'd been captured by the police while fleeing the scene. There, staring back at him, was a very sullen Mark Atkinson.

"Idiot!" Ares shouted at himself. He leaned back in his chair and thought, *I just tried to call Viper twice, and the cops are sure to have his phone! How stupid can I be?*

Ten minutes later the crushed remains of his Boeing Black were sitting on the bottom of the Potomac River.

****

Politics is a brutal business, and the electorate can be very fickle. The number of voters in a presidential campaign who are committed ideologically to a specific philosophy of governance is rather small. These are the "true believers," ideologues, whose loyalty is not attached to political parties but to a specific vision of government. They won't vote for a candidate who does not share their values, regardless of party affiliation.

The next larger group are the pragmatists. They are less interested in ideology and more interested in candidates whose ideas are perceived to "work." Party loyalty means more to them—simply because they typically find that the policies which accomplish purposes they can align with are concentrated within one party or another. But party loyalty is still not the deciding factor.

The largest group of voters are those who identify closely with a major party. The association means more than the platform. Even when the party's platform seems to contradict their own preferences, they'll find reasons to remain associated with the party. After the nominating convention identifies the party nominee, these are the base voters who can be relied upon to fall in line even though they might find disagreements with their nominee.

There is a big wild card in any presidential election—a wild card large enough to decide a closely contested race. These are the undecideds. They're pulled by a multitude of pros and cons, and simply can't decide which are most important to them. Sometimes it's because the issues are truly complex. Sometimes it's because they have not spent enough time investigating the candidates. Though the number of unde-cided voters usually shrinks as the day draws near, many will wind up deciding who to vote for when they're standing in the voting booth.

Within the undecided block of voters, there are a signifi-cant number that political scientists suspect simply want to go with the winner, whoever it is and whatever they stand for. No one really knows how large a portion of the undecideds these comprise—they just know they're there. The candidate they perceive to be winning as Election Day draws near is the one they'll pull the lever for.

Regardless of Marshall's announcement that his campaign would continue, by Tuesday afternoon national polls were showing he'd dropped five points. Joshua Cummings studied the results with a sinking heart and commissioned a poll of his own. The results came back on Thursday, and showed that the voters were unconvinced Henry Marshall would make it all the way to Election Day.

****

On Thursday evening, September 29, Henry Marshall flew to Columbus, Ohio, for a series of campaign events beginning on Friday morning. Starting in Columbus, he would then swing through Cincinnati, follow up with an event at the Wright-Patterson Air Force Base, and then wrap up the day with a major campaign rally at the UD arena in Dayton.

Saturday he would travel to Indianapolis for a presidential debate, facing off with Hastings and Bushnell.

The senior members of his campaign staff, as well as his children, would arrive Friday afternoon in time for the rally at the UD arena. Sandy Jackson would stay with Haley, who was scheduled to be released from the hospital on Friday.

Ashton Bancroft picked him up at Port Columbus International Airport. Carlos Estrada and two Secret Service agents accompanied Marshall. "Thanks for picking us up, Abe."

"No problem, Hank. How are you feeling? That's quite a wringer you Marshalls have been through lately."

Marshall laughed. "You know the Marshalls, Abe. We always lead with our head. Seriously, though, we're all improving. I think Haley's coming home from the hospital tomorrow. Her speech is still a problem, she's still in a wheelchair, but thank God she's alive. As for me, well, I'm feeling great. Other than the fact that babies cry and children run away when they see me, I'm fine."

"They were doing that *before* you were injured,"Bancroft chuckled.

"Thanks a heap, pal."

Bancroft glanced over at Hank as he drove. "Too bad about Tim Hardy, Hank. I couldn't believe it when I heard the news. How's the investigation going?"

"Pretty well, I suppose. I don't keep up with it. They formally arrested Tim on Tuesday morning. I feel so bad for him—he's ruined his life," he acknowledged, shaking his head.

"Yes, well, he's ruined quite a few other lives in the process."

Hank sighed. "Yeah, I know. He's realized that and is now cooperating fully with the police."

"Angling for a plea bargain?" asked Bancroft dubiously, as he pulled on to I-270.

"No, I don't think so. Tim knows what he did was wrong. He's not making excuses and he's accepted the fact that he deserves to spend the rest of his life in jail."

"I'll say," Bancroft muttered. He changed the subject. "How does Olive Garden sound for supper? The local Ruth's

Chris has closed."

"Sounds perfect."

Bancroft had been acting as Hank's senior foreign policy advisor. He was based in Dayton, but often traveled with Hank to campaign events. His main job over the next two days was to get Marshall ready for the debate Saturday night in Indianapolis.

"Why didn't the whole crew come out tonight, Hank? I understand we'll be meeting them in Dayton tomorrow afternoon."

"I needed some time with you, Abe. Want to bounce some ideas off of you without distraction," Marshall said, somewhat evasively.

"Fire away," offered Bancroft.

"No. Let's eat first. I can't think when I'm starving."

When they arrived at the restaurant, Hank put Carlos and the Secret Service agents at a separate table close by. He and Bancroft were seated in a small booth where they could talk privately. During supper Hank asked Bancroft about his experiences in Vietnam.

When supper was cleared away and they both had a cup of coffee, Hank said, "I got your list of veep recommendations two months ago, Abe. You did a great job, both in advocating and vetting. Josh, Buford, and Tru all gave me their lists as well. I also asked Elizabeth Montgomery to make up a list. So I've had two months to think and pray about this. A month ago I made my pick, and for the last four weeks I've had a team of oppo researchers digging up all the dirt, looking under all the rocks, checking out all the closets. No skeletons, no bodies, no scandals waiting in the background. My guy came out absolutely clean. I figured he would."

Bancroft sipped his coffee, then offered, "That's great—sounds like you've done your homework, Hank. Who's it going to be?"

Hank smiled. "It's the name that has been on top of my personal list from the beginning. It's the only name that appeared on everyone's list except yours."

"You mean I totally whiffed? Bummer. So, who is it?"

"You, Ashton."

Bancroft looked at him and blinked. "Me? Seriously?"

"It never even occurred to you, did it? And if I read you right, you don't even want it, do you?"

"No, and no."

"That's one of the reasons I want you as my running mate, Ashton, other than the fact that you are so uniquely qualified. While you really ought to be the man in the left-hand seat— you're much more skilled and accomplished than I am— you've got the humility to sit in the right-hand seat and be the copilot, the number two guy."

Ashton Bancroft was silent. He really did not want to go back to Washington. But he also knew he could bring a lot of experience to the ticket. And he believed in Marshall and what he was trying to do. Marshall was the one guy he'd truly feel privileged to serve.

"I'm not going to be coy, Hank. I don't want to go back to Washington. But I'll talk to Margie about it tonight. If she agrees, I'll be honored to be your running mate and I'll do everything in my power to force a four-year change of address on both of us."

****

The crowds on Friday were large and enthusiastic, but none so much as the crowd of Marshall supporters that showed up at the UD arena for the 7:00 p.m. campaign rally. The platform was decorated with red, white, and blue bunting and American flags. A paraplegic veteran of Afghanistan warmed up the crowd with a funny monologue of political satire that had the audience rolling in the aisles. No one was exempt from his razor-sharp tongue, including Marshall.

Sergeant Carson rolled out on the platform. He was wearing a wireless throat mic. "Good evening. I'm Sergeant Jack Carson. I'm a veteran of Afghanistan, and I left my legs there. I assure you, it was unintentional."

When he said this, the large crowd gave him a standing

ovation.

When the audience was seated again, he said, "I'm supposed to get y'all riled up, so Henry Marshall can come out in a few minutes and put you to sleep." Chuckles rippled through the gathering.

"When I got home from Helmand Province, I went to a VA hospital and asked if they could help me get a motorized wheelchair. The little lady sitting across the desk from me asked if I had any evidence of disability. I said, yeah, I ain't got no legs. She said, no, I mean, do you have any *documentary* evidence of disability. I said, you mean, like a picture of me without legs? She said, yeah, that would probably do it. So I pulled out my phone and took a selfie, and then pushed the phone across to her. How's this, I says. She said, fine, that's all I needed to see. That was three years ago. Still haven't seen that motorized wheelchair.

"I called the VA a month ago to ask about it. She says, okay, we've got you on the list. I said, that's what y'all told me last year. She says, no, no, last year you were on the list to get on the list. This year we moved you from *that* list to THE LIST. THE LIST! Do you understand, she asked me."

Carson paused until the laughter died down, and then continued. "Ma'am, I said, this is year three. I've been waiting three years. Wasn't I put on a list right away? Oh yes, Sergeant, you were. So I asked her, well, what list was I on the first year? Oh, that list, she says, that list was the documentary evidence list. You have to start on that list." More laughter.

"I asked her, ma'am, you didn't happen to command my battalion in Afghanistan, did you?" The crowd roared with laughter.

"One of the reasons," Carson said, "that I'm voting for Henry Marshall next month, is because he has promised that he will *not* fix the Veterans Health Administration. He will not fix it. Did y'all get that? He said he won't *fix* it, because he's gonna *kill* it. He's going to dismantle it. He's going to fire the doctors and nurses and all the administrators and bureaucrats, sell the buildings, and shut it down completely. Henry Marshall has promised to push for legislation that provides veterans with healthcare vouchers that they can use with any hospital or any healthcare plan. Veterans won't have to wait in lines or on lists anymore. We can go to the doctor just like you can." The arena erupted in applause and cheers.

"You folks don't mind a few political jokes, do you? I mean, we don't have to set up a safe zone for anyone in here, do we? You folks ain't troubled by microaggressions are you? Man, I sure wish it was a microaggression I'd stepped on in Afghanistan rather than an IED. I wish it was microaggressions that the mujaheddin had been shootin' at us. We might have come home with a wounded self-image, but at least we'd still have our fingers and toes and arms and legs. Okay, I'll ask you again. Can I tell a political joke?"

Someone in the crowd shouted out, "Yes, please do!"

Carson looked over his way and grinned, "Thank you! Y'all know what Jay Leno said, don't you? Leno said that if God had wanted us to vote, he woulda given us candidates." The crowd was silent other than a few guffaws.

"Okay, might take some of y'all a little while to figure that one out. Here's one a little easier. You know what the problem is with political jokes? Y'all want to know?" Carson waited until someone shouted, *yes!* "Problem with political jokes is they get elected." The arena reverberated with laughter.

Sergeant Carson waited for the noise to subside, and then grinning, said, "I'd like to introduce you to my favorite political joke: Henry Marshall, welcome to Dayton and the UD arena!"

Marshall strode out onto the platform to ringing applause and shook Carson's hand, and then stepped to the podium. "That's a brave man," he said as Carson was rolled off the platform. "That's the sort of men and women we have serving in our military. They are an honor to our country. Sergeant Carson suffered horrific battle damage that will be with him for the rest of his life. But he can come home and poke fun at himself and his condition. That's a man of rare courage. We owe him and others like him more than we can ever repay. Let's give Sergeant Carson a hand."

After the applause died down, Marshall smiled and looked

back in Carson's direction. "He'd make a good press secretary, wouldn't he? With him at the podium, no one would want to miss a single White House press conference." Marshall paused and looked over the crowd.

"One of the reasons I'm running for office is because we have military men and women like Sergeant Carson who wait for years for the VA to treat their medical conditions. I'll be honest, folks, that's frankly outrageous. It's time to eliminate large chunks of the Veterans Administration, and one of those chunks that needs to be utterly shuttered is the Veterans Health Administration.

"But the VA is merely symptomatic of a larger problem. Because of the Civil Service system and government employee unions, it has become virtually impossible to fire a government worker. If a government employee engages in a proven instance of sexual harassment, they don't need sensitivity training, they need to be fired. If a government employee looks at pornography on their computer at work, they need to be canned, not reeducated. If a government employee is consistently late for work, they need to be terminated. If a government employee drags their feet on a Freedom of Information request, they need to be shown to the door. If your momma did not teach you how to behave, then we don't want you working for Uncle Sam. And this goes for anyone from clerical workers to managers and even political appointees."

Marshall spoke for fifteen minutes, and the theme of his speech was *don't fix it, eliminate it*. He concluded his remarks and then said, "We have a special treat for you tonight. The campaign promised we'd have a major announcement tonight and we won't let you down. This evening, here in Dayton, Ohio, I am going to introduce to you my running mate. He happens to be an Ohio boy." Thunderous applause interrupted Marshall at this point and he was forced to wait until it subsided.

"This man has served his country in the Special Forces. He is a marine who served in the 1st Reconnaissance Battalion as a sniper. He is still something of a legend in the sniper community. In Ohio he's been a prosecuting attorney. He served as the attorney general for the state of Ohio. He served five terms in the US House of Representatives, where he chaired the Intelligence Committee and also served on the Foreign Affairs Committee. Of course you know by now of whom I speak. He's a man of great accomplishments and even greater character. I am honored to introduce Ashton Bancroft as my vice presidential running mate. Please welcome him."

The arena went wild with applause. Bancroft had been a favorite son of Ohio for years and was well respected on both sides of the aisle. Abe spoke for ten minutes to enthusiastic applause, and the event ended with some high-energy music, a balloon drop, and confetti.

Chapter 19

AS THERE IS A DEGREE OF DEPRAVITY IN MANKIND
WHICH REQUIRES A CERTAIN DEGREE OF
CIRCUMSPECTION AND DISTRUST, SO THERE ARE
OTHER QUALITIES IN HUMAN NATURE WHICH JUSTIFY
A CERTAIN PORTION OF ESTEEM AND CONFIDENCE.
REPUBLICAN GOVERNMENT PRESUPPOSES THE
EXISTENCE OF THESE QUALITIES IN A HIGHER
DEGREE THAN ANY OTHER FORM. WERE THE
PICTURES WHICH HAVE BEEN DRAWN BY THE
POLITICAL JEALOUSY OF SOME AMONG US FAITHFUL
LIKENESSES OF THE HUMAN CHARACTER, THE
INFERENCE WOULD BE, THAT THERE IS NOT
SUFFICIENT VIRTUE AMONG MEN FOR SELF-
GOVERNMENT; AND THAT NOTHING LESS THAN THE
CHAINS OF DESPOTISM CAN RESTRAIN THEM FROM
DESTROYING AND DEVOURING ONE ANOTHER.

James Madison, Federalist #55

Saturday evening, October 1, 2016

To say that Henry Marshall was nervous was an under-statement. He'd already thrown up twice. It was his first presidential debate and he knew—better than anyone else—what he *didn't* know. Depending on the questions asked, he could be made to appear incompetent and unready for the Oval Office. Whether or not the questions were relevant to the task of being the country's chief executive didn't matter—if you got stumped or chumped on national TV you could kiss the race goodbye.

There were a lot of facts Hank didn't know. For instance, he didn't know who the current president of Burundi was, nor who would be his counterpart in Swaziland. He'd have to consult Google even to place Swaziland on the map. He did not know what the annual budget of the city of Chicago was, nor the name of the attorney general of South Dakota. But these were just facts, as Ashton Bancroft reminded him, and he would have people in his administration who knew the answers.

The important thing is that he knew the Constitution and he knew American history and he knew how the government was supposed to function. And most importantly—he knew where the federal government had gone off the rails and what needed to be done to get it back on track.

Fox News was moderating the debate. They'd try to turn it into a political brawl, he was sure, rather than an honest debate, and he was determined not to cooperate. His opportunity came early on.

"Mr. Marshall, this question is for you," said Clifford Rose, one of three Fox News personalities on the panel. "In July, Wayne Bushnell's campaign released an audio recording in which your goal appeared to be securing a spot as Bushnell's running mate, rather than a making a legitimate run at the presidency. The Bushnell recording was later exposed as a fraudulent editing job. Your campaign released an unedited recording of the same meeting in which you can be clearly heard turning down his offer of the veep slot. What do you have to say to Senator Bushnell this evening, and what do you think that incident reveals about his character?"

Marshall looked at Rose without smiling and replied, "Cliff, the Bushnell campaign has sincerely apologized for that incident, and I have accepted their apology. Consequently the matter is closed to further discussion and I have no comment on it.

"But I have a question for you, and for Fox News. How does your question address what Senator Bushnell, Senator Hastings, or myself intend to do when in office? How does that question address our platforms or plans, or the problems the average American faces? With the US national debt approaching twenty trillion dollars, with the current budget deficit hovering around half a trillion, with US military personnel deployed in Iraq, Afghanistan, and other danger zones around the world, with China, Russia, North Korea, and Iran rattling their sabers, and with illegal aliens flooding our borders, is Fox News really unable to find a question of greater importance to the American people? Really, Clifford, the three of us on this platform have two hours to convince the American public that we're up to the task of governing this great country. Do you really want to be asking questions submitted by the National Enquirer?"

The entire auditorium leaped to their feet and gave Marshall a standing ovation, and both senators looked at Marshall and smiled and nodded their agreement.

When the applause died down a red-faced Rose indignantly replied, "The National Enquirer did not submit that question, it was written by Fox News."

"In that case I am very disappointed in Fox News, Cliff. What can I say? Did you have a question of substance for me?"

Rose scowled at Marshall, and asked Senator Hastings about her plans for the education budget. For the next twenty minutes, the panelists directed all their questions to the two senators. Marshall realized that he was being punished for confronting Clifford Rose. Finally Mary Overlund threw a question his way.

"Mr. Marshall, you are on record as opposing crop subsidies for farmers. Do you stand by that statement, sir, and how do you think American farmers respond to that idea?"

"Yes, I stand by that statement. But I want to assure the farmers that other segments of American commerce will share their misery because I intend to do everything in my power to end virtually all federal corporate subsides in every marketplace and every sector of the economy. It's not the job of the federal government to prop up commodities or ventures that can't withstand market forces. Rather, the job of the federal government is to get the devil out of the way of business and let the American people be productive as only Americans can. Not only will I attempt to end federal government subsidies, I also intend to turn the lights out on as many of the intrusive government regulations as I can get my hands on. Some regulations are necessary and good. But many regulations are designed to limit entry to the marketplace, or discourage competition, or to simply exert power and authority over the citizenry. These must be rolled back, and the myriad regulatory agencies need to have their hands slapped. For those agencies that have exceeded their legislative mandates, heads need to roll, ranging from the political appointees to the clerks writing the regulations."

Clifford Rose said, "I have a follow-up on that question for you, Mr. Marshall. It's the opinion of many that you are hostile toward the federal government. Your answer to Mary's question seems to display that hostility. How do you answer that accusation, sir?"

"I *am* hostile to those elements of the federal government that have pushed beyond the sphere of authority assigned them by the US Constitution. I've said many times that my intention is not to fix Washington, DC but to dismantle it. I stand by that statement. The federal government envisioned by the Founders—as represented by the US Constitution—is one of the most beautifully balanced institutions in human history. The ugly leviathan that currently occupies our capital is in many ways a far cry from what the Founders created.

"The usurpation of power by the federal government is the single best explanation for why we have a budget deficit and a ballooning debt. I intend to go into Washington with a chainsaw, not a scalpel.

"So, yes, Cliff, I am hostile to the federal government inasmuch as the current government in DC represents an abandonment of our Constitution. I love those aspects of our government that are working hard to uphold our Constitution."

"Can you name any, sir, that are upholding our Constitution as you see it?" Cliff asked.

"Yes, the US military comes to mind. I have the greatest respect for our armed forces. They have protected this country well for many years. The primary job of the military is to break things and kill people, not to promote current cultural fads nor build democracy among peoples who have no desire for it. The most successful military is the one that's sufficiently powerful and sufficiently ready that it's never needed and never used. That said, our military has been of late deployed on missions that are of doubtful value to our national security. They've had their hands tied by rules of engagement that severely curtail their abilities. As commander-in-chief, it would be my hope to change that.

"It is also my intention to retire many of the high-ranking officers who've betrayed our front line troops by rolling over and playing dead while the current administration turns our armed forces into a feminized social sciences experiment. I also want to commence an overhaul of the Pentagon's purchasing and procurement practices.

"Another part of our government I have a great deal of appreciation for are the judges who adjudicate according to strict constitutional interpretations. It will be my intent to only nominate strict constitutionalists to the bench—in fact that will be my litmus test for judges."

The moderators managed to provoke a series of angry exchanges between the two major party candidates over the issue of reforming the government-controlled healthcare plan. Bushnell insisted that the plan of the current administration was not working, was inordinately expensive, and involved too many government mandates. Hastings doubled down on the current administration's plan, arguing that the plan needed to be given more time to work, and that the solution was more, not less, government control. Marshall was not asked his opinion.

Later analysis of the debate showed that Bushnell received thirty-seven percent of the air-time, Hastings thirty-one, Marshall sixteen, and the moderators sixteen. The opinion of most pundits was that Marshall had not helped himself during the interchange, and polls taken several days later seemed to confirm that viewpoint.

****

On Sunday evening, Marshall, his security detail, and several senior staff flew to San Antonio. Plans for Monday included a campaign blitz through the state. He'd come a day early because the president of TEXGREX, Texas Green Energy Exchange Corporation, had asked him for a private meeting. They met at the Ruth's Chris Steak House at La Cantera Plaza.

Barney O'Donnell was a fascinating character. His parents had immigrated from Belfast, Ireland during the height of the bloodshed between the British military and the Irish Republican Army. His father found work in the oilfields of Midland, Texas, where Barney was born. Barney grew up working as a gopher for a drilling crew during high school. After graduation he worked nine years of eighty-hour weeks, accumulating a nest egg. When the stock in the small oil company he was working for went public he put all his eggs in one basket. Ten years later he sold out, becoming a millionaire. Hard-driving, hard-working, and at times hard-drinking, Barney was a Texan from the tip of his Heritage Limited Edition handmade cowboy boots to the top of his white Stetson hat.

And then he discovered wind energy and the insanely lucrative subsidies the federal government was ladling out. According to a government website, the subsidies for wind energy actually exceeded the wholesale price of energy in Texas. And so Barney started Texas Green Energy Exchange with some highly leveraged cash. Thanks to Uncle Sam, Texas Green hadn't been running in the red for three years. It was becoming highly profitable, with slightly less than forty percent of its revenue coming directly from the federal government.

Henry Marshall was threatening to end that sweet deal by eliminating government subsidies. Without the federal portion of the revenue, TEXGREX would not survive. If Marshall was elected the entire green energy market, primarily solar and wind, would lose their subsidies and most companies would fold. The fossil fuel industries would lose their subsidies, too, but they'd been running at a self-sustaining revenue level for years—as long as they could survive the regulatory attacks, they would continue to be viable businesses.

O'Donnell could read the political winds as well as anyone, so he'd formed a lobbyist consortium to represent the green energy companies in Washington. They'd already bought and paid for Hastings and Bushnell; now it was Marshall's turn. Only Barney was going to do this job himself.

They were eating their dessert when O'Donnell put down his fork, grinned, and drawled, "Hank, sir, I 'spect your campaign is gettin' mighty shy of funds 'bout now. Those political campaigns must be surely expensive. So how's the donor situation? Ya'll got enough cash to get through October?"

"Oh, Barney, I expect it's tight for everyone right now. We'll survive," replied Marshall. He'd smelled a rat within five minutes of sitting down with the expansive Texan, and had an idea of what was coming. He was glad he had his digital recorder running in his pocket but hoped he wouldn't wind up needing it.

"I know some people, Hank, fine upstanding American citizens—red-blooded patriots. You just say the word and we could fund one of the political action committees pushing your policy initiatives with five, mebbe six million dollars. I know what the law says—you can't coordinate your actions with 'em, but since they are for the same thing you are, it would help your campaign. I would not be surprised if within ten days that five mill' could grow to ten, and it would all be supporting your platform." Barney winked and nodded at Henry, grinning.

Henry spread his hands. "Well, what are you waiting for? If you believe the same things I do, surely you don't need a nod from me. Go ahead, man, call your patriots, pull the trigger," he urged, grinning back at the former oilman.

Barney slapped the table with his open palm, "You don't know how much I'd love to do that, Hank. Why, I'd love to get on my phone right now, call a dozen of my friends and get that money rolling in right now. With PAC help I know you'd win Texas, anyway. An' some of my friends are in Californy— you'd probably take that state, too. Just think, all those electoral votes goin' your way. If we got behind you, man, you'd probably win the whole enchilada." He shoveled a Texas-sized portion of apple crumb pie in his mouth.

"Well, that would be downright wonderful," Hank said, toying with the man. By now he realized what the Texan's gambit was. "Let's do it, Barney!

"Just a li'l problem, Hank. It's your darn, cotton-pickin' opposition to those subsidies. Without federal subsidies, Hank, I'm finished. All of us in the green energy field are. Now, if we could just get a li'l exception carved into your plat-form—just enough to save green energy subsidies—well, the problem goes away faster 'n a coyote after a jackrabbit."

Hank nodded. "Is that all, pardner? Is that all I'd have to do?"

"That's it. That's all. You promise that, and I'll turn on the PAC money spigot, pardner."

Hank looked down at the check the server just brought. "You got the tab, Barney?"

Barney grinned, thinking he'd just bought himself another politician. "Oh, yeah. I got it."

Hank stood up. "Good, because we're done. No deal. Not now, not ever. I don't sell my integrity, O'Donnell. If I get in office and if I can convince Congress to back me, you can kiss your subsidies goodbye, pardner." He fished the digital recorder out of his pocket and showed it to the Texan, "And don't even think about trying to pull any dirty tricks with this conversation, because I've got the whole thing right here.

"Now, O'Donnell, here is my promise to you. If I am elected, your subsidies will dry up. But I will do my dead-level best to get the federal government out of your way as a busi-ness man. I'll do my best to create an atmosphere in which businesses like yours can flourish. But it's going to be on a level playing field. The feds aren't going to pick the winners and the losers."

Long after Marshall had left, Barney O'Donnell remained at the table, sipping his coffee and thinking. He was remem-bering his hard-working boyhood in the West Texas oilfields and how his daddy had taught him to give the Man a full day's work for a full day's pay. He remembered the time he shoplifted candy from the town's only Seven-Eleven. His mom found the candy, extracted the truth, gave him a whipping to remember, and dragged him down to the store to confess. Not only was he made to pay for the candy, his mom made him go every night for a week after the store had closed for the evening and sweep their parking lot.

Something in Marshall's words brought back memories of the man he once was. *What happened to that guy I used to be?* O'Donnell wondered. He looked at his hands in disgust. They were soft now, the calluses long gone. *What have I become?*

****

At 9:30 on Monday morning SJ Bergman's cellphone rang, displaying the grinning face of Bill Sylvester, who was calling from the FBI's Investigative and Operations Support Section in Quantico, Virginia.

"Yo, Billy-boy, whatcha got for me?" SJ asked.

"Well, I tracked down that batch of Composition 4 you asked about, and wound up kicking over a few hornets' nests while I was doing it. Haven't had this much fun since I flushed an M80 down the toilet in the girls' dorm at Cal Tech."

"You never told me about that one, Bill," SJ chuckled.

"That's because certain details remain, ah, classified, meaning that I'm not real sure if the statute of limitations has expired yet."

"So what's with the hornets' nests?"

"No one I contacted initially wanted to talk to me. So I called Congressman Norman Mayfield. Not only is he the FBI's strongest ally in Congress, he also chairs the House Committee on Foreign Affairs. He called around and kicked a few butts, and voila! Suddenly I had all the cooperation I needed."

"Must be nice to have that kind of clout," Bergman mused.

"I wouldn't know. But the short story is this: what you want to know about that batch of C4 is classified at the SECRET level. I know you are cleared for it, but you won't be able to share it with local law enforcement. I've sent you my report via SIPRNET. It's pretty interesting reading, especially the last page. Call me back on the secure landline, and I'll tell you what I found."

SJ walked over to the Denver Field Office's Secure Room and called Sylvester. "Okay, William, tell me all about it."

"Bear with me, SJ, for a little bit of background. The State Department and the DOD are collaborating on something called the Global Security Contingency Fund, or GSCF, which was authorized by Section 1207 of the fiscal year 2012 National Defense and Authorization Act. GSCF is essentially military and judicial foreign aid. The mission of the GSCF is to prop up countries at risk by training and supplying their military and implementing rule-of-law programs.

"In 2012, the SecDef and SecState, after a request by the President of Nigeria and our own ambassador, decided to assist the Nigerian army in their fight against the Boko Haram terrorist organization. That assistance consisted of military weaponry and munitions, and a company of US Army Rangers to train the Nigerians how to use it. It was paid for under the auspices of the GSCF. Since 2012 there have been additional training evolutions, all conducted by elements of the 75th Ranger Regiment, based out of Fort Benning. Charlie Company of the 3rd Ranger Battalion was deployed in June, and they're over there right now.

"The training has moved into a much more aggressive posture. Charlie Company is teaching the Nigerians how to conduct offensive operations against Boko Haram strongholds. That's where your C4 comes in, SJ. Included in the latest funding authorization were munitions for training in breaching and demolition. Sixty M183 demolition charge assemblies were ordered from the Swiss manufacturer *Suisse Explosifs AG*. The GSCF only uses Swiss-manufactured explosives in its programs because of the identification micro-taggants the Swiss use in the manufacturing process. If any of the explosives are stolen or captured by terrorist groups, or—God forbid—sold to terrorists, the microtaggants can tell us where they came from.

"This is where the story gets really interesting. Your Composition 4 came from that shipment bound for Nigeria this past June. The M183 demolition package is made up of sixteen separately packaged blocks of C4, each weighing one and a quarter pounds. In military parlance, they're known as M112 demolition blocks. In July, the commander of Charlie Company called home and notified his boss at Fort Benning that one of the M183 demolition packages had arrived in Nigeria with only eight M112 blocks, instead of the normal sixteen. Apparently someone had unpacked the kit, replaced the M112 blocks with identically sized wooden blocks painted army green, each weighing exactly one and a quarter pounds. The only reason Charlie Company discovered it is because during a classroom training exercise they broke open an M183 assembly to show the Nigerians what was inside. They just happened to pick the one that had been tampered with," Bill explained.

"Hmm," SJ mused, leaning back in his chair. "Whoever stole those M112s went to quite a bit of trouble to cover their tracks. I wonder where those missing eight blocks are?"

"That's just it. Nobody knows. None of it has ever turned up until the bombing of Flight 1356.

SJ paused, thinking. Then he affirmed, "Good job, Bill. What about the chain of custody?"

"It's detailed in the report, but I can give you the summary: *Suisse Explosifs AG* manufactured the C4 and provided a heavily armed escort to the airfield on June 7, where it was loaded on an Army C20G guarded by a squad of Rangers. It was flown directly to Fort Benning. At Fort Benning it was stored in a guarded ordnance bunker until it was transported to Nigeria on a C17 along with a load of other military equipment, arriving on June 22 at the same time as Charlie Company. From that time it's been locked in a guarded bunker in Nigeria. At every step of the process, from the manufacturing facility in Switzerland to the ordnance bunkers in Fort

Benning and Nigeria, any and every access to it is recorded in logbooks. The report I sent has digital scans of all the bills of lading, sign-offs, and acknowledgments of receipt."

"Who would have access to it while it was in the bunkers?"

"The Rangers' quartermaster and commanding officer. The man running the GSCF operation, Byron Gillespie, would also have access. Gillespie is a former SEAL and would know how to handle C4. But there's no record he was ever near it."

"Great work, Bill. Don't close the book on this one, yet. I might be calling you back. By the way, contact Charlie Company and see if you can get them to put those blocks in evidence bags and send 'em to us. Forensics might be able to lift something off of them."

****

Monday night, October 3, was a rare night at home for Henry Marshall. He'd flown home from a day of campaigning across the Lone Star State, winding up in Austin with Texas Senator Elizabeth Montgomery and Ashton and Margie Bancroft. Between his security detail, the ever-present Joshua Cummings, and Buford Jackson, the campaign was purchasing whole blocks of airline tickets and it was getting harder to get everyone on the same commercial flight.

Sandy Jackson was practically living at the Marshall residence helping Haley get accustomed to the new reality of a wheelchair. Hank had a contractor install a wheelchair lift on the stairs, which eliminated the upstairs-downstairs barrier for his wife. The neurologist was hopeful that Haley would continue to regain function over the next twelve months, possibly including her mobility. Her speech was already a little better, and mentally she was as sharp as ever.

On Sunday Hank had declared that Monday night was going to be game night. The boys were coming home, Charity was coming home, Lucy Gillespie had been invited, and Buford and Sandy would be there. For an evening they would forget the campaign and just have fun.

The doorbell rang and the twins answered the door. Lucy Gillespie stood on the doorstep. She was wearing blue jeans, a Broncos sweatshirt, and sandals. Lucy looked from Charlie to Conner and announced, "Wow. You really *are* identical."

The boys glanced at each other and grinned—mirror images of one another—and turned back to Lucy. "Yup," they agreed, in unison.

Conner held out his hand. "You are Lucy," he said gravely. "I recognize you by your cast. Welcome, and please come in. I'm Conner."

"Your dad must have said something about me," she said.

"Oh, yeah. We got the whole story," said Charlie. "I'm Charlie, Lucy. Pleased to meet you. I'm the good brother. That," he said, pointing at Conner, "is the evil brother."

Lucy laughed and looked at Conner sympathetically. "Does he always make you be the evil twin?"

"Oh, no. We both get to play the role. About halfway through the evening tonight, Charlie and I will disappear upstairs for a few minutes, change clothes—and roles—he'll be the evil Conner and I'll be the good Charlie, and," he said, looking around and dropping his voice to a conspiratorial whisper, "nobody will know the difference."

She stepped back and raised her eyebrows, looking at the two. She retrieved a pen from her purse, pointed at Charlie, and said, "You. Give me your hand."

He looked at his brother quizzically and shrugged, then held out his right hand. Before he could snatch it away, she drew a big X on the back of his hand. "I'll know," she said airily, and stepped into the house.

Charity ran up and hugged her. "Lucy, I'm so excited to meet you! I'm Charity. Did you get the job?"

Lucy laughed again, "I did! I'm so excited to be working for the Broncos! I actually started today."

"That's awesome!" Charlie said. "Do you get tickets to any of the Broncos' games?" he asked.

"Every home game," she said, smiling.

"Come on back to the den," Charity said, "and I'll introduce you to Mom and the Jacksons. The pizza is almost ready."

They walked back to the den, and Charity said, "Mom, this is Lucy."

"I'm so pleased . . . to meet you, Lucy! Hank has . . . told me all about you. I'm so . . . glad . . .your injuries weren't any worse," Haley said warmly, clasping the girl's hand in both of hers.

"Mrs. Marshall, how do you do? I feel really privileged to meet you, ma'am. I read about your accident in the papers. I'm praying that you enjoy a full recovery." Lucy sat on the couch next to Haley's wheelchair.

"Lucy, I'd be delighted if you . . . called me Haley. And thank you . . . for your prayers. I am grateful to be alive."

The twins walked into the room. Charity looked at her brothers and asked in the slightly disdainful voice that older sisters reserve for brothers when they act like nitwits, "What did you two do to your hands?"

The twins held out their right hands. Each had an identical black X on the back of their hand. "Oh, nothing," one of them said. "Just a little accident with an ink pen."

Lucy shot them a dirty look, but said nothing. They grinned innocently.

"Dear Lucy, how are you doing?" Henry said. He'd just come in from the kitchen. He and walked over and gave the girl a fatherly hug. "Did you get your job?"

"Started today," she said with a big smile.

"Good for you!" he said enthusiastically. "I'm not surprised you got the position. Lucy, allow me to introduce you to some of our dearest friends. This is Buford and Sandy Jackson. Buford is my chief of staff, but really he is my mentor, more like my older brother."

Buford looked at her sternly and asked in his gravelly voice, "Are you the girl who crashed the airplane?" He winked at her with the faintest hint of a grin working at the corners of his mouth.

Sandy said, "Ignore him, Lucy, he's not happy unless he's crabby."

"I'm very happy," Buford objected, looking at his wife.

"You're very crabby, dear."

The group chatted as they ate pizza and salad. After dinner they played *Apples to Apples*. Before long the den was filled with howls of laughter at the inane comparisons being made. Lucy couldn't remember the last time she'd had so much fun.

Hank's cellphone rang just after nine o'clock. It was Mike Trujillo.

"Hank, are you watching the news?" asked Trujillo.

"No, why?"

"You just got three big endorsements. John Calhoun, governor of Texas, Nancy Peterson, governor of Florida, and Admiral Jason Branson, who was chairman of the Joint Chiefs until he retired last month."

* * * * * * * * * *

"Oh, we had a time of it! The Soviets had us chasing our own tail. They were masters of disinformation and we took the bait, hook, line and sinker. Your daddy and momma finally got us straightened around, SJ. Unfortunately, it wasn't before some lives were lost. It was a close thing." Jim Stewart paused, stirring his coffee, lost in his thoughts.

"Oh, that was a case! One of the toughest I ever worked on. The Sovs were telling us one thing, Falcon was telling us another. It was an international *he-said-she-said*. The whole episode was finally declassified in 2012 when it hit the twenty-five-year mark," the old agent said, stirring his coffee again, a faint smile on his face as he remembered events from 1987.

"So did you believe this guy—what was his name?"

"His nickname was Falcon."

"So did you believe Falcon's story?"

A gravelly chuckle escaped Stewart's lips. "Son, I didn't know what to believe." He stirred his coffee.

SJ smiled. "Mr. Stewart, the waitress brought our coffee ten minutes ago and all you've been doing is stirring it. You never even put sugar in it. Probably cold by now."

Stewart blinked and shook his head as though awakening

from a reverie. "Huh? Oh, that. I've already had a cup. I just like the smell of it. Now, listen, boy, almost forgot why I dragged you out here."

Stewart had called SJ Bergman and invited him to an early breakfast at IHOP on Wednesday morning. SJ grabbed at the chance to talk to the retired FBI special agent.

"You let me do the talking, SJ. If you open your mouth, son, you're going to violate federal law and a whole raft of FBI regulations regarding classified information. You'll get your butt in serious trouble. I know you've got a SECRET classification. When I retired, my classification was TOP SECRET. So I'll do the talking, you'll do the listening, and you won't get yourself in trouble.

"I know about the microtaggants, I know about Mark Atkinson's Boeing Black and the two times it rang. I know about Nigeria and the missing M112 blocks."

SJ turned pale. "But how—"

Stewart dismissed his objection with a careless wave of his hand. "I know every detail of your case. Don't ask me how, because I'm not going to tell you other than to say I've still got friends in the Agency going all the way up to the director."

"You know I can't comment on anything you said," Bergman responded indignantly.

"*Of course* I know that, son! I used to work for 'em, too, remember? Now you've gone and got your dander up. You just put that thing right back wherever you store it, shut up, and listen. Capiche?"

SJ sighed. "Sure, Mr. Stewart. I'll listen to what you have to say."

Stewart nodded. "Good. Okay, your case is stuck. But it doesn't have to be. You've got a perfect case to take to a FISA court and get authorization for the metadata on that phone call."

"But—"

"Close your trap, son. Legally, you're not allowed to tell me anything. So you just sit there and listen to your Uncle Jim, okay?"

SJ smiled reluctantly. "Okay, *Uncle Jim*," he said, rolling his eyes.

"As I was saying, it's a perfect case. Here are your two problems. One is that Atkinson is an American citizen. The other is that the phone calls to that Boeing Black might have originated from within the United States—you don't know. Those two items would dispose the FISA judge to say *no.* But there are stronger mitigating circumstances that might cause them to say *yes.* First, the microtaggants indicate that the C4 came from Nigeria, a country known to have a significant terrorist element. Second, it was used in a bombing that brought down an aircraft, killing thirty-five souls. Third, that aircraft had a United States presidential candidate aboard, which raises the stakes. Fourth, while Atkinson is a US citizen, his permanent residence is the Cayman Islands, which is outside the US. In other words, there is a strong possibility that this was a terrorist plot from outside the US.

"Now here's what you do. You contact the Agency's lawyer who's got the best record with FISA presentations—here's his name." Stewart slid the card across the table. "You talk to him, ask him to handle the FISA court. Within twenty-four hours, you'll have what you need to access that metadata from the NSA.

"Don't nod, shake your head, or say yes or no. Just get up, get out of here, and get to work. I've got the tab." Stewart winked at him.

SJ stood up, grinning, and pocketed the attorney's card. He winked back and left the restaurant without another word.

Chapter 20

> . . . IN QUESTIONS OF POWER THEN, LET NO MORE
> BE HEARD OF CONFIDENCE IN MAN, BUT BIND HIM
> DOWN FROM MISCHIEF BY THE CHAINS OF THE
> CONSTITUTION: . . .
>
> *Thomas Jefferson, The Kentucky Resolutions
> of 1798*

Sunday evening, October 9, 2016

"Tonight on MSNBC *Special Report* we're taking an in-depth look at Henry Marshall, the man who's running for president as an Independent. I'm Patty Holmes. A little later in the program we'll be talking with journalist Adam MacKenzie who's written over three exclusives on Henry Marshall, and who seems to have his finger on the pulse of Marshall's campaign. Ezra Klinghoff, senior political reporter for the *Washington Post* is also with us tonight, and I'm looking forward to his thoughts on Marshall.

"It was just twenty months ago that Marshall threw his hat in the ring of what seemed to be a standard presidential election cycle. While he'd been a wildly popular conservative blogger since late 2004, he was relatively unknown in the circles of Washington, DC's powerful and influential. It might, actually, be inaccurate to say he was *unknown*, perhaps *unacknowledged* would be a better term. In the halls and chambers of powerful people, Marshall was—and is—unwelcome. He's a constitutional gadfly, making the case that the federal government has vastly overstepped its bounds and has usurped the rights, power, and authority of the fifty states.

"As you might imagine, that message is not popular in the

Capital. So tonight we want to ask—and answer, if possible—just who is this man that has climbed to twenty-seven percent in national polls, and is threatening to shutter vast portions of the government in DC?

"We turned *Special Reports* investigative journalists loose on Marshall, his campaign, his family, and his background. And this is what they came up with." Patty swiveled around in her chair and watched the big screen behind her as the director went full screen with the pre-recorded segment.

The piece was exceptionally well done, and traced Marshall's steps from his graduation from high school. He joined the Marines in '72, served in Vietnam, and was eventually honorably discharged at the rank of sergeant. His first marriage, to Rose Bruckner, ended tragically when she was killed in an auto accident by a drunk driver. Henry spent the next year in an alcohol-fueled fog. He then had a "religious experience," as the investigative team termed it, which cured him of the booze and got his life back on track. Fast forward eleven years later to 1990, and he'd acquired a college degree in Electronic Engineering, a wife—Haley—and a fat nest egg from a Silicon Valley startup that made it big. Marshall parleyed his know-how and his money into his own hi-tech startup—Econnect, Inc.—which he sold in 2004 for hundreds of millions of dollars.

From that time, Marshall had been splitting his time between his blog and his charitable work. For over twenty hours a week he was swinging a hammer as a volunteer in a Denver-based charity—Build Denver, Inc.—that refurbished homes for citizens living below the poverty line.

Marshall's blog became a sensation, with over twenty million regular followers. Because of its strict constitutionalist positions, it had become very *unpopular* in DC. In 2013 Marshall was tapped to be a domestic policy advisor for Ohio Congressman Ashton Bancroft, and moved to DC for the duration of that appointment. The Marshalls returned home to Colorado in late 2014, just before Bancroft's term expired. But between his blog and his work in DC, Henry Marshall had come to the attention of some powerful people, and in late

February of 2015 he was recruited to run as an independent candidate for president by one of the most well-known and well-respected political consultants, Joshua Cummings, as well as a handful of other politicos, including Bancroft.

The video segment spent the final five minutes examining Henry Marshall's family, faith, and charitable work. When the segment ended, MSNBC went to a commercial break and then returned to the live show.

"This is Patty Holmes, and you're watching MSNBC *Special Report*. As we have done for Senators Hastings and Bushnell, we are devoting tonight's program to an examination of Henry Marshall and his candidacy. With me in the studio are Adam MacKenzie, senior political reporter for the *Chicago Tribune*, and Ezra Klinghoff, senior political reporter for the *Washington Post*.

Patty turned from the camera to her guests. "So, gentlemen, in this campaign we have two fairly standard representatives of their respective parties, Hastings and Bushnell—and I hasten to say that referring to them as 'standard' is not meant in a pejorative or negative sense. What I mean by that is they represent their parties' platforms well, with no surprises. So we have Hastings and Bushnell—and then we have Marshall, who's frankly hard to categorize. Adam, you go first: what do you think of Henry Marshall, the man?"

MacKenzie was dressed simply in a pair of khakis, a black turtleneck shirt, dark brown coat, and brown loafers. He shrugged and responded, "Well, Patty, I must admit he's somewhat of a puzzle to me. I've never known anyone quite like him. Look, let's be honest: no one rises this high on the political ladder with his integrity perfectly intact. Somewhere on the way to becoming the standard-bearer of your party as a presidential candidate, you've broken some promises, told some lies, made some backroom deals that maybe wouldn't pass moral muster. Both parties know this, the average voter understands this, and news reporters realize it—we all get it, okay?

"But, Patty, that's where Marshall is so radically—and I mean, radically—different. First of all, he didn't climb any political ladder. Other than serving Ashton Bancroft in a background role, Marshall appears on the scene out of the blue. He's never even run for dogcatcher. The first political office he runs for is also the highest, the most powerful office in the world. Now you might think that means he's unqualified, and in a certain sense you're right, but it also means he's not compromised. He hasn't been bought and sold. He owes no favors.

"Patty, I have to admit it—I'm a self-identified liberal—but I find myself really liking Marshall. I don't agree with his positions, but I love his character and integrity."

"Oh, come on, MacKenzie, you're drinking the Kool-Aid," snorted Klinghoff. He turned to Holmes, waving his hands for emphasis. "Patty, I disagree. The only special 'integrity' that Marshall's got is that he hasn't been under the public microscope long enough for us to know where the bodies are buried. But they are there somewhere, I assure you. Closets are for hiding skeletons, and my bet is that Marshall has plenty of closets."

"So are you saying he's a fake, Ezra?" Patty asked.

Klinghoff grimaced, "No, not exactly a fake. He's just not Saint Henry, okay? I'm sure he's a nice guy and everything, but I've yet to meet a pol that's not up to their ears in at least some low-level of corruption."

"But Ezra, have you ever met Marshall?" asked MacKenzie.

"No, and I do regret that. But the I-95 corridor is my beat, and I missed him the brief time he was in Washington serving Bancroft. You've got the Midwest beat, MacKenzie," Klinghoff said with a wistful grin. "You're one lucky dude."

"I've met him, and he's given me three or four exclusive interviews. You might change your tune if you spent some time with him," MacKenzie insisted.

Ezra Klinghoff just shrugged, and turned back to Patty Holmes.

"Okay, gentlemen, we've learned about his background. We've had a little dust-up about his character. What about his campaign? Ezra, you first this time."

Klinghoff compressed his lips and nodded. "Look. He's got Joshua Cummings running the circus and Cummings is far and away the best there is. And it shows; the Marshall campaign is doing a terrific job staying on message. Nearly everyone in America can quote Marshall's slogan: *I'm not going to fix Washington, I'm going to dismantle it*. That's a really popular idea, by the way. It's off the charts in the poll-testing that both Hastings and Bushnell have commissioned. And his Tenth Amendment shtick is popular, too. Yeah, Patty, Cummings runs a tight ship and that sort of discipline seems to serve Marshall's campaign very well."

Holmes looked at the Chicago reporter and asked, "Adam, what do you think?"

"Ezra just made my point about Marshall's character." He turned to Klinghoff and asked, "Do you know who did *not* poll-test that slogan? And do you know who did not poll-test the Tenth Amendment 'shtick,' as you call it?"

Klinghoff wrinkled his nose in irritation, "What do you mean, Adam, *do I know who didn't poll-test it*? Sure, three hundred fifty million Americans didn't poll-test it. So what! What's that got to do with anything?"

"Oh, but it does matter! The Marshall campaign never poll-tested either of those, simply because that slogan and that *shtick* reflect who Marshall really is. It wouldn't matter to him *how* they poll-test. The man is an ideologue, he's a true believer in his own positions. This is a guy who stood up in a meeting of five hundred Iowa farmers and told them point-blank that if elected he was going to try to put an end to their crop subsidies."

Adam turned back to Patty, "But I do agree with Ezra about the campaign and Josh Cummings. So far they haven't made a misstep. And picking Bancroft as his running mate was an outstanding move. Bancroft has a stellar reputation, he's got great foreign policy chops, and this isn't his first rodeo."

Ezra nodded, "I agree—Bancroft's a great pick. Between snagging Cummings and Bancroft, Marshall has made some really good moves."

"What about the polls, gentlemen?" Patty asked. "Before the series of accidents several weeks ago Marshall was at thirty percent. He slipped down to twenty-five and then clawed back up to twenty-seven, where he seems stuck. What are his chances, and how did the accidents affect his campaign?"

Klinghoff shook his head sadly and spread his hands, "Patty, the accidents were—and continue to be—devastating for him. I'm not for Marshall, but I hate to see anyone experience the trouble he's had," affirmed Ezra. "He lost at least two weeks in the hottest part of the campaign. That's huge. His lovely wife Haley is his best asset, and she's confined to a wheelchair, no longer able to campaign for him. I pray that she has a full recovery. His scar—it's healing now—is off-putting to look at. He's lost his data guy, who is now facing criminal charges and was somehow allegedly involved in the bombing of Flight 1356. All in all, these accidents have been an unmitigated disaster, Patty, and he won't recover from them, not by November 8. Right now this election is Pamela Hasting's to lose. Bushnell picked up a few Marshall voters, but it won't be enough to put him over the top."

"You agree, Adam?" asked Holmes.

MacKenzie pulled at his lip for a moment, thinking, and then said, "No."

"No?" repeated Ezra with surprise. "Why?"

"You're right, Ezra, about how the accidents have hurt him, and I agree with you there. But you're not thinking about how they have *helped* him." Adam turned to face the anchor. "Listen, Patty, one of the worst deficits Marshall faced when he got into this race was name recognition. He was well known among conservative blog readers, but relatively unknown beyond that smallish circle. Nobody knew who Henry Marshall was.

"But that's no longer true. Because of that trio of accidents, he's become a household name. And we're not done hearing the news about Flight 1356, nor about his IT director. It's quite likely he'll get free play in the news media four days out of every five between now and the eighth simply because of the ongoing reporting about the accidents. It's not just a political story—more importantly it's a human interest story that's captured our country's imagination. And the Marshalls have conducted themselves so admirably folks can't help liking them, even rooting for them. Many people are hearing his name, becoming curious about who he is, googling him, researching him, visiting his website, and thinking about his positions. And some of them will like what they see."

"So you think he has a chance?" Patty asked.

"He didn't, not before September 23. But he does now. In fact, I think he'll have a late surge. And here's the interesting part: it just might be late enough that none of the polls pick it up. We could have a historic upset."

****

The FISA Court's approval came on Tuesday evening. Wednesday morning Bergman picked Bill Sylvester up at the airport. He'd requested Sylvester from the FBI's IOSS Division to handle the research end of the case.

"Did you bring your hi-tech toys with you, Willy?" asked Bergman, as they stood at the baggage carousel in the airport.

"I did, indeed. Never leave home without 'em. Never know when a Stingray might come in handy." The Stingray was a device that mimicked a cellphone tower, coaxing all the nearby cellphones to broadcast their Electronic Serial Number (ESN) and their International Mobile Subscriber Identity number (IMSI), as well as other bits of data.

"Excellent. We got all the approval we need from FISA. As soon as you can lift that Boeing Black's ESN and IMSI, you can log onto the NSA database from our secure room and start cross-referencing the metadata. With luck you can narrow down the location of the phone that originated those calls on September 27."

When they got back to the FBI building, Bergman set Sylvester up in the secure room and then retired to his own office, leaving the IOSS man to perform his digital wizardry without unnecessary interruption.

A few minutes later his cellphone rang. It was Grady Wilson from the Golden PD. "Hey, Grady, what's up?"

"Our bad boy wants to talk to you," the police detective said. He chuckled. "Apparently I don't count. He's not interested in talking to me, says he wants to talk to the feds. His lawyer can be here in thirty minutes, if you're available. What do you say? Can you pop over?"

"Sure, I'll be over in fifteen."

****

Wilson and Bergman walked down the hall toward the interrogation room, as Wilson caught the FBI agent up to date with the latest news on their prisoner.

"He's been pretty much a model prisoner, cooperative, no threats, other than one incident. Some muscle-bound punk— one of those MMA types—tried to get tough with Atkinson. The punk was serving time for robbery and aggravated assault. I'm telling you, SJ, this kid was big—six four, maybe two twenty, really built. Atkinson is maybe six feet, one seventy, wiry. Anyway, this punk starts pushing Atkinson around, talking trash to him. Atkinson was ignoring him. So the kid takes a poke at him. Atkinson took him apart in less than ten seconds. Broke one of the punk's arms, a wrist, and a knee. Some of the guards managed to talk Atkinson down while there was still enough left of the kid to take to the hospital. I saw the incident on the security video. There was no contest, Atkinson walked all over him. And fast? Oh, my. I can see why they say the SEALs are the best in the world.

"Ever since then we've had Atkinson in shackles—don't want him getting a notion of going after our own people. In any case, we didn't charge him with anything new. It was the punk's fault. That kid will be spending an extra six months in the slammer, after he gets out of the hospital."

The two men chatted outside the interrogation room while the lawyer and his client conferred privately within. Finally the lawyer stuck his head outside. "We're ready," Cavenaugh said.

Wilson turned on the video recording equipment, checked the settings, and then he and Bergman entered the room.

"I'm ready to talk," Mark Atkinson said. The tough veneer he'd exuded previously was all but gone. Apparently the thought of thirty-five counts of murder, along with the other charges associated with bombing a commercial airliner, was weighing heavily on his mind.

His attorney, Patrick Cavenaugh, nodded. "He is. Provided you grant full immunity, he'll turn State's witness and spill the beans. The whole story. Anything you want to know." Atkinson nodded.

"Hmm. Full immunity," SJ muttered as he stared at Atkinson. He thought for a moment and then shook his head. The price was too high. "Full immunity? No. Maybe limited immunity. If you can give us the guy who gave you the battery for the laptop, we'll talk limited. But full is off the table."

"Why?" asked Cavenaugh.

"Why? Because we're maybe ten days from putting the other guy in the bag without his help," SJ said, motioning to Atkinson. SJ wasn't sure his claim was true, but Cavenaugh wouldn't know that—neither would Atkinson. "Atkinson's testimony might put the nails in the coffin, but I don't think we'll really need it. Limited is the deal."

"What would limited involve?" asked Cavenaugh.

"Well, obviously I'd need to clear this with the US attorney, but I suspect it might take the thirty-five murder charges off the table. You'd still be facing the attempted murder charges with respect to Timothy Hardy," Bergman said, looking at the former SEAL. "In fact, anything related to the Hardy case will stick. But we might be able to get you off the hook for all of the charges surrounding Flight 1356."

Cavenaugh started to answer, but Atkinson cut him off. "No. Full immunity. That's the deal. I walk out of here a free man."

Bergman picked up his legal pad and stood up. He shook his head. "A free man? I don't think so. You lost that option a long time ago." The agent turned to Grady Wilson. "Grady, I've got a lot to do, so I'm gonna run. Let me know if

Atkinson changes his mind." He acknowledged the lawyer with a slight tip of his head, "Counselor," and then left the room, shutting the door behind him.

****

Sylvester walked into Bergman's office with a big grin on his face, plopped down in the chair and put his feet up on the desk. Bergman frowned, and swept his friend's feet off the desk. "My desk," Bergman said. "My feet only. What's with the silly grin, Bill?"

"I've got to think of a way to make this case last until Monday. That way I'm in colorful Colorado with Saturday and Sunday to bump around the mountains on the Agency's dime. Sweet," the researcher chortled.

"You think you'll be done before this weekend, researching those phone calls?" Bergman asked, raising his eyebrows.

"Oh, I'm almost done now. And I've pretty much pegged your bad boy's little friend."

Bergman sat up straight, incredulity on his face. "Really? Already?"

"Yep. Once the Stingray gave me the IMSI for the Boeing Black, the rest was pretty easy. I filtered the NSA metadata for all calls to that IMSI, and then cross-referenced the NSA data using the time and date you provided for the two incoming calls. That gave me the originating phone's IMSI, and no surprise, both calls came from the exact same phone. And the digital signature indicates it's another Boeing Black. Nearly everything from those phones is so heavily encrypted we can't access it. But I should be able to take the IMSI for the originating phone and access cell tower records to triangulate its position at the time of the calls. That's going to take another day or so, shaking loose that data from the providers. I could hack it in a couple hours, but I'm guessing you're going to want to use it in court, so I'll do it the legal way."

Bergman grinned. "You want to hang around till the weekend, so you've got Saturday and Sunday to enjoy the

Rockies, Willy? I'll make it happen. You just keep turning over stones, buddy, and collecting all the slimy things crawling underneath in the dark. Never know—you might even wind up with two weekends here."

****

The official investigation into the downing of Flight 1356, comprised of Yates' NTSB team and Dalton's FBI ERT, was experiencing relentless pressure from the media. Any tragedy involving a commercial airliner captured the public's attention anyway, but when rumors began circulating that the bombing was connected with an attempt to assassinate a candidate for the presidency of the United States, the effort to restrict leaks became impossible. A joint decision was made at the highest levels of the NTSB and FBI to hold a press conference and provide enough selected details to derail some of the inaccurate reporting that was already circulating on the Internet.

Friday morning, October 14, dawned under rain-sodden, windy skies in Chicago. The two investigative teams took time out from their work to cordon off restricted areas containing the wreckage of Flight 1356 in the old FedEx hangar building at Midway International. They set up neat rows of chairs for the press. The charred fuselage of the destroyed 737-800 served as the backdrop for the podium. A large detachment from the Chicago PD was deployed along the cordon, an officer every ten feet or so, to keep overly aggressive reporters and camera crews away from the wreckage. A carefully selected set of photos taken by the ERT was prepared for distribution. The hangar was opened at 9:00 a.m. to allow television crews to set up, and then the press conference began at 10:00. All the seats were taken, and at least thirty reporters and journalists were standing behind the last row of chairs.

"Good morning. My name is Roland Yates, and I am the NTSB Investigator-in-Charge of the investigation into the crash of Flight 1356. I have a prepared statement, and then Special Agent Sarah Dalton, who's leading the FBI's Evidence

Response Team, will also make a statement. We will then entertain your questions.

"On Friday, September 23, shortly before 9:00 p.m. local, Southwest Airlines Flight 1356, bound for Denver, departed the gate and taxied to Runway 31C. After receiving clearance for takeoff, the aircraft began its takeoff roll. As the pilot rotated the aircraft an explosion occurred, stunning the pilots into momentary unconsciousness. Debris from the explosion was ingested into the left-hand engine, causing it to flame out. The right-hand engine continued operating at takeoff power, causing the jet, which was still on the ground, to veer left off the runway and begin spinning. The co-pilot regained consciousness and immediately shut down the engine, but by this time it was too late to save the aircraft. The sideward skid of the jet on the grass between 31C and 31L ripped off the landing gear as the plane continued to rotate. Finally the right wing dug into the ground, rupturing the fuel tanks and igniting a fire under the wing, which eventually spread to the passenger compartment.

"Thanks to quick action by passengers who escaped injury and first responders on the scene, the aircraft was emptied of passengers before the cabin space caught fire. We are fortunate that the casualty count was limited to thirty-five people. Our heartfelt condolences and sympathy go out to the families of those victims.

"Working closely with the FBI we've determined that the source of the explosion was a bomb that had been placed in a passenger's laptop. Special Agent Dalton will say more about the bomb so I'll turn the microphone over to her."

Dalton stepped to the podium, and continued the briefing. "I am Special Agent Sarah Dalton, and I'm leading the FBI Evidence Response Team. Here is what we know at the present time: a bomb employing Composition 4 was detonated in the forward closet at one second after 9:00 p.m., causing the chain of events resulting in the crash of Flight 1356.

"There have been multiple theories floating about the news outlets about the explosion. I'd like to put those to rest.

One report claimed that a terrorist wearing a suicide vest jumped from his seat, ran up to the forward closet and cried *Allahu Ackbar* immediately before detonating the bomb. That didn't happen, period. This bombing was not a terrorist event.

"Another news outlet interviewed an alleged witness who claimed to have seen a shoulder-launched missile fired toward the jetliner. There is no truth to that claim.

"Here's what we do know: the bomb was not intended by its makers for Flight 1356." When Special Agent Dalton said this, a collective gasp could be heard among the media. "The intended target was Henry Marshall, one of the candidates for the presidency in the current election. The bomb, which had been planted in his laptop battery, was supposed to detonate at 9:00 p.m. on the 23rd while he was alone in his hotel room in downtown Chicago. However, when Marshall received news that his wife was rushed to the hospital after a bad accident in their home that afternoon, he changed his plans and booked a flight to Denver. That flight was Southwest Flight 1356. Whoever was trying to assassinate Marshall never intended to bring down an airliner. The FBI is currently trying to identify a suspect."

Roland Yates joined Dalton at the podium and said, "We'll take your questions now." He pointed to a journalist in the front row.

"Mary Overlund, *Fox News*. Agent Dalton, has a motive been established as to why someone would want to kill Henry Marshall?"

"No. We do not have a motive at this time. Next question. Yes, go ahead."

"Matt Johnson, *CBS*. Is there a relationship between this bombing and the suspect in custody in Colorado, who allegedly tried to kill Mr. Marshall's IT director?"

"I cannot comment on that, Matt, other than to say that we are following all leads. Next question."

"Andy Rutledge, *Denver Post*. This question is for Mr. Yates. Was the black box recovered, and what sort of shape was it in?"

"Yes, Andy, we recovered both the cockpit voice recorder

and the flight data recorder. They were in excellent condition, and the data from both devices is what led us to the current level of confidence we have about what happened to Flight 1356." Yates pointed to another reporter.

"Ellen Merrow, *Politico*. Are you presently pursuing any leads that might implicate either the Democrats or the Republicans in this tragedy?"

"Absolutely not," the FBI agent said firmly. "There's not even a hint of political involvement in this, and I would appreciate it if all of you could make that point clear in your reporting. At no time have either the FBI or the NTSB run across anything that implicates either party." Yates nodded his agreement, then motioned to MacKenzie.

"Adam MacKenzie, *Chicago Tribune*. My sources are claiming that the C4 explosive has been positively identified as having come from Nigeria. Agent Dalton, can you comment on this?"

"No, I'm afraid I cannot, Adam," Dalton said firmly.

"Can you at least confirm that the FBI has found micro-taggants in the residue left from the explosion?" he persisted.

"No, I cannot. I'm sorry, but I can't answer any questions on this subject. Next question."

The press conference continued for another thirty minutes, after which the reporters were allowed to photograph the wreckage from behind the security cordon.

Two days later an exclusive appeared in the *Chicago Tribune* under MacKenzie's byline. The article claimed that Timothy Hardy had been allegedly bribed to replace the battery in Henry Marshall's laptop on the fateful day, and that the replacement battery contained a bomb, unbeknownst to Hardy. The attempts on Hardy's life were intended to eliminate the principal witness to the battery scheme. The explosives in the battery were manufactured in Switzerland, and had been sold to Nigeria. This last detail was in fact incorrect—the explosives had been sold to GSCF—but most of the other points of MacKenzie's article were accurate, so much so that the FBI launched an internal investigation to identify the leaker, an in-house effort that consumed them for the next three months. It came up empty.

****

On Friday afternoon, Bill Sylvester was finally able to mine the cellphone tower data from the areas in which the two originating phone calls came on September 27, the calls that were placed to Mark Atkinson's Boeing Black. The software application he was using triangulated the data from four towers, and came up with two points on the map. He brought up Google Earth and plotted the two circles, each having a radius of about two hundred twenty meters.

"Oh, boy. That's not good," Sylvester muttered to himself. The first circle encompassed the Harry S. Truman building in downtown Washington, DC—in other words, the US State Department.

The second circle took in most of Runner Road, a semi-rural residential area of Great Falls, Virginia. Sylvester accessed a database of government employees and filtered for home addresses on Runner Road. One name came up—Byron Gillespie.

Sylvester stared at the name and muttered to himself, "Well, surprise, surprise: Byron Gillespie! I know who you are —you're the State Department dude directing the GSCF operation in Nigeria from your comfortable desk in Foggy Bottom. Small world indeed."

Sylvester recorded the results of his research and then shut down the computer. He gazed at the darkened monitor for a moment, thinking. *This is really going to mess up Gillespie's day, and I'm betting it won't be pretty. The man's a former SEAL. He's gonna be a hard target. Better find SJ.*

Bill Sylvester poked his head in Bergman's office. SJ was on the phone, and he motioned his friend to take a seat. After his call was completed, SJ asked, "What's up, Bill?"

"I was just thinking, SJ, you look like you could use a donut. C'mon, I'm buying." Sylvester said.

"Bill, it's almost five—time for supper. I don't want a

donut, but thanks anyway."

"Then you need supper. C'mon, I'm buying," the IOSS man insisted.

SJ looked at his friend suspiciously. "What's with you, man?"

Sylvester looked around. No one was within earshot. He raised his eyebrows and stared at intensely at his friend. "Come. With. Me. Now!" he said quietly, emphasizing each word.

A few minutes later they were walking west on East 36th Avenue, heading for Famous Dave's Bar-B-Que. It was a brilliant, clear afternoon and the sun was sitting above the peaks in the west.

"What's up, Willy? Obviously you wanted me out of the office, but I'm going to hold you to your word about supper. Have you ever eaten at Famous Dave's before? Are you a fan of barbecue?" Bergman asked as they strolled down the sidewalk of the busy street.

"Oh, yeah. Love it. Never eaten at this one, but we've got one in Falls Church."

They walked another half-block, enjoying the afternoon, until SJ finally said, "Okay, Bill, cough it up. Why are we out here?"

"SJ, I've managed to locate where those two phone calls came from. And, ah, let's just say that the plot thickens."

"That's why you wanted to discuss it outside of the office, Bill?" SJ asked, shooting a curious glance at his friend.

"Uh, yeah. Just in case. Didn't want anyone eavesdropping. If by some remote chance this was an official action I have no idea how high it might go. You and I could become targets ourselves simply by poking our noses into it."

"What are you talking about, Bill?" asked SJ, scrutinizing the IOSS researcher.

"SJ, the earlier call originated from the State Department in Washington. *The State Department*, for crying out loud! The second call originated from a residential area in Great Falls. I cross-referenced the government employee database for that residential area, and only came up with one name for

State Department employees. Luckily the area is semi-rural, otherwise I'd have probably gotten quite a few hits. Anyway, the name is Byron Gillespie."

Bergman stopped and looked at his friend. "The GSCF guy?" he asked incredulously.

"Bingo, baby. He is the chief facilitator for projects on the African continent. Just in case your geography is a little wobbly, Nigeria happens to be in that landmass."

"No kidding," SJ rejoined sarcastically. "Hmm. Sounds like Byron Gillespie bears looking into."

"Yeah. But you'd better tread carefully. He's a former SEAL. Those guys have a well-honed sixth sense. You start investigating him, he's probably gonna know it within two, three days at the most. And what if this was some sort of official sanction? That wouldn't go well for either of us."

"You've been watching too many Jason Bourne movies, Bill. If this had been officially sanctioned, Marshall's death would have been arranged to look like an accident, not a bombing. No, there's something else going on here. Quit your worrying!"

Twelve hours later, Byron Gillespie was under court-approved FBI surveillance. All known phones were being monitored, his home had been bugged, and his whereabouts were being tracked.

Chapter 21

THE INTERNAL EFFECTS OF A MUTABLE POLICY ARE STILL MORE CALAMITOUS. IT POISONS THE BLESSING OF LIBERTY ITSELF. IT WILL BE OF LITTLE AVAIL TO THE PEOPLE, THAT THE LAWS ARE MADE BY MEN OF THEIR OWN CHOICE, IF THE LAWS BE SO VOLUMINOUS THAT THEY CANNOT BE READ, OR SO INCOHERENT THAT THEY CANNOT BE UNDERSTOOD; IF THEY BE REPEALED OR REVISED BEFORE THEY ARE PROMULGATED, OR UNDERGO SUCH INCESSANT CHANGES THAT NO MAN, WHO KNOWS WHAT THE LAW IS TODAY, CAN GUESS WHAT IT WILL BE TOMORROW. LAW IS DEFINED TO BE A RULE OF ACTION; BUT HOW CAN THAT BE A RULE, WHICH IS LITTLE KNOWN, AND LESS FIXED?

James Madison, Federalist #62

Wednesday, October 19, 2016

Henry Marshall, Buford Jackson, and Joshua Cummings sat in the living area of their hotel suite, relaxing before the rally planned for later that evening. Haley was taking a nap in the bedroom, and Sandy was taking a shower.

"I had no idea we had the sort of voter strength in Pennsylvania that I've seen in the last few days," Marshall said, sipping on a Coke.

"Agreed," said Buford. "Capturing Pennsylvania is clearly a possibility. It's a surprise to me, too."

"I had a notion that you actually did have the support we've seen, Hank," confessed Joshua Cummings. "I've been watching not only the raw polls, which are pretty strong by themselves, but the issue polls, too. If you take away the problem of party labels, your platform positions are exactly what the people of Pennsylvania have been asking for, Hank. But you're battling party identification. Party stalwarts feel guilty if they vote for someone not on their party's ballot."

The latest polls were demonstrating that Pennsylvania was in play. It was a twenty-electoral-vote plum that Cummings wanted to pick. He'd organized a three-day whirlwind campaign swing through the Keystone State.

One of the states they would not be visiting, however, was New York. Hastings and Bushnell were running neck and neck there, with Marshall a distant third. Cummings' strategy was to give Bushnell a chance to take it away from the Democrat, so that its twenty-nine electors weren't added to Pamela Hasting's total. Hastings had already locked up California (fifty-five electoral votes); neither Bushnell nor Marshall had much traction there. Texas (thirty-eight electoral votes) was in the bag for Marshall. His message of getting the feds out of the way resonated with the people of the Lone Star State. Once Elizabeth Montgomery had endorsed him and begun campaigning for him there, Marshall built an unsurpassable lead in Texas.

Texas was the linch-pin of Cummings' strategy. The states completing the Big Six—Illinois (twenty) and Florida (twenty-nine)—were toss-ups, and would be getting a great deal of attention from Marshall in the next several weeks. If he could capture both those states, as well as Pennsylvania, it would give Marshall one hundred seven of the two hundred seventy electoral votes needed to win the election. Just as importantly, it would deny them to his opponents.

When they entered Hersheypark Arena several hours later, it was already packed. The venue's official capacity was thirty thousand, and as Joshua Cummings surveyed the crowd he guessed the arena was ninety-five percent full. The group stood behind the curtain, chatting until it was time to start. Sergeant Jack Carson was with them. Carson had done such a great job in Dayton in September, prepping the crowd with humor, that Cummings had secured him for major rallies for the remainder of the campaign. The sergeant was the most popular speaker at each event, sprinkling his comments with sharp-elbowed humor, usually aimed at Marshall and Bancroft. What Carson didn't know is that Marshall was seriously considering him to head up the VA and oversee the shuttering of the Veterans Health Administration.

"Are you ready, Sergeant?" Hank asked, putting his hand on the veteran's shoulder.

"Ready to rock and roll, sir," he responded with a grin. Carson looked over at Haley sitting in her wheelchair, and asked impishly, "Wanna go to a barbecue, babe?"

She laughed and said, "You bet, Jack. Let's do it."

"What do you mean, a barbecue?" Hank asked, as the two started rolling toward the curtain to make their entrance.

Carson stopped and looked over his shoulder at Marshall. "She's the charcoal and I'm the grill." He turned and rolled a few more feet, then called over his shoulder just as he rolled through the curtain, "And you're the turkey!"

The two rolled out to the podium to uproarious applause, and immediately began trading lighthearted jabs and quips at each other's disabilities. Tonight's event was the first time that Haley and Carson shared the stage, and the first time Haley had been on the platform since her accident. The audience loved it. At one point Haley went blank trying to think of the punchline for one of her jokes. Laughing infectiously at herself, she admitted that she'd forgotten the line. The crowd roared with laughter. In an election season filled with special interest grievances, college safe zones, trigger warnings, and other emotionally crippled nonsense, it was clear that the public was longing to hear from people who were comfortable in their own skin, disabilities notwithstanding.

When Marshall came out to the platform he received an enthusiastic standing ovation. "Good evening. It's great to be here in the Keystone State. People have been kind and gracious to us all across Pennsylvania. My wife has been lobbying for an executive action for my first day in office, if I'm elected. She wants me to declare chocolate the official food of the White House. I'm seriously considering it. I told her that I thought it was definitely worth twenty electoral votes."

After a few more light-hearted comments, Marshall gave a twenty-minute, detail-laden speech filled with specifics about his intentions to dismantle Washington. As he concluded his remarks, he said, "I've been asked if I am a populist. Perhaps you've noticed, populism is all the rage now. The answer is no, I am not a populist. The Founding Fathers of this nation did not give us a pure democracy, but a democratic republic, in which we elect people to serve us in the House of Representatives and the Senate. James Madison wisely said, in *Federalist #55, In all very numerous assemblies, of whatever character composed, passion never fails to wrest the sceptre from reason. Had every Athenian citizen been a Socrates, every Athenian assembly would still have been a mob.*

"Madison's contention was that the larger the group legislating—which in a pure democracy would be the entire body politic—the more prone it would be to the passions of the mob, rather than the carefully debated and considered reasonings of a smaller, representative legislature. I think Madison was correct; the republic the Founding Fathers gave us is demonstrably the best government in the history of mankind, balancing freedom, opportunity, justice, protection, rights, and responsibilities as no other government ever has done.

"So, no, I am not a populist. But I also don't believe that Jefferson, Madison, Adams, and others of our Founders envisioned a perpetual, professional ruling class seated in Washington, DC. They very carefully considered what length of term would be proper for the House of Representatives, settling on two years as the best figure that would give a representative enough time to learn the ropes and be effective, but short enough so that the people could easily give his office to another if he abused it or was deaf to their wishes.

"Unfortunately, because our legislators are not term-limited we have developed a political class that virtually lives in Washington, and an incumbency that's nigh unto impossible to dislodge. That is not in the best interest of our states or our federal government, and it undergirds the development and growth of a corrupt system of crony capitalism and rent-seekers. I support a constitutional amendment that would set term limits on US senators and congressmen." Marshall's speech concluded to enthusiastic applause.

Ashton Bancroft took the podium next, and delivered a fifteen-minute speech setting forward a foreign policy that would limit US military intervention to matters of direct and demonstrable national interest, or matters required by treaty or alliance. Nation-building exercises did not qualify. Bancroft also pledged that when the Marshall administration deployed the armed forces, it would do so with consistently aggressive rules of engagement. Foreign aggression would be met with a swift and lethal response of overwhelming force, and except where treaty obligations required otherwise, the decision to commence military action would be determined unilaterally using constitutional procedures. Israel, Britain, Canada, Australia, and Japan were identified as major allies, though by no means the only ones. The European Union was fore-warned that from now on it would be responsible for a much larger financial commitment to its own defense, as well as to NATO, if NATO was to remain a meaningful organization. In conclusion, Bancroft warned that without immediate major reforms at all levels, a Marshall administration would withdraw the country from the United Nations, and ask it to move its headquarters out of the US.

When Bancroft was done, the crowd began chanting "Marshall! Marshall! Marshall!" Marshall's whole entourage came out on the platform and waved at the crowd, and then Henry, accompanied by a very nervous Estrada and two Secret Service agents, came off the platform and mingled with the crowd, signing autographs and posing for pictures. It was clear the message was resonating with those gathered at the Arena. What wasn't clear is whether it would be adequate to carry the campaign to victory in November.

****

Among the former SEALs who occupied the very

shadowy world of the international mercenary community, there was a strict code: you didn't rat on your brothers. Period. This code was looked upon as an inviolable rule, and it wasn't because of the sterling integrity of the men who upheld it. It was because your end would be swift, sure, and unpleasant if you broke the code. If you violated this rule, you became a target not only of the man you turned in, but of the whole community, because you were perceived as a danger to everyone. If you could be induced to turn on Billy-Bob, so the thinking was, you could also be persuaded to turn on Bubba, and anyone else.

It was for this reason that Gillespie was not particularly concerned that Mark Atkinson would give him up. And it was also for this reason that Atkinson's next request, had total immunity been granted, would have been for the federal Witness Protection Program. But as it was, both men were safe because total immunity had not been granted.

That wasn't to say, however, that Byron Gillespie wasn't upset. He was. He was coldly furious. Three days ago he'd become aware that he was under surveillance. The boys tailing him were doing such a poor job of it he'd thought of stopping them once or twice and giving them some helpful hints. Hint number one: *for crying out loud, don't use a black Suburban—nobody uses them except the government anyway!*

Then, two days ago he'd gotten a call from a paid informant in the CIA. Ares' little weapons-fund-skimming operation would not be looked upon favorably by either the SecState or SecDef—it was, after all, their money he was pocketing. So Ares had recruited a mole in the CIA, a man that he'd turned with the help of some cold cash, to let him know if anyone was on his trail.

"Gillespie," said Byron, irritated that the man would call him at work.

"Byron, you'd better be checking six, man."

"What are you talking about?"

"Somebody's doing some discreet snooping, but not discreet enough. They're checking out your banking and financial records, international movements for the last three years, and so forth. It smells like FBI. Don't say I didn't warn you."

It looked like things were heading for a showdown, and while Gillespie had supreme confidence in his ability to either evade or fight his way out of any situation, if he took that sort of definitive action against agents of the US government, he was finished. He'd have to flee the States and he'd never see Lucy again.

It was this recognition that finally pushed Ares over the thin line of irrationality he'd been approaching since his wife died. His rage required a suitable target, and he found one in Henry Marshall. His anger burned with a volcanic, violent, unreasoning fury. It was all Marshall's fault, beginning with the initial threat to Gillespie's illicit income and extending to the investigation that was now on the verge of exposing Gillespie as a murderous criminal. To top it all, Lucy had fallen in love with the Marshall family. It was simply too much. From Gillespie's fervid perspective Marshall was stealing the only person left in this world that Gillespie loved, his beloved Lucy.

In some still-sane portion of his mind, Byron was aware that his rage was irrational. He'd attempted to murder Marshall but had failed in the effort, killing instead thirty-five innocents. He'd given himself away by foolishly calling Viper's Boeing Black, not once, but twice. And it wasn't Marshall carrying out the investigation closing in on him. It wasn't Marshall who'd ordered the surveillance. Though he tried to suppress the thought, deep down Gillespie knew his calamities were his own doing.

Didn't matter. It actually increased his anger. As far as he was concerned, because of Marshall he would be denied the love and respect of his daughter for the rest of his life. He would be exposed for what he truly was and Lucy would be horrified at the revelation.

Byron Gillespie secured his safe, extinguished his office lights and locked the door for the last time ever. Outwardly calm, inwardly seething, he walked through the massive building headed for the 21st Street exit. In his head he could hear his own voice screaming, *Marshall! You have taken my daughter from me! I will take yours from you!*

Gillespie exited the building through the Virginia Avenue/E Street exit. A muscular young man wearing blue jeans and a black UnderArmour sweatshirt, with a Washington Redskins ball cap parked backwards on his head, was hanging out in Galvez Park. As Gillespie headed for 23rd Street NW, the fellow followed a block behind. "Don't get too close, punk, or I might feed you that ball cap," Byron muttered under his breath. He knew there'd be another agent in the Foggy Bottom Metro Station that the young man would hand him off to.

The former SEAL boarded the Silver Line bound for Tysons Corner. A young woman carrying a black attaché case boarded the train behind him. She looked like an attorney, but Gillespie knew she was an FBI agent. She might as well have worn her credentials on her forehead. If he got off at any station other than Tysons Corner, she'd follow him. If he debarked at Tysons, she would stay on the train and another agent would be at Tysons to follow him home. Gillespie frowned and shook his head. *Do these silly people really think I haven't spotted them? What do they take me for, anyway?*

At Tysons Corner he located his black F-150 in the parking lot and headed for a Walmart on his way home. He'd planned the manner of his escape that afternoon in his office and he was going to do it in style. He bought two plastic five-gallon jerry cans, two full twenty-pound propane tanks, two propane pigtail hoses, and a spool of quarter-inch nylon rope. On the way home he filled the truck and the jerry cans with gasoline. A black Suburban tailed him until he turned right from Arnon Chapel Road onto Runner Road. The Suburban continued on. A Time Warner Cable van was parked about a hundred feet from his driveway with a good view of his front yard. Gillespie smirked as he drove past it and turned into his driveway. He parked the F-150 in the garage and shut the door.

Once in the house he moved quickly and silently, figuring the FBI had probably bugged the place. Retrieving his go bag from the pickup, Gillespie added a Heckler & Koch HK45 Tactical pistol, Ti-RANT suppressor, and a dozen magazines to it. From his wall safe he emptied an assortment of passports, driver's licenses, credit cards, fake credentials, and cash —some fifteen thousand dollars' worth—into the go bag. He had enough identities to live off the grid permanently.

Grabbing a backpack, he loaded it with tactical gear, additional weapons, several changes of clothes, his laptop, and other items. His packing complete, Gillespie wandered around his house, knowing it would be the last time he would see it. He lovingly removed the pictures of his wife and daughter from the walls and carefully wrapped them in clothes, placing them in the backpack. A few other small keepsakes and heirlooms also went into his pack. Mementos of the life he once had.

Byron put his pack and go bag by the back door. It was a straight shot into the woods and he wouldn't be in view of the agents in the van when he abandoned the house. He wasn't quite ready to go out the back door; when he did there'd be no coming back. It was now around ten o'clock, and he was approaching the point of no return. The rest of his life would be spent on the run under an assumed identity. There would be no more normal, not for him.

There was some leftover cherry pie in the fridge, so he made a cup of coffee and sat on the back deck, enjoying the calm before the storm. When he was done he called Lucy and talked for ten minutes, just catching up. As he wrapped up the conversation, he said, "You know, sweetie, you've been through some really rough times in your life. Losing Mom was the toughest thing that ever happened to both of us. And that crash a month ago, that was awful."

"I know, Daddy, but I think these things happen to make us stronger, you know?" she said.

Byron longed to hug her one more time, but she was eighteen hundred miles away. He knew he'd never see her again. "That's right, Lucy, they do—and you've become a very strong young woman. I want you to know how much I love you and how proud of you I am. No matter what should ever happen to me or to you, just remember—that will never change. I'll always love you and I'll always be proud of you. I've got to run now. Goodbye, babe." Fighting down a lump in his throat, he wiped his eyes and went inside, putting his cup and plate in the sink. It was time for the final preparations.

He'd moved into this big empty house two years ago, and as far as he was concerned the bank owned it. He had little equity in it and he'd never be able to claim it anyway—not with the murder charges soon to be filed against him. His pickup truck was less than six months old—the bank owned that as well.

Ares had decided that if he couldn't have his possessions, the bank couldn't either. Besides, his offshore accounts were bursting with cash and he could replace everything without blinking an eye. But first he was going to rip off the Man. Ares was so consumed by anger and bitterness at the world that he saw his actions as perfectly justifiable.

Gillespie disabled the monitored fire alarm system and then went around the first floor opening all the windows. Next he turned on the whole-house fan, located in the ceiling of the second-floor hallway. He retrieved a jerry can of gas from the back of his pickup and carried it upstairs to the master bedroom. Removing the cap, he carefully set the can upright on the bed. He tied one end of the quarter-inch line to the jerry can handle, then unspooled the line down the stairs to the back door, cutting the rope there. He did the same with the other jerry can, placing it on the bed in the second-floor guest bedroom. He left both rope ends by the back door.

The propane tanks and pigtails he retrieved from his truck. He screwed the pigtail fittings into each propane tank, and then chopped off the other ends of the pigtails with a hand axe. Both propane tanks he took downstairs to the unfinished basement and placed them on either end, feeding the open end of each pigtail up to the exposed floor joists, securing it with duct tape.

As he surveyed his handiwork a voice in the back of his brain—the remnant of his sanity—was screaming at him. *What are you doing, Byron? Stop! This is crazy! This won't solve anything!* "SHUT UP!" he shouted aloud furiously,

"JUST SHUT UP!" The agents in the van, listening, looked at each other and shrugged.

Before he could have second thoughts, he opened the valve slightly on one propane tank and used his lighter to ignite the gas coming out of the pigtail. Then he opened the valve all the way, bringing a roaring flame to bear on the exposed joist. He ran over to the other tank and got it going also, then raced upstairs to the back door. Grabbing each rope, he tugged on them until he felt the jerry cans tip over. Picking up his pack and go bag, Byron Gillespie ran into the woods and hid, watching to see what would happen.

Soon smoke was coming out of the attic vents. Within five minutes the first floor was lit with an unnatural light. Seconds later there was a mighty *whump!* and all the windows blew out of the house as the gasoline fumes ignited. Another sixty seconds and the whole house was transformed into a raging inferno.

Gillespie grinned. So far there were no sirens. It would take a few more minutes for the fire department to arrive, and by then the blaze would have destroyed the house. He turned and walked further into the woods. It was about a mile to the clubhouse of the River Bend Golf and Country Club. The links, of course, were deserted this time of night but there was a lot of action at the clubhouse. Gillespie hung back in the shadows, and called a cab. Ten minutes later he was on his way to the Marriott at Dulles. He checked in under an assumed name and fell into bed, exhausted. Very early the next morning he grabbed a shuttle to Enterprise Rent-a-Car and rented a Jeep Renegade, using yet a different name.

Gillespie drove to Norfolk and ate a late lunch at a Burger King on Little Creek Road, not far from the Joint Expeditionary Base. Just before leaving, he used the ATM machine inside the store to withdraw the maximum amount—eight hundred dollars—from his main checking account. Moments later he was headed west on I-64.

****

It was only a little after six in the morning, but SJ Bergman's cellphone was already buzzing angrily. The call finally went to voicemail. When Bergman returned from his five-mile run he saw the message light blinking. It was a call from FBI headquarters in DC.

"Hey, Valerie, sorry I missed your call. Was out running. What's up?" Valerie Marquette was the special agent in charge of the Gillespie case in Washington.

"SJ, Byron Gillespie committed suicide last night. Apparently he burned his house down with him inside. Firefighters finally got the blaze under control a couple of hours ago, but so far no one has been allowed into the hulk to look for a body."

"Wow. Was he aware that he was under surveillance?" Bergman asked.

"Yeah. We were making it obvious to put some pressure on him, hoping to provoke him into making a mistake. We didn't figure on anything like this."

"You're making a leap, Val, with that suicide idea. It's far more likely he's on the run and burned the house down to cover his tracks."

"We had a surveillance team on site," she objected. "They claim he didn't leave the house."

"Ten to one he's on the lam, Val. You're not going to find a body. You'd better detail some agents to start checking airports."

"But SJ, his truck was in the garage and that burnt up with the rest of the house. If he's on the run, he's not getting far on foot," she insisted stubbornly.

"Think, Val," SJ explained patiently. "All he's got to do is walk away from the house and call Uber. That's it."

There was silence on the other end of the phone. Valerie Marquette was a little green, but she wasn't dumb. She was a good agent in a scrap or a shoot-out, but unimaginative when outside-the-box thinking was called for. Her team had made a mistake and she didn't want to admit it.

"Look, Valerie, you lost him, okay? It's not surprising; the man is, after all, a former SEAL and he's been trained in surveillance and how to evade it. Let the police look for the body at the house. You put your people to work checking all the transportation hubs. Take his photo to all the car rental agencies within an hour of his house. Make a Hotwatch request to his bank and get real-time monitoring on all his accounts—although I doubt he'll make the mistake of using them. Talk to his associates at State. Find out if anyone knows alternate identities that Gillespie travels under. We need to find this guy, Val. He's got a nine-hour head start on us.

"Gather the best photos we have of him and submit them to Homeland Security's facial recognition database. I want an alert immediately if he's spotted."

"Okay," she said. Her voice was subdued. "We've got some good photos of him. I'll submit 'em to Homeland as soon as I hang up. Look, I'm really sorry, SJ. I thought we had him buttoned up tight."

"Could happen to any of us, Valerie. And Gillespie is well motivated to disappear—by now he realizes that he's got thirty-five first-degree murder charges hanging over his head. You lost him, but don't let it distract you. Concentrate on reeling him in."

****

As Gillespie had intended, his ATM withdrawal soon came to the attention of the FBI. It was after two in the afternoon on the East Coast when Marquette called Bergman back.

"SJ, we got a hit," Valerie said. "Gillespie withdrew cash from an ATM outside of the naval base at Little Creek. He must be headed south, somewhere."

"Whoa, wait. Let's close the loop on the house, first. What did you find out?" Bergman asked.

"You were right. Tysons Corner PD combed the site. There's no body. And we checked with the bank: both the house and the truck were purchased within the last two years. Gillespie had nothing to lose, really, by torching them. It was a diversion," she acknowledged, "and it worked. Completely snookered me."

"Okay, good job checking the bank info. Now, what about the ATM thing?"

"He made a big withdrawal—the maximum, eight hundred dollars—two hours ago from an ATM located inside a Burger King on Little Creek Road, about four miles from the Joint Expeditionary Base. So he's headed south somewhere," Marquette concluded.

"No," SJ replied, after thinking for a moment. "It's a misdirection play. He wants us to *think* he's headed south. There's no way Gillespie would be this obvious. He's too smart and too well trained. But this time he's overplaying his hand."

"Could it have something to do with the fact that this was his base when he was a SEAL?" she asked.

"No. Listen, Val, a guy like this doesn't make rookie errors. He used the ATM there on purpose, knowing we'd find out. He wants us to know he was at Little Creek. He's probably playing with our head, thinking that we'll waste time trying to figure out why he's at Little Creek, maybe hoping we'll commit resources to tracking down and interviewing the guys in his former unit. And to a certain degree, he'll be successful. Good police work demands that we follow all the leads. So set up a small team of agents researching Gillespie's time at Little Creek when he was a SEAL. Have them account for the whereabouts of each of his former team members. Let's see what they can dig up. But I don't want you and your main team distracted with grunt work. Delegate it to someone else.

"At the very least, though, Gillespie has done us a favor. We know exactly what time he was there, and we also know he can't go any further east. I think he's headed west, but to stay on the safe side we'll have to look north and south, too."

Two hours later another clue surfaced. A desk clerk at the Dulles Enterprise Rent-a-Car recognized Gillespie's photo. Marquette's team now knew he was driving a white Jeep Renegade, and they had the license number.

What they didn't know was that the Renegade had been abandoned in the parking garage at Chippenham Hospital in

Richmond, Virginia, and that Gillespie had rented a silver Ford Escape and was now entering West Virginia on I-64.

****

Late Friday evening Bergman called Carlos Estrada.

"Carlos, it's SJ. Listen, man, Byron Gillespie has dropped off the grid. We have no clue where he is at the moment."

"When did this happen, SJ?" Estrada asked. He was cleaning his handgun in his hotel room, and had the phone cradled between his shoulder and ear.

"Last night. The surveillance team in Virginia was a little too green, and he outwitted them. He used an ATM machine at Little Creek late this morning. That was our last clue."

Estrada chuckled. "Let me guess: it was located in a Burger King on Little Creek Road, wasn't it?"

"How'd you know?" Bergman asked, surprised.

"Oh, we all used that BK. It was close to the base and it had an ATM machine. Our SEAL team ate there many times. Did he use his regular bank account?" Estrada deftly reassembled the gun and wiped it down with a clean cloth.

"Yes."

"He's playing with your mind, SJ. Byron doesn't make mistakes. He intended for you to place him there, and that means he's not anywhere close to Norfolk now."

"Yeah, that's what I figured, too. Anyway, I wanted to warn you," the FBI agent said.

"You think he's coming after Marshall?" asked Estrada, frowning, as he reloaded the weapon and put it in his shoulder holster.

"I don't know. It's possible. We still don't know his motives for trying to bump Marshall off in the first place. I thought I ought to at least warn you. Where are you guys today?"

"We're in Chicago tonight. We've got events in Peoria, Bloomington, Champaign, Decatur, and Springfield over the next couple of days."

"Is Marshall's itinerary published anywhere?" asked the

FBI agent.

"No, but it wouldn't be hard to find. It's not secret."

"Okay. You might want to raise your security another notch. Ask the head of your Secret Service detail to give me a call, if you would, so I can brief him. I think we'd better play it safe."

"Roger that. Will do."

****

Henry and Haley had changed into jeans and sweatshirts and were sitting on the bed in their hotel room, chatting with Joshua Cummings and Buford and Sandy Jackson. The rally that evening at the Jones Convocation Center had been exciting. All seven thousand seats had been filled with an enthusiastic crowd, and the atmosphere was electric.

It was the first rally in which they had faced a large number of noisy, well-organized protesters—over two hundred. Nearly all of the protesters were wearing Hastings' campaign buttons and hats. The protest was a clear indication that Hastings' campaign was getting nervous about Marshall's momentum.

Most of the protesters were students organized by professional political activists. The biggest bone of contention was Marshall's plan to shut down the federal student loan and grant programs. Much to the activists' dismay, Marshall agreed to meet with the students for an hour after the rally. The hour turned into two hours, with the result that when the protesters left the venue they felt like they'd been heard. Though most did not agree with his position he earned their respect by listening to their complaints and taking them seriously. Mutually respectful interaction had not been what the organizers had in mind.

There was a light knock on the door leading to Estrada's room. "Come in, Carlos," called Marshall.

Carlos Estrada entered the room and glanced around. "I'm glad you're all together. There's something important we need to talk about."

"What's up?" Marshall asked.

"I just received a call from Special Agent Bergman. It hasn't hit the news yet, because the FBI is keeping it close to the vest, but they have identified the chief suspect in the plot to kill you, Mr. Marshall. I can't tell you how much it pains me to tell you this, but it's Lucy Gillespie's dad, my old friend, Byron Gillespie."

The color drained from Hank's face. "Surely there's some mistake, Carlos. That can't be," he insisted.

"There's no mistake, sir, and the evidence tying him to the attempt is very solid—conclusive, actually. Lucy knows nothing about her dad's activities. Her feelings for you, Mr. and Mrs. Marshall, are quite genuine. This news will devastate her when it gets out. And the irony is that in attempting to assassinate you, sir, Byron nearly killed his own daughter on Flight 1356."

"That's tragic," murmured Haley. "She should be with . . . us . . . when she hears this. When her dad is arrested, she'll have . . . virtually no family. Her heart is going to break. Poor girl."

Hank added, "I agree, Haley." He studied Carlos' face and could see that his chief of security wasn't done yet. "But there's more, isn't there, Carlos?"

Estrada nodded. "Yes, sir, there is. The FBI has had him under surveillance since last Friday. Last night he managed to elude them and now they have no idea where he is. He actually burnt down his own house as a diversion while he escaped. Bergman thinks he's not entirely rational, that something has pushed him over the edge. I remember when he was on SEAL Team 8 and we had to encourage him to resign because he was getting a little strange then.

"Anyway, the worst part is Bergman thinks he might try again," Estrada concluded.

"What do you mean *try again*, Carlos?" Buford asked.

"They think it is possible that Gillespie's coming after Mr. Marshall again."

Silence hung in the air for about two seconds, then

everyone in the room started talking at once. Marshall finally raised his voice and said, "Whoa, folks! One at a time!"

He looked at his chief of security and asked, "What is your recommendation, Carlos?"

"Sir, I think you should go ahead with your planned schedule. I've already talked to the Secret Service. The head of the detail has contacted Bergman, and in an abundance of caution he's taking Bergman's concerns seriously and asking for two more agents—so by tomorrow sometime you'll have four Secret Service agents guarding you.

"But I recommend that you allow me to escort Mrs. Marshall and Mrs. Jackson back to Denver tomorrow morning. I think that Mrs. Jackson and I, plus Jim Stewart, should remain with Mrs. Marshall at your residence, twenty-four seven, until this threat is eliminated."

Buford nodded his head. "That's a good plan, Carlos." He turned to Marshall, "I think you should do exactly as your chief of security is recommending. That is, after all, what you hired him to do, Hank."

"Haley, what do you think?" Henry asked his wife.

"If we don't do it," Haley said, "I think you would . . . be distracted, because you're worried about me. I'm . . . for it."

"Sandy, is that okay with you?" Marshall asked. "You'd be staying at our house helping Haley."

Sandy smiled, "I'll be glad to help Haley." Buford nodded his agreement.

Marshall considered the alternatives briefly, and then decided. "Okay, that's what we'll do. Thank you all. The longer this campaign goes on, the more I find myself in an unre-payable debt to my friends." He turned to his security chief. "Carlos, my man, make it so."

"Yes, sir."

"I'll call Momma, Carlos, and have her book your tickets," Buford said. "First class," he added with a wink.

****

Byron Gillespie spent the night in Beckley, West Virginia, in a hotel just off Interstate 64. He was up early the next morning and soon after six was on the road. He hoped to make Kansas City before stopping for the night.

Meanwhile, the Marshall campaign continued its swing through Illinois with growing and enthusiastic crowds. Security around the candidate was much tighter, but the only ones to notice were the few who knew what to look for. The rest hadn't a clue.

Interstate 64 ended at St. Louis, where Gillespie picked up Interstate 70. He was a little less than an hour from Kansas City when he pulled off the road at the Concordia Rest Area. He had to use the bathroom, and he was having trouble keeping his eyes open. He pulled the Ford Escape into the parking area, and then headed for the bathrooms in the small hospitality center. When he came out of the bathroom, he examined the giant I-70 map and then wandered aimlessly around the rest area, just glad to be out of the car. It was an unusually warm evening for late October, with clear skies and no breeze. He sat on a picnic table and watched the sunset before he resumed his westward drive.

A security camera was located in the ceiling just behind the I-70 map. Unbeknownst to most people, including Byron Gillespie, Missouri was participating in a pilot program cosponsored by the FBI and the Department of Homeland Security, in which the video feeds from Missouri rest areas, bus and train stations, and airports were sent via a fiber-optic link to the FBI field office in Kansas City, where they were examined by facial recognition software running on a distributed network.

A perfectly clear high-definition video of Gillespie sat in the server's queue, waiting for an available computer. Soon it was distributed to an idle processor. The system quickly analyzed all the frames of the video, settling on the best eight frames. Gillespie's face was divided into datapoints and reduced to a series of mathematical distance and angle relationships. The resulting data was compared with a database of desired targets. Sorting through thousands of records, a match was swiftly located. After the match was recorded in the "hits" database, a compressed version of the video was automatically emailed to the requestor—in this case, SJ Bergman.

Once in Kansas City Gillespie stopped at a steak house for supper, then found a parking garage downtown. He parked on the highest covered level and wiped down the car. After locking the keys inside, he went down to street level and took a cab to the airport. There he rented yet another car. He drove forty miles north to St. Joseph and checked into a cheap motel. Gillespie was beginning to get paranoid. He couldn't explain why, but a sixth sense told him to get away from Interstate 70. Tomorrow he'd let the FBI know where he was, but not tonight. It was too early. He wanted to achieve tactical surprise.

****

Carlos' phone vibrated in his pocket. The Jacksons and Haley were sitting in the family room reading. He stepped into the kitchen and shut the door to the family room, then answered. "Estrada."

"Carlos, it's SJ. Listen, man, we just received some new information. Gillespie was tagged by facial recognition software in Missouri, just the other side of KC, in an I-70 rest area on the westbound side. It's a good bet he's headed your way. I think we ought to prepare a welcoming committee. What do you think?"

Estrada sighed. Gillespie had been a friend and a brother-in-arms, but like an overripe apple he'd gone bad. It had started with the death of his wife. Somehow Byron had taken a turn on the wild side, and there was no coming back. *If I have to, I'll kill him*, thought the former SEAL, *but it will kill me to do that.*

"Yeah. Let's do it. Can you hang on a minute?" He muted his phone and stepped back into the family room.

"Sir," he said, addressing Buford. "I need to move you three out of here. We either need to get a hotel room for you, or head for your house." The two women looked up in alarm.

"What happened, Carlos? What's going on?" asked Jackson.

"Gillespie has been spotted around KC, and he's headed this way. I want to move you all out of here and go somewhere safe, somewhere he won't look. A team from the FBI will come here and be ready for him if he shows up," Estrada said calmly.

"You think he's coming after Haley?" Buford asked, raising his eyebrows.

"I'm sorry, sir, but I don't know what his intentions are. I'm just not going to leave anything to chance. We need to leave this house until I feel it is safe," Estrada replied.

"Couldn't we leave in the morning? Kansas City is almost nine hours away," the lawyer objected. He wanted to keep Sandy and Haley as comfortable as possible.

"Nine hours by car, sir, but he could be here in two or three by air. We have no way of knowing what his plans are. In my opinion we should leave as soon as possible."

"Okay," Buford agreed. He turned to the women. "Ladies, let's pack up. We're gettin' out of Dodge while the gettin' is good." He winked at Carlos. "Let's head for Fort Jackson."

Carlos grinned. "Thank you, sir." He stepped back into the kitchen and unmuted his phone. "Okay, SJ. We're leaving here and going to the Jacksons'. I'm going to call the Golden PD and request some extra protection from them so we don't spread your team too thin. Jim Stewart will meet you here and give you a set of keys."

"Excellent. My team will be there in the next ninety minutes."

"Sounds good. Listen, SJ, was that facial recognition stuff done from a video or stills?" Estrada asked.

"Video," the FBI agent responded. "Why?"

"Can you send it to my phone?"

"Yes, but why are you interested, Carlos?" Bergman persisted.

"Let's just call it threat assessment. Gillespie and I served together on SEAL Team 8. Whenever he was about to go into combat he would get an involuntary twitch on the left side of his face. I want to see if that's going on in this video," Estrada explained.

"Huh. Okay. I'll send it. Let me know what you see."

A few minutes later the video landed on his phone. Carlos watched several times, but there was no sign of the twitch. He texted SJ,

> *no twitch. he's not doing anything tonight. But we'll go ahead with our plans to move anyway. can't hurt.*
>
> *roger that. thanks.*

****

Assistants guided Henry Marshall to the proper chair on the set, affixed his microphone and did several sound checks, balancing volume and tone. Patty Holmes was making last-minute adjustments with the program director, but then took her place on the set. The interview was being recorded at an NBC affiliate in Springfield, Illinois for later broadcast.

"Mr. Marshall, it's great to see you again. I know your schedule in these last several weeks is brutal—thanks for taking time for us," she said with a warm smile.

"Thanks, Patty, I appreciate the opportunity to be on your show. You always ask great questions, and you've treated me with an even hand."

"How is Mrs. Marshall doing? You all have had quite a time of it the last month or so."

"She's improving. You might have noticed that several video clips of her have shown a halting tendency in her speech—well, that's almost gone. And she's been undergoing physical therapy to keep her leg muscles from atrophying. In the last week the therapists have noticed a return of sensation in her legs, and she's been able to move her toes and ankles. We're quite hopeful for a full recovery."

"That's wonderful! Please give her our best wishes." She pressed her finger to her earbud and listened to some instructions from the program director and responded. "Got it, Phil," she said. "I was just about to make sure he understands." She directed her attention to Marshall again and said, "We're almost ready. Now remember, Mr. Marshall, we aren't live. This interview will air next Sunday night, the 30th, but we're recording the introduction now. During the intro, I'll be speaking from the perspective as though this next week has already gone by, and you'll hear me explain to the viewers that we recorded your interview 'last week.' Then we'll cut to allow affiliates to insert a commercial break. When we come back we'll begin your interview, and we'll do it from the correct frame of reference, as it actually is, today, the 23rd.

"Now, even though this is recorded, the ground rules are simple: you don't get any retakes. If you garble your words or your answers, what you say is what we will broadcast. We will not do any editing of your answers. Do you understand?" She raised her eyebrows quizzically.

"I do, and I'm ready," he replied confidently.

"Okay, Phil," she said to the director. "We'll start on your countdown."

From off-set somewhere, Hank could hear a "Three, two, one, recording." The red RECORDING light flashed twice and then remained illuminated.

Patty looked at camera one. "Good evening. I'm Patty Holmes, and tonight we have an extended, ninety-minute edition of *Special Report*. Three weeks ago we aired a segment on each of the major candidates, examining their character, their background, and their campaign. Tonight, just nine days before Election Day, we are providing each candidate with twenty minutes to make their case to the American voter.

"First up will be Henry Marshall, the conservative blogger from Colorado who's taken the political world by storm in this election cycle. Though long popular in the world of conservative blog-readers, Marshall was unknown to most on the Beltway circuit, and unwelcome to those who did know him. I caught up with him a week ago in Springfield, Illinois as he was wrapping up a campaign swing through that state. You'll see my interview in just a moment.

"Marshall threw his hat in the ring in February of 2015 after being recruited by political luminaries as notable as Joshua Cummings, Ashton Bancroft, and Mike Trujillo, the former head of the Colorado GOP. In the intervening months, Marshall has endured a combination of setbacks ranging from political dirty tricks to a triple set of near-tragedies that have affected his campaign and even his family. Despite all, he's climbed in the polls to the point that he now threatens the virtual headlock the Democrats and Republicans have had on the political process for more than one hundred years. Is he a new kind of citizen-politician? Is he a harbinger of things to come? Stay tuned, as we share with you an inter-view I recorded with Henry Marshall last Sunday. We'll be right back."

The RECORDING light went off, and she spent a moment studying her notes. The program director reminded her, "We can go anytime you're ready, Patty."

"Thanks, Phil, I know. I just want one last look at these so I don't stumble." After another moment she looked at Marshall, and he nodded. "When you're ready, Phil."

The RECORDING light came on, and she began. "With me in the studio tonight is presidential candidate Henry Marshall. Welcome, Mr. Marshall."

"Thank you, Patty, it's a pleasure to be with you."

"Mr. Marshall, you've become famous for saying that you don't intend to improve Washington, you intend to dismantle it. That's become a virtual slogan for the Marshall campaign. It's on bumper stickers, campaign buttons, yard signs—every-where, it seems. Some of the political action committees supporting your positions have even put up billboards advo-cating that position.

"I'm interviewing you tonight in Springfield, Illinois, the Land of Lincoln. What would Abraham Lincoln have thought of your slogan?"

Marshall laughed. "Great question, Patty. Well, it is inar-guable that Lincoln greatly strengthened the federal government in his prosecution of the Civil War. His suspension of the writ of habeas corpus, his actions as commander-in-chief prior to the special session of Congress on July 4, 1861, and the Emancipation Proclamation, were all executive actions the legitimacy of which historians have debated for years.

"But in fairness to Lincoln, he was faced with the very real possibility that the United States was about to be destroyed, not by war from without but by rebellion from within. In a sense, the rebellion of the southern states took us completely off the map of the Constitution, and Lincoln was faced with responding in keeping with the spirit of the Constitution, rather than the letter. The spirit of our Constitution has always resided not in the document itself, but in the Declaration of Independence, the document that truly gave rise to the founding of our country. In a piece that appeared in *National Review Online*, David French wrote, 'If our Constitution is our law, then our Declaration of Independence is, in Timothy Sandefur's memorable phrase, its conscience.' The question of slavery, which sparked the Civil War, was a fatal contradiction between our two most significant founding documents. Lincoln was faced with the task of righting that terrible wrong.

"In a letter Lincoln wrote to Henry Pierce on April 6, 1859 —before the war started—it was clear that he could see the trouble coming. Lincoln said, 'This is a world of compensations; and he who would be no slave, must consent to have no slave. Those who deny freedom to others, deserve it not for themselves; and, under a just God, cannot long retain it.'

"Even Madison, when explaining to Jefferson his position on the Bill of Rights in a letter dated October 17, 1788, said 'Supposing a bill of rights to be proper the articles which ought to compose it, admit of much discussion. I am inclined to think that absolute restrictions in cases that are doubtful, or where emergencies may overrule them, ought to be avoided.' Madison specifically named the possibility of the suspension of a writ of habeas corpus in a time of rebellion, saying that 'no written prohibitions on earth would prevent the measure.' Lincoln was faced with just such a situation.

"The bottom line for me, Patty, is that Lincoln's actions were proper and needful. He certainly did strengthen the hand both of the presidency and the federal government. The federal government alone was capable of eliminating the contradictions between the Declaration and the Constitution. But Lincoln would have never argued for the sort of federal overreach that plagues our government today. He would have been aghast at what Washington has become."

Marshall smiled. "And permit me, Patty, if you will, to turn the question around. Here we are in Illinois, the Land of Lincoln. Do you know what the unofficial state motto of Illinois is? They say it is unofficial, even though it appears on the official state seal."

She laughed, "I do not. What is it?"

He winked at her. "*State sovereignty, national union.* If it wasn't already taken by Illinois, I might adopt that as my campaign slogan," replied Marshall. "I am convinced that the key to correcting the federal government is a proper, constitutional restoration of state sovereignty."

She glanced at her notes. "That brings us to the principal points on which you are campaigning. Please explain to our viewers where you believe the federal government has gone off the rails."

"Certainly. The Tenth Amendment says this: *The powers not delegated to the United States by the Constitution, nor prohibited by it to the States, are reserved to the States respectively, or to the people.* Most of the powers granted to the federal government are enumerated in Article 1, Section 8. The Founders specifically intended that the several states retain as much of their power as possible. *The Federalist Papers*, in which Hamilton, Madison, and Jay argue for the adoption of the Constitution over the old *Articles of Confederation*, clarify why power is to be reserved to the states. Just as the three branches of the federal government serve as checks and balances against each other, so the opposing power of the states and the federal government constitute another means to protect the people from tyranny, whether arising from a state government or the federal government.

"But our modern government has virtually ignored the Tenth Amendment. Its involvement in education is a prime example, as well as its involvement in agriculture, healthcare, and a host of other areas. The result has been a sprawling federal bureaucracy that attempts to control everything from the sort of light bulbs that can be manufactured, to the use of drainage ditches on your property, to how many miles per gallon your car must get, to the language on safety tags that come with your appliances. It's insane. Someone needs to say it, Patty, it's just insane. It's ridiculous. It's worthy of a thousand seasons of *Saturday Night Live* parodies."

"How did our government get this way?" Patty asked. "I mean, there are some aspects of it that really *are* stupid. My mattresses come with a tag that says, *do not remove under penalty of law.* That's absurd."

"In fairness, Patty, that law prohibits mattress sellers from removing the tag, not the retail consumer. And it has to do with the fact that mattress sellers in the past have been like used car salesmen—you never know what you're really getting inside that mattress. If we had time we could talk about how our culture is on track to remove the obligation of personal responsibility from the individual. Unfortunately our legal system does a far better job of protecting people from their own irresponsibility than it does enforcing consequences for illegal or irresponsible behavior. But that's another discussion.

"There are two main things that have contributed to the encroachment of federal power and the ignoring of the Tenth Amendment, Patty. First, the courts have been overly broad in their reading of the Constitution. Things like the commerce clause have been stretched beyond all recognition, effectively bringing all commerce, interstate or not, under federal control.

"Second, the Seventeenth Amendment destroyed the balance of power between the states and the federal government. Prior to 1913, when the Seventeenth was passed, US senators were appointed by the legislatures of their state. They served the interest of the state, and could act as an effective balance against federal power. They knew their job was to represent the concerns of their state to the feds. When the

Seventeenth Amendment passed, the selection of senators transferred directly to the popular vote of the people; the state legislatures were no longer involved. This fundamentally changed the conception of the function of a US senator. They began to represent the federal government to the people, and their identification with their own respective states and their interests became secondary. As a consequence, the balance of power swung decisively to the feds. It is precisely the resulting imbalance which explains why the legislative branch no longer acts effectively as a check on the other two branches to limit the authority of the federal government."

"But," Patty objected, "in a democracy shouldn't all our federal legislators be chosen via popular vote?"

"No, Patty, they should not. First, we aren't a democracy, we're a democratic republic. Democracy is what you see in things like state referenda—citizens voting directly for or against laws. There is a place for that. Unfortunately the federal courts have had a field day illegitimately overturning popularly approved referenda—but that, too, is another discussion.

"The government at the federal level runs by representation. We elect representatives who then legislate on our behalf. Prior to the Seventeenth, the citizens of a state chose their US representatives by direct election, but their US senators indirectly through the men and women they had voted into their *state* legislatures. This arrangement kept our US senators accountable to the state.

"Hamilton, Madison, and Jay recognized the opposing interests existing between the two layers of government—state and federal—and considered this tension necessary to the proper functioning of our government, indeed, they thought of it as a protection of liberty against overreach and tyranny. But because of the Seventeenth Amendment, we are now dangerously unbalanced on the federal side."

Patty Holmes nodded. "Okay. Can you boil it down for us in a sound bite or two?"

Marshall nodded. "Sure. If elected it will be my intention to ensure that all acts of Congress abide by a conservative reading of the Tenth Amendment, and my goal will be to repeal all legislation that runs afoul of the Tenth. Secondly, I intend to lead the charge to repeal the Seventeenth Amendment. Third, I promise to appoint no judge to the federal bench, at any level, who does not adhere to a strict interpretation of the Constitution as it was written, regardless of prior precedent. And if you want to call that a litmus test, I'll gladly accept the term."

****

Ares rose early on Sunday morning, October 23. He was looking forward to the day. This evening he would commence his brief reign of terror against the Marshall family. He had fully subdued the voice of conscience—no longer did he hear its voice or feel its pricks. Gillespie was not only resigned to doing evil, he was positively anticipating it. He never for a second entertained the possibility that his intention to commit murder would bring lifelong grief and shame on Lucy. On one level, it really didn't matter. Revenge was the important thing, the main thing—no, the *only* thing. Marshall was denying him a lifetime of happiness with Lucy, the joy of walking her down the aisle, of grandkids, of watching a beautiful, intelligent woman come into her own. And so, in Gillespie's perverse logic, he would even the scales by denying Marshall the same thing. He would make Henry Marshall suffer.

All but forgotten was his original motivation to stop Marshall from stealing his livelihood by threatening to turn back the flood-tide of US foreign aid military expenditures. It had been overshadowed by the bungling of his attempt on Marshall's life. When his role in that crime was exposed, a normal life would become impossible for Gillespie. He'd always be on the run, always looking over his shoulder. He'd never be able to enjoy being a part of his daughter's life.

And for that, Marshall must be punished.

A little after six in the morning, Ares pulled onto US 36 west. Using the red-line road instead of the interstate meant that the normal nine-hour drive from Kansas City to Denver lengthened to eleven—but he became harder to spot, if the FBI had somehow managed to track his movements.

When he arrived in Denver he went straight to the airport's short-term parking. He didn't bother to wipe the car down. He put on the pack and grabbed his go bag, and strolled into the ticket counter area, looking for a security camera. Spotting one, he stood below it and removed his ball cap and sunglasses and looked into the camera, grinning and waving. He stayed in place for five minutes, and muttered to no one in particular, "Now we'll find out how good the FBI really is."

He took an escalator to the ground transport level and got into a cab. "Hyatt Hotel on East 40th, please." The cabbie nodded. A few minutes later, he was deposited at the door of the hotel. He waited until the cab moved on, then walked down the street to the Cambria Inn, and called Uber. When the driver arrived, Gillespie requested, "Take me to the Best Western in Castle Rock." There he caught one more cab to the Hilton Garden Inn, near the Colorado Springs Airport. He was confident that no one would be able to track him down. After checking in, he dumped his gear on the bed and called Uber. Thirty minutes later he was prowling the streets of Colorado Springs in his latest rental, a dark blue Ford Escort, looking for a good place to eat.

****

Bergman was watching the Seahawks' second drive against the Cardinals when the call came at quarter till seven. It was his work phone. He groaned, and set his beer and cheese nachos down on the TV tray.

"Bergman." He tried not to let the irritation he felt find expression in his voice. *Goes with the job*, he thought philo-sophically.

"Gillespie's in Denver. A security camera caught him at the airport. We've got a thirty-minute-old video you've got to see."

"Why do I have to see it?" he grumbled.

"You just do," the agent said.

"Okay. I'll be there in a few. In the meantime, put out an all-points-bulletin on Gillespie to the state patrol and all the local police agencies in the state."

"You got it."

Darn, he thought. *I really wanted to see this game. Might as well DVR it.* He set up his electronics to record it, then called Carlos Estrada.

"You watching the Seahawks' game?" he asked when Carlos picked up.

"Naah. It's my turn to keep an eye on Mrs. Marshall. But I'm recording it. Did you know I've recorded all the Broncos' and Seahawks' games this season, but haven't got to see a single one yet? I need Mr. Marshall to win the election so I can hand him off to the Secret Service and get back to my football."

"I hear ya, man! Priorities, right?"

"Darn straight. What's up, SJ?"

"You tell Jim Stewart to take your watch, and meet me down at the Agency in ten, would you? The duty agent just got a fresh video of Gillespie at the Denver Airport—says we have to see it. I figure you'll be able to interpret it better than me, since you know the guy."

"I'll be there. But first I'm calling the Golden PD, and asking them to beef up security here, maybe give us a few more men."

Ten minutes later Estrada was being escorted through the FBI's facility to the secure room.

SJ greeted him as he came in. "Yo. My man, Carlos. Benji, meet Carlos. He's a former SEAL, so watch yourself around him. Carlos, meet Benji. Fresh out of Quantico, one of these days he's gonna be a great agent. We're still waiting for him to get his first shave, though."

Estrada grinned and shook the younger man's hand. "Benji, don't you mind this curmudgeon. When he jumps on you about your youth, just keep reminding him, he'll reach sixty long before you do."

SJ turned to the young duty agent and said, "Show us what you got."

Benji switched the feed to the large flat screen monitor and ran the video. Soon the screen filled with a picture of the big SEAL waving at the camera, wearing a Cheshire cat grin.

"What's he doing?" asked Benji.

"He's sending us a message: *I'm here and there's not a darn thing you can do about it*," murmured Bergman, watching the recording.

"Um-hmm," agreed Estrada. "That's exactly what he's doing. Look! There! You see it? His left cheek is twitching."

"So what!" exclaimed Benji. "That doesn't mean anything."

"Oh, but it does," explained Estrada. "We were on SEAL Team 8 together for five years. Whenever we'd go into action, his cheek would do that twitchy thing. We started calling him Twitchy, until he nearly put one of the team members in the hospital.

"Yeah, that twitch means he's planning on hurting someone. I'd better make some calls."

"Okay," the agent said. "Let's go down to my office, you can make your calls from my phone." SJ turned to Benji and patted him on the back. "You're a good kid, even if you did interrupt my Seahawks' game."

While Bergman notified his team at the Marshall residence and got the manhunt for Gillespie rolling in Denver, Estrada warned the contingent at the Jackson residence, and then called the Boulder and Fort Collins police departments. Soon each of the Marshall children had two police officers guarding them. Even though everyone was convinced that Haley was the target, Estrada was not taking any chances. The twins would have to skip classes, and Charity would have to skip work until Gillespie was apprehended.

****

Monday morning, October 24, dawned clear and cold

under sunny skies in Colorado Springs, but the Front Range to the west was shrouded in clouds. Every now and again the clouds would part to reveal a burnished silver peak, coated in a dusting of snow.

Gillespie put on his ballistic and tactical gear. It felt good to be going to war again. Never mind that the target was a relatively helpless twenty-two-year-old girl. In his twisted mind, he was on a mission—and she represented the enemy. Byron pulled on a Denver Broncos' football jersey over the bulky ballistics vest, and stepped into a baggy pair of blue nylon warm-up pants, in an attempt to make his gear less obvious. He threw his bags in the rental and left the hotel without bothering to check out. After going through the drive-in at a local McDonalds, he headed north on Interstate 25.

Two hours later Ares pulled off at the Longmont Conoco Truckstop to gas up. Going inside to pay cash, he decided to get a cup of coffee. While he was pouring his coffee a car pulled up and parked. It was one of those unmarked State Patrol cars that are obvious even though unmarked. The driver stepped out and entered the store.

Byron kept his head down, wishing he'd kept his sunglasses on. When the officer moved toward the coffee machine, Gillespie casually turned away and headed for the back hall where the restrooms were. The patrolman took note of the bulky clothing and the obvious attempt to avoid him, and suspected that Gillespie was a shoplifter. He followed Gillespie back to the bathroom and waited.

Byron stepped into the restroom and locked the door behind him. From various pockets in his tactical clothing he produced the HK45 and the suppressor. He filled the suppressor with liquid and then screwed it on the barrel, racked a round, and tucked the gun behind his waist, with the baggy Broncos jersey draped over it.

When Byron opened the restroom door, the cop was standing outside. He said to Gillespie, "Sir, what are you hiding under that clothing? You know that shoplifting is against the law in Colorado, and everywhere else, for that matter."

"I didn't take anything," Byron responded quietly in his most whiny voice.

"Just lift your shirt, sir, that's all I'm asking," the trooper asked.

"Look, this is embarrassing," Gillespie objected. "Could you at least step into the bathroom so I don't have to do it in front of everyone?"

The officer looked down the hall, "There's no one there to see, sir."

"Please," Byron pleaded. "You caught me, okay? At least let me retain a little dignity—is that too much to ask?"

"Fine," said the officer, stepping into the bathroom and shutting the door. When he turned back he was staring into the silencer on Gillespie's HK45.

"Not your lucky day, officer," Byron observed as he shot twice, coughing loudly with each pull of the trigger to mask the sound of the shot.

Returning the gun to his waistband, he pulled the body into the stall and sat the officer on the toilet, then closed the stall door. He wiped up the blood with paper towels, and then buried them below the other discarded towels in the wastebasket. As he exited the restroom he made sure the door locked behind him. When he walked out into the store it was apparent no one had noticed anything. He completed his purchase, got back into the car, and continued north on I-25.

****

"Carlos, this is SJ. Just got a report of a Colorado state patrolman shot to death at a truckstop on I-25 at Longmont. The officer was found in the restroom, double-tapped. The store clerk heard no gunshots."

"Suppressor," Carlos observed.

"Obviously," Bergman agreed. "That's got to be our man."

"Oh, my—" Carlos exclaimed with horror, as it registered that the truck stop was *north* of Denver. "Oh, no! It's not

Haley, it's Charity he's after! Why didn't I see it earlier? SJ, have you guys got a chopper?"

"Yes, wh—"

"Put together a small tactical squad. Bring gear for me. I'll be there in ten. We've got to get to Fort Collins immediately."

"Carlos, the police—"

"They'll be sitting ducks, clay pigeons, for a man like Gillespie. No offense, SJ, but if you've never seen a SEAL in action you don't have a clue. This guy is a killing machine, and he's clearly gone over the edge. I'll be there in ten. Call the Fort Collins police for me. Warn them!"

****

Charity sat in her apartment reading a book. She was bored. Yesterday when the news came from Carlos that the police department would be placing guards at her house, it was kind of exciting. It made her feel like she was someone important. She blushed to think how shamelessly she'd casually dropped the information to some of her Facebook friends. "Ah, Lord God, give me a humble heart," she murmured.

But now the increased security made her feel trapped. They didn't want her to go anywhere. She couldn't go to work. She couldn't go for a run. *Blah!* Two Fort Collins policemen were patrolling somewhere outside her apartment—she wasn't quite sure where. Occasionally she'd see one walk by. She turned away from the window and looked at her book sitting on the chair. *Boring!*

There was a knock at her door.

"Who is it?" she asked, not quite sure if she was allowed to open the door. She was new to this kind of security thing. She looked through the peep hole, and there was a big man dressed in black military-looking clothes.

"Special Agent Russell Smith, with Her Majesty's Secret Service," the man said, chuckling.

"Who?" she called out, wrinkling her nose. *Do agents*

make jokes in times of stress? She didn't know. She thought they were all deadpan-serious.

"I said, 'Special Agent Russell Smith, with YOUR Majesty's Secret Service!'"

"What? Who is this?" She was stalling, not knowing what to do. *And shouldn't the police be with this guy?* she asked herself.

"Oh, for Pete's sake, Miss Marshall! Open the blankety-blank door. Carlos Estrada sent me. I am in fact a Secret Service agent. Look, I'll hold my credentials in front of your peep hole."

She looked, and sure enough, she saw credentials with the strange man's picture on it, showing he was with the Secret Service. She opened the door and he quickly walked in, shutting it behind him.

"Sorry about the light-heartedness, ma'am. I didn't want to alarm anyone who might be listening in. We are actually in a bit of a crisis. The man who attempted to murder your dad is somewhere in the area even now, and we think he's coming after you. We need to leave immediately. I'm taking you back to Denver, where it will be easier to keep an eye on you."

She stared at him, confused. "Okay, sure, but—"

"I need your cellphone."

"What? Why?"

"He's tracking you with it. All I want to do is take out the battery. Don't want him to find you. Let me have your cellphone."

"That's ridiculous. I'm at home, and he must know where I live already."

"Miss Marshall," the agent asked, cocking his head, "did you argue this much with your daddy when you were living at home? If you did, your dad has my sympathy. Now give me the stupid phone, please."

She handed it to him and he stripped the batteries out and handed it back to her. He dropped the battery in his pocket.

"See," he said, "that was easy. Now pack what you need in a small suitcase. We're leaving in five minutes. I don't want you to be here when that guy shows up. He's supposed to be a real bad actor."

While she was packing, he located her landline phone and unplugged the cable from the wall. As she packed she talked to him from her bedroom.

"I don't understand, Agent Smith. There are two policemen out there guarding my house right now. What more do I need? I'm safe enough right here—although it is getting really boring."

He could hear her in the bathroom, and figured she was packing cosmetics. He rolled his eyes and shook his head. Just like his daughter, he thought. "No, Miss Marshall, they are out there but they aren't guarding anything."

She walked into the living room where he was sitting. "What do you mean they aren't guarding anything?"

He grimaced. "Miss, I am so sorry to tell you this, but they will never guard anything again, ever. Apparently the assassin got to them first. I must have scared him off when I drove up, but I'm sure he'll be back soon. That's why we have to hurry."

Charity turned pale and started to sway. She grabbed a chair back to steady herself. "You mean, you mean, they're de —" She couldn't bring herself to finish the word.

He nodded gravely.

"Oh, my. Oh, my." She rushed back into her room and finished packing. She emerged carrying a small red suitcase. "I'm ready. Let me turn off the lights."

Agent Smith was looking out the kitchen window, his eyes fixed on a small dot in the sky coming out of the south. It was a chopper. "NO!" he insisted. "It will buy us some time if he thinks you're still here. Let's go! Now!"

He grabbed her hand and they raced out the front door. Charity could see that one policeman was slumped over in the police car. She couldn't see the other one. They jumped in his Ford Escort.

"Buckle up," he said.

"An Escort?" she asked as she buckled in. It seemed so incongruous. Everything about the day seemed surreal. "You've got to be kidding. Somehow I didn't imagine that Secret Service agents drove Ford Escorts. I thought they all used big black Suburbans."

"You read too many spy novels, Miss. This," he said, motioning to the car, "is the result of budget cuts. Budget cuts that will get even worse if your daddy becomes president," he grumbled, raising his eyebrows in an expression of reproof. He turned toward her to look behind the car as he backed out of the driveway, and she noticed his cheek was twitching.

****

The helicopter landed in the open field behind the house, and Estrada, Bergman, and a four-man tactical squad emerged, running toward the condo, weapons at the ready. Two men positioned themselves at either side of the back door. The others went around front. Estrada gently tried the front door handle. It was unlocked. They burst through the door, Carlos rolling left, Bergman rolling right, followed by the other two members of the team.

"Clear!" Bergman said. They moved through the rest of the apartment, and within thirty seconds it was obvious. She was gone.

"We'd better go check on the cops," Bergman said.

"Yeah," Carlos agreed, grimacing. "But I can already tell you what you'll find. Each will be double-tapped to the head, the second shot from close range."

Bergman nodded. He pulled out his radio. "Johnny, contact Fort Collins PD, the Larimer County Sheriff, and the State Patrol, stat! Have them set up road blocks at all major exits from Fort Collins. I think we just missed them, and we might be able to stop them before they hit any of the bigger highways." He turned to Estrada. "At least we have a vehicle description, Carlos." The clerk at the truck stop had reviewed the security video of the fuel pump cameras and provided the police with the description and license plate.

Chapter 22

> IF IT BE ASKED WHAT IS TO BE THE CONSEQUENCE,
> IN CASE THE CONGRESS SHALL MISCONSTRUE THIS
> PART OF THE CONSTITUTION, AND EXERCISE
> POWERS NOT WARRANTED BY ITS TRUE MEANING, I
> ANSWER, THE SAME AS IF THEY SHOULD
> MISCONSTRUE OR ENLARGE ANY OTHER POWER
> VESTED IN THEM; . . . IN THE LAST RESORT A
> REMEDY MUST BE OBTAINED FROM THE PEOPLE WHO
> CAN, BY THE ELECTION OF MORE FAITHFUL
> REPRESENTATIVES, ANNUL THE ACTS OF THE
> USURPERS.
>
> *James Madison, Federalist #44*

Monday, October 24, 2016

Gillespie avoided looking at the girl in the passenger seat. He didn't want pangs of conscience weakening his resolve. But he couldn't avoid the comparison—Charity reminded him of Lucy.

He wanted to murder the girl in her parents' home. He wanted it to be horrific for them to discover her mutilated body there. He wanted to ensure that they could not go on living in their home, just as he would not be able to live in his.

But, he rationalized, stealing a glance at Charity, he would not make the girl suffer. A quick bullet to the head when she wasn't looking. But it had to be done in Henry Marshall's home. He had to maintain the charade long enough to get her down there, otherwise he'd have to shoot her right here, in the car.

He drove down East Harmony Road, and decided that I-

25 was not a good route. It would be crawling with cops soon.

"I thought we were headed for my mom and dad's," Charity objected, as they passed the on-ramp to I-25 south, and continued east.

"We are. But I don't know who the assassin is or how many people are working with him. I don't want to risk him finding us on I-25, so we'll go to your parents' home by a different route."

"Are you taking US 85 south at Eaton?"

"Right," he nodded.

****

Bergman was planning the next move with his tactical team and a small mob of Fort Collins' police officers. Helicopters were already in the air, one from Denver flying north and one from Cheyenne flying south. Interstate 25 would be covered in both directions. State patrolmen and county sheriff personnel would be watching all the roads east, particularly to Sterling and Wray. A combination of choppers and sheriff's deputies would handle the roads west out of Fort Collins. The Fort Collins Police Department was devastated and angry. Estrada knew that if the local boys caught up with Gillespie, they might go down but they'd go down shooting.

Estrada walked away from the knot of men and called Buford Jackson.

"Jackson," the lawyer answered crisply.

"Mr. Jackson, this is Carlos. Are you alone?"

"No, but I can be. Just a minute." A moment later he answered, "Okay, what's up, Carlos?"

"Sir, Byron Gillespie has kidnapped Charity."

"Oh, dear God help us! What happened, Carlos?"

"We all thought he was coming after Haley, sir." Carlos stepped up on the curb to move out of the way of a police cruiser leaving the scene. "I didn't realize that his actual target was Charity. I'd asked the Fort Collins PD to put a couple of officers outside her apartment, just in case. My mistake—I should have moved her to a different location. Gillespie killed both officers and grabbed Charity."

"Did he leave a note? Is he making demands?" asked Jackson.

"No, sir. There's not been any communication from him."

"Oh, that's not good. Do you think he's going to kill her, or use her as a bargaining chip?" asked Jackson.

"If he's backed into a corner he'll use her as a chip. Otherwise, he'll kill her. I didn't put two and two together until just a few minutes ago. Gillespie is all about revenge—always has been, even when he was with the SEALs, even before his wife died.

"If I am figuring it correctly, he knows his crimes will keep him from his own daughter, so he's going to steal Marshall's daughter from him, kind of a warped tit-for-tat." Carlos looked back at Bergman, who was standing on the bed of a pickup, organizing the manhunt.

"But why, Carlos? Why does he hate Henry? Why is he blaming Henry for his own troubles?" asked the lawyer.

"I don't know, sir. Haven't a clue. I don't know how Mr. Marshall even got on Byron's radar in the first place. Listen, I've got to go, we're about to get into the chopper to start the search. Would you take care of informing Mr. and Mrs. Marshall, sir? Please let them know we're doing everything we can to recover her safely."

****

The more she thought about the whole situation, the more uncomfortable she became. If the assassin was so dangerous, why did they send just one man to escort her to Denver? Why not a pair, or even a team? Why didn't Mr. Smith communicate with anyone to let them know he had her, or to get the latest threat assessment? Why didn't he even notify the Fort Collins Police Department about the men who were killed? None of it made sense.

And then she had a terrifying thought. What if Russell

Smith was the assassin? What if it was he who killed the two cops? She knew all four members of her dad's security team; this man was not one of the four.

"I haven't been home for several months, and I've not been keeping up with Dad's campaign staff. How long have you been there, Agent Smith?" she asked, as though making conversation.

"Well, first of all, Miss Marshall," he responded, looking sideways at her, "I'm not on your dad's security staff, I'm a Secret Service agent. I work for the Treasury Department, and I go wherever they send me. But I was detailed to protect your dad three weeks ago, and have been out here ever since."

"Welcome to Colorado," she said with a smile.

"Thanks. It's a gorgeous state. Think I'd like to retire here," he said, grinning back.

It was as simple as that. The man might be friendly, but he was an imposter. Carlos had explained to her back in September that there was a security briefing each morning, and the principal piece of intelligence they covered every day was the whereabouts of each family member and their movement plans. The entire security detail participated, both Marshall's campaign security staff and the Secret Service guys —even when they were on the road. If they weren't at headquarters they participated via a conference call.

Charity had been home every weekend since her mom's accident. Agent Smith would know that—if he were really part of her dad's security detail.

She fought down her fears and tried to stay calm, but her mind was racing. *Now what? This man is the assassin. What should I do?*

****

Joshua Cummings terminated the call. Buford had just informed him of the situation with Charity. Cummings closed his eyes and shook his head. *Oh, Lord,* he prayed silently, *please have mercy on that sweet, beautiful girl. Protect her from all harm.*

Henry was wrapping up a rally in Springfield. They were about to head for the airport and grab a flight to Florida for two days of campaigning there. Ashton Bancroft was stumping in Ohio. While Marshall was showing strong in Bancroft's home state, they didn't want to take Ohio and its eighteen electoral votes for granted.

As soon as they were in the car, Cummings said, "Sir, I'm so sorry to tell you this, but something terrible has happened."

Marshall became very still. "Go ahead, Josh. Tell me." Cummings was pale as a ghost, so Hank knew it was going to be really bad.

"Byron Gillespie has kidnapped Charity, sir. There's been no word, no ransom note, no communication from him. I just talked to Buford. Haley knows, and she is waiting for your call."

Marshall groaned. "Oh, dear God, not my daughter. Please, God, not Charity." He put his hands over his face for a moment while he struggled with his emotions. When he looked up his face was firm and bleak. "Josh, cancel tomorrow's appearances in Florida. We'll make a decision on Wednesday's meetings later. Have Carly cancel the Florida tickets and book us on a plane back to Denver."

"Yes, sir." Cummings hesitated. "Sir, I've been praying for Charity ever since I heard the news. I'm so sorry."

Marshall reached over and squeezed his friend's shoulder. "Thanks, Josh, that means a lot. Keep praying, please, until this is resolved. One way or the other."

"You know I will, sir."

Hank dialed Haley, and for a moment all either of them could do was weep. Then Hank cleared his throat, and said hoarsely, "We're headed home, babe, as soon as Carly can book us some tickets." They prayed together, and spoke quietly for a few minutes, then Hank terminated the call.

****

"Oh, oww, I think I'm going to be ill." Charity clutched her stomach and bent over, belching loudly.

"What's wrong," Gillespie asked, irritated.

"I picked up some sort of a stomach bug last night—you know, barfing, diarrhea—it was a real mess. I thought I was over it, but I'm cramping up again. Oh! I need a bathroom, quick, or I'm going to make an awful mess in your car. I'm so sorry." She belched again and bent over as though in pain.

Not much could make Gillespie panic, but this sort of thing did. They were passing through Fort Lupton, and he saw a Shell Station and Convenience Mart on the left. He pulled up to the store and said, "Go on in, I'll wait for you."

"Oh, thank you. I'll probably be a few minutes."

"Take your time. I'll be right here."

He tensed as he watched her walk into the store. He couldn't hear the words, but he could see the cashier pointing her toward the bathrooms. Then the lady appeared to take Charity's arm and help her to the bathroom. Gillespie relaxed. As long as the girl was convinced he was her protector, there would be no problems. She had no reason to try to escape, and every reason not to. Better to stop for a few minutes than travel with a smelly mess in the car.

****

Charity went into the store clutching her stomach. "Ma'am, can you direct me to the bathroom?"

"Yes, ma'am, it's right down that hall," the cashier said, pointing.

"Oh! Could you help me, please? I don't think I can make it by myself." Charity was hunched over, grimacing, trying to look like someone in pain.

The cashier came around the counter with a look of genuine concern, and said, "Dearie, you look terrible. Should I call 911?"

"No, no, that's not necessary. But can you help me to the bathroom?" The woman took her arm and gently led her to the ladies' room, and then Charity said, "Oh, thank you. I hate to ask, but could you do me one more favor? I need to call my doctor and I don't have my phone. I'm afraid I'm going to lose the baby."

"Baby? Are you pregnant? Oh, my! Sure, honey, you can use my phone, let me get it."

The woman hurried back to the cash register and picked up her iPhone, and brought it to Charity.

"Are you going to be okay? Do you need anything? Just call if you get in trouble. You can bring me my phone when you're done."

"I don't know how to thank you," Charity answered, gritting her teeth.

"Don't worry about it, hon. Just holler if you need me, and I'll come runnin'."

Charity shut and locked the door. *Oh, Lord, forgive me! I've told more lies in the last five minutes than I have the last five years.* She looked down at the phone and thought for a moment. The only number she knew by heart was her mom's.

> *mom, it's charity. do NOT call, text ONLY. I'm in the bathroom of a shell station, corner us85 and cr27 in fort lupton. a man claiming to be a ss agent is waiting outside for me, dark blue ford escort. I think he's fake, mom. don't know what to do. scared.*

A moment later the phone vibrated.

> *this is buford. stay put. lock door. do not go back to car, man is very dangerous. carlos will text you.*

Terror was welling up inside, threatening to make her panic. She never dreamed she would be the target of a killer.

The phone vibrated again. It was Carlos, and he had sent a picture with his text.

> *is this the man?*

yes

> *very dangerous. do not go back to him. describe his clothes.*

black, bulky, lots of pockets. looks military.

There was a loud, insistent knocking at the door. "Miss Marshall! Miss Marshall! Are you okay?" It was Agent Smith!

"Yes, yes. Still sick," she belched for emphasis. "Give me a few more minutes."

"You told me it was a stomach bug. The cashier said you told her you're pregnant, and she loaned you her cellphone. Do you have a cellphone in there?"

Lord, now what do I do? She panicked, mind racing, and then it came to her.

"Oh, Agent Smith, please, please, promise not to tell my parents! I don't know what I'm going to do! I lied to you because I didn't want my parents to find out." She let out a sob, and hoped it sounded real. "Please don't tell them," she pleaded.

"So, you've got what, something like morning sickness?" he asked through the door.

"Uh-huh. It's so awful. I've, well, I've never been pregnant before. I'm so sorry I lied to you, I just didn't know what to do."

Gillespie stood in the hall, chuckling. *Good grief, here I am, set to kill this girl and she's practically making me a member of the family. At least she's bought my story, hook, line, and sinker.* "Relax, Miss Marshall, your secret is safe with me. So why did you need the cellphone?"

"I'm so sick, I needed to call my doctor to find out if this is normal. He assured me it is. I hope I'm not making you late for anything, Agent Smith. I'll just be a few more minutes."

"Oh, for crying out loud, take your time. My only job today is to get you back to Denver safely. Good grief!"

She could hear him retreating down the hall. *Oh, Lord, that was close.*

The phone vibrated again.

ten minutes out. lay flat on floor, might be shooting. do not get up until you hear me or the police. do not open door unless you hear this password - zulu.

She wrinkled her nose. The floor was really dirty. *Oh, well, I can always take a bath later.*

****

"It's him all right. She just verified it," Carlos said into his throat mic. Bergman nodded and gave a thumbs up.

Sheriff's deputies and the state patrol had been deployed at intersections surrounding the target on a three-mile radius, so they didn't spook him. No sirens. They were hoping to retain the advantage of surprise.

"What's the report, Bobby?" requested SJ over his radio. Bobby McKinnon was an undercover state police officer who looked like a bearded mountain man. He had just driven by the Shell station in an old beat-up pickup to do a little reconnaissance.

"The car is parked on the east side of the station, close to the front door. The target can't see anything approaching from the west. He's sitting in the driver's seat of the car looking very alert, maybe a little nervous. North of the station is a junkyard. An old semi trailer is parked in it, about sixty meters north of the target. It would make a good perch for a sniper, with a good field of fire. The station has a back door, and it's usually unlocked."

"Okay, thanks. All units, we're landing three miles west of the station, at the intersection of 14th Street and CR 21. ETA in two minutes. There are three pickup trucks waiting for us. Alpha team will deploy behind the large building on the southeast corner of 14th and Denver and take up positions there. Bravo has the sniper, and will deploy in the junkyard. Charlie will park on the west side of the station, out of sight of the target. Charlie's job is to secure the hostage.

"All teams, remain out of sight. Report when you're in position. Once we engage, if the target pulls a weapon or tries to escape, take him out immediately. We think he's wearing ballistic gear, so a head shot will be needed to bring him down. Any questions? No? All right then, good luck!"

As the chopper was landing, Bergman looked at Carlos and said, "You're with me on Charlie. Your job is to secure Charity." Carlos nodded.

****

Gillespie sat in the Escort, wishing Charity would hurry up. But he didn't want to get rough with her, as he needed her cooperation until the moment he put a bullet in her head.

He noticed a mud-caked pickup with knobby tires approaching the intersection from the west. *Some teenager's toy. Bet daddy paid for it. Looks like he's been four-wheeling,* he noted idly as it turned north and disappeared behind the junkyard. A moment later, another pickup approached from the same direction, and pulled behind the building southeast of the intersection.

Gillespie sat up. *Something's wrong.* Then he realized nothing was driving by on US 85, and aside from the two pickups there hadn't been any local traffic either for at least ten minutes. He looked through the windshield into the store. No sign of the cashier. *Oh, boy. This is not good.*

He sat for a moment, examining his surroundings. *If I was running a team, I'd put a sniper on top of that old semi, shooters in that building across the street, and somebody on the other side of this station, where I can't see, to rescue the girl.* A slight movement to his north attracted his attention. He looked out of of the corner of his eye, at the top of the old semi. *Yep, sniper. Okay, Ares, old boy, new mission. We'll call this one 'Live to fight another day.' Forget the girl, let's get your butt out of this trap.*

The bulk of the town was to his south. It would be easier to lose a pursuit there than in the wide open spaces outside of town. *South it is. I'll get past their net, then ditch the car. Can always steal another.*

He reached into his backpack in the back seat, withdrew an MP5 and a handful of magazines, and then started the car.

****

Bergman sat with Carlos in the pickup on the other side of the store. His teams reported that they were in position. It was time to roll. "Bobby, call the cashier using the store's number. Tell her to casually walk out the back door."

A moment later the woman emerged from the door, looking confused. Bergman said, "FBI, get in the truck, please, and stay down."

Carlos peeked in the back door, and realized the hall could not be seen from Gillespie's vehicle. He crept to the bathroom door, tapped on it, and whispered, "Zulu, zulu, zulu, Charity. Open up!"

The girl opened the door and started to cry. Carlos grabbed her arm, pulled her down the hall, and put her in the truck. Bergman gave him the keys and said, "Get her to the chopper, now."

Estrada started to object, but remembered that his mission was the security of Marshall and his family. He nodded, climbed in, and drove off.

"All teams, all units. The hostage is secure, repeat, the hostage is secure. Now let's—" SJ was cut off by the simultaneous sound of squealing tires, and the sniper reporting that the target had started the car.

****

Gillespie threw the vehicle in reverse and gunned it. He lay down in the seat and grabbed the rearview mirror with one hand while steering with the other. He raced south down Denver Avenue, going backwards.

Pop! Pop! Pop! The windshield fractured as the sniper started shooting. The agents in the southeast building peppered the car as it flashed by.

A hundred yards down the street Gillespie threw the car into a J-turn and sat up. He continued south, pedal to the metal. The windshield was a dense spider web of cracks, and he couldn't see through it very well but he could hear just fine. Sirens from all points were converging on his position.

Ahead he saw a freight train pulling out of a lumber yard, blocking the street. It was accelerating, and Ares thought, *That's my ticket out of here. Couldn't have timed it better if I'd planned it.* Slamming on the brakes, he grabbed his go bag and the MP5 and abandoned the car, racing for the train. But Ares stumbled as he leapt for an open boxcar. Screaming in terror, he fell under the wheels of the train.

＊＊＊＊＊＊＊＊＊＊

"This is *CBS This Morning*. People across the country are waking up to the news that presidential candidate Henry Marshall and his family narrowly escaped yet another tragedy yesterday. No one knows why Byron Gillespie, a State Department employee and decorated former SEAL, targeted Marshall's family. But it has become apparent that he was behind the assassination attempt in late September, a laptop bomb that was intended to kill Henry Marshall, but instead destroyed Southwest Flight 1356, killing thirty-five innocent people, and, ironically, nearly killing Gillespie's own daughter.

"The FBI suspected Gillespie of being involved, and last week placed him under surveillance. Last Thursday night, however, Gillespie burnt down his own house and in the confusion managed to escape.

"The FBI has been desperately trying to locate him. Yesterday he turned up in Colorado, leaving a trail of bodies behind him, including a Colorado state patrolman and two Fort Collins police officers, before kidnapping Marshall's twenty-two-year-old daughter, Charity. Authorities believe he was intending to kill her, as well.

"Charity Marshall was rescued yesterday afternoon, unharmed, by an FBI tactical team that had cornered Gillespie in Fort Lupton. As he fled the scene, Gillespie accidentally fell beneath the wheels of a moving train, and was crushed to—." Marshall turned the television off and said, "We don't need to hear any more of that."

A moment later Lucy Gillespie walked into the kitchen in a bathrobe, her face tear-streaked. Haley and Sandy had broken the news to her the night before, and insisted that the lonely, heart-broken girl stay at the Marshall residence.

Henry walked over and wrapped his arms around the disconsolate young woman. She squeezed him fiercely and wept. When the sobs subsided he sat her in a chair at the kitchen table and poured her a cup of coffee.

"Oh, dear sweet Lucy. There's nothing I, or anyone else, can say to take away the pain and grief you feel," he said to the girl. "But Haley and I want you to know that we love you and we want to treat you as our own daughter. If you'll let us, we'll be your family. You aren't going to be alone. I know we can't replace your mom or your dad, and we're not trying to do that. But we want to be there for you, from now on."

She stared at her coffee cup and sniffed. "I'm so angry at my dad. I can't believe that he would do all these terrible things—but he did! I feel like I hate him—but I miss him. And I love him, and I'll never see him again. I didn't even get to say goodbye." The tears started again. Charity sat down next to her and put her arm around the weeping girl.

"Sweetheart," Marshall said, "your dad is not defined by his actions of the last several months. By all accounts he served his country well and he was a great, devoted husband and dad. Somewhere along the way, more recently, he gave full play to the darker side of his nature, what the Bible calls sin. I suspect he went over the edge when your mom died.

"I understand that. I lost my first wife, too, in a tragic car accident. And like your dad, I gave way to bitterness and anger. I turned to alcohol. But Jesus Christ rescued me from that. Your dad never turned to Christ, and so he never had resources that were more powerful than his grief and anger.

"Weep for him, but don't hate him, don't be angry with him. Remember the great man he was, before his rage took over, and love the memory.

"If you'll permit it, I can ask my pastor to do the funeral. He'll preach the gospel to give people an opportunity to find hope in Christ, and I know he'll honor who your dad was before he became so entrapped in his sin and bitterness."

"I'd like that," Lucy said softly, staring at the table, tracing circles with her index finger.

****

On Tuesday, October 25, RealClearPolitics released the latest national average of the major polls. Pamela Hastings was at thirty-eight percent, Bushnell was at thirty-one, Marshall at twenty-eight. However, when pollsters asked, *Which candidate do you admire most?* Henry Marshall led with a stunning sixty-eight percent. The sample size was over two thousand, all of whom were classed as likely voters.

The sky was brilliant blue, and a strong westerly wind was buffeting the building as Buford Jackson stood looking out the windows of the conference room of Western Law Associates. The forecast was calling for snow in the high country that night, and maybe up to an inch in Denver. But as of the moment there was not a cloud in sight.

Buford wasn't thinking about the beautiful view, however. He was replaying in his mind the high points of his relationship with his friend, Henry Marshall, since the day Marshall had picked him out of the phone book and put him on retainer as his corporate lawyer twenty-six years ago. Somewhere along the line—it must have been a consequence of Marshall's blogs—Jackson had become convinced that Henry Marshall was the man the nation needed to rein in DC.

An outlandish dream from the start, Marshall had done far better than anyone would have predicted. But now, two weeks from Election Day, it seemed clear that Marshall would fall well short of the votes needed to secure the presidency.

"No regrets," he muttered to himself. "Hank has run a great campaign, we all have our integrity intact, we've surmounted incredible odds and vicious opposition, and very nearly pulled it off." He gazed at the beautiful Front Range, solid, silent sentinels. "Whether we win or lose, God will still be on His throne, those gorgeous mountains will still be there, and life will still be blessed. No regrets," he repeated. He heard the door open behind him, and Cummings, Trujillo, Bancroft, and Marshall filed in, followed by Carly Johnson with her ubiquitous legal pad.

Cummings immediately took charge. "Two weeks from today is Election Day. It's what we've been working for since February of last year. This is our last lap, and our last chance to convince the voters that Henry is their man.

"Henry, I'd like to send you, Haley, and Jack Carson to Florida for several days. We've still got a good chance of capturing that state.

"Mike, it looks like Hastings will take Colorado, but her support has been trending down the last several weeks. I think we might be able to take it from her. I'd like to set up some rallies for you here. We should focus our efforts on Denver, the Springs, Loveland, Greely, La Junta, and your stomping grounds around Pueblo. I wouldn't spend much time on Fort Collins or Boulder—Hastings has both towns sewn up. Are you available?"

"Of course. I might be able to pry loose a few late endorsements, too," Trujillo promised.

"Excellent. Ashton, Ohio appears to be ours but Pennsylvania is on the bubble. I've got you scheduled for rallies in Cleveland, Youngstown, and Pittsburgh tomorrow. Scranton, Allentown, and Philly on Thursday, and multiple events in the Harrisburg area on Friday."

"You mentioned to me on the elevator that you were going to share a shocker with us, Josh. What was that all about?" Trujillo asked.

Cummings didn't respond right away. He got up and walked over to the window. After a moment he turned around and said, "New York."

"What about New York?" Buford asked.

Cummings smiled broadly, "I think it's in play."

"What?" exclaimed Hank, sitting up straighter.

"New York is in play. Three weeks ago I started to see a softening in Pamela Hastings' numbers, and two weeks ago the bottom fell out of Bushnell in New York. I commissioned some of our own polling to find out what was going on, and here's what I discovered: as Election Day draws near, Hastings' voters are having second thoughts, particularly on the character and trustworthiness questions. There's a downward trend in her numbers among registered voters, from sixty-five percent to fifty-eight. Those voters aren't moving into anyone else's column—they're becoming undecideds.

"At the same time, Bushnell is having his own problems. Adam MacKenzie published an article on October 10 exposing the ties that Russian oligarchs have to Power Without Carbon, Inc. PWC is a New York corporation that purports to be an energy middleman, buying excess wind energy and reselling it. But financial filings have shown that they spend relatively little money in that endeavor, and reap even less revenue. What MacKenzie exposed is that PWC appears to be a shell corporation that receives capital from foreign investors—i.e., the Russians—and then spends it on anti-fracking initiatives and other green political actions. PWC donations are heavily tied into several political action committees in New York that largely support Bushnell initiatives. The bottom line is, the Russians can flood PWC with capital, which then becomes available as a donation to PAC efforts supporting Bushnell. MacKenzie tied this with Bushnell's position opposing sales of American gas and oil to foreign nations. What the Russians gain, if US energy stays off the international market, is protection from America's energy boom. If our gas and oil can't be sold on the worldwide markets, it bolsters the global price of a barrel of oil, which helps the Russian economy, as well as their military efforts in the Crimea and Syria.

"Since that article came out, Bushnell's numbers in New York have been in free-fall. He's got both the frackers and anti-frackers mad at him—which I think is a pretty significant accomplishment. New York voters on both sides of the aisle are beginning to pool in the undecided column. Add to that the fact that, in the state of New York, *seventy-seven percent* identified Marshall as their most admired candidate."

Cummings paused for a moment to let what he'd said sink in. Then he continued, "Here's what I'm recommending. Let's take the rest of our campaign funds and do an ad blitz in New York this week. Then we'll spend Sunday through Friday doing rallies in New York, and close out with rallies in the remainder of the Big Six on November 5, 6, and 7. If we can capture New York, we just might win this thing!"

****

Thursday night, November 3, found Henry and Haley Marshall in Buffalo and Ashton and Margie Bancroft in Albany. Joshua Cummings remained at Marshall campaign headquarters to coordinate all the last-minute efforts. Sergeant Jack Carson was in Poughkeepsie with Mike Trujillo.

"Are you sure you want to try it?" Hank asked his wife, as they got ready for the rally that evening.

"Positive," she answered brightly. "Look, honey, what's the worst that can happen? So I trip and fall in front of thousands of people and look like an idiot. No big deal, right?" she said, laughing at herself as she made final adjustments to her makeup. "I'll be fine."

In the last week, her speech had improved to the point where she no longer had the pauses and halts. Although she'd been using a wheelchair for safety's sake at the rallies, she was walking in the hotel room with a walker, and doing therapy without any artificial assistance. She'd proposed to Hank that she walk onto the platform unsupported, for the first time since her accident.

"If you think it's time, let's do it. But tonight, you and I walk out together," he suggested.

She turned and put her arms around his neck and smiled up at him. "That's a deal, buster."

An hour later they were waiting behind the curtain. Elizabeth Montgomery, the Republican senator from Texas got the program started, and then she introduced the Marshalls.

When the crowd saw the two walk out together, with

neither wheelchair nor walker, they stood and cheered. Haley stood at the microphone while he stood behind her and to the left, ready to step in if she started to sway.

"Good evening," she said. "It's great to be in Buffalo tonight. I bring you greetings tonight from the—." She paused. "I stopped to make sure I had your attention. I bring you greetings tonight from the Denver Broncos, the best football team in the NFL!" Good-natured boos reverberated throughout the audience. "I'm bringing you greetings from them, because your Buffalo Bills won't be seeing them during the regular season. But I'm hoping for your sakes—and for ours—that you'll see them during the playoffs." The crowd had no idea where she was going with this, but cheers sounded through the hall.

"The AFC championship game this year is January 22, two days after Inauguration Day. I'm hoping to watch it in the White House. I understand the Situation Room's got a pretty big screen. Wouldn't it be great to see the Bills and the Broncos in that game?" Loud clapping and cheers.

"And then see the Broncos go on to win the Super Bowl on February 5?" Groans and boos rang around the great hall again.

"Wait," she said, looking confused. She looked back at Henry, who also had no idea where she was going in her comments. "Am I supposed to be talking about you?" she asked. "The Broncos are much more interesting." Laughter all around. Haley was clearly a crowd favorite.

She turned back to the microphone and waited for the audience to quiet down, then said, "Now that I've thoroughly insulted everyone here tonight, including my husband— . . ." There was more laughter and clapping from the crowd. Once they grew quiet again, she continued more seriously, "I want to tell you why I'm voting for my husband, and why I'm hoping you will, too." She spent the next five minutes talking about Marshall's character as a dad and a husband.

"But that's not the only reason I'm voting for Hank. I'm voting for him because I believe his plan for America is the right one. I believe his commitment to reduce the size of government is the right commitment, along with his commitment to the Constitution. When he says he's going into Washington with a chain saw and not a scalpel some have criticized, saying he's not sufficiently nuanced. Well, let me tell you something: those people have nuanced us into a nineteen-trillion-dollar debt. I think I'm tired of nuance—aren't you?" The entire hall erupted, and jumped to their feet, clapping and cheering.

She waited until they grew silent. She turned to Hank and said with a big smile, "They're pretty rowdy. Think you can handle 'em?" She turned back and said with all seriousness, "I'm so proud to present to you the man I love, and the man I think our nation needs at this hour—my husband, Henry Marshall."

Marshall spoke for twenty minutes, detailing the agencies and cabinet departments he would eliminate, a speech that was frequently punctuated with applause and cheers.

By Saturday, the national polls had significantly shifted, due in large part to Bushnell's troubles with his PACs. Pamela Hastings was at thirty-eight percent, Marshall had moved to second place at thirty-two percent, and Bushnell was third at twenty-six percent, with four percent in the undecided category.

****

"Henry, have you seen the news this morning?" a breathless Joshua Cummings practically shouted into the phone. It was Saturday, November 5.

Henry held the phone away from his ear and raised his eyebrows at Haley, who'd looked up from texting the kids. "Umm, no, Josh, don't believe I have. Why?"

"You're not going to believe this, Hank, but the *Chicago Tribune* published an opinion piece in last night's paper—and it's on the website, too, ENDORSING YOU!"

Henry sat down on the bed, shocked. "You've got to be kidding!"

"Nope. And tomorrow night on *Campaign 2016 Special Report*, Adam MacKenzie is going to explain the paper's position."

****

"Good evening, and welcome to *Campaign 2016 Special Report*. I'm Susan Wyatt. Tonight we'll be hearing from our expert panel, Rosalyn Jansen-Canford, Democratic political consultant, Thomas Bayfeld, Republican strategist, and Adam MacKenzie, the senior political reporter for the *Chicago Tribune*.

"The last ten days has seen a pretty dramatic shakeup of our three main candidates. It was hard to conceive a year ago that we'd ever use the expression, '*three*' main candidates, but here we are. It's now just two days to Election Day and we do have three candidates, and while there is a clear front-runner, all three have a legitimate shot to win.

"Thomas, what about the polls? And what happened to Bushnell?"

Bayfeld looked unhappy. "Susan, this has been a classic collapse. Adam's article a week ago, exposing the link between Bushnell and the Russian oligarchs was devastating. I've looked at the data and talked with Adam about this privately, and I cannot dispute his conclusions. It makes Bushnell look very bad, I have to admit it. And apparently, the voters feel the same way, because Bushnell is tanking." He compressed his lips and shook his head sadly.

Susan turned to the Democratic consultant. "Rosalyn, you on the other hand must feel very good about your candidate's position, with less than thirty-six hours before voting begins."

"Yes and no, Susan," Jansen-Canford said, wrinkling her nose.

Wyatt frowned. "Why *no*, Rosalyn? Hastings is clearly at the top of the polls, and a little beyond the margin of error. Why are you so cautious?"

"If you are a poll-hound, Susan, like some of us, you're

seeing an unusual trend. Voters are dropping off Bushnell, but they're pooling in the undecided column. Normally they would simply jump to another candidate—but they're not. If some major event happens in the next thirty-six hours, it's that growing pool of undecideds that will be swayed. They could swing as a group, and if they do, all bets are off."

"So, you would characterize the current situation as volatile?" the host suggested.

"Very much so."

"So, Adam, what in the world is going on at the *Tribune?* A year ago Marshall was a nobody, a green-behind-the-ears gadfly who was good for a few laughs but not much else. But now look at him."

"Well, Susan, I don't agree with your characterization of who he was a year ago. But you're right that one year ago Marshall had little name-recognition beyond the blogosphere. Today he's nipping at Hastings' heels, and could very well overtake her to become the forty-fifth President of the United States."

"So how did it happen that the *Chicago Tribune* endorsed him?"

"I think the biggest reason, Susan, is that the editorial board took two months to study his positions. They've reread the Constitution, *The Federalist Papers*, and other significant materials. They met four times for discussion during that period and have concluded that Marshall's principal contentions about the government and the Constitution are in fact correct. Once you've worked through the analysis and arrive at that conclusion, you immediately realize that the other candidates have nothing to offer that will actually correct the overreach of our government. The other two candidates are just kicking the can down the road."

Susan was so nonplussed she had no follow-up.

Bayfeld rescued her with his own follow-up question. "So, the *Tribune* endorsed him based on their analysis?"

MacKenzie nodded.

"Incredible," Bayfeld mused. "What are your thoughts, Adam?"

"About the endorsement?"

"Yes, about the endorsement."

MacKenzie was silent for a moment, considering how to respond. Then he said carefully, "Thomas, if your goal is to perpetuate the current reach of government, and maybe make incremental improvements, either of the other two candidates will be the best at accomplishing your goal. If on the other hand, you are thoroughly convinced our government is too big, that it's spending too much money, that it's become too intrusive into the private affairs of its citizens, then there is only one choice, and it's Marshall. The other two simply don't have the philosophical commitments to our Constitution to make any meaningful changes."

Susan finally found her voice. "Adam, are you willing to tell us where you come down on this issue? Who are you going to vote for?"

"Normally, as a journalist I wouldn't answer that question. But we're only two days out, now, and I guess it won't hurt. Look, I am a self-identified liberal. But over the last year of watching Henry Marshall there are two things that have made my decision. First, I've discovered that I am not a big-government liberal. I want to see liberalism done well, but I think it can be done well without a bloated government. I think it can be done better on a state and local level than on the federal level. The only way that's going to happen is to put someone in office who will go to Washington with a chainsaw instead of a scalpel. Second, Marshall seems to me to be utterly uncorrupted. I believe, I truly believe, that he is an honest and honorable man. And I, for one, would like a man of integrity in the White House even if I disagree with his politics. It's about time.

"So I am voting for Marshall on Tuesday, because I am convinced that he will leave the White House, the presidency, the government, and the country far, far better than he found them."

****

It was snowing in Denver on Election Day, a wet sloppy stuff that would be gone by the following day. News crews were camped out on the front lawn of the Marshall residence to capture pictures and comments when they went out to vote, but the whole family plus Lucy managed to sneak out the back without being caught.

Colorado united around its new favorite son. Even those who were voting for one of the major-party candidates were proud of the Marshalls and the campaign they had run. Marshall had shown that it was possible to disagree agreeably. The Marshall campaign had made its case exclusively on the strength of issues, and had said very little about the other candidates. If they won nothing else, they did win the hearts of their fellow Coloradoans.

Voter turnout across the nation was extremely heavy, even though the East Coast was experiencing torrential rains. The Midwest was gripped by an arctic air mass. Temperatures in Chicago dropped to single digits the night before the election, and the wind was icy. The usual allegations of fraud and irregularities cropped up here and there, but most reporters and poll workers felt that it was a fairly smooth election with no major problems.

****

The venue chosen for the Marshall campaign election night party was the Grand Ballroom at the Brown Palace on 17th Street in Denver. Campaign workers had labored throughout the day to decorate and prepare the place. Win or lose, Henry and Haley wanted to give their staff and volunteers a memorable evening as a thank-you for the countless hours spent on the campaign's behalf.

The Marshall family started the evening at home, with plans to make their way to the Brown Palace around eight. The atmosphere there was electric. The twins had created spreadsheets to record the returns as they came in, and the family room was festooned with whiteboards and charts.

Charity was as excited as the twins, but she was content to watch the returns on Fox and listen to the commentary.

Lucy had joined the family. With Charity's permission Hank and Haley had turned their daughter's room into Lucy's room, and she moved in. Hank installed bunk beds so Charity would have a bed whenever she came home from Fort Collins. Though nothing was ever said, it was obvious to Lucy that the family did not hold her responsible for her dad's actions. The unconditional love she received removed all questions and discomfort from her mind. Soon she began attending the Marshalls' church. There was something real, something tangible, something immensely powerful in their faith, and she wanted the same thing for herself.

One of the things Lucy loved most was talking to Carlos late at night. He always took the late shift watching over the family. Often they would sit in the kitchen drinking coffee, and Carlos would tell her about her dad's heroic exploits on SEAL Team 8. He wanted her to know the kind of man her dad was before the blackness had overtaken him.

"Okay, here we go! The polls in Indiana and Kentucky just closed!" Charlie shouted from the family room. It was only four o'clock, and the twins were the only ones watching.

Charity was excited, too, but as the big sister it wasn't cool to show it. She rolled her eyes and smiled at Lucy, and hollered down from their room, "Hey, you nitwits! You've got at least two hours before ANYTHING is really rolling. All you're going to hear between now and six are talking heads saying the same stupid things over and over."

"Well . . ." Conner responded, shouting up from the family room. The silence that followed told Charity that they knew she was right and just didn't want to admit it. "Well—it's not every day your dad is about to be elected president, you know," he kind of trailed off.

Hank and Haley were sitting in the master bedroom, chatting.

"I'm feeling almost giddy," Hank said to his wife. "And it's not because I think we're going to win—I don't, actually. It's because this marathon is finally over. It has dominated our lives and our family for the last eighteen months. I feel like I just completed the final exam and tomorrow I get my diploma. It's over, babe, it is finally over. Thank God it's over!

"Tomorrow, I'll go into the campaign office later in the morning and start writing dozens of thank-you notes, and I'll start shutting the whole operation down. Tomorrow afternoon I'm going to talk Buford into going for a run. Tomorrow night I'm going to come home and plan a Thanksgiving family vacation for us. Tomorrow morning, Haley, we'll wake up and go back to normal life."

She smiled at him and ran her fingers through his hair. "Do you remember the last time you said to me that we'll go back to a normal life after this campaign?"

His eyes narrowed. "No. You mean I've said that before?"

Her eyes got a faraway look, and she answered softly, "Yes, you have. You said it on the morning of September 23, the day I had my accident and you had your airplane crash. You probably don't remember how I answered you. I said, *this is the new normal.* I told you that you'd become the spokesman for the opposition to the two political parties, and that you are one of the few people out there who can challenge the status quo." She focused on his face, looking into his eyes. "I'm with you, Hank, every step of the way. Whatever it takes, whatever it costs. Some things are worth fighting for. This country is one of the last bastions of religious freedom left, and even here that freedom is in danger." She kissed him, and put her finger on his nose. "Besides, we're going to win this election and tomorrow you will start putting together your administration."

"Oh, dear Lord," he said, putting his head in his hands, "winning might be worse than losing. What in the world am I going to do if I win?"

"Is God still on the throne?" she asked, raising her eyebrows.

He smiled and nodded. "What would I do without you?"

"I don't know, but don't try it, buster. Now saddle up. We've got a party to go to."

****

Indiana and Kentucky were called for Marshall by 5:00 p.m., putting his electoral vote total at nineteen. The twins whooped and hollered and raced around the house, making sure everyone knew.

By seven thirty, the northeastern states had been called for Hastings. Massachusetts, Rhode Island, Connecticut, New Jersey, Delaware, Maryland, DC, Maine, Vermont, and Virginia were firmly in Hastings column, giving her seventy-two electoral votes.

South Carolina and Alabama were called by CNN for Bushnell, giving him eighteen. Fox had called Louisiana and Mississippi for Bushnell as well, but CNN was insisting they were too close to call, so the boys didn't mark them in the Republican's column yet.

In rapid succession, West Virginia, Ohio, and Texas were placed in Marshall's column. The twins had Marshall's tally standing at eighty of the two hundred seventy required to win. By this time the Jacksons, Joshua Cummings, the Bancrofts, the Trujillos, and all the Marshalls were standing or sitting around the television in the family room.

A few minutes later, Mississippi and Louisiana were resolved and added to Bushnell's total, bringing him to thirty-two.

Florida, Georgia, North Carolina, Tennessee, and Indiana were each locked in a virtual dead heat between Bushnell and Marshall, first one leading, then the other. New York and Pennsylvania were in the same situation, but between Hastings and Marshall. *Too close to call* became a gut-wrenching expression as the evening wore on. Right before the whole crew left the house for the ballroom, Michigan, Wisconsin, and Illinois were called for Hastings, and Kansas, Missouri, Arkansas, New Hampshire, and Oklahoma for Marshall, bringing their respective totals to one hundred eighteen and one hundred thirteen.

Marshall's party entered through the main doors and circulated through the ballroom, greeting friends and workers.

Every time a state was called, it would be announced over the loudspeaker to groans or cheers, depending on whom it was called for.

Colorado was called for Marshall, followed quickly by New Mexico, and then Fox News called Minnesota and Iowa for Hastings, and both Dakotas and Nebraska for Bushnell.

By ten o'clock, Hastings had accumulated one hundred thirty-four electoral votes, Marshall one hundred twenty-seven, and Bushnell forty-three.

"How's it looking, Josh?" Hank asked his campaign manager.

"Well, it's definitely not looking good for Bushnell. It's going to be mathematically impossible for him to get to two hundred seventy, since it is a three-way race. Bushnell's only chance at this point, and it's actually a good one, is that no one gets two hundred seventy electoral votes and the election is thrown to the House of Representatives. If that happens Bushnell is a lock because the House is dominated by the Republicans, and he's their boy."

"But how is it looking for us?" Henry asked.

"Pretty goo—" Josh started to say, but he was cut off by an announcement over the loudspeaker.

"Florida and Tennessee have just been called for us!" The floor of the ballroom erupted in cheers. Marshall's count now stood at one hundred sixty-seven. The cheering was so loud they almost missed the next announcement, "Fox News is now projecting that Hastings has won New York and Pennsylvania." That quieted the crowd immediately. Everyone knew that their only realistic hope was to win at least one of those two states. Hastings' total now stood at one hundred eighty-three.

"Well, Hank," Joshua said, "I was about to say our chances were looking pretty good, but now, not so much. When you figure that Hastings has got California's fifty-five delegates wrapped up—they don't even need to count the votes, as far as I'm concerned—then she's getting really close to the magic number."

As soon as he'd said that, the loudspeaker sounded again,

"CNN just called Georgia for us, and both Fox and CNN confirm North Carolina is in our column!" Twenty minutes later, Indiana was added. Marshall's tally had now reached one hundred ninety-eight.

At 11:00 p.m., Wayne Bushnell made his concession speech. It was by now mathematically impossible for him to reach two hundred seventy, and his campaign manager had assured him that, based on their own numbers and projections, Pamela Hastings would be the forty-fifth president of the United States.

Bushnell stepped to the podium. "I want to congratulate my colleague this evening. It's been a tough, bruising, exhausting campaign. Pamela ran a gritty race and, let's face it, she won fair and square." Boos could be heard coming from the people in Bushnell's venue. "No, no, let's not have any of that," he said. "We are all Americans, after all. And I pledge to work with President Hastings to restore this country to the prosperity and unity we have seen in years past."

Bushnell went on for another twenty minutes, but people soon tuned out and even the commentators and analysts at the various news shows turned him down and resumed their own commentary. Joshua Cummings noticed that one name Bushnell never mentioned in his entire speech was Henry Marshall. *If Hank is able to win this thing, we'll have a powerful enemy in the Senate*, he thought to himself.

It was almost midnight, and the two remaining contenders still could not tell who was going to win. CNN called California and Arizona for Hastings, bringing her up to two hundred forty-nine. New Mexico was still on the bubble, with Hastings and Marshall trading leads.

At midnight the calls started rolling in. Wyoming, Montana, Idaho, Nevada, and Utah all went into the Marshall column. His electoral count was now at two hundred fifteen, but by now the eventual outcome was obvious.

The final blow came when New Mexico, Washington, and Oregon went into the Hastings column, giving her two hundred seventy-eight electoral votes. Still not yet in were Alaska and Hawaii—they would eventually go to Marshall and

Hastings, respectively—but it didn't matter. The race was over.

Tears were running down the girls' faces. The twins looked crestfallen. Some out in the ballroom had taken up the chant "Marshall! Marshall!" but it was not the cry of victory, merely of loyalty.

The inner circle was in a private room behind the stage, preparing to enter the ballroom. "Come on, bring it in close," Marshall said, motioning to those in the room with him. They all stood and gathered close to him. He looked around the circle at Buford and Sandy, Joshua Cummings, Mike Trujillo, Ashton and Margie Bancroft, Lucy, and his own precious family.

"Listen to me. First of all, thank you. It has been an incredible run, and we were this close." He held up his thumb and forefinger. "We nearly did it. It's been a historic campaign. We got our message out, and for many it has resonated. But tonight the verdict is clear, God has not granted us the win. His purposes are good even though we don't understand them. He is always faithful. Let's pray and thank God for the wonderful opportunity He gave us, and pray for our next President, Pamela Hastings, that God will be pleased to favor her administration over the next four years." He lead them in a simple prayer, and then turned and strode out to the platform, his family following.

His supporters took up a chant, "2020, 2020, 2020!"

Marshall held up his hands for quiet, smiling. "One campaign at a time, okay?" The crowd grew quiet. "Thank you for all your hard work, your dedication, the long hours, the sacrifices." He spent a few minutes thanking the workers, the staff, and the volunteers. Many he singled out by name.

"I want to extend my congratulations to Senator Hastings, now President-elect Hastings. It is my hope that the Lord will be pleased to pour His common grace out on her administration. I hope that she will get a chance in the coming months to think about some of the points I have made regarding the federal government and the Constitution. Perhaps she will find something of use to help her in the next four years.

"I want to congratulate Senator Wayne Bushnell for a

hard-fought campaign. As he returns to his work in the Senate for the remaining two years of his term, I pray that the Lord will also bless Senator Bushnell's work.

"You and I worked hard. You and I were faithful. But in the end we fell short of the goal. The American people have spoken, and we must accept their verdict. We have nothing to be ashamed of—we gave it our all. Good night, God bless you, and God bless America."

Epilogue

Friday, January 20, 2017

It was a cold, snowy Friday. The wind blew hard, and sleet rattled against the window-panes. Hank and his family and friends had gathered for the inauguration.

They watched the television as the commentators talked about the long history of the inauguration, and the fact that America was one of the few countries in the world with an orderly transition of power every four years.

"Wow, it looks cold out there," said Conner.

"I'll say," Charlie agreed.

Hank looked at the spectacle on the television and said to Haley, "Well, babe, we gave it our best shot."

"That we did, buster. I guess it's about time for a new chapter isn't it?" she said, smiling at the man she loved.

"Yep."

The door opened, and Buford Jackson entered in a heavy overcoat. A few flakes of snow followed him in. He stood in front of Hank and straightened his friend's tie. He studied Henry's face, and said, "They're ready for you, Mr. President."

As they filed out, Vice President Bancroft whispered to Josh Cummings, "I still can't believe that New York and Pennsylvania wound up in our column the day after the election. They were too close to call and when the media called them on election night, it called them the wrong way. That was a *really* close vote."

"Yes, it was," Cummings agreed. "And I expect it was a bitter pill for Bushnell when the final tally in Nebraska moved the state from his column to Henry's. The funny thing is, Hank didn't even know he'd won until the next day when Adam MacKenzie called him and asked for an interview. None of us were watching the news!"

The ceremony began and before Marshall knew it, he was placing his hand on the Bible and reciting the oath of office: "I do solemnly swear that I will faithfully execute the office of President of the United States, and will to the best of my ability, preserve, protect, and defend the Constitution of the United States." And he added, "So help me, God."

Afterword

I hope you have enjoyed *The Candidate*. But I must confess, I wrote it with the motive of getting a simple point across: ideas have trajectories, they have legs, they are going somewhere. This is specially true in political philosophies.

Much mischief has been done in the government because men and women didn't pause to fully consider where an idea would take us. A good example of this would be the vote for the Seventeenth Amendment. Many of the politicians who pushed for it probably never considered how it would affect the finely-tuned opposing balance between the federal government and that of the states—a balance that the Founders intentionally designed into the Constitution. It's clear from *The Federalist Papers* that the decision to entrust the state legislatures with the selection of US senators was explicitly intended to *prevent* the concentration of federal power. We are witnesses of what happens when that design is thwarted.

The Candidate is my attempt to demonstrate the trajectory of ideas in a captivating way. I hope this tale kept you up past your bedtime. I hope you were ensnared in the lives of the book's characters, in whom you can probably see yourself or your friends. But most of all I hope that reading *The Candidate* has reminded you of something that you probably already knew but which may have gotten lost in the busyness of life: ideas have trajectories—they are going somewhere and *they will take you somewhere.*

And consequently, I hope that you might be motivated to take a second look at your own ideas about politics, government, and, yes, even Jesus Christ. Thanks for reading!

ABOUT THE AUTHOR

Chris Cobb's resume reads like a patchwork quilt. He's driven a forklift, worked as a technician doing component-level repair on digital circuitry, been a programmer-analyst, a data-center shift operator, taught high school science and mathematics, and been an Information Technology Director at a graduate school. Most of his career he's been a pastor.

He lives with his wife, Doris, in western Ohio, and is presently one of the pastors at Bible Fellowship Church in Greenville, OH. They have three adult children, and two fine sons-in-law and daughter-in-law, all of whom are actively engaged in the arts.

Chris received Jesus Christ as his Savior in 1974, and seeks to incorporate a biblically faithful worldview into everything he does, including his writing.

You can find Chris on Facebook, or find other works by him at chcobb.com.

A FALCON NOVEL

FALCON DOWN

C. H. COBB

Sometimes what you don't know really can hurt you . . .

While flying unarmed over international waters, Major Jacob "Falcon" Kelly's F-16 is downed by a Soviet missile. Captured after ejecting from his aircraft, Kelly is incarcerated in a secret interrogation center in Siberia, where he discovers the most daring and ruthless program of international espionage in the history of the Cold War. He faces torture, interrogation and certain death—unless he can escape. Escape seems impossible, but the Soviets' dossier on Kelly is missing two vital facts . . .

The complete Falcon Trilogy is available at chcobb.com and Amazon.com:

> *Falcon Down* (book 1)
> *Falcon Rising* (book 2)
> *Falcon Strike* (book 3)

Praise for *Falcon Down:*

"Cobb . . . has clearly done his research on multiple counts and, like Tom Clancy or Dale Brown, masterly intertwines military technology and behavior into a tightly plotted narrative in which every development follows logically and smoothly from what came before. This deft touch extends to the characters: . . . . This first installment chronicling the adventures of Maj. Jacob Kelly turns out to be an undisputed success." – *Kirkus Reviews*

OUTLANDER CHRONICLES

BOOK ONE

PHOENIX

C.H. COBB

Survival and scavenging. Those are the two bywords for a world reeling from biological warfare. The future of humanity is in doubt, when one young man decides that there must be more to life than mere survival. He encounters a mysterious mentor who buys in to his vision and the two collaborate to reestablish civilization. They might be successful—if they don't kill each other first.

Print copies signed by the author are available at chcobb.com. Also available on Amazon.com in print or Kindle formats, or Barnes and Noble in Nook format.

Praise from readers for Phoenix:

"The characters are well developed, peeling back layers one at a time just as happens in real life when you meet a person and remain associated with him for many years. You care about the characters because you can see yourself in each of them.

The story moves at a steady, quick pace. Once you start reading, you'll lose track of time until you're done. And identifying who is the Outlander is a good literary quiz for the reader.

In short, a very fine work . . ."

"This is a well paced voyage into a future devastated by biological warfare. The survivors are divided between those who seek to retain a moral code and thereby rebuild civilization, and those who don't. Combining thought-provoking dialogue and brisk action, this book is a must-read for anyone who wants a peek into what the world could become if the west's moral force continues to erode."

"An enjoyable and thought-provoking read."

"I couldn't put the book down until I had read through the whole thing! Very well written . . . , and it seems as if it could almost be prophetic, considering the awful world we live in. Can't wait to read the next volume!"

"Starting on page one you had my attention and it was a page-turner all the way through."

"I picked up your book on Saturday and couldn't put it down! I really enjoyed the book. Great mix of entertaining and thoughtful, suspense and interpersonal relationships, etc."

". . . this is coming from a guy who historically doesn't like to read fiction....in fact he doesn't like to read....but, I thoroughly enjoyed Phoenix. . ."

"I just finished your book. I LIKED it! The story moved along at a good, crisp pace; it was well written; the characters truly lived; the dialogue rang true and didn't get bogged down . . ."

Made in the USA
Middletown, DE
26 September 2023

39215748R10261